"Sasha Lord weaves a most imaginative tale."
—Bertrice Small

Kalial was lost to the music. Her bare feet moved languidly with a tinkle of tiny bells. Of their own volition, her steps brought her infinitesimally nearer to Ronin, as if the pull of his gaze could physically move her.

Ronin sank to his knees when a white silk scarf brushed his cheek. Kalial gazed longingly at him while her body continued to undulate. She twirled so close that the forty-nine scarves gracing her hips fluttered around him. She twisted her handheld scarf and lightly snapped it at his chest where his silk shirt was open. Her ivory skin glowed. Ronin's eyes deepened to the aqua color she had seen earlier. She turned her back to him and looked over her shoulder. She ran her hands down her hips over her heated skin.

Ronin's eyes followed her hand movements, yet he remained still. The rule of this dance was clear. He could not choose her—she must choose him. Although his every muscle ached with the effort to keep from taking her, he disciplined his body to obey. He could not risk the chance of scaring off this exquisite creature.

UNDER A WILD SKY

SASHA LORD

A SIGNET BOOK

SIGNET
Published by New American Library, a division of
Penguin Group (USA) Inc., 375 Hudson Street,
New York, New York 10014, U.S.A.
Penguin Books Ltd, 80 Strand,
London WC2R 0RL, England
Penguin Books Australia Ltd, 250 Camberwell Road,
Camberwell, Victoria 3124, Australia
Penguin Books Canada Ltd, 10 Alcorn Avenue,
Toronto, Ontario, Canada M4V 3B2
Penguin Books (N.Z.) Ltd, Cnr Rosedale and Airborne Roads,
Albany, Auckland 1310, New Zealand

Penguin Books Ltd, Registered Offices:
80 Strand, London WC2R 0RL, England

First published by Signet, an imprint of New American Library,
a division of Penguin Group (USA) Inc.

First Printing, February 2004
10 9 8 7 6 5 4 3 2 1

Map by Patricia Tobin Fein

 REGISTERED TRADEMARK—MARCA REGISTRADA

Printed in the United States of America

PUBLISHER'S NOTE
This is a work of fiction. Names, characters, places, and incidents either are the product of the author's imagination or are used fictitiously, and any resemblance to actual persons, living or dead, business establishments, events, or locales is entirely coincidental.

BOOKS ARE AVAILABLE AT QUANTITY DISCOUNTS WHEN USED TO PROMOTE PRODUCTS OR SERVICES. FOR INFORMATION PLEASE WRITE TO PREMIUM MARKETING DIVISION, PENGUIN GROUP (USA) INC., 375 HUDSON STREET, NEW YORK, NEW YORK 10014.

I dedicate this story to the person who made all my dreams possible because she gave me faith to believe in myself. I love you, Mother. You gave me a big, beautiful, wild sky to play in.

ACKNOWLEDGMENTS

First and foremost, I would like to thank Denise. Your help and encouragement were invaluable, and without you, I would never have used my computer to delve into Kalial and Ronin's world. You also introduced me to Marlene Howard, cofounder of the Oregon Writer's Colony, who in turn gave my manuscript to Jennifer McCord, who became my advisor, my advocate and my friend. Through Jennifer, I met my agent, Bob Mecoy, a strong Manhattan man with enough fire to match the characters in my novel. And finally, I want to acknowledge Ellen Edwards, my editor, whose tireless efforts helped apply the final polish to my wild imagination.

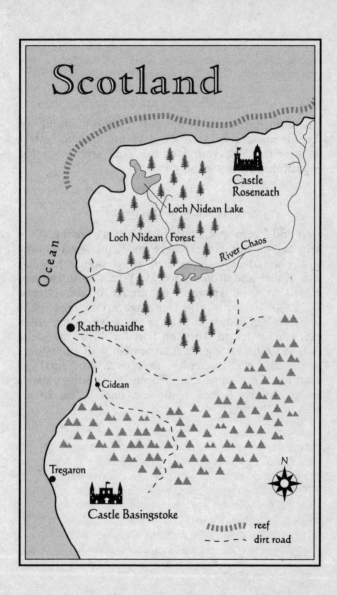

PROLOGUE

The great hall of Castle Roseneath, towering over the Scottish coast, echoed with the screams of the dying. The invaders showed no mercy, no compassion. Hounds ran after the attackers, their fangs snapping, but the marauders slashed them with great slices of broadswords and bludgeoned them with heavy cudgels as they advanced into the castle hall and murdered the unsuspecting inhabitants. Children toppled forward as knives were thrown into their backs. Women lay littering the ground, their silk dresses pooling around them, mixing with their blood. The defending warriors dripped with sweat and blood and some with tears as they valiantly stood their ground. Their comrades fell underneath the butchery of the onslaught, yet not one would retreat. With the final few standing, they blocked the entrance to the master staircase to give the fleeing McTaver women a chance to take their own lives in honor.

High in the tower Evelyn McTaver frantically sought the vial of poison for her daughters. She located it, and in a part of her mind curiously removed from the horror around her, she marveled at the delicacy of the scrollwork ornamenting the glass vial. The juice of roots carefully selected and prepared for their soothing potency glittered in the waning daylight shining through an arrow slit in the high reaches of the tower.

One by one the five girls lined up to take a careful draught of the potion. Evelyn's hands shook as she watched her precious daughters drop silently to the floor. Underneath her feet the heartbeat of battle throbbed to a crescendo when the heavy oak door was splintered from without, raining sprung iron shards and timbers into the room. A length of iron whipped in front of Evelyn as she held her arm out to her final daughter, slashing through her flesh and bone. Evelyn stood still, shock overwhelming her as her severed hand fell to the floor still holding the lovely glass vial, its contents soaking the floorboards.

She slowly raised her eyes to her last daughter, the youngest. Laureen had the smooth, creamy skin of a schoolgirl. Her light blue eyes blazed with terror. The sweet dimples on her cheeks stood out starkly against the whiteness of her face and the purity of her demure dress.

Father and son stumbled back into the room, desperately trying to protect the women. Laird Robert of Roseneath looked older, wiser and weary. Next to him stood his successor, his son, Ronin. Ronin's face was strong, powerful and furious. His jet-black hair curled on his forehead, wet with sweat, flecked with his enemy's blood. His eyes were blue like his sister's, yet the softness of the girl's eyes contrasted with the rage boiling in his.

The men stood side by side with the tips of their swords arcing in a defensive dance. The attackers slowed, hindered by the closer confines of the open stairs and the menace of the two weapons. Then suddenly the attackers parted and a man dressed in the tartan of the Serpent stood at the foot of the stairs. Laird Robert saw him first and slowly lowered his weapon. Glancing behind him, he saw his wife, Evelyn, sink to the floor as the life force poured out of

her. He saw his darling Laureen swaying amid the
finery at her feet. The great tear rolling down her soft
cheek made him choke on his failure to defend the
castle and protect his family. Turning back, he gave
the age-old sign of surrender by carefully turning the
sword around and holding it out toward the Serpent,
hilt first.

"Lothian," he called out, "I give over my castle in
exchange for my remaining family's life."

"Why would I grant you that, Robert, when I have
you helpless already?" Lothian's voice hissed through
the air. His beady eyes were cold and unfeeling, yet the
twist of a smile spread across his face. Ronin surged
forward, enraged, but Robert gripped his shoulder and
held him back.

"Find some honor left in your soul, my old friend.
Why must you kill us all? Why the children? The
women?"

Lothian dropped the pretense of a smile and snarled,
"I know all about the Scottish Gold. I know its secrets
are buried along this heathen coast." He took another
step up the spiral stairs, and his chest heaved with
agitation. "I have traced the legends and know that
the fortune is here!"

"You know nothing, Lothian. You never did." Robert looked down in contempt. "As a boy you were
obsessed with money, wealth, power. You still do not
understand and most likely never will. I do not know
where the Scottish Gold is, nor did any of the other
families you murdered in your vicious path up the
coast. You have blackened your name and heart for
nothing."

"You do know of it, for I heard that you hold the
second tapestry. Lie not to me, Robert." Lothian the
Serpent glared up at the pair, his gaze sliding past
Robert to rest briefly upon Ronin. "You," he said
abruptly, "you will tell me or you will watch the last
of your family die."

Robert swung around, his old eyes suddenly bright with purpose. "Ronin, the Scottish Gold is not to be taken, plundered or squandered. It is our greatest legacy and you must protect it at all costs."

" 'Tis only a fable!" shouted Ronin. "It is a story for young maidens to whisper in spring orchards! This is beyond foolish—"

"Tell me where it is!" shouted the Serpent. "It should be mine!"

"It was never meant for you, Lothian. Why would you think you deserve such fortune?"

"I am the strongest. You, with all your family peace and tranquility . . . you have failed. The Scottish Gold should go to a man who is powerful enough to use it!"

Robert bowed his head before the maniacal gleam in Lothian's eyes. Ronin, seeing the slump of defeat, shouted, "I vow upon all the beasts of the forest, I will never let you breathe upon the Scottish Gold with your foul lungs!"

Robert looked up and shook his head, glancing at both men in despair. "You do not understand . . . the Scottish Gold is priceless. You, Lothian, are too greedy and you, Ronin, are too young."

"Will you give me the tapestry, Robert?" Lothian hissed again.

Laird Robert of Roseneath glanced around the room one final time. His beautiful wife and daughters lay dead upon the floor. His gaze met Laureen's and held it for long moments. She trembled at the fatality she saw in his eyes just before he turned away.

"No, Lothian of the Serpents. I will not tell you the way to the Scottish Gold," he finally said.

The Serpent smiled. He lifted his hand and threaded a dart in his crossbow. While Ronin watched in disbelief, the dart whispered through the air and sank through his father's chest. Stunned, Ronin was slammed to the planks as the men on the stairway rushed into the tower, attacking him. As he fell, he saw his father double over, gasping for breath, then crash heavily to the floor. Suddenly galvanized into motion, Ronin arched off the rushes and bucked one man off only to be set upon by two more as other soldiers surged through the door. A flash of light glinted off a dirk that sang through the air toward his struggling form. Laureen screamed, her voice shrill with hysteria. Ronin dropped his broadsword and rolled to avoid the dagger's murderous path. A soldier placed his booted foot against Ronin's chest while three others pinned him to the floor. The man who had thrown the dirk yanked it from the wood and raised it to finish the besieged Ronin.

"Wait!" Lothian's ominous voice snaked out. "I might need him." The man with the dirk paused, hesitated, and a second hiss from Lothian forced him to step back, allowing the Serpent access.

The soldiers hauled Ronin to his feet, tightly gripping his sweat-slick skin. They all breathed heavily but Ronin's breath burned with a special intensity. His struggles were increasing, his movements frantic and furious as Laureen's cries echoed in the small space. Finally, abruptly, he stilled and glared at the Serpent. His deep blue eyes glittered darkly while the whites of his eyes shone crisply, fringed with thick, spiky lashes like iron shards set in vicious defense upon a castle wall. Lothian grinned, nodded and climbed the last steps to stop directly in front of Ronin.

"Bind them while we search. Tie them together, she on the bed, he beside her."

Laureen was thrown roughly on the massive walnut bed and tied to the carved bedposts, face down. Both arms were spread above her head but her legs were left free. She tugged weakly against the headboard before lying still in submission. Ronin's left wrist was bound and then tied to the same bedpost while his other arm was strung tightly to a metal ring in the wall far to the right. The bonds cut deeply into his skin as he struggled and his fingers began to tingle almost immediately. Laureen's frightened eyes met his and he stilled.

"Why are they here, brother? What has happened?"

"Shush, little sister. Do not talk now." He watched the tears well up in her eyes and looked around at their sisters lying upon the floor, their mother whose blood had ceased to flow, their unfairly slain father. His anger simmered as he silently acknowledged the devastation around him. He stared at each family member, burning the image into his mind. Then he looked fiercely into Lothian's triumphant face. "I will remember every moment of today, Serpent, and I vow you will regret what you have done here."

The soldiers left as Lothian signaled them away, and Ronin watched helplessly as Lothian swept his gaze first over himself, then insolently over Laureen's backside. Lothian watched Ronin's furious expression, then chuckled and sank down on the bed beside Laureen. His sour odor wafted over to her and she gagged in disgust. His sightless left eye shifted as his pale right eye focused upon Ronin.

He slid his hand up her skirts in one quick, fluid movement. She shrieked and jerked away as far as her bonds would allow. "Ronin!" she cried. Ronin tore frantically against his restraints as his sister pleaded for help. "Oh God, oh God! Have mercy!" she screamed. As she struggled, her dress rode higher and the hiss of the Serpent's breath came faster, yet his gaze remained fixed upon the man and not the girl.

Lothian continued to watch Ronin as his hands reached higher and ripped at her thin white woolen stockings and fragile undergarments. She squirmed and cried helplessly. The cords on Ronin's neck stood out starkly and the veins on his forehead bulged as he strained and fought against the bonds. His black hair whipped around as he yanked his head back and forth, trying to rip the bolt out of the stone wall where the rope was secured. The Serpent climbed up on the girl and roughly spread her legs. Her bottom glowed in the fading light, but the Serpent's one eye trained itself on the maddened man. "Ronin! Help me!" Laureen whimpered.

"Get away from her," Ronin growled. "Leave her be!"

"Give me what I came for. I want the tapestry of the Second Hunt. I will find the Scottish Gold, and I need your tapestry to show me where it is hidden."

"I swear I will never give it to you!"

"You misunderstand, Ronin McTaver. I will have the Hunt tapestry or you will watch me ravage this sweet child."

"It is nothing but a useless piece of cloth!" Ronin shouted. A thunderous roar filled Ronin's ears as he watched the Serpent pull his kilt aside and extract his swollen member. A welling of despair filled his heart as familial duty warred with brotherly love. "Stop! Leave her be . . . leave her be and I will give you what you seek!"

The Serpent paused in spreading the struggling girl's legs and looked up with a satisfied glow. The black hairs covering Ronin's chest lifted in a prehistoric show of animal fury and blood dripped freely from the bonds around his wrists. The stones in the wall trembled where his tether was bound. Ronin growled and shouted in an explosion of rage as the Serpent bent over Laureen once more.

Ronin surged forward again, his muscles leaping and straining, when suddenly the stones beneath his feet shook and the slabs in the wall broke free. A burst of dust showered the room as stone by stone the castle wall crumbled, tumbling into the gap that Ronin had inadvertently created. The tower sighed and the wall behind Ronin collapsed. The floor tilted and he scrambled to climb the incline, stones rocking and shivering, as he focused on his only goal—reaching and killing

Lothian the Serpent. But the forces of gravity overpowered Ronin and the floor sucked him down, snapping the bedpost to which his other arm was bound and hurtling him downward among the rock and mortar. As he fell, his sister's cries were abruptly silenced by the heavy collapse of stone.

PART I

Loch Nidean Forest

CHAPTER 1

Kalial watched the stranger weave among the dense trees on his massive warhorse. The sounds of pursuit had halted at the edge of the forest. The froth-flecked horses of the nine men in bloody tunics that had thundered after the stranger now milled just beyond the shade. The men yowled and shook their battleaxes at the darkness, but none of them made a move to enter after the stranger. He glanced back at the final flickers of sunlight glinting off the rusty armor emblazoned with the symbol of the Serpent, and then nudged his horse forward. A hint of animosity wrinkling her brow, Kalial watched him from her hiding place in the branches of an old, gnarled oak tree.

His back was bare and drenched with sweat. Every muscle rippled and bulged with his movements. Long midnight hair stuck to his sticky skin that was maimed by scratches and bruises now healing. Just before he turned away from her she saw one strand of hair plastered along his cheek and down a supple neck. She judged that he was nervous by the way his eyes continuously scanned the forest and by the frequent flicking of his horse's ears. A howl from a nearby forest beast caused the horse's tail to swish, and it balked. The man stroked the crest of the dark mahogany steed and encouraged the horse forward into the darkness.

"You'll never get out alive, McTaver! You'll wish for the mercy of my blade before the night is over!" shouted one of the Serpent's men. His horse reared and struck out with its hooves.

Another man called, "The forest dwellers will rip you to pieces and feed you to their beasts! Come out while you still can for we offer swift death, a mercy you will not see in Loch Nidean forest!"

"You forget I was born next to this cursed place! It does not frighten me, you cowards," Ronin shouted back, although he looked around nervously.

"You are a fool, Ronin! Everyone knows that Druid powers guard the forest."

"I fear naught! Go on your way, mercenaries, and tell Lothian that you saw me eaten by the beasts of Loch Nidean." Ronin leaned down, peering through the branches as he slowly entered deeper into the forest, leaving the soldiers behind.

Kalial's amber eyes narrowed as she watched the Serpent men confer, then circle and move off. Her face was black, coated with grease mixed with dank earth. Her hair, too, hung heavy and dank with the concealing grease. She leapt nimbly to a lower branch and swung her body to the forest floor. There she froze as a black jaguar paced around a tree and stared at her.

Kalial reached out her hand and placed it upon the great cat's nose. "Let us follow him, my pet," she whispered in a soft, singsong voice, "and drive him from our sacred trees, for no stranger is allowed within Loch Nidean forest." As she started forward, seven equally black bodies sprang down from their hiding places and spread out behind her. The birds that had rustled and cried out warnings as Ronin McTaver moved past them settled into forest song in the presence of the silent followers.

"God help me in this evil place," Ronin McTaver grumbled aloud. He shifted in his saddle to check his meager load. In a worn saddlebag he had thrown what food and tools he could find in the stable where he had crawled after the tower had collapsed around him. He had been in agony. His shoulder had been wrenched from its socket. His ribs had throbbed and at least two were broken. His skin still ached from contusions and was scored with multiple abrasions.

However, his memories pained him most. His family, his clansmen . . . their deaths had driven him, crawling, out from under the stones of the collapsed tower. His hatred had settled into a seething force in his soul and had given him strength to wrap up an old saddlebag, a hunting knife, a flint and a rope trap. Hatred had given him the will to slam his shoulder against the wall and silently endure the white-hot pain of the bones grinding back into place. With fingers still tingling he had lashed the saddlebag and his sword and crossbow onto a saddle.

Then, leading a stallion and carrying his bundle with his aching arm, he had crept with quiet stealth to the family church, pried up several planks from the altar and removed a beautiful, golden-threaded tapestry. Eyes burning in fury and pain, he had rapidly rolled it in concealing dust, then placed it upon the back of his mahogany steed disguised as a saddle blanket. He had ignored the urge to touch the material as he recalled the horror of his family's destruction. He had clenched his fists in fury, then knelt upon the altar as he held the reins of the restless stallion.

A silent vow of vengeance had come from his gut and blazed through his soul. The church air froze and dust fairies fled in frightened panic when he surged abruptly to his feet, swung up upon the warhorse and galloped out of the holy sanctuary. As he burst through the arched doors, the Serpent mercenaries attempted to converge upon him, grabbing his thighs and seeking to trip his horse. A scream of fury trumpeted from the stallion's throat and he struck out with both hind legs then leapt above the ground. The men scattered and Ronin clamped his legs around the angry stallion, causing him to gallop madly away from Castle Roseneath.

For three weeks the Serpent men pursued him as he slipped in and around the shifting waters of River Chaos. Then despite his skill, two hours ago the mercenaries had closed in, and Ronin McTaver had decided upon a daring gamble. Racing his exhausted horse to the west, he headed for the dreaded forest that flanked the coast from his castle lands to just north of the port town of Rath-thuaidhe.

Loch Nidean forest, the wilderness shielding the sacred Nidean lake, was a land of witches and ferocious beasts. Tales of the place had beguiled him since childhood. The mysterious forest dwellers—ancient Druids, people said—fiercely guarded this domain from any intruder and no one risked penetrating its thick growth. Yet, with no other choice but to run until his horse gave out beneath him, or fight until the attackers carved the flesh from his body, Ronin had plunged his steed into the Loch Nidean forest.

Stories told of a magical, mystical land that vibrated with shapeshifters, animal speakers and invisible spirits. Legend spoke of the bottomless Nidean lake that swallowed man and steed, such that any who entered the forest never returned to the Scottish moors. Intermixed with such tales was the legend of the Scottish Gold, which was said to have been hidden and lost within the dangerous forest long ago.

The legend was old . . . older than any person Ronin had known and older than any *they* had known. As such, truth and fiction had merged. Only children played at searching for the legendary Scottish Gold, for once they were adults, such frivolity was discouraged. Besides, no matter what soothsayer spoke of it, no one knew the secret to finding it, or for that matter, what the treasure truly entailed.

Ronin's childhood fascination with the treasure had abruptly ceased one early morning many years ago. Waking him in the wee hours, Laird Robert said, "Ronin, my son, it is time to teach you about our family. You are a McTaver, and that means you must one day be master of all around you. Our lands abut the Loch Nidean forest, and our destinies are forever entwined. What I tell and show you must be kept secret forever. Do you understand the responsibility I give you this day, my son?"

Solemnly, Ronin nodded and followed his father outside. No hound stirred from the fireside, no servant milled in the courtyard. The two men walked quietly out to the church where Laird Robert latched the door from inside, locking them in. Then, motioning Ronin forward, Laird Robert pulled up the altar boards and extracted an exquisite length of fabric—the golden tapestry.

"This, more than the castle or these lands, is your legacy. A long time ago, our ancestors made an uncommon union between our ancient line and that of an ordinary woman traveler who wandered into our land while lost in a horrific storm. The woman and the laird of the castle fell in love, and from that marriage sprang a wealth that has not been seen since. The wealth of the Scottish Gold. In jealousy, a feuding clan killed the McTaver laird in search of the riches that flowed from this union, yet despite ransacking and torture, they could not find the place where the gold was hidden.

"As the mother of our clan lay trapped in the tower, awaiting her fate and sorrowing for the loss of her beloved, she wove three tapestries, each telling a part of the tale that would lead to the heart of the Scottish Gold, so that her descendants could one day reclaim it from its hiding place. Of the three, only this one remains in our possession. It is the Second Hunt, the intermediate map that now has no beginning and no end, and thus, without its mates, is useless in anyone's search for the hidden treasure. The greedy still seek it, but such hatred will only destroy it. Know that the Scottish Gold dwells within our family, my son, and that this treasure is your destiny and that of your children. Someday the other tapestries will surface, and when they do, you will be bound to protect and guard the treasure they describe."

Ronin grimaced at the remembered warnings and shook his head to clear the sorry thoughts. His hand strayed to the hilt of his sword. The coolness of its familiar presence steadied his nerves. He looked up to judge his direction by the sun, but was met by lush foliage through which seeped only glimmers of light. He slowly pivoted his steed while keeping his eyes closed to feel the infinitesimal differences of heat and wind upon his bare back. He stopped where the warmth was strongest and glanced around at the moss on the trees. It was thickest on the shaded side, indicating the northern direction. With a silent salute to the spongy plants, he set off northwest—toward the ocean on the other end of the bleak Loch Nidean forest.

Kalial's worry grew as the man got his bearings and proceeded into the heart of the forest. A shiver raced through her as his eyes passed over the bush where she was hiding. She felt the hairs on the back of her neck tremble when his gaze paused and seemed to bore through the fronds. He stroked the jewels on his warrior's sword and slowly turned his eye past her. He was watchful but relaxed now as he bent over his horse's neck to avoid a low hanging branch. The velvet undersurface of the leaves stroked him as he rode beneath them. She could see the sheen of his body oils on the leaves as they swung back into place behind him.

The musk of his body teased her nose. He was big! She had never seen such a large man. His thighs bulged as thick as her waist. His shoulders were near two lengths across. Even his powerful jaw was imposing. A call from her left startled her and she creased her brow in annoyance. She whistled back and her seven followers started after Ronin, forming a large, moving circle around him and his horse.

Ronin felt something. His heart started to pound and his senses sharpened. He knew someone was nearby. When the sharp cry of a bird to his left was immediately answered by a whistle behind him, he knew that others now tracked him. He deliberately kept his muscles soft and his eyes unfocused. He could see vague movements around him. Most of the movement was undirected and natural. Birds took flight, long strands of moss waved, leaves rippled. But one, two . . . multiple dark shadows moved with a purpose that matched his own. He could not keep track of any one shadow in particular as they weaved in and out of the forest greenery as if they were part of the land itself, but he was well aware of their deliberate pace. He began to anticipate where he would next see a flash of dull black.

His horse stumbled with fatigue and Ronin swore under his breath. He subtly altered his course toward a break in the trees ahead. The open meadow would afford no hiding places for his uninvited traveling companions. There he would stop and rest his horse. A fire should keep the forest animals away. Perhaps it would also deter the followers.

Kalial stroked the fur of the black cat beside her. She checked her clothes. The band around her breasts was snug. She had discovered that as she grew and her small, pert breasts became full and round, she was better able to run and fight when they were bound tightly under a shapeless, loose black tunic. Dark leggings covered the telltale whiteness of her long legs and the fur foot coverings hardly made a sound when she stalked her prey. Kalial dug her fingers into the rich loam beside her and spread the earth over her cheeks, forehead and nose. She ground more dirt into her hair and then tied it back with a small leather thong. Only her brilliant yellow eyes marked her as separate from the night.

She waited until the warrior ate and settled down to sleep. Soon he slumped forward. The fire was left to smolder. She commanded the cat to wait, and then moved silently toward the mahogany horse. She nickered at the stallion and blew warm air through moistened lips. The horse arched his neck and shook his mane at her. She smiled in the darkness and called again. This time the horse took short steps toward her, emerging from the circle of firelight. When the man did not move, Kalial wrinkled her nose in disgust. Only a fool would allow his beast to be so easily taken.

With the stallion blowing in her ear, Kalial reached down and sliced the hobbles around the horse's fetlocks. Freed, he pawed the ground and nipped at her shoulder. She led the magnificent horse out of the meadow and into the forest where a comrade materialized to take the steed. The horse snorted his dismay when Kalial turned away, but a soft touch soothed him. She melted back into the tall grasses of the meadow.

A cluck from the back of her throat called the great cat forward. The black McCat, a Scottish jaguar, had appeared on Kalial's second birthday as a kitten partially grown. She was as dark as the new moon, with subtle stripes upon her hide, and long canines that were only partially covered by her whiskered lips. Woman and beast hunted and played together as they grew together. Now they worked together as Kalial accepted the responsibilities of her birth. She was the protector of the secrets of Loch Nidean forest and dhu Cait, the jaguar, was her familiar.

No one had ever ventured so deep among the trees

and Kalial wondered how to deal with the intruder. She had never killed a man before, relying upon her forest beasts to frighten and injure careless stragglers. Yet she knew her duty. This man must either be driven out of the forest, or captured and brought to Loch Nidean and dumped into its fathomless depths.

A faint snore reached her ears. The man must be exhausted. She whistled into the night sky and began her final advancement. She intended to grab his hair, yank back his head to expose his throat and hold her dirk to it while the others trussed him by hand and foot. She could see the others moving with her as she reached the faint edge of the firelight and went silently to his side.

She had reached up and grasped his hair when her whole body froze in shock. Two deep indigo eyes gleamed up at her. They were rich and deep and very alert. In that brief pause he sprang up and crashed his fist into her abdomen. Kalial collapsed in the grass and struggled vainly to gulp in air. Her eyes widened in terror as the jewels on his sword hilt winked in the firelight as he swung his weapon toward her.

The forest around them erupted into chaos. Screams from her people blasted upon her ears and a jarring clang of metal upon metal filled the air above her head. She saw two swords locked together in front of her eyes when suddenly the jeweled sword flicked forward and into the gut of the man trying to save her. A breath finally burst into her lungs and she rolled over to avoid her comrade's falling body. Three more men sprang at the warrior, but his arms outreached their own and he kept the men at bay. Kalial struggled slowly to her feet and leapt clumsily onto the man's back, her dirk held high to plunge into his neck.

His bellow of rage vibrated through him and coursed along her legs wrapped around his waist. She felt her wrist being clenched tight. Almost instantly her fingers went numb and the dirk fell harmlessly to the ground.

He grasped her thighs, wrenched them apart and swung her to the earth where she crashed, headfirst. A haze clouded her mind and she struggled to clear her thinking.

Ronin grinned ferociously. The attacking forest dwellers were swift, stealthy and clever, but they were small and not skilled in hand-to-hand combat. They were untrained young men whose talent lay in surprise and mental intimidation. Their blackened faces and shapeless tunics created a resemblance to the demons of yore or to the sexless, shapeless beasts of the under-brush. Yet Ronin had already been fighting his version of demons for three weeks, and the forest dwellers caused barely a flicker of unease in his soul. Instead, he poured his anger at the Serpent into his sword as he fought the hapless forest dwellers with deadly intent.

Ronin lunged forward and opened the arm of an-other attacker. He sensed someone approaching from behind and turned to fling his dagger into his chest. The man hung still for a moment with a confused expression before he collapsed. Ronin heard a sudden series of birdcalls, and then felt a shift in the direction of the attackers. They all surged to the right, toward their fallen companions, leaving the left flank clear for his escape. Ronin almost dashed through the open avenue when he saw his horse standing in the trees, yet battle instinct made him hold his ground.

The remaining forest fighters became vicious as they closed in upon him. A thrown dirk hit his sword arm and his swing faltered, but to his surprise they did not take advantage of his momentary lapse. Instead, they reached toward the one who was just now struggling to rise for a second time. Suddenly deciphering the boy's importance to the forest men, Ronin lunged for-ward, his sword tip raising the chest of the man who was trying to grab the fallen comrade from the ground. The man fell back a step while holding an edge of the boy's shapeless tunic. Abruptly, Ronin's sword flashed down and severed the cloth, separating the tenuous bond between the two males.

The boy stumbled again, unbalanced by the abrupt tear of his tunic. He fell down in front of Ronin whereupon Ronin slammed his booted foot onto the boy's leather bound hair and jammed it into the churned dirt. The boy screamed in anger and tried to jerk away. The other forest dwellers rushed forward with their swords and dirks leveled at Ronin's chest.

His eyes cold, Ronin lowered his sword. The eyes of one of the attacking forest men gleamed with triumph as he closed in for a fatal thrust, but then he saw the direction of the warrior's blade, pressed into the throat of his comrade. The advancing man froze and barked out a warning to the others in a strange voice. They instantly ceased their attack and glared at the warrior holding their comrade with his booted foot.

Kalial jerked and pulled at her hair until she was sure her scalp would be wrenched off her head. She looked up past the powerful thighs, past the rippled stomach and up to his face. His gaze was deadly. As blue as the depths of Loch Nidean, it held the same promise of mercilessness that filled the lake waters.

"No!" Kalial screamed at her men. "Sacrifice me. He must not survive!" But the men continued to fall back.

Ronin saw a few flames start to lick at the boy's tunic and realized why the fighters had suddenly stopped pressing him. He kept his sword on the boy's throat and waited until the others fully understood that his captive would soon be ablaze. The man in front of him visibly trembled.

Kalial felt heat on her leg and through her tears of frustration she saw the hungry flames. She arched up to try to escape the fire and consequently drove Ronin's sword through the first layer of skin on her throat.

A trickle of warm blood soaked the tip of his sword at the boy's struggles and Ronin lifted its deadly point a fraction higher. With the boy squirming underneath him, Ronin withdrew a skin of water from his belt with his free hand.

"Allow me safe passage," he commanded, "and I will allow this boy to live." The forest dwellers started at his words. "I demand no interference from here until the ocean. You will not attack or hinder me in any way, or your boy dies with flames scorching his flesh." A drop of water splashed on the flaming tunic edge and the hiss was audible even above the boy's screams of rage and fear.

One man quickly nodded. "We will not seek to harm you. We will be true to our word." He spoke in a strange accent. The man glanced anxiously at the boy who had finally fallen still. Ronin kept his blade against his skin.

An arch of crystal clear water flowed out of the bladder skin and down onto Kalial's clothes. The shock of the cold water made her gasp. The warrior reached down and hauled her to her feet with a strong hand wrapped around her slender arm. A few strands of her hair still caught on his boot and were ripped out of her scalp, adding pricks of pain to her bruised and battered body.

Ronin noted that the boy was smaller than the others, not even old enough to shave. He shook his head.

"I will keep him with me to ensure that you keep your word." The boy glared at him and spit on his cheek. Ronin's eyes grew cold. "And if any attempt is made to rescue him, I will not rest until I have ripped out his liver."

Kalial watched as the thin line of spittle dripped from his cheek and onto his chest level with her eyes. She saw him take a breath as his chest expanded and a piercing whistle called forth his mahogany horse. The stallion danced forward and blew on Kalial's face in bestial apology. Kalial expelled her pent-up breath in a snort not unlike that of a frustrated bull.

The warrior wrapped one arm around her neck and used the other to place the dusty saddle blanket and saddle upon the stallion's huge back, then lashed on his saddlebag. He tossed her face down over the horse's withers. The ridge of the leather dug into her already aching belly, but she did not have time to concentrate on that displeasure when she felt him swing up behind her and her head started spinning again. At a slight clench of the warrior's thighs the warhorse sprang forward into a controlled canter. Before Kalial sank into unconsciousness, she twisted her head in order to see her men standing still, passively watching as she was taken away. Her last thought was for her great cat, padding silently beside them just out of sight.

CHAPTER 2

Ronin was forced to slow his horse to a walk as he entered an even more dense area of the forest. The night sky was obliterated from view by the leafy canopy so that even the sliver of moonlight no longer guided his way. The boy was still draped across the saddle, his slight form wedged tightly against Ronin's thighs. Ronin's nose wrinkled at the smell of animal grease mixed with charred cloth that wafted from the boy. Clearly cleanliness was not a requirement of the forest dwellers. The boy's dank hair hung in a ragged queue down to the forest floor, catching on branches and bushes as they passed.

A massive set of tree roots loomed up ahead. The upended tree must have fallen many years ago as the roots were moss covered and the hole in the ground where the roots had been was now soft with many layers of fallen leaves. Ronin pulled up next to the lee of the roots and pushed the boy down onto the spongy bed. A quiet groan signaled the boy's return to consciousness. Ronin swung off his horse. He unraveled the rope trap he carried, and used it to bind the boy's legs together. He then bound the boy's arms at his back and pulled both arms and legs together with his final piece. The end was secured to a twisted root embedded in the ground. Ronin surveyed his handiwork and tested the knots. Satisfied, he turned to gather wood for the second time that night.

Kalial's head was swimming and her abdomen ached terribly. When she heard the man move away she carefully opened her eyes a slit and waited for the shadows to stop spinning. She opened them wider and peered into the gloom around her. The man was not in sight. Oddly, she could not even hear him in the darkness.

For a man so large, it was not right that he could move with the grace of a wolf in the dark, she thought irritably. Her jaguar's tail twitched on a branch overhead. With the confidence of a person who knows she will be understood and obeyed, Kalial silently asked the cat to follow the man and ambush him. The cat simply sat on the branch. Kalial frowned and clucked quietly, her signal for the cat to come forward. The jaguar lowered her head onto the branch and rubbed her cheek against the bark before leaping softly to the ground next to Kalial.

"Dhu Cait, my wild Scots McCat of the night," she whispered aloud. "Go after him." The cat tilted her head. Her whiskers fluttered and a twitch of her lips revealed a glimpse of startlingly long, white teeth. Kalial looked at her incredulously. "No?" she whispered again, this time more loudly. "Why not? He has captured me, my friend, and is our enemy. He, like the others of the legend, must not be allowed to enter the forest. It is our duty to protect the creatures and secrets of this land. Now, go after him and then rejoin me to free me so we may return to guard our borders."

The cat twitched her upper lip again and looked away. Kalial stared at her in amazement, then anger. "You have never failed me. Why do you ignore me now, when I need you most? This man is a threat to me! I felt it when he took his very first step into the forest. Can you not sense the danger of this man?" The cat looked back at her beloved mistress and blinked slowly. Then she turned and with a gathering of her haunches, glided back up to her place in the trees above.

"Why? Why, my dhu Cait?" whispered Kalial into the darkness.

An image of the man's face slipped into and out of her mind so quickly she almost did not see the message.

What does he have to do with this? she answered silently.

The image returned and Kalial latched onto it. She closed her eyes in concentration. The man looked out over fields of burned wheat. Bloated sheep lay on their sides, dotting the black ground with splashes of white. His head turned slightly and she saw a forest lit behind him with flickering tendrils of orange fire. Then the image faded.

I know the legend, my friend. The legend warns us of strangers destroying this land we love so dearly. I remember the fear of fire we all share. I have not forgotten the treasure we guard. I know I must protect the forest and the sacred loch. That is why we must not allow this stranger to pass through. His presence here will only draw more men and more destruction. Help me, my cat. Let us work together! The last words were almost spoken aloud as Kalial strained upwards in her fervor.

Ronin returned to find the boy contorting himself in the ropes with his eyes scrunched shut and his lips moving soundlessly. He dropped his armful of wood onto the ground with a resounding clatter.

Kalial froze. She opened her eyes and stared across the small clearing at the hulk of the man who had punched her, held a sword to her, knocked her head so hard it still pounded, carried her off and, for some inexplicable reason, made her dearest friend betray her. She glared at him.

"Good," he said, "you appear to be well." He

strode over to where Kalial was tied. She attempted to move back but instead she knocked her head against a jutting root and cursed loudly. Shaking the loose, greasy strands of hair out of her face, she saw the man grinning.

"Perhaps you should rest awhile, lad." Ronin watched the boy's face grow tight with anger. A small trickle of blood dripped down the smooth cheek. "Come now, boy, if you will just behave, you will not hurt yourself." Ronin turned back to the firewood and began to build up a pile of kindling, adding a stick covered in santeen moss over the top of the pile. When he pulled out his flint, the boy jerked in surprise, his oddly colored yellow eyes fixated on the pile of wood. He looked frightened. Ronin sighed and turned to the boy.

"You can not light that," the boy said in a high, youthful voice made thick by the unusual accent.

Ronin tilted his head, trying to place the sound. It was not of the Scottish lowlands or highlands. Clearly, it was an accent unique to the Loch Nidean forest. "Why not? Do not worry, I will not hurt you with the flames." Ronin smiled encouragingly, trying to soften his face. If he had to cart this boy with him to ensure his safe passage through the forest, then there was no reason not to try to get him to relax. A hostile, angry prisoner would be more trouble than an obedient one. Ronin had decided during his walk in the dark that he would be kind but firm to the young boy. That was how his mother had handled young squires who came to train at his father's castle.

The boy grunted in disgust. "You are a fool!" he said scathingly. Ronin's eyes narrowed. This might be more difficult than he had anticipated. "That is santeen moss," the boy stated.

Ronin was nonplussed. "Is that supposed to mean something to me?"

"Of course it should, since it is the season when the

leaves are turning color." The boy shifted positions so that he could lean against the tree. Ronin turned back to the wood and started striking the flint, irritated that he could not understand the youth. A spark flew off, landed on the dry grasses underneath the wood and started to smolder. The boy stared at him incredulously before burying his face in the damp earth at the base of the upended roots. Ronin saw the boy fall forward and took a step toward him to help him right himself. At that moment a huge crack resounded behind him and a shower of sparks blasted around him, singeing his back as embers pelted him with the force of a small explosion.

With a roar Ronin reached down and grabbed the neckline of the boy's tunic. His small, frail body was rippling with laughter. Ronin shook him hard until the boy gasped and stopped laughing in favor of shouting, "I told you, you idiot. No one is stupid enough to light santeen moss in autumn. It is just a shame you turned away at the last moment or you might have lost an eye or two!"

Ronin shoved the boy face down into the dirt. The boy's head twisted back and forth as he struggled to draw breath through the dirt clogging his throat. "You will NEVER do that—" Ronin began but a low rumble at his back made him whip around and draw his hunting knife. A giant black jaguar stood at the upper lip of the depression Ronin and the boy occupied. Behind him, he heard the boy sit up and cough to clear his throat.

"Scoot back, boy," Ronin said. "I will block you." He crouched down in a fighting stance. The giant cat stood with her head lowered to the ground, her jaws opened slightly. The cat's red tongue flicked out and licked at her nose. Ronin shifted the knife in his hand. The cat remained standing, watching him. "Just a little longer . . ." Ronin whispered. He slowly raised the knife into throwing position.

"No!" screamed the boy. "Go away, dhu Cait, leave now!" The cat sprang up over their heads and onto the top of the roots just as the hunting knife sailed from Ronin's hand. It landed with a twang deep into the earth where the cat had been standing not a moment before. Ronin jumped to where his sword lay and snatched it up. He spun, expecting attack, and was surprised by the calm regard of the jaguar above him. The cat batted the air with her claws extended, folding her small ears flat against her skull and hissing. Ronin stepped over the boy sprawled on the ground and lifted his sword. With a low growl, the great cat leapt off the roots and into the darkness. Ronin stood still for some moments, scanning the trees for movement, then glanced down at the boy in fury.

"You call me stupid when you warn a hungry jaguar away from my blade? No doubt that beast will return. You should be grateful I value you enough not to feed you to it." Ronin stepped away and kicked the boy's back with his boot.

Kalial rolled up and sputtered at him, "I only wish she had ripped you to pieces. I can not imagine why she did not!" Kalial's gaze swung around the forest. Dhu Cait's sudden absence made her brow crease in worry and confusion. The McCat had been more of a friend to her than any human. Their close love had developed from a mutual interdependence and although Kalial could talk to her as she could with any forest animal, they often had no need of such simple communication. Their link went deeper, for they were both bound by the same destiny—to protect the forest from intruders. Though the jaguar did not understand the nuances of Kalial's duty, she was devoted to her mistress and thus equally committed to keep Loch Nidean forest from the filth of invasion.

Raised in lonely isolation, Kalial had found her closest friend in dhu Cait. Simple play, simple pleasures had been denied her in favor of strict tradition and unrelenting instruction. She was kept always apart from the other children such that now she hardly noticed her lack of closeness to any human. Her life-blood sang with generations of protectors as each mother passed the knowledge and duty down to her daughter.

Kalial accepted her role without protest. She did not feel the urges that rippled through the young girls of her home tribe. She did not return the longing glances of the male youths in her band. She set herself apart, alone and aloof. She was the princess of Loch Nidean forest, born to uphold the tradition of isolation. She knew the darkest secrets of the lake and why foreigners were never permitted within the leafy canopy, and she had shared her duty with the black cat.

Yet now the McCat had abandoned her, leaving her helpless with this threatening man. Kalial glared up at her captor, feeling her control slipping away. She shivered, the unfamiliar anxiety making her frightened.

"Such blood thirst in a boy of what, twelve summers?" remarked Ronin with a lift to his eyebrow.

Kalial glanced back at Ronin in surprise. Boy? Twelve? The few earlier references to "boy" clicked into place and Kalial's thoughts sharpened. She glanced down at her bound chest, grease-covered skin and loose tunic, and sneered at Ronin from beneath her lowered lashes.

Morning came with bright shafts of sunshine and joyful birdsong. Ronin glowered at the boy sleeping peacefully in a most uncomfortable position. Ronin had not slept soundly all night. He had kept a watchful ear out for the jaguar and was frankly puzzled that it had not returned. Overnight his resentment of the boy had grown. If only his blade had sunk into the chest of that beast, he would not have had to worry about it all night.

The boy's eyes slowly opened. For a moment Ronin

was stunned by the brilliance of their golden depths. Then the dusky lashes fluttered down and the boy groaned. Ronin stood and shook his head. Of course this crazy boy-child would have funny-looking eyes. He was just surprised at how catlike they appeared after his nightlong vigil watching for the jaguar, he told himself.

"Here," Ronin said, "let me untie you so you can stretch."

Kalial felt uncomfortable with her shoulders pulled back. The position jutted her chest forward. She turned on her knees and presented her back to Ronin. She felt the cold metal of a blade at her neck and saw the sunlight glancing off the hunting knife he used. When Ronin was assured of her attention, he skillfully untied the ropes around her legs and wrists. Holding the knife in his left hand, he quickly relooped the rope around her neck and secured it with a sliding knot.

"There. Now understand this. This knot will only get tighter with tension. It will not loosen, so do not try to struggle or run. Your neck is too tiny as it is. I would hate to see you squeeze it smaller." Ronin frowned at her. "Go piss and then we are moving on."

Kalial gaped up at him. She stumbled to her feet and swayed for a moment as the blood swept back into her calves. She grabbed hold of a root and started to move behind the nearest tree. A slight tug and faint tightening of her neck collar stopped her.

"Where are you going, boy?" asked Ronin in irritation.

"Behind the tree."

Ronin glowered even more fiercely. The boy looked even younger than he had thought last night. His skin was filthy yet his bones were delicate and underdeveloped. His voice was soft—too soft for a fighter. "Blast you! Must you be shy as well as a baby? Go then, but be quick." Ronin drew open his leggings and pulled out his cock.

Kalial's mouth dropped open. Her eyes shot upwards to Ronin's face and she saw him mocking her.
A splash drew her eyes down again and she saw an
arc of urine landing at her feet. She yelped and dashed
behind the tree as far as her tether would allow, the
warrior's laughter following her.

Ronin headed the mahogany horse in a westerly
direction. Kalial trudged behind, tossing dark and
angry looks at Ronin's back, which swayed gracefully
with the horse's movements. Periodically he stopped
and allowed his horse to graze while he climbed a tree
for a vantage point. Kalial remained lashed to the saddle and was obliged to walk with the horse's meander-
ings or have the rope around her neck tighten. She
had stumbled twice that morning so consequently the
rope was tight enough to make a slight indentation in
her throat. After the second time she slid her fingers
into the noose and tried to loosen it but the rope
would not budge. Her fingers explored the rope in a
effort to untie it, but the twists eluded her understanding.

Ronin sprang down from the tree. The boy appeared surprisingly strong and fit for such a tiny fellow
since he had managed to keep up with the horse without seeming to tire.

"What is your name, boy?"

"My name?" The boy's voice was raspy and deep
due to the bruising of his throat. He averted his eyes
for a moment and scuffed his boot in the dirt.

"Would you rather I call you 'boy'?"

"No, I mean yes, that would be fine. I do not intend
to be with you long enough for it to matter," he replied. He looked up swiftly with a defiant glare. Ronin
tilted his head slightly and contemplated the boy. His
gaze traveled slowly down the youth's frame, from the
slender throat to the scrawny, blackened arms and finally to the coltish legs covered in leather leggings.
His gaze then returned to stare into the pair of golden

eyes. The boy gazed back unflinchingly. Ronin felt oddly disturbed, uncomfortable. He turned abruptly away.

"Tell me your name, boy," he demanded as he tightened the warhorse's girth.

"Kal," Kalial finally replied, not daring to show more disobedience.

"An odd name," he muttered, mostly to himself. He swung up on his horse again and without another word he started the threesome off.

Kalial stood frozen for a moment, the sudden heat flushing her skin catching her by surprise. When his eyes had raked her she had been certain he would see the truth, for her body had trembled and her chest had heaved.

She stumbled after him. "I do not know who you are," she tossed at his bare back, her voice sweet and lilting. She coughed at the sound and tried to deepen the tones.

"McTaver," Ronin growled over his shoulder. "I am Ronin McTaver of Roseneath."

"When will you release me?" Kalial persisted.

"When we reach the ocean."

"The ocean? It is too far. I can not go there," she stated firmly and planted her feet for a moment. The tug on her neck forced her to continue almost immediately but the fear of the ocean made her chatter quickly.

The forest was her home, the high trees, the dank air, the shadows and leaves and fronds. Even the mysterious Loch Nidean and the waterways that flowed into its banks were familiar to her. But the ocean was the antithesis of her safe haven. It was wide open, endless, bright and bereft of the forest creatures she knew so well. To a woman who knew every leaf, every stream of her homeland, the concept of stepping out of her forest and seeking the open seas was horrifying.

"I will be nothing but a burden to you," she insisted. "I mean, you would make much better time without me," she said, fear entering her voice.

"Yes, I am sure I would be much faster without you. But without the protection your presence grants me, my time upon this earth would be too short for my liking. I am quite aware of your distaste for me in your land. I have no desire to be here either. I find the leaves too dense, the trees too numerous, the air too damp and the wildlife too unpredictable. However, I must reach the ocean and thence travel across it to reach my cousin. His force is large and strong. I will ask him to grant a small army so I may reclaim my lands."

Kalial looked at Ronin's back as he talked. She saw a thin line of tree sap drip onto his shoulder and trace a short, sparkling path down the middle of his back. She marveled once again at the man's immense size. She had never seen someone so massive yet composed of solid strength and firm musculature. It frightened her, yet also soothed her. Perhaps even the ocean would be intimidated by his strength.

"A man like you should not need to hide behind a scrap of a *boy* like me," Kalial challenged. Her voice broke on the last word when she turned her head sideways to view the flash of black that was keeping pace with them.

"A man like me is too smart to be goaded into releasing you to prove my courage. You will remain with me until I make it safely to the shore. Then you can rejoin your heathen camp and need never recall me to memory again. Do not worry. As long as you are well behaved, I will find no need to punish you."

Ronin chuckled quietly, in better spirits than he had been in weeks. He could almost feel the growing frustration of the boy behind him. He was not quite sure why he teased Kal. Perhaps because he had not talked to anyone in so long and felt reasonably safe for the first time since the awful day his family had been murdered.

Ronin snuck a glance over his shoulder to see how the boy was faring. He followed the path of Kal's eyes into an area of heavy ferns. For a moment he thought he saw the outline of a large cat's head, but then it disappeared. Kal looked away.

"What did you see, Kal? Is that cat tracking us?" When the boy did not answer, Ronin drew his crossbow out and strung a dart. Ronin saw Kal grow pale.

"Do not tell me that you wish to kill me but can not abide the thought of hurting a beast," Ronin said scornfully. His eyes swept the bushes and ferns surrounding them, but he could not spot the black shadow of the cat.

"I see no compelling reason to kill the animal," Kal replied.

"Are not our lives a compelling reason?"

"That cat will not hurt me. Nor apparently will it hurt you," she finished in a disgruntled mumble.

"And why not? Because you are a forest dweller? Because you are such a part of this dark forest that the wild animals leave you in peace?" Ronin's tone was sarcastic. His eyebrows were raised in mockery. Kal glowered at him.

"Of course the animals will attack me if they are hungry. I just meant that . . . ah . . . that the cat does not appear hungry. Yes, she clearly is not hungry."

Kalial smiled in triumph at Ronin. She had no intention of letting this stranger know how she communicated with wild beasts, especially this jaguar. The skill gave her a certain advantage over this hulk of a man who had bested her again and again. She knew that her ability was unusual. Many of the forest dwellers had a connection to the forest, but her ease of communication transcended the normal.

It was her heritage, as her mother before her had

also spoken with the great beasts. Her gift gave her the eyes of the sparrows, the vibrations of the bees and the nostrils of the wolves, and with her help, the forest people located intruders. They could silently encircle a victim and scare him back out of the trees, or ambush him and throw him into the Loch. The beast talk was important to her for two reasons: it allowed her to protect her forest and it gave her companionship when she felt isolated from her own people.

This man was the only one who had ever escaped her band of men and animals, and now the beasts refused to obey her silent commands. She could not get the ants to crawl up his trousers or a nearby snake to spook his horse. And there was the complete betrayal of her beloved cat, who would not show herself in order to frighten this man away. The situation was utterly galling and utterly incomprehensible.

"The beast is not hungry?" Ronin's voice broke into her thoughts. "I suppose you can tell by the way it is following us that it wants nothing to do with us?"

"It is probably following me," Kalial replied with sudden inspiration. "I am sure it senses that I am injured. If you would leave me behind, I am certain it would leave you alone."

Ronin laughed aloud. Kalial thought with annoyance that he seemed to laugh at her a lot.

"I will not leave you to be devoured by a jaguar that is not hungry but is stalking a poor, injured, young boy. Even if I did not need you, I would not do that to you since you have no weapons other than your sharp tongue with which to defend yourself."

"You could return my dirk," Kalial replied sulkily.

Ronin smiled again while shaking his head. At least the lad had spunk. He nudged his horse forward while scanning the forest carefully. He listened to the hum of insects and the rustling of leaves for any change in tempo or cadence which might signal a predator's presence. He kept his crossbow handy, although not strung. It would not be useful unless he saw the cat at some distance. If it pounced on him from above, his short-handled knife would be his best choice.

They traveled in silence for some time. Ronin could not see the sun reach the zenith but he could feel the heat penetrating the canopy with more force. Every now and then he would spare a glance for his mute companion walking behind him, the darkness of Kal's skin, hair and clothes making him blend in with the forest. Ronin made a note that should he ever want to hide in a dark space, he too would use dark grease and dirt to camouflage his skin. It was no wonder that he had failed to spot the group of men before they had attacked.

A sudden jerk on the boy's rope and a choked-off gasp made him whip his head around. He saw Kal falling forward with his leg caught around a devil's foot hidden in the ground. His eyes were wide with fright and one hand was flung forward to stop his fall while the other was flying to his throat where the rope was choking off his air as the noose tightened roughly, swiftly.

Sparkles of light darted in front of Kalial while a dull, red haze clouded her vision. A sharp pain tore through her ankle caught in a tangle of roots. Her free hand ripped at the rope around her throat and left furrows of scratches where her nails caught. She heard a curse from far away, then her face slammed into the packed earth. The last breath was forced out of her lungs in a whoosh.

Ronin leapt from his horse and drew his knife in one fluid movement. He hauled Kal up by his long hair, then wedged the point of his knife under the rope. Kal's body thrashed and reaching his hand up, his palm accidentally slid along the knife-edge. The rope sprang apart as, with a strong jerk of Ronin's forearm, he pulled the finely honed blade through the multi-twined rope. Kal gasped, struggling to draw air into his chest. Ronin dropped his hair and let his head sink to the ground. Kal rolled over on all fours and struggled to draw breath.

Ronin watched him heave. He rubbed his forehead and ran his fingers through his hair. He glanced around him, expecting to see the forest's inhabitants bearing down on him for harming this boy. He saw a glimpse of two orange eyes and a flickering black tail framed by dark green leaves, then it was gone. Ronin sheathed his knife and bent over the boy.

"Are you alright, Kal? Here, let me untwist your foot." Ronin squatted down and gently disentangled the boy's ankle from the devil's foot. He heard him catch his breath in pain but when he looked up, Kal just clenched his teeth and ducked his head lower.

Ronin slid Kal's soft boot off his foot and studied his ankle. It was slender and fine. He stroked the delicate indentations above the heel, checking for breaks. Then he cautiously rotated the ankle with one hand on Kal's lower calf and the other encasing the ankle. He felt Kal's calf muscles twitch under his warm hands and he stared down at the sight, surprised by the creaminess of the skin compared to the filth covering his arms and face. A dusting of golden hair made the lower limb silky. His hands moved down and he felt the high arch of the boy's foot and then closed around his petite toes. He felt each digit separately, starting with the big toe and ending with the tiniest one. He wiggled each one back and forth and felt them carefully for heat. He then ran his fingers along the bones of the foot, ensuring that each one felt smooth and uninjured. Convinced that nothing was seriously damaged, he continued to stroke the mysterious valleys and hard hills of Kal's ankle, mesmerized by the soft texture.

Kal jerked his foot out of Ronin's hands. Ronin sat back, startled, and looked up into Kal's angry golden eyes. "I am fine. Nothing is broken, just sprained,"

Kal squawked, his voice harsh and raspy. He shifted into a sitting position and rolled his wrist in small circles, then pressed the fingers of his other hand into a tight fist around the cut palm. A rope burn encircled his neck. Ronin stood abruptly. A dull flush stained his neck and a blood vessel pulsed at his temple.

"Yes. Good. I am sorry," he mumbled. The hand that had been stroking Kal's ankle shook slightly. He turned away to hide his face and walked over to his horse, standing patiently nearby. He pulled out a waterskin and returned to Kal. As he handed it to him he noticed with stupefaction that his palm, too, had a cut on its callused surface. He faintly recalled Kal's fingernails tearing at his hands in the instant before the rope was released.

Kalial grasped Ronin's hand with hers to pull herself up since her ankle would not fully support her weight. The second the bloodied palms clasped, a shock ran through each of them. Their eyes locked. Time was suspended while they felt a pulse throb between their hands and race throughout their bodies. Ronin watched a glow suffuse Kal's face and body and he stood entranced while a deep roar echoed in his head.

Kalial shivered as bolts of electricity raced through her fingertips and down to her belly. Her mouth went suddenly dry yet her skin was covered with a fine sheen of sweat. She felt her thighs slip against each other as Ronin continued to pull her up to a standing position. Staring into his midnight eyes, she was reminded of whirlpools on cloudless nights. She lifted her other hand to brace herself against his bare chest and dimly felt an electric shock arc between them.

Ronin felt a sharp sting when Kal's hand accidentally touched his nipple and he leapt back, dropping his palm in haste. Kal swayed as if he were falling once again. Ronin stepped away quickly, not trusting himself to assist the boy again. He felt a terrible sense of shame that he had reacted to a young boy in such a manner. Although he himself knew many good knights who preferred the companionship of boys to that of women, he preferred soft, meek, sweet-tongued ladies. Ronin looked at the scrawny, filthy boy in front of him and shuddered. He turned away and walked into the forest, leaving Kal balancing on one foot in the clearing, alone.

Kalial watched him go with an overwhelming sense of relief. The tingling in her body remained and she was certain that had he continued to stare at her in horror, she would have burst into tears. She limped over to a nearby tree and collapsed against it, closing her eyes. She soon felt a raspy tongue stroking her cheek and a furry face rubbing against her brow.

Kalial tilted her head against dhu Cait's solid flank. A deep rumbling emanated from the cat's chest, soothing her. Kalial breathed slowly. The smell of damp leaves wafted to her nose along with stray wisps of cat hair. Kalial sneezed. Twice. Then she smiled ruefully.

"Steady me, my friend." Dhu Cait gazed deeply into Kalial's eyes. Orange eyes met gold and a wealth of communication flickered back and forth. Kalial transmitted her uneasiness, her fears and her strange stirrings. Dhu Cait replied with calm reassurance. When Kalial leaned her head back against the tree, her breathing was even, although her thoughts were not. She was the forest princess, she reminded herself. She had no time for womanly feelings, and most certainly not for a stranger. She must push these unwelcome feelings away and concentrate on her duty.

A long time later Kalial pushed herself off the tree. Dhu Cait melted away into the forest. Kalial took one tentative step after her.

"Oh!" she cried when a shaft of pain raced up her leg. A glance down at her ankle revealed extensive swelling. Kalial scolded herself. *How stupid I am to be sitting here while a chance to escape slips by?* She wanted to stomp her feet like a child, but such a release of emotion was not allowed. She was trained to be in control at all times. She was bred to defend her emotions against everyone, for her maternal line was not to be distracted by unruly feelings. She had no known father. The mothers of her line mated during the fertility rites just as she expected to mate when it was time. Her flicker of interest in this male warrior was not to be tolerated, she berated herself. She was hard. She was strong.

Finally convincing herself, she dropped down on her hands and knees and peered carefully around, tilting her head to listen for any sound in the undergrowth. One wrist was still tender but it could support her weight. She crawled as stealthily as she could toward the underbrush. After reaching a thick clump, she squirmed underneath and looked behind her. Ronin McTaver was nowhere in sight and she breathed a little easier. She spent precious moments wrapping her disheveled hair into a quick knot so the strands would not get tangled in the brush, thus hindering her escape, then she crept along the forest floor, using the thick carpet of leaves to muffle her progress. She was familiar with most of the forest, but this was not an area where she traveled often so it took her a while to sort out her direction. In addition, she was accustomed to using the trees as her main route of travel. Everything looked quite different from this low perspective.

She came across a mud pool ringed by horsetails and suffused with a mild scent of sulfur. Kalial crawled over to the mud and plunged her aching ankle into the squishy depths. The coolness instantly soothed the throbbing. She remained in that position for many minutes. During that time she gingerly felt around her raw neck and reapplied mud to her face, hair and limbs. Satisfied that her skin would not gleam in the darkness, Kalial withdrew her foot and reexamined it. The swelling had decreased but the ankle was not ready for walking. Perhaps, she thought, if she allowed it a bit more time, she would be able to use it in the morning. After slathering a final handful of mud onto her ankle, Kalial commenced her slow crawl toward home.

Ronin returned to the clearing where he had left Kal and found it empty save for his horse nickering softly at his arrival. The grim lines around his face deepened into furrows. On the ground he saw tracks of a large cat and the blurred image of human handprints. He followed the tracks to the edge of the surrounding bushes where thick brambles and a heavy carpet of leaves hid their direction.

Unease at his sexual response to the young boy lingered in his gut, and he was relieved that Kal was gone. His walk in the woods had calmed his groin, but he remained uncomfortable. The boy clearly knew how to survive in the mysterious Loch Nidean forest and Ronin could sense the change of environment that signaled the nearness of the ocean. Perhaps, if he traveled quickly, he could reach the edge of the forest before nightfall and be rid of the strange feelings that both the boy and the forest evoked.

Ronin turned toward his horse. He slid his sword out of its scabbard, then gently brushed the blade free of dust upon the gilded threads of the tapestry concealed as his saddle blanket. He leaned his head down, pressing his forehead against the fabric. A shudder went through him as his memories rushed back.

" 'Tis time to move on," he muttered. "I have more important concerns than that forest lad." He stood up and lifted the sword. He turned it slightly so that its reflective surface caught the scant sunlight peeking through the trees and swung his eyes upwards as the shiny reflection danced off his sword and played with the green and brown leaves overhead. A flash of light sparking off his saddle blanket caught his eye. A sliver of gold embedded in the tapestry threads reminded him of Kal's golden eyes blinking in the sunlight. With a sigh, Ronin deliberately ignored the tracks in the earth, sheathed the sword, then swung up on his horse and headed toward the ocean.

CHAPTER 3

Kalial's knees were bruised and torn. Her hands did not feel much better. She was sweaty and hungry. Overall, the day had not been favorable. Her grumpy thoughts circled around one person.

If that man had left me be, I would not be crawling along like some earthworm. I would not be burning inside because of some odd clasp of his hand. I would not have been separated from my companions. I would not . . . She paused, trying to think of other things to blame him for. In all fairness she could not blame him for being hungry—she often was. Nor could she really blame him for all her injuries since she was always injured in some way. *I would not have a burning throat and a voice like a old crone!* There, it was fair enough to blame him for her neck injury since she would never have placed a noose around her *own* neck.

Kalial avoided thinking about her part in her capture. It was not satisfying to recall that she had initially attacked him. Instead she preferred to list how he had harmed her. Yes, that was much more pleasing.

When she suddenly came across a wild strawberry patch, her negative thoughts came to an abrupt halt. With a grin of delight, she settled herself in the center of the patch and began gobbling up the bright, red berries. She ate without delicacy, smearing berry juice over her chin and creating wide stains on her fingers and palms. When she had stuffed herself, she flopped back into the strawberry leaves and closed her eyes. *What a difference a full stomach makes.* The afternoon sun dipped lower as she drifted in a lazy doze.

A sharp cry from a blue jay brought her to jarring wakefulness. The cry signaled danger. Kalial sought out the bird with her mind, but the bird's dull thoughts only revealed generalized fear. Kalial swung her mind farther, trying to connect with the other animals around her. A rising disturbance stirred the air. Kalial could even hear the clicks of the wood bugs tapping alarm signals back and forth. Kalial strained harder, trying to find a focal point. A rabbit dashed through the strawberry patch, its mind a jumble of pure panic. She rose up to her knees, ignoring the sting of strawberry leaves digging into her scrapes. The vibrations in the forest began to hum in her head so loudly that she clamped her hands over her ears and squeezed her eyes shut.

Deprived of sight and auditory stimulus, Kalial concentrated on her other senses. She felt a warm breeze brush along her mud-covered skin. She felt a trembling in the ground beneath her. Then she smelled a faint wisp of smoke. Her eyes flew open in horror. Looking up, she saw birds and insects traveling rapidly but without clear bearing. The rabbit that had sped by a moment earlier now dashed back into the patch. It tripped and tumbled against Kalial's leg before springing up again to dart off in yet another direction. Kalial rose to a standing position. Her ankle hurt but held her weight.

She felt the creatures' fear start to overwhelm her and struggled to keep sane. The legend had warned her but she had failed to protect the forest. She trembled, her sense of self slipping away, replaced by an aching loneliness and fear. She cast out for the familiar comfort of her jaguar, yet even dhu Cait was gone.

Drawing a shaking breath, she tried to calm herself, to think clearly.

An image of her mother drifted to her. *Never forget your duty, daughter. You are to protect Loch Nidean and the beauty that she shields. The legend speaks of blazing heat that will seek to destroy everything we hold sacred, but remember, daughter, heat is powerful in many ways. Do not fight what you cannot fight, and turn the fire into your strength.*

Kalial shook her head, feeling helpless. She inhaled the smoke and coughed. She limped over to a nearby tree with many handholds and exceptional height.

"I must," she gasped as she gripped the tree bark with shaking fingers. She deliberately steadied her breathing and focused her mind. "I must be strong. It is my duty." The trembling in her fingers subsided and she felt her mind clear as the strength of her will suffused her. "Mother," she called out, "we live by legends and traditions, yet none tell of what I must do now. Guide me!" Kalial closed her eyes, seeking the answer to her plea, but the voices in her mind were silent. "Mother! Ancestors!" she cried out again.

Finally Kalial felt a whispered response. *There is no path preordained for you. I have no answer for you. For hundreds of years we have lived as we are, isolated, protected and alone. But the legends always spoke of this day and now it has come. You were chosen to be the one to live the legend instead of retelling it. Only you will know how to survive it.*

Kalial bowed her head. The memory of the warrior touching her ankle made her shiver and she looked up. "Very well," she whispered aloud, her voice gradually gaining strength. "I will do what I must, on my own. I will protect this forest, our people and our secret, even should I have to travel beyond these realms."

With effort, she hauled herself up the tree, taking the weight on her arms whenever possible. She reached a branch above the lower canopy, and inched along its length with her feet while holding onto the branch above with her hands. The smell of smoke grew stronger. An owl huddled in a hollow of the tree, her feathers fluffed and her beak open. Underneath her sat two owlets who were unable to fly away like the other birds. Kalial's heart skipped a beat as she stared into the mother owl's beady eyes. The owl blinked and Kalial turned away.

The forest before her was a tableau of chaos. In the distance, from every direction, blackened vistas encroached, following a line of blue-orange fire. Smoke streamed out, flooding the sky. The wind picked up as the fire greedily fed from the air around Kalial. She frantically searched for how or why the fire had started, but the smoke shifted and the heat warped the distant view. Her newborn strength faltered as paralyzing fear, such as a mother feels for her threatened children, swept over her. She desperately scanned the area for escape, but the panic infiltrating her mind from the beasts around her made her eyes glaze and her thoughts waver. She turned to the owl and stared at her, both of them frozen in the branches of the dry tree while the fire raced relentlessly toward them.

Ronin felt his horse dance nervously beneath him. His large calves wrapped more firmly around the horse's girth and he sank his heels down to brace himself. A moment later the horse shied sideways with the suddenness of a snake strike, but Ronin's body moved fluidly with him. He reached down and stroked the horse's neck and felt small muscle fasciculations running over the horse's hide. The horse calmed under his soothing touch but continued to flick his ears as Ronin halted him.

A hush had enveloped the forest. Ronin turned his horse on its haunches to make a full circle, scanning the thick trees with piercing eyes. His mouth dropped open and his breath caught. In front of him, sitting regally like a pampered house cat, was the huge black jaguar that had tracked him for the last two days.

He stared at the beast, watching her thick tail flick lazily and her eyes blink slowly. She was less than one easy jump away. Ronin considered pulling out his sword but instantly rejected the thought. The cat could have torn him to shreds moments ago when his back was turned, and even now could be upon him faster than Ronin could brace his sword in defense. While Ronin watched, a thin shaft of sunlight broke through the trees and highlighted the cat's dark coat, illuminating faint black striations. The light shifted as the leaves moved in the warm wind high above him, and flickered over the cat's brilliant ginger-orange eyes. The jaguar's nose twitched, causing her whiskers to shake. At the same moment Ronin became aware of an odor that was at odds with the forest.

Smoke. Dangerous, destructive smoke coming from his left and rear. He whipped his horse to the right at once and dug in his heels. The stallion leapt forward with a squeal at the rough treatment, then abruptly reared and screamed. Ronin fought for control. Slipping, he grabbled fistfuls of mane and flung his weight forward to force the warhorse down on his front feet. The horse crashed his hooves to the ground and tossed his head up in a spiral. His pole smashed into Ronin's face, splitting his lip and causing him to swear viciously. Ronin glared at the enormous jaguar that had sprung in front of his horse and now paced back and forth in front of him, jaws wide, teeth glistening.

Ronin jiggled the horse's bit to get his attention, and then turned him a few more degrees to the right. The jaguar's path widened as she blocked his passage once again. Ronin backed his horse toward the billowing smoke. The cat sat quietly and gazed at him.

"You bloody beast. Is this your revenge? Send me into the fire and force me to burn?" Ronin swung his horse to the left and smacked him sharply. Man and horse surged forward. Ronin saw a blur of black beside him, then felt an impact similar to that of four warriors thump against his back. He went hurtling forward, falling clear of his bucking horse. He felt soft fur under his nose as he rolled and then a sharp sting where a claw grazed his cheek. He rolled to his feet and spun around to wrestle the beast but she suddenly sprang away from him. She turned to face him after one bound, placing his body between her and the fire. Ronin snorted with disgust. An answering snort came from his horse standing next to him. They both glared at the cat.

For the space of an instant, Ronin thought of the boy he had left behind. He blinked. His heart started to pound. He envisioned the injured boy caught in the flames he himself wanted to avoid and felt a pang of guilt. A fleeting memory of his sister Laureen came to mind. He had been trained as a warrior. His duty was to protect those who were weaker than he. He had failed his family. Perhaps destiny was asking him to redeem himself by saving this young boy.

Ronin's skilled senses told him that the forest fire was immense. Not much would survive. The famous Loch Nidean forest would soon be a graveyard. He imagined small, fragile human bones, burned and crumbled, and golden eyes forever dulled. He took one last look at the black cat whose fur would soon match the ruined forest, and then turned his back on her.

Leading his horse behind him, he swiftly retraced his path to the clearing. Although he moved swiftly toward the blaze, his heart was light and his steps were sure. He did not need to see the cat bounding along behind him to keep him moving deeper into the forest. The image of youthful, golden eyes drew him onward.

Kalial did not know how long she had stood on that branch, staring at the mother owl, but when she smelled the stench of burning feathers, she began to move. The owl flapped around, then started ripping at the tree bark. A muffled peep ended abruptly when the mother hopped forward onto one of her babies in an effort to protect it from the fire. She flapped her wings so rapidly that the leaves of the tree burst into flames from the added oxygen.

Kalial reached forward and scooped up the crumpled owlet. Its heart was still. She gently placed it back into the nest and lifted the other baby. It huddled in her palm in a tiny ball of white, downy feathers. Kalial dropped it into an inner breast pocket of her tunic.

A screech next to her ear caused Kalial to leap back and slip. The feathers of the mother owl began to smolder. Kalial caught herself by grabbing a burning branch. She jerked her hand back and sank it into her muddy hair to cool the burn. Kalial sent a brief thank you to the forest for earlier providing her with an insulating layer of mud before she began to make her way down the tree. She ignored the slight pain of her ankle when she jumped the last few feet to the ground. The air was clearer on the forest floor and she took a deep breath. Even so, she coughed from the smoke entering her lungs.

She started to run north, but a wall of towering flames loomed ahead so she veered east. A symphony of cracks rocked the treetops and hundreds of branches began to rain down all around her. Kalial twisted frantically to avoid them, but one thumped her on the shoulder before rolling to the ground. There the fiery branch fed flames to the hungry leaves and an inferno swept the forest carpet. Kalial jumped onto a granite boulder and scrambled to the top. When she looked up around her, she saw nothing but red, orange and blue. She gasped, struggling to draw breath.

Without warning, there was no air left. Kalial's lungs strained to no avail. Black dots floated in front of her eyes as the flames suddenly sank back, as desperate as she for the life-giving oxygen.

Ronin raced low to the ground, overwhelmed by a need to hurry. He skirted crawling tendrils of flame that reached for him and continued relentlessly forward. He felt a cool breeze and darted over to a stream feeding a mud pool surrounded by human foot and handprints. He rolled in the water, drenching his clothes, hair and skin. He spent a few precious moments filling his water skin, then flung the strap over his neck, held a wet cloth over his nose and mouth, and continued following the tracks.

His gaze was drawn to the crumpled carcass of an owl at his feet. Thunder roared as hundreds of branches showered the ground. His horse was well trained, as all warhorses must be, but even he shuddered at the collapse of the canopy and would go no farther. Ronin heard the yowl of a cat in pain and saw flames lick up the jaguar's coat. Without thought, he grabbed the cat and flung her heavy weight to the ground, smothering the fire. A pink tongue darted out before she struggled to her feet. Her side was slightly charred, but the flames were gone. Then Ronin heard a dark rumbling and felt a stiff wind suck at his feet. He took a full breath, then plunged into the flames blocking the eastern forest.

Within the flames, Ronin felt strangely alone. He saw the red, the green and the blue flames lick around his body and he felt the burn of steam as the fire instantly dried his clothes. Then the strange rumbling was replaced with a *whoosh* so intense that he was knocked off his feet. He rolled up, ready to beat off the flames, when he saw the fire sweeping back in an immense backdraft. Holding his breath, he looked up at the house-sized boulder in front of him and saw Kal collapse.

The boy sank to his knees, then twisted and started to tumble off the rock. His body gained momentum and then hurtled through the air toward Ronin. He braced his legs and caught Kal against his chest, stumbling backwards only two steps. Kal's dazed eyes stared up at him for a moment before they closed in an exhausted faint.

Ronin spun around and started to run back toward the stream. He could feel the fire reorganizing, could almost sense its malevolence building as he stole Kal from its clutches. An explosion shattered the air behind him and a fifty foot arc of flame leapt over the area where Kal had been and landed in the treetops above Ronin's head. A hollow tree next to him imploded. A shivering whinny called Ronin over to his horse and, still holding the boy in his arms, he sprang up by grasping a handhold of flaxen mane. The black cat struck off in nimble leaps ahead of them. Ronin's knees guided his horse to follow close behind. The four of them surged across another wall of fire lining the banks of the stream before they finally splashed into the healing water.

Ronin immediately jumped down and plunged Kal into the cool liquid. Kal sputtered, coughed and flung his hands out in front of him. Ronin hauled him up and turned him so he could look into his face. The golden irises, regarding him in surprise and shock, reflected the flames and intensified their natural color. He suddenly realized that Kal's lips were moving.

"Let's go!" he heard the boy choke out. Ronin smiled broadly and clasped his hand. They turned downstream and began running over the slippery stones. He felt Kal falter when his hurt ankle twisted on the uneven surface, but Ronin gripped his hand tighter and kept running. The fire now spun above them, tossed back and forth from one stream bank to the other. Soon he knew the width and depth of this stream would not protect them.

They came to a Y in the stream and hesitated.

"This way! That way leads to Loch Nidean! This comes from the smaller lakes near the village, and leads out to the sea." Kal motioned. Ronin glanced at him, then at the thin stream division that he indicated. The other side looked wider. On an impulse, he shrugged his shoulders and followed the boy's guidance. The horse trotted behind them and, with a grimace of distaste, the cat bounded into the water as well.

Around a bend two other streams merged with theirs and formed a flowing river. The current swept them downstream as Kalial lost her footing. Ronin fell too, for Kalial would not relinquish her tight grip on his hand. They bobbed in the river, feet pointed downstream to push off the rocks they crashed into. The horse and cat swam behind, each involved in its own struggle to survive.

As the water washed over them, the clods of mud covering Kal's face disappeared in dirty rivulets. A boom overhead signaled the descent of a large, man-sized branch into the river just ahead. Its leafy branches were singed so that only the thick, main trunk remained. It sizzled as it hit the water. Ronin and Kal grabbed at it in unison. With hands still clasped, they hung on to the log and watched the fire rage above them as they were swept downstream.

Kalial felt a tiny stirring in her inner tunic breast pocket as the baby owlet snuggled into a comfortable, if somewhat wet, position.

The fire continued to whistle and crack around them. Ronin slid the belt from his waist and wrapped it around their bodies, lashing them to the log. The river tumbled along, filled with falling debris and panicked animals trying to escape the inferno. Ronin and Kal could only cling to the log and to each other while they watched the fire destroy the once deep, dark and beautiful forest known as Loch Nidean.

Kal gazed around in shock. He clung tightly to Ronin's hand, causing the blood to decrease its flow to his fingertips. His once blackened visage now shown with golden health as the flickering flame brought his face into relief. Smooth cheeks were shaped by shadowed cheekbones. A high brow was framed by dark blond tendrils that sprang into loose curls once the mud was washed away. A fan of gold spun in the water behind his head. His skin gleamed orange and yellow with occasional flashes of bright white from the water's reflections. His lashes swept over golden eyes with each blink, causing spiky shadows to lengthen then shorten along his cheeks. A wide mouth with generous lips was held slightly open as Kal watched the fire running along the riverbanks.

Ronin had never seen anyone so exquisite.

His heart started to race. He dragged his eyes away from the boy and concentrated on guiding the log down the river. He looked down at their clasped hands and then at Kal's strong forearm. He shook his head in frustration. The arm of his companion was powerful. It had wielded a knife and had sought to strangle him. The biceps were well shaped—not large like a warrior's but firm and well defined. These were not the arms of a female, Ronin reminded himself. The boy may be very pretty, but he was still a boy. Ronin felt one of Kal's legs graze his as he kicked at a rock they bumped into. He felt a shock run up his leg straight to his groin.

He immediately gritted his teeth and willed the sensation away. He must have groaned aloud because Kal looked at him questioningly. His clear gaze added proof to Ronin that this golden child had to be male. No female would ever look upon a man so directly. His years with so many sisters had taught him that all females were soft, pliant, weak and vulnerable. This person was none of those things, thus, despite his girlish looks, he must be a young boy.

Ronin deliberately moved his muscled leg against Kal's so he could feel the young strength. Although Kal's skin was softer than his, Ronin convinced himself of Kal's masculinity by feeling the bunching of his thigh muscles when he swam, the tightening of his calves when he braced against an obstacle that floated near.

Ronin recalled the two-day hike Kal had endured without complaint. He remembered Kal's knowledge of the forest and his male companions. He forced his awareness of his beautiful face to change from a sexual longing to fierce protectiveness. He told himself that his feelings for the boy stemmed from the excitement of danger, of battle lust. Every man felt it.

He turned to look again at the boy, who gazed back with a deep sadness. Ronin gripped the boy's hand tighter yet, and swore to himself that he would watch over this golden child with his life if need be. He swept all his protective emotions together and concentrated them on Kal. Ronin had lost everything, and now, so had this boy. They were linked, bonded. He smiled back reassuringly and placed a chaste kiss on Kal's creased brow.

Kalial lowered her head onto the log, and let herself be lulled to sleep by the rocking waves and the sense of safety she felt snuggled next to this big warrior who had saved her from the surrounding terror. Despite the catastrophe that raged around her, she felt a blooming trust for this man that she had never felt for anyone before. He was overwhelmingly strong and powerful and she believed in his potency. She had never been rescued or protected by anyone. For the first time in her life, she breathed a sigh of relief, and relinquished absolute control into another's capable hands. She breathed softly, sleepily, feeling safe.

They drifted downstream throughout the night. Slowly the red and gold of the flames gave way to the pink and copper of the sunrise. The acrid scent of smoke gradually drifted away as a silky, salty wind whispered up the river from the sea. Kalial stirred when she felt Ronin gently shake her. She opened her eyes and looked around. The landscape was completely unfamiliar. The forest trees were gone. In their place were acres of undulating green fields dotted occasionally with bushes or small groves of leafy trees. A rhythmic crash of ocean waves beating on the beach could be heard ahead.

The vastness of the land frightened her. Never had she been able to see for miles. Never had she seen such light. It glimmered off the water and caused her to blink rapidly. The huge vista seemed to leave her suspended in midair, without support. The sky above sparkled with brilliant colors and sunshine, bearing down on her with heat and dryness. Kalial started to tremble.

Ronin watched the boy's face undergo a surprising transformation. His eyes had first gazed around with wonder, but then shifted to fear when he realized that he was no longer hidden within his beloved forest. Ronin thought that blunt conversation would be best, as all men like to hear the facts straight.

"This is the ocean. We will travel south along the coast until we reach Tregaron where my cousin has a castle. There I will place you among the squires, an enviable position, and they will provide for you and teach you the ways of the fighter. You will learn fast and well. With your skills you should be able to hire out to knights and thus make your fortune. It will be a hard life, but a good and honest one. You will be happy. It is the dream of every boy who is not nobly born."

Kal looked at him in amazement. Ronin took the expression to mean that he was dumfounded at his luck. He felt proud of his decision and thus began to move toward the shore. When Kal did not swim with him, he looked at him in annoyance. To his complete surprise, Kal's eyes glittered with anger. He pulled his hand from Ronin's grasp and kicked him hard between his legs.

Such betrayal! her mind shrieked. *To have thought he would take care of me! What idiocy to even desire such a thing from a stranger!* She ducked under the water and struck out for the shore before Ronin's first bellow of rage was completely formed.

She reached the shore quickly and leapt out, scattering water droplets in every direction. She could still hear him roaring in the middle of the river, so she did not glance back but instead began to run. She ran in no particular direction at first, just away from the river, until she saw a small thicket of trees. She darted toward it, seeking the security of the woods. The twinges in her ankle disappeared as she stretched out into a fast run. She felt the odd, sharp beach grasses slice at her soles and cut her calves since she had lost her fur-lined boots in the river. When she reached the trees she made to leap up into the branches. Instead, she stumbled to a halt and stared up at the thin, spindly wood that would not hold her weight. She spun around and saw the empty terrain she had just run across. Looking in another direction, she saw similar, indistinguishable emptiness.

Ronin gasped for breath and clenched his fists as he emerged from the water, his testicles throbbing. In the distance Kal was racing toward some trees. Closer, he noticed his loyal horse splashing along the riverbed. He whistled and the horse picked up its pace to trot up to him. When Ronin swung up, his groin hit the horse's withers and elicited more bellows of pain and anger. He spun the horse toward the fleeing boy and set off at a full gallop.

"You stupid, ungrateful bastard!" he yelled as he reached the boy. "I could leave you here and let you be set upon by thieves, or let you lose yourself in the sand dunes. I could skewer you through and pound you to the tree for the vultures to pick upon. What ridiculous reason do you have for maiming *me*? I saved you and am providing you with a home. You lost yours, or do you not remember? Do you think your family still lives? Do you believe your home will be standing? What do you intend to do once I ride off and leave you to rot in this sun?"

Kalial was faintly surprised that Ronin had not already attacked her but decided that if he did, she would fight until he killed her. "I do not care what you do and I will not be dragged along by you to some *castle*!" she spit out. "I will never live inside walls like you land dwellers do. You are weak creatures who need walls to protect you. I live in the trees where the forest—" She broke off suddenly as she saw the pity in Ronin's eyes. "The deepest part of the forest remains," she continued stubbornly, "and I will return there. I must."

"Not today you will not. I will take you, either willing or not. Once you have served my cousin, you can return if you still so desire. Do you not wonder at the fire's beginnings? Do you not think it curious that such a large fire raged through Loch Nidean from so many directions at once?" Kalial arrested her steps. "Come now," Ronin continued, "you are not foolish. The fire was set. Those who set it must still be near, waiting to see if anything was flushed out. Most likely 'twas me they wanted, but do you think they would hesitate to harm you if they found you? These men are evil. They kill and destroy without thought in order to achieve their ends. You would be butchered in an instant." A fleeting memory of his ransacked home flashed in Ronin's mind as he spoke, lending a harshness to his words.

"No," Kalial said faintly.

"Aye," Ronin answered loudly, thinking that Kal was refuting his statement.

"No," she repeated, "they did not come for you,

although your coming was the sign that the fire would rage. They burned my home for its secrets."

Ronin looked the boy quizzically. "I was wronged you must truly be an idiot. All the more reason to take you with me." He reached out and grasped his arm. "We are both landless for the moment," he added softly, "and we must work together to help each other."

Kalial pulled against him, her yellow eyes sparkling with anger and a delicate film of tears. "I have never been helped by someone. I am the protector. I help others!" she declared.

Ronin stared at the boy for a moment, saying nothing. He reached out and grasped Kal's hand that was still raw from the knife wound. He stroked it gently and looked away, over the ocean waves that rolled relentlessly against the coast. Kal followed his gaze, then shrank back against his chest. At the brief contact, Kal pulled away and faced Ronin. "I have lost my home."

"And I have lost my family," Ronin answered. "I mean only to offer you a new home, for I cannot recreate your family." He fell silent at the boy's swift glance of animosity. He sighed and dropped Kal's hand. "You can tell me what you think the men meant to gain by destroying the forest, although I think you overestimate its importance."

Kalial swung her leg back to kick him again. Abruptly Ronin grabbed her tunic and brought her body up against his. Kalial froze. She sucked in her breath and tried to sink her chest in by rolling her shoulders forward, then sank her weight down so that Ronin would not feel the lack of male parts between her thighs.

Ronin's eyes were hard. "Do not think you can run away again. I warn you now. I will not allow disobedience from one as young and untutored as you. When you can beat me in a fair fight, you will win your freedom. Until then, you will remain in my charge and conduct yourself as befits a squire. Your lessons begin now. The first rule is never, *never* dare to strike me unless you are ready for my full retaliation. And hear this clearly. My response will be measured tenfold in blood. If you kick me, I will beat you senseless. If you run from me, I will whip your back until it is scarred. If you attack me again with your dirk, I will slice you twenty times with the edge of my sword. I am done catering to your childish antics. You look too much like a girl to act like one too. Now stand up and stop cowering. It does not become you."

Kalial lifted her head and yanked her arm out of his hand. "Do not cower? After you have told me that if I have the courage to try to escape you, you will carve my body with your broadsword? You are right. I am too small to fight you now. But hear *me* well. If you intend to let me learn how to fight with your weapons, I will come one night and slay you in your sleep!"

"I said a fair fight, boy," Ronin gritted out through clenched teeth. "There is no honor in defeating your enemy unfairly."

"I am not talking about honor, you beast! I am talking about revenge. You are as deceitful as any other. You promised to take me only until we had reached your ocean. Well, here we are. Now let me go. Show me your *honor*," Kalial ended sarcastically.

"Do you think there is honor in that?" Ronin gestured toward the road that wound along the coast. Kalial gasped and was silent. Along the road, four men on horseback dragged another man behind them. The beaten and tattered man wore the dark clothing of one who lived among her kind in the forest of Loch Nidean.

His clothes were scorched and torn such that they barely covered his form. His body was limp. A rope was wrapped around his shoulders and then tied to a saddle horn. With each step of the horse, his body was jerked forward. The men on horseback had scraggly beards stained with wine and food, and they wore black and red tunics bearing the emblem of the Serpent.

Ronin drew her down, then tugged on his horse's bridle with a whispered command and it too sank behind the concealing trees. "This is why I kept you near," Ronin whispered harshly. "I will not hold you against your will, for if you truly want to escape me, then do so."

Kalial looked up at Ronin's hard face. The slight raspiness of new beard growth darkened his chin and cheeks. She could feel his chest expand as he took deep breaths to cool his temper. A tremble ran over her legs and she abruptly slid closer to his form.

She stared out at the sand dunes and glanced behind her at the blue ocean. This world was so different, so broad and . . . and exciting. Her life had always been simple and predictable. She was the forest princess. She had one and only one role in life, to protect the secrets of Loch Nidean. Now, due to forces beyond her control, she was alone in a strange land with a handsome and powerful man by her side, protecting her and caring for her, despite his belief that she was a he. A new and utterly beguiling sense of freedom filled her being, and she gasped aloud at the awesome feeling.

CHAPTER 4

With a fierce glower, Ronin shushed her; however, the glint of the sunlight on Kalial's blond hair drew one of the men's eyes toward their hiding spot.

"Derek, look o'er there. I think I be seein' gold in that there thicket. Think you that someun hid a piece of somethin' for us to find?" The men chuckled as they ambled over to the grove. Ronin let go of Kalial and drew his sword from its scabbard. The hiss of steel halted the men.

"Ho there," another man said loudly, "we jus' be thinkin' that you might need some help, stranger. Why don' you step out un meet us friendly like?"

"Yah, mayhap you is injured like our comrade here." The first man jerked his head behind him at the man he was dragging. "Mayhap you need a helping hand." He guffawed loudly at his joke. Kalial tensed to leap at him but Ronin lifted his sword slightly to block her path.

"Wait," he whispered. Kalial glowered at him angrily, but grew still. He knew this land, this type of fight, whereas her skills lay in subtlety and stealth. Perhaps he knew better how to handle these rogues. She subsided to wait for Ronin's command.

"You cut the rope if I engage them . . ." Ronin spoke so quietly, Kalial took a moment to understand him. Biting her lip, she slid her dirk from Ronin's waistband. He grabbed her wrist and jerked it, but Kalial glared at him defiantly. Finally, with a smothered oath, he reluctantly released her hand while whispering a threat. "If you are so foolish as to use it upon me, then may God let you perish as you should!"

Kalial huffed. "Do you think I lack any sense of self-preservation? Despite the pleasure I would get out of seeing your shocked look, I have come to . . . to somewhat respect you and am only taking my weapon in hand to assist."

Ronin's blue eyes swung to lock with her golden ones. A flash of heat swirled in Kalial's belly and she quickly dropped her gaze. Ronin, apparently satisfied that she appeared sufficiently cowed, looked back at the men. Suspicious, the first man drew his ax and sword. Behind him, the other men did the same with a wide array of weapons.

With a sigh of disgust, Ronin stood up. His black hair gleamed with dripping water. His broad, bare chest rippled with battle-honed musculature. A line of fine black hair swooped down his navel to disappear under his breeches, which hugged a narrow, lean waist. The muscles of his sword arm were tensed.

"Excuse me, gentlemen. I am afeared you caught me napping or I would have come out to greet you. Why do you travel this lonely road?" Although Ronin's voice was mild, there was a steely glint in his eyes. The men shifted in their saddles and looked around at each other.

"We thought we did see a wee flash of gold in this here thicket. Mayhap you need escort to the village? For a price, we could stray from our journey and lend you our service."

"You must have seen the hilt of my sword flashing in the sun. It sleeps beside me like a lover. It needs no escort other than my hand where it nestles most comfortably. But I thank you for your generosity, gentlemen." Ronin nodded mockingly to the men. They hesitated. The leader craned his neck to see if he could see ought else.

Kalial rose from the shadows with her dirk in hand. Although her dark form was not nearly as large as Ronin's, the men could count and two was definitely more than one.

"Well then, I guess we'll be on our way. G'day."

The man turned to leave when Kalial called out, "You have no more need of that man. Leave him here and we will tend him." The man swung back around, arrested by Kalial's foreign accent. Ronin thought dark thoughts about his companion, then took a deep breath to calm himself.

"The boy means that we would like to reward your kindness by relieving you of your burden. Should you come across rogues and need to fight or run, his body would only hamper your efforts. Surely it is embarrassing for noble knights like you to be dragging a half-dead peasant behind your steed. We offer you our services . . ." Then Ronin added, "For a small price," so the man would misconstrue his interest.

"Ah, now I understand." The man chortled. "You think to get me to part with me coins. Well, tell your strange friend here that we be smarter 'en that. You get nothin' from me, but you get a body weight too!" The men laughed all around, happy now that they had tricked Ronin and Kalial. "We tried to ransom him at the village, but no un knows who he be. A bloody foreigner like you, I s'pose." The leader chopped at the rope, then rode away, still chucking at his cleverness. The backs of the four men disappeared over the next hill.

Kalial tried to ignore Ronin's glower as she walked over to the barely conscious man on the ground. "Quinn? Can you hear me?" The man's eyes flickered at the sound of her voice. He groaned and lifted his hand to her tunic, then slowly traced the faint markings hidden beneath the grime.

In tones of reverence, Quinn whispered, "You still carry the Secret upon your back." His fingers continued to trace the fine fabric. The yellow and gold, the sprinklings of green and red, and the delicate hues of blue were faded, but his eyes could follow the pattern easily.

"Tell me," he pleaded. "Remind me of that day you became—"

Kalial placed her fingers over his lips to stop his speech, fearing Ronin's reaction to anything he might reveal. She looked up, silently asking for privacy. Nodding in understanding, Ronin moved away. He stared out across the ocean, recalling his own sorrow over lost loved ones.

Kalial leaned down, softly stroking Quinn's face.

"Princess?" he whispered. "Is Loch Nidean lost?"

"No, I am still alive and while I breathe I will find a way to keep what is left protected. Fear naught, brave man."

Quinn smiled softly and gazed reverently up at her. "I have always loved you," he stated quietly.

" 'Tis your duty to love your princess."

"Remember? Remember the weave? The rite of your maturity?"

Kalial sighed and nodded and stroked his face again. "Of course I remember, Quinn. Your family is important to mine."

"Tell me. Tell me the story before I die." His eyelids fluttered closed as his hand dropped. Behind the closed lids he could see the colors upon the loom in sharp relief. He could see the grimy tunic as it once had been, before it had been made into a shirt, when it still hung in the village.

Kalial created a vivid picture for him. "No one knows when the reigning princess will retire and allow her daughter to ascend to leadership. It is a time that happens but is never planned. One day when the leaves were fresh and the flowers were new, my mother approached yours and spoke silently to her. You and I stood nearby for we both sensed that something important was about to happen."

Kalial glanced around her, confirming that Ronin was a safe distance away. Quinn's breathing slowed and she frowned before continuing. "Your mother was a very skilled weaver, as are you. But then you were young and had not formed calluses on your palms. After my mother communicated with yours, the loom was moved from the village center to the sheltered grove where our people gather their strength and power. There your mother began to weave the most glorious piece ever seen.

"The card slipped in and out of the strings for nine days, and your mother wove in a trance, stopping only to eat once a day. She wove swiftly with her eyes closed as each color merged together to create a unique if baffling mosaic. The village, too, ceased its activity while she weaved. The adults chanted and sang while we children somehow knew the natural rhythms well enough to join our voices to theirs.

"There were moments when the village fell quiet as the adults bowed with reverence. It was frightening, was it not, Quinn? But it was beautiful. It was magical.

"Later I understood. This ceremony is repeated once a lifetime at the time of the new princess's elevation. It is the way we pass the most important secret from one generation to the next. It is the link that ties us back to when Loch Nidean was found to be in need of protection. Although each tapestry is unique, each holds the same markings of beast and land.

"You did not understood the high ceremony that surrounded the weaving, nor did you comprehend the significance of my isolation. You thought me a lonely, unapproachable girl in need of friendship. You were very kind, Quinn, and I have never forgotten."

Quinn opened his eyes and stared up at Kalial and repeated his earlier words. "I have always loved you, Princess. I wanted you to reject the title so you could be like the other children."

"Hush, that is not something to think, much less say aloud. We do not choose our destiny and must be content with who we are. Think instead of the richness of the hues, the vibrancy of the threads, the silence of our forest . . . those are the things you must think of now."

Quinn closed his eyes again, accepting her orders. She was the leader, the holder of secrets, the Protector. She understood the meaning of things he could not.

Kalial continued. "The beautiful fabric was left in the sun and rain for over a year, ignored yet never forgotten while I took on my new responsibilities. Gradually the colors faded. You learned the craft of weaving while I spent my time in the forest, working with the animals and honing my forest skills. While you spent day after day playing with threads and experimenting with colors and patterns, I trained to track and hunt. Our childhood camaraderie vanished with the coming of the spring flowers."

"I never stopped worshiping you," Quinn murmured. "You blossomed like the spring honeysuckle and I was always in awe of you. So when Mother made the tapestry into a tunic for you, I gladly helped edge the cut ends." He spoke very slowly, his words slurring.

"Quinn! Open your eyes again. Please wake up." He lifted his heavy eyelids.

"Kal . . . you must keep it safe . . . the village is gone . . . everyone is gone . . . the Serpents came and destroyed all. Only the North remains. The legend foresaw this, and you *must* survive. You must live beyond the traditions and protect Loch Nidean!" Quinn rolled his eyes toward Ronin as the warrior approached, his muscled chest and strong legs encased in leather, his glittering sword held loosely in his hand.

A snort from the warhorse drew Quinn's gaze. The long, rippling mane flowed over the crossbow and darts, spilling over the saddle blanket. Quinn reached toward the horse, causing it to shy away.

"The blanket . . ." he whispered. Kalial dashed for the horse, who jumped sideways until he heard a low command from Ronin.

"Hold," said Ronin as he watched Kal in confusion. The boy tugged at the blanket but could not drag it from beneath the saddle. He whimpered in frustration, while casting quick glances behind him at the man on the ground. Ronin walked over to him. "What are you doing?" he asked.

"The blanket, he asked for it. Please help me lift the saddle and get the blanket for him." Kal continued to tug frantically.

"Why?" he growled, moving to guard the precious tapestry.

Kalial looked at him incredulously. "He is dying," she hissed, "and wishes to rest his head. Are you so hardened that you can not allow a dying man some comfort?"

Ronin reached under the horse's girth and loosened the strap. With both hands he elevated the saddle slightly so that Kal could sweep the blanket from the horse's back.

She spun around and pulled it over to Quinn. He reached his hand upward and clutched at it. Kalial gently removed his hands and rolled the blanket into a pillow for him. He turned to press his cheek into the blanket and breathed deeply. A soft smile graced his lips.

Ronin glanced at Kalial with a question in his gaze.

"He is a weaver. He must appreciate the quality of your horse blanket. He has always been interested in unusual cloth." Kalial touched the blanket while stroking Quinn's matted hair. She felt a tangled web of horsehair overlaying the double-layered blanket.

Ronin saw a few strands of Kalial's own blond hair caught in the threads and horsehair, creating a shimmer of gold highlights. He roughly plucked them from the fabric, feeling unaccountably angry with this man Quinn as Kal caressed his cheek and murmured soft, soothing sounds.

Gradually the injured man grew still. His breathing slowed, then stopped. Kal stared at him solemnly. On her knees she clasped her hands together in front of him, remaining quiet for several moments. Then he looked up, and gazed thoughtfully back toward the smoldering forest.

Ronin watched thoughts flicker over the young boy's face. He was amazed at how expressive he was. Even in this moment of sorrow his eyes were mesmerizing. Ronin's own heart ached with Kal's, even though the dead man meant nothing to him. Then Kal switched his perusal to Ronin's face. For several seconds Ronin stood still, entranced. When Kal started to shake, Ronin moved to hold him in his arms, but abruptly stopped and dropped his hands. The beautiful boy looked up at him with wide, sparking eyes overflowing with sorrow. Ronin swallowed, stunned by the softness in the young boy's face. His mouth went dry and he swallowed again.

"Ronin?" asked Kal. Ronin closed his face. Forcefully ignoring his inexplicable reactions, he held out a hand to assist. He clasped his hand briefly as Kal rose, then squeezed it once in a manly gesture of support. "Ronin, is my forest truly gone? Are my home, my family, my Loch Nidean destroyed?"

Ronin pressed the boy's hand once again before dropping it. "They are gone, boy. The forest may regrow and some parts may have escaped total destruction, but for now consider it no more." His voice was gentle.

Kalial shivered at the wide-open beaches extending beyond her vision. "I cannot survive out here," she stated. "There are no trees, no shade. I have no family and no friends." Her voice trailed to a whisper and she looked about forlornly.

Ronin felt an ache in his lower chest as he watched the boy's face. The surge of protectiveness he felt for the helpless youth was part instinct, part pity, part understanding.

"I will care for you, little one. When I took you, I made you my responsibility. Do not fret any longer. I, too, have lost my family and home, but together we can reclaim what we can. I will teach you our ways and make you strong enough to survive and then you will return to your home with skills you can teach the others when your forest rejuvenates. I can place you in a home with kind people. To squire is an honor." From the corner of his eye, Ronin saw the now familiar black cat stride through the waving beach grass toward them.

"I suppose it is only right that I tell you who I am and thus the dangers of traveling with me," Ronin continued. "You are unlikely to know the affairs of greater Scotland, now are you? I am now Lord McTaver, Laird of the McTaver clan, such that it remains, and Earl of Roseneath. My father, the former Laird Robert, was murdered several weeks ago by a vicious clan that seeks to rule my land and others bordering it. So far he has annihilated three clans, the Dougals, the Evans and the McGregors. They all lay in a line, stretching farther than the eye can see on a clear morning.

"Roseneath was the most naturally protected. As you know, it was bordered on the west by Loch Nidean, whose dense growth and unfriendly inhabitants made an almost impenetrable barrier." He smiled slightly, although a faint shadow of pain in his eyes was evident, then continued. "The north was equally difficult to approach as the ocean curves from the Loch Nidean forest and forms a barrier with its rocky shores and dangerous reefs. The south edge abuts the McGregor land. It is traversable, but certainly not hospitable, especially if you are not a McGregor. The east section is riddled with treacherous waterways and sinkholes. The actual boundary is marked by the River Chaos which shifts direction with the phases of the moon and changes its currents haphazardly. Many a soul has drowned in its deceitful waters.

"I admit we were complacent in our security. Lothian, head of the clan of the Serpent, is the man responsible for this wreckage. Your destroyed forest, your man's death, my presence here on the beach with you are all because of the events he set in motion. Lothian murdered my family, my people. I warned my father that he had become crazed in his search for wealth and power, but my father would not believe that his childhood friend could become so evil.

"Down the coast we heard rumors of Lothian's . . . quest . . . for a hidden treasure my clan is reported to possess, but we never expected him to destroy lives in order to find it. Even as word of his fight with the McGregors reached us, my father was convinced that should Lothian make it to our land, we would fight off his army with our superior might. We failed."

Kalial listened, hearing the sorrow in his voice. She could understand the loss of one's home only too well.

"What happened?" she asked when he was silent for a while.

"They came. They came so swiftly we had no warning. We were celebrating the harvest. Families from all over our lands were gathered in our hall. Children were there to receive blessings. Several upcoming weddings had been announced, including that of one of my sisters to the O'Bannon family. The bridge was down to welcome visitors for on harvest day we fed all comers, noble or peasant. I do not know how it was that our sentinels did not see the army. Were they drugged? Killed? I do not know and will likely never find out.

"My family was killed but I was spared for torture and questioning. My baby sister . . ." His voice broke.

"How did you escape?"

"I am not sure. The tower collapsed and pulled me down with it. The stones should have crushed me but by some miracle I landed on top. I was able to break free, get my horse and some supplies and escape.

"The tower was very old. Mortar weakens with age and I pulled a brick from its supporting structure while trying to break free." He shrugged. The how of his escape was not important to him; what he would do with the unexpected boon was.

"But I do not understand your ways. Why did the Serpent want all of that land?" Kalial's voice was puzzled. "And why did he give you the opportunity to escape?"

"He was not after the land, and I told you," he said shortly, "I was being questioned about a treasure."

"Treasure?" asked Kalial.

"Does it matter?" he snapped at her. "I lost my family and my home and was lucky enough to escape. I will return and avenge my family's deaths and retake my castle. That is my only goal and I will not rest until I am successful . . . or dead."

Kalial took a deep breath and then slowly let it out. Her eyes became more focused and resolute. "I do not understand the politics of what you say. Such monetary motivations seem trivial compared to the wealth of a forest or the power of a waterfall. But I do understand what it means to protect something of value, and in that we are similar. You are bound to protect a treasure as I am bound to protect my home. We are more alike than I thought."

Ronin looked into Kal's eyes, surprised at the wisdom he saw there. Finally he nodded. "Yes, we are similar, although it surprises me to realize it."

Kalial slowly rose up on one foot so that she remained kneeling on the other. She bowed her head. A fall of golden hair slipped over her shoulder. She placed both hands, clasped, on her upright knee. When she spoke, her strangely accented voice was deep and strong.

"I will travel with you, for now. I freely give you my vow not to seek to harm you while the moon remains high in the sky and the grasses stay green in the fields. During that time I will lend you my assistance and that of my beastly companions.

"We have a common enemy," she stated with a flinty look, well aware that in Ronin's eyes she was a young man. She knew that his reactions to her would be much different if he determined that she was female. Silently she accepted the continuance of the façade, and looked up at him with bravado.

"When the serpent coils to strike, much is harmed, the strong as well as the meek, the fighters as well as the defenders. I have my destiny to fulfill, and I *will* return by the next solstice. You also wish to return and right the wrong done to your family. You know this strange land and I do not, but you have shown respect for the forest and its creatures. Therefore, I will do as you bid. I will squire, as you call it, but I will only squire for you for I will grant my service to no unknown master." At that Kalial looked up, her slender throat arched upward as she craned her neck to meet Ronin's eyes.

Ronin did not hesitate. He lifted his sword and laid it heavily upon the boy's right shoulder. Kal did not sag beneath it, although its weight was consider-

able. Ronin held the boy's gaze and spoke in ring-
ing tones.

"Kal, do you swear to serve me in all that I ask?"

"Yes, until it is time."

"Do you swear to follow my guidance?"

"Yes, in all matters of warfare."

"Do you swear to protect me with your life in exchange for the same from me?"

Kalial paused. The seconds mounted but neither
Ronin nor Kalial broke eye contact. The crash of the
nearby waves rolled over them. The soft sea breeze
ruffled through Ronin's midnight hair and Kalial's
golden mane. Two seagulls cried out overhead as they
swooped in the air currents. Kalial looked down at her
palm where the knife slash of yesterday still burned.

"We have shared blood," Kalial whispered. "I could
do no less."

Ronin lifted the sword and touched Kal's left shoulder. He then plunged it into the ground. Its bejeweled
hilt quivered. Ronin reached down and lifted Kal's
hands. He turned them over, palm up. Choosing the
hand with the fresh laceration, he curled it around the
hilt and covered it with his own hands. Kal stared at
their clasped hands.

She rose to her feet. The hilt of the sword was level
with her heart and she leaned forward into it.

Ronin could feel the boy's heart beat through the
heavy layers of fabric and the softness of his chest
sent fine tremors up his arm.

"Yes, I swear," Kal repeated powerfully and then
stepped back. Ronin released their hands and the
young boy slowly uncurled his fingers from around the
sword. The black jaguar weaved in between their legs
with her back arched. A low purr rumbled from her
chest as she rubbed her cheek against Ronin's legs
and then turned and did the same to Kal. Ronin
looked down and tentatively placed his hand upon her
head. The jaguar pushed up against his hand while

lifting her two front feet off the ground. Ronin stroked the cat's silky fur and peered at Kal in wonder.

"I talk to them," Kalial said hesitantly. Then she smiled and reached into her breast pocket to withdraw the baby owlet. His eyes blinked sleepily in the bright sunlight before tucking his head underneath its wing.

"Here. He would not be alive if it were not for you. Will you accept him as a token of my gratitude?" Kalial queried.

Ronin stepped back in surprise. The delight in his eyes made the blue color sparkle. His wide smile caused tiny laugh lines to appear around his mouth and eyes, something that rarely occurred. He reached out eagerly but then suddenly stopped.

"How do I hold him? What if I crush him? He looks so tiny, how can he survive without his mother?"

"Do not worry so. He has chosen you and so it is done. I will carry him for you until he can fly." Kalial glanced down at Ronin's tight breeches and giggled. "You do not appear to have any place to carry him now." She reached down and lightly touched the bulge in Ronin's leggings. "Unless this is a pouch for storing extra items of need?"

Ronin felt his member jerk at her touch and he flushed in embarrassment. Kalial grinned in amusement. "I thought not," she continued while replacing the bird into her pocket. "You will be surprised at how fast he will grow."

Ronin narrowed his gaze until he perceived that Kal was talking about the owlet again.

"Soon he will be a night guard for you and your only worry will be how to get his downy feathers out of your hair." Kalial tossed her own golden strands behind her. Ronin reached out and grabbed its length. He twisted his fingers around, shortening the length by increments and forcing her to step nearer.

"You should carefully consider the wisdom of being flippant, Kal. Your words could land you in a morass of difficulty, and your actions . . . well, you had best be wary of how you toy with me or you will find yourself in situations you can not control. Boys that look as pretty as you do can discover disturbing aspects of the male nature." Kal was brought up against Ronin as he wound the boy's hair one final turn.

"And I strongly suggest that you either cut this mop upon your head or bind it into submission. It is entirely too full of freedom which will cause you the lack thereof." He jerked the boy's head at his last words to make an impact upon him. Tears sprang into Kal's golden eyes but his lips pressed together and he held his body rigid.

Ronin released Kal's hair abruptly, uncomfortable with his closeness. He turned and jerked his sword out of the ground, then wiped the dirt off against his leather boots. He slid the sword into the scabbard on his saddle, silently reminding himself that he was not attracted to the blond boy-child, but rather felt strong brotherly protectiveness. He withdrew the saddle blanket from the dead man's head and resaddled his stallion. Knowing that Kal was handling Quinn's body in the manner of the forest people, he left him alone for several minutes as he stared out over the ocean once again.

He was a virile man, as anyone who knew him could testify, but these abnormal stirrings around his new charge were disturbing and unwelcome. Ronin briefly imagined Kal as a woman, the golden eyes and hair atop a plush female body. He rubbed his eyes and sighed. It was poor of him, he thought, to create fantasies. Women were big, round and soft. Kal was thin, lithe and supple. There ought not to be any confusion! Kal was a young boy with the ill luck to be pretty. He must obliterate these odd notions from his mind, and seek female companionship soon. Perhaps all he needed was to sink his cock deep into the velvet sheath of a willing woman from the nearby town. Once he lay with a woman again, any strange yearnings would disappear.

Once he had his unusual reactions under control, he turned back and motioned to Kal. The boy walked forward cautiously, perhaps wary of the burning look that smoldered deep in Ronin's indigo eyes. He grasped the boy's hand firmly and pulled him forward. With a quick toss, he grabbed him around the waist and swung him up in front of the saddle. Before Kal could slide down, Ronin jumped up behind him and tightened his calves about the horse's belly. "We ride for Rath-thuaidhe," he told the boy gruffly. Then they shot off at a gallop, dhu Cait loping beside them.

CHAPTER 5

Kalial felt every line of Ronin's bulging muscles press against her back as he rocked with the motion of the charger. He leaned forward slightly to shift his weight off of the horse's back and up onto its withers and thus ease the strain of their combined weight. Kalial clung to the flaxen mane and tried to hold completely still. She watched the ground spin under the flying hooves and gasped. Her long legs clamped down to hold herself in place, and the horse responded with another surge in speed. The unfamiliar feel of horse-flesh between her legs caused her to laugh out loud.

Ronin felt a delicious emotion ripple through him at the sensual sound, which he immediately suppressed. He wrapped one arm around Kal to hold him steady, and then guided the horse to the ocean edge. The horse pounded along the shore and then splashed into the waves. It leapt a small tidal pool without breaking stride and gathered its haunches for a soaring jump over a pile of driftwood. Kal would have fallen if not for Ronin's firm hold upon her waist.

They shot forward with the crashing waves tumbling around the horse's legs. The splashing water drenched both Kal and Ronin and caused the mahogany color of the horse's hide to darken to black. Along the coastline, the jaguar loped with them, her coat rippling, her movements graceful and swift. Kal's hair whipped in the wind and mingled with the white mane of the horse so that Ronin felt both Kal's soft, silky strands and the horse's coarse, thick strands snap at his face in a medley of sensation.

In fascination, Kalial let go of her death grip and reached up and out to grab at the salty spray. The newness of it all—the wide vistas, the vast ocean, the closeness of the warrior that was unlike anyone of her knowledge—made her feel frightened and thrilled. She soon began to smell the scent of horse sweat. With it there merged another richer smell rising off the skin of the man behind her. She breathed in deeply and knew that the wild part of her would always remember—and seek—that scent.

Gradually the horse slowed to a canter, and its rocking motion was infinitely comforting to both of them. Kalial sank back against Ronin's chest and let his body guide her motions so that she could learn the rhythm of the horse's gait. Without words, Ronin taught her the subtle weight shifts that told the horse to turn or veer in a new direction. He showed her how to lean forward or back to increase or decrease the horse's speed. He taught her to play lightly with the reins for added control. Her natural skills and his teachings merged and she began to learn the art of riding.

Throughout, their thighs lay snuggled next to each other and Kalial's hips were pressed tightly against Ronin's groin. The firmness pressing against her buttocks combined with the rubbing of the horse between her legs caused a trickle of moisture to spring from her center, and moisten her inner thigh. A faint heat spread up and over her body. Kalial gloried in the freedom and in the unique feeling. Her soul sang with exhilaration despite the flicker of guilt the excitement caused.

Finally Ronin pulled the horse to a walk. They rode quietly until the sun spread a fiery array of glorious colors across the sky. That evening saw them in a glen hidden behind the sand dunes. The moon was visible through an opening in the trees and its reflection glimmered on a still, freshwater pool centered between two large overhanging rocks. The grass surrounding the pool was thick. A day-old deer bed indicated that they were not the only creatures that viewed this spot as a lovely place to rest. Kalial walked slowly over to the edge of the pool with the horse, and like him, she sank down to drink from its refreshing depths.

When she lifted her head, she saw Ronin standing atop one of the rocks, naked. The moonlight shone on his skin. Kalial stood, stunned at the sight. Her eyes roved up and down his body. His flat nipples were dark red and puckered from the breeze. Following the line of black chest hair downwards, she saw a faint line separating his sun-kissed, bronzed chest from his paler waist. His backside muscles bulged as he paced forward to the edge of the rock. Kalial had an urge to run her hands down his back and over his muscular buttocks. Her eyes peeked at his manhood dangling in a bed of dark hair before she averted her eyes. She felt her breath quicken and her breasts tingle underneath the tight bindings.

Ronin stood poised for a moment more, then he dove into the deep pool with a quiet splash. For a brief second, Kalial could not see him, and then his face broke the surface. He shook his head roughly. By the time he looked over to where Kalial was drinking, she had risen and stalked angrily off into the trees and toward the beach with her black jaguar beside her.

It was the tiny peeping of the owlet on a low branch that woke them later that night. His huge eyes dwarfed the petite body as its head swiveled back and forth. He would attempt to hop forward, but invariably toppled over before righting itself again. Then the persistent peeping would recommence. Ronin lay still with his eyes closed, trying to place the reason for the owlet's disquiet. Soon, he felt the vibrations on the ground beneath him.

Riders approached.

Kalial turned over and looked at him nervously. With a fluid movement born of years of practice, Ronin rose with sword in hand. He crept stealthily toward the glen edge and looked down the coastal road. Kalial moved up behind him while quickly plaiting her hair into a long, single braid down her back. Ronin nodded in approval. She flashed him a quick smile and tucked her dirk into the sleeve of her tunic.

Together they watched the approach of a small caravan. Outriders dressed in black leggings and colorful shirts rode upon several brown and white colored ponies. One man wore a bright red scarf tied around his head while another had a yellow one around his neck. Five wagons lumbered along the road between the outriders. They were brightly painted in a dazzling array of colors. As the second wagon rolled over the rutted road, its many pots and pans swung against each other, creating a loud racket. A young woman sat on the wagon seat and stared over toward the glen. She wore large, golden hoops in her ears and multiple strands of golden chains around her neck. Her sultry eyes bore through the trees to where Ronin and Kalial stood hiding. As the caravan drew to a halt beside the glen, people started to pour out of the wagons. Each was dressed in brilliant colors and unusual fabrics. The black-eyed woman from the second wagon drew out a deck of tarot cards and flicked up the top card. Her ruby lips curled into an inviting smile when she looked at the figure on the card. She then beckoned at the hiding figures.

Kalial looked at Ronin in bewilderment. She had never seen such an odd but intriguing band of people. Ronin's face was grim. "Gypsies," he declared. "One never knows just what they will do. Come on, they know we are here. It is best to show no fear and to play along with whatever they want to do. I only hope they do not try to steal my horse and sword." Ronin glanced over at Kalial, whose amber eyes were wide, but she followed him readily when he strode out to greet the Gypsy band.

The sultry one moved up to Ronin and twitched her hips to imaginary music. She swirled around in front of him, dipping her shoulders with a tilt of her head. When she moved close enough to brush her body against him, Kalial stepped forward, her golden eyes narrowed and her glare malevolent.

"Who are you?" Kalial demanded. The woman responded by licking her red lips with a pointed, pink tongue and pressing her breasts forward against the already straining fabric of her blouse while gazing at Ronin.

Kalial grabbed her arm and swung her around and away from Ronin. Her anger was palpable. The Gypsy girl laughed low, her voice heady with invitation. She tilted her head again, this time in a slight nod before gently removing Kalial's punishing grip.

"Peace," she murmured. "I am only trying to make your acquaintance." Her eyes roved over Ronin's bare chest and Kalial's tightly bound one. "You are an interesting pair. My cards speak of you both and thus you are welcome to join us. You," she pointed at Ronin, "are welcome in my wagon. But you," she pointed to Kalial, "would perhaps like something else. Stay here and my cousin will help you. Come, handsome one," she invited Ronin, "let me introduce you to my father, the king." With that, she turned in a soft swish of silken scarves and swayed her hips. She tossed an enticing smile over her shoulder and started toward the first wagon. Ronin watched the undulation of her hips and moved to follow.

Kalial stared at his back with golden daggers. Her

petite frame vibrated with fear and anger. Her strong stranger was being whisked away by some other female! They had made a pledge! Not only was she in a strange land, but now she was among an alien group of people. In fury, she watched Ronin walk away, leaving her just as a stallion scenting a mare would abandon his fellow colts. She felt the familiar presence of dhu Cait beside her, lending her a small measure of courage for a whisper of awe spread through the camp at the appearance of her cat's dark, sleek body. Making a quick decision, Kalial cocked her head upwards in arrogance, and sauntered after the pair. Around them, the Gypsies vied for position to better see the hulking warrior with the jeweled sword followed by the black jaguar and the golden youth.

At the entrance of the wagon, Ronin turned to Kal. "Wait here, squire." He handed the boy his sword as his eyes swept Kal's angry face. Oddly, he felt pleased by the boy's reaction for he was still at a loss regarding his own bewitching attraction to him. "I can not bring this in, for to bring a weapon inside is to invite disaster, so you must guard it carefully. Do not trust them at all, although they appear friendly. Call out if you suspect danger."

He raised his eyebrows at Kal when he immediately opened his mouth, so he shut it sullenly. Ronin looked over at the cat next to him. She stood almost as tall as Kal. Her clubbed face and long whiskers combined with the gleam of white fangs were intimidating, and the sheer beauty of her deadly frame was enough to protect Kal. "The Gypsies are a superstitious lot," he murmured. "Your power over the jaguar should guarantee your safety."

Kal replied with a humph, and glared harder at the female Gypsy who waited. The woman blinked her black eyes slowly, the inside corners closing slightly before the outside corners, giving her a feline look.

She smiled and reached out to stroke Ronin's chest. Kal jumped forward but Ronin caught his shoulder. "Stay here. It is a command."

"Then it must be obeyed," Kalial spit out, "but only because I have no wish to enter that hellhole with you!" A low growl from dhu Cait was directed toward the Gypsy woman, who dropped her hand and stepped back with a small twist to her red lower lip, slanting a knowing look at Kalial. Kalial pulled out of Ronin's grasp and turned her back on the Gypsy. She heard them knock at the wagon's door, and then enter at a hearty reply.

Kalial stood looking around for several moments. A flock of Gypsy children scampered up. Kalial put her hand down to still the great cat's rumbling growl. The boldest of the children reached out to touch her white skin. "You are as pale as the moon! And your hair is as bright as the sun! Your eyes are like topaz! You are the most beautiful woman I have ever seen!" Kalial started. She was so used to Ronin only seeing what he believed he saw when he looked at her that she had forgotten that others might see her for who she was. She peered anxiously behind her.

"Do not fret, beautiful one." An outrider rode up and swung off his pony. "You have reasons for your masquerade that we are not privy to, but we will respect." At his look, the children rapidly dispersed. "My name is Romeo, and I would be pleased to call you friend."

He stared deeply into her eyes. His swarthy skin was darker than Ronin's and although he was not as large, his body was strong and lean. His hair was dark as well, with a hint of red in its depths. "I suspect you will travel with us until the town up ahead. This is no road to be traveling alone in these troubled days. The king will decide if we should offer you shelter, but I rather expect he will if his daughter has anything to say on the matter." Romeo paused. He watched a

golden tendril escape its braid and flutter across Kalial's face. She reached up absently to push it behind
her ear. "Are you hungry?"

Kalial glanced up quickly. A quiet rumble of her
belly answered for her. Romeo offered his hand.
When Kalial hesitantly took it, he looked carefully
over at the cat whose orange eyes tracked him unerringly. Kalial turned toward the beast and stared into
her eyes, sending a quiet message that felt like a faint
breeze to Romeo. When the cat growled but slunk off
into the glade, Romeo turned and led her off to a
small fire.

A pot of simmering stew balanced over the flames.
A flash of fear rocketed through Kalial's mind as she
recalled the forest fire of yesterday and she halted.
Romeo dropped her hand and walked up to the pot.
He acted naturally around the fire, casting reassuring
glances at her from beneath heavy brows. Kalial
watched him and the fear fled as quickly as it had
appeared. She shook her head and walked up next to
him. This time her belly grumbled louder and Romeo
smiled. He ladled a generous helping of rabbit stew
into a pottery bowl.

Kalial dropped down cross-legged and placed the
bowl in her lap. As soon as Romeo handed her a
spoon, she began to devour the food. Romeo sat next
to her with his bowl. He broke off a piece of bread
that another Gypsy handed him and gave half to Kalial. Presently, the Gypsies wandered over to this fire
or another, and ladled out their portions. Many stared
at Kalial, but none were threatening so she ate peacefully, slipping choice bits to the owlet in her pocket.

"You appear to be camping rather late," Kalial remarked. She scooped an unknown vegetable out of
the soup and peered at it. Romeo laughed, then flung
his arms wide and leaned back against a wagon wheel.

"We do what we want, that is the beauty of the
Gypsy life. If we want to camp today, we will. But if

we have no reason to stop, we will not. Today has been dull so we moved along until we found something of interest. And look! We found you and your companions. Tell me, what is your name?"

"McTaver calls me Kal," Kalial answered.

"Why does that wild cat accompany you?"

Kalial shrugged as she spooned in another mouthful. "She is my helpmate, my mother and my friend. She is my guardian just as I am the guardian of her home."

"What do you guard?"

Kalial paused in her eating to look up, considering. "I guard its secrets. I failed to protect the lands . . ." she murmured unhappily.

"You are from Loch Nidean forest," Romeo stated as if the realization explained much. "That secret was hidden away centuries ago and is to remain so until the Time. Not even we Gypsies know what you guard, but we have never dared to enter your domain." Romeo regarded the mournful look on Kalial's face and smiled gently.

"The secret worries me," Kalial admitted softly, "for although I guard it I do not understand it."

"You are a powerful woman to live within Loch Nidean and to command such a creature as the Scottish McCat. I hear your sad heart. Power often comes at such a price, my dear. Yet despite your awesome duties, your heart is wild, am I not right? You are free of your duties for now. Relax, let an unknown destiny sweep you away. Lend me your palms and let me trace their markings."

Kalial scooped the last bite into her mouth and then carefully placed the bowl and spoon on a rock next to the fire. She cocked her head to the left and looked warily into his dark eyes. She pressed her palms against her thighs and rubbed them up and down to wipe away the dust and grime, then held out her left hand first. His hand was warm where he grasped hers and he used his other hand to lightly stroke the palm.

The sensation was pleasant. It tickled in an enjoyable way. When the corners of Kalial's lips turned up in a slight smile, Romeo's own eyes grew warm with desire. He looked down and concentrated on the lines.

"This palm is your past. I see joy and loneliness. I see that you grew up early and became a leader before you became a woman. Your sense of responsibilities and familial obligations run deep. I see a lack of spontaneity throughout your girlhood days. You worked hard and your mind was clear. Perhaps I see loneliness. You do not have siblings, correct?" he asked. When Kalial shook her head, he continued, "You have no other family anymore?" Again, Kalial shook her head.

Romeo smiled at her sadly, thinking of the huge families in his camp. "I can not imagine living so alone as you must have lived." When Kalial did not respond to his sympathy, he shrugged and continued. "This line here indicates a significant event that occurred when you were a young child." Romeo looked up. Kalial's face was blank. He pulled her palm closer to his eyes. "It shaped your actions and decisions nonetheless. I believe it influences you still."

Romeo gently returned her hand to her lap and reached for the other. Kalial closed her fist for a second, then let Romeo uncurl her fingers one by one. He stroked each fingertip with his own until her four fingers were matched tip to tip with his. Observing the tension in her face, he tried to convey reassurance. His soft black eyes lowered down her straight, petite nose and over her firm chin, along her lithe arm and up to her upturned palm. His fingers jerked and clenched her fragile fingers at what he saw. When Kalial made to pull her hand away, Romeo forcibly relaxed and stroked the surface with his thumb.

"This cut is new. It was made by a blade of finely honed metal like that of the sword you guard. It bled profusely but was not stitched. It heals well despite

the lack of care. . . . Kal? Did he harm you? Is he
the one who marred your beautiful skin?" Kalial
averted her eyes and remained silent. "This cut tran-
sects your life line and obliterates the rest of its path.
It dips down to merge with your line of love. The
crease here is bumpy and beginning to scar. I fear
your path will be troubled. However, scars form in
many different ways and this one is young and unde-
termined. Perhaps with proper care and tenderness it
will smooth out.

"This line here double links your line of love to the
area where your life line ought to be. It is a potent
symbol. It means that your love could become your
life, or your life could become forfeit for that of your
love." Romeo looked into her topaz eyes. "This man
you travel with could destroy you. Stay with us for
awhile and learn to be free. Let us teach you how to
dance and sing. I will play my violin for you and I
will dress you in silks from the Orient. Let your duty
find its own way for a time, and discover the rapture
of personal sovereignty."

He leaned forward and blew softly on her lips. When
she did not move, he let his lips brush against her. His
tongue flicked out to wipe at the moisture glistening
on her lower lip. Kalial watched him lean back. A
small line of sweat beaded along his upper lip as well.
She reached out and touched it. The bead rolled onto
her fingertip. She rubbed her thumb and finger together. The salty drip slid down her finger and onto
her laceration. Kalial frowned at the stinging sensation
and she shook her hand to remove it. She gazed levelly at Romeo, and then rose regally and walked away,
toward the king's wagon where Ronin was emerging.

Ronin looked around until he spotted Kalial walking toward him. He was wearing a white silk shirt that
molded to his chest as he moved. The top was opened
in a vee, allowing Kalial to view a portion of his

bronzed skin. The long sleeves billowed softly and then buttoned at his wrists. He wore a new belt as well. This one was in black leather with semiprecious stones set in swirling patterns. Only his worn breeches and boots remained the same, for the Gypsies were smaller in size. He held some clothes out to Kalial. She stared at the soft silk shirt and black leggings and knew she could not wear them without revealing her secret. Her eyes showed her longing but her words refused them.

"I am happy with my garments." When Ronin looked at her in amused disbelief she continued, "They are my last possessions from the village and I value them dearly."

Ronin shrugged. "It is your loss, my friend. The Gypsies are camping here for a time. They are going to be joined by another family in the next few days. The king tells of an army occupying the coastal village of Rath-thuaidhe where we intend to procure passage to Tregaron. It is advisable to wait here until they are gone. For some reason the Gypsies feel generous and are welcoming us to their celebration. I suggest we take advantage of their hospitality for the time being." He slapped Kal on the back. "I think we could have a good time here. I do not believe it will be a hardship. Gypsies are free and beautifully sensual. Try to relax and get that frown off your brow. You should be used to this kind of living. Or are all of the forest dwellers as tightly wound as you?"

Kalial drew her brows together in a slitted, yellow glare. She thrust the heavy sword at Ronin so hard that he stepped back with a laugh.

"I can be more wild than you can ever dream! I, too, want to stay here and *make friends*, so do not concern yourself with my wishes. You do not have to mock me in order to encourage me to stay. Asking my opinion and requesting my compliance would have been entirely sufficient. You will regret teasing me so!" Her accent thickened with her rising anger and Ronin felt the rich tones snake down his back.

"Remember your vow, my wild one," he admonished lightly. "You have sworn to do me no harm, if you recall." He stepped closer and towered over her, his very nearness causing Kalial to tremble.

"I recall, but there are ways to cause you distress that do not exactly hurt you. You said that I should learn to fight you with your own weapons."

"Indeed? Do you not think that is stretching the specifics of your vow to suit yourself?"

"Indeed." Kalial then bowed at her waist to Ronin. "McTaver."

"Laird McTaver," Ronin corrected. Kalial ground her teeth in frustration. "Say it, squire," he demanded.

"No! I have no choice but to travel with you, for I have nothing, no home. This land is perplexing and the people—even the foods—are strange to me. However, you are not my lord and I'll not say that you are. I call no one lord!"

Ronin grabbed the boy by his shoulders and lifted him so that his face was level with his own. "You will call me so, for that is the truth of what I am," he answered in a calm but determined voice.

"Never!" Kal squirmed in his grip but could not break free. In frustration, Ronin flung him over his shoulder and strode over to a large drum of steaming water. The nearby Gypsies rose to watch the great warrior and his squirming blond baggage. They started to stomp and clap while laughing at Kal's helplessness. The clamor drew additional attention and soon some of the women began beating sticks together in rhythm to Ronin's walk and the bounce of Kal's golden braid.

"I fail to see why not. I *am* your lord and master by your own admission. Now call me by my title!" Ronin commanded once again.

Kalial beat her fists against his back and cried out

in rage. The rising Gypsy beat swirled up into the night sky and some young Gypsy girls tossed scarves in the air in front of his path.

Ronin brushed through them and felt their silken texture brush against his cheek. The softness of Kal's body angered him further and he gripped more tightly to punish him, pressing the curve of his bottom onto his cheek.

"Release me!" screamed Kalial.

"What will you call me?" Ronin stood next to the drum. He had to shout over the thunderous noise around him. When Kal did not respond, he flung him into the steaming water.

Kalial sank down over her head until her feet touched the hot bottom. She shot up, sputtering in anger. "You cowardly beast!" she screamed at him.

He leaned down with both hands on the lip of the barrel and placed his eyes level with hers.

"What did you say?" he ground out.

Kalial sank back down in the water with widened eyes. She stared at him in silence.

His gaze flicked over Kal's frightened amber eyes and flushed cheeks. Kal's feminine facial structure made Ronin narrow his gaze and he reached out to grab the boy again as suspicion wormed through his mind.

A sudden delicate touch made him whip around and glare furiously behind him to locate the cause. The sultry Gypsy girl had her hand upon his arm. "Come now, the poor *boy* is scared. Leave *him* to his bath and let me feed you some meat from my fire." She pursed her lips and winked slowly. For a moment Ronin stood still, his emotions strung taunt. He closed his eyes and drew a breath to calm himself, an action he found himself doing more often since he had met Kal. He focused on the sultry Gypsy. Then, with a slight push against the drum, Ronin stood up.

"This conversation is not finished, little squire," he said in a low, threatening voice. "Stay away from me until the next moon so my anger will ease. Until then I am not sure I would not wring your neck should it fall conveniently into my hands." He scowled at Kal again before giving in to the gentle enticements of the Gypsy woman.

As Kalial watched them move away, she felt crestfallen. A wave of familiar loneliness swept over her. As angry as she felt toward him, part of her clung to him like a baby cub fearful of the great outdoors. He was all she had now, her only human companion, and she felt fiercely, guiltily, aggressively proprietary toward him. Her eyes followed Ronin's progress until he moved behind a wagon and was lost to sight. The Gypsies around her cheered loudly and tossed her sympathetic looks. An older woman with kind, dark eyes moved up next to her with a motherly smile.

The woman pulled a screen from where it had been resting against a nearby tree. It was made of black silk with white embroidered flowers and was stretched over a six-by-four-foot leather-hinged frame. She wrapped it around the barrel so that Kalial was hidden from view. She quietly rolled up her sleeves and picked up a bar of soap. Kalial watched her movements. The heated water felt relaxing and she had no immediate desire to jump out into the cool night air, so when the woman began to ease off Kalial's clothes, she remained pliant.

She reposed with a sense of tranquility. She pulled her knees up so that her bottom rested on the base of the drum and her back against the side. Just the tops of her knees and her shoulders peeked above the water. The woman gathered her golden hair and slowly unbraided its length. It rippled down over the side of the dark wood. With incredibly soothing hands, she wet it and lathered it, developing a rich foam. As Kal's hair soaked, the woman proceeded to run the lather over her body. She started with her shoulders.

The deep massaging motion smoothed away Kalial's tight tension.

The woman ran her thumbs down Kalial's neck and spread them over her back. She then soaped Kalial's arms and hands, making sure that each finger received equal attention. She picked up the soap again and slid her hands over Kalial's slippery skin to wash her belly in wide, firm circles. Underneath the water, the woman picked up each of Kalial's feet, and ran the soap over them multiple times. She slid her fingers in between Kalial's toes before abandoning them and sliding up her calves to her thighs. Kalial's eyes were closed. The steam brought a faint flush to her cheeks. She purred in contentment.

Kalial heard someone lift pitchers of warm water and pour them over her hair until all traces of soap were gone. Then the soothing massage began again, only this time the hands were slick with scented oil. Her neck and throat were rubbed with the oil, then her shoulders and back. This time each leg was unfolded and draped over the barrel edge so that her thighs were parted slightly. The oil was rubbed into her feet and calves. The sensitive place behind her knee was caressed with smooth, circular motions, causing Kalial to groan softly. Then the oil was spread up her inner thighs and out in sweeping strokes.

Kalial felt a dribbling of oil on her collarbone next, and she could feel it slowly making its way down to her breasts. She felt arms come around her from behind and smooth the oil down, over the hollow in her throat. The hands slipped boldly under the water and over her breasts to cup each of them. Kalial's eyes shot open and she jerked forward. She scrambled for a moment to untangle her legs and then turned to stare at the culprit.

The sultry, black-eyed Gypsy girl stood behind her with a bottle of heated oil in her hands. Her small hands were shiny and covered with oil. The gold hoops in her ears gleamed in the firelight and her red lips were parted in a smile.

"What were you doing?" asked Kalial in shock.

The girl raised one hand, palm up in a gesture of innocence. "Assisting you in your bathing." She blinked in her unusual way and smiled. "Do you want me to stop?" she asked. Kalial looked around for her clothes but could not find them. She looked at the woman suspiciously. The woman handed Kalial a thick, quilted robe and a cup of steaming tea. "Your clothing is still wet, darling. Remember, you started this bath in an unconventional manner. You do know that the water had been heated for me? Never mind, I am glad to share. Here, drink some tea while you dry in the comfort of this wagon. The owner said that you could use it at your leisure."

Kalial could not see anyone due to the heavy screen. She pondered whether to stay in the cooling water, or take the offered robe. She decided upon the wiser course and rose from the bath. The oil on her skin caused the water to sluice off her body, highlighting her sleek muscles and sinuous curves. The black eyes of the Gypsy girl ran boldly over her ivory skin. She licked her lips before holding out a hand to assist her. Kalial took a few deep swallows of the tea and forced herself to relax.

"Your body is very strong," the girl said. "It is no wonder that your man has mistaken you for a boy. Such muscularity in a feminine form is truly remarkable. What do you do that makes you so sleek and formed? Your belly is firm but incredibly soft. Ah, but perhaps the men, the men they prefer a fleshy pillow like me, huh, rather than you? You see, me, our warrior would never mistake as a male." She laughed throatily. "And your poor breasts, they must ache to be bound so during the day. You must need to rub them at night to return the blood flow. Perhaps they will be damaged forever, ah?"

Kalial slipped her arms into the robe with her back facing the girl. Part of her listened to the husky taunts, yet half of her felt as if she were floating, drifting to another place where she could no longer hear the woman's voice. She turned back to face her new nemesis. Taking another sip of her tea, she felt her lids drift closed. She snapped them open and looked longingly at the wagon flap.

"I have no need to be like you, Gypsy woman," she answered. "I am a hunter and a protector. I am the princess of Loch Nidean forest. I travel the forest by day and night, as one with my surroundings." Kalial glanced pointedly at the bright wagons around them. "My body is what I have become. McTaver's blindness is, for me, a blessing. I prefer the anonymity"—Kalial's voice trailed off, and the touch of loneliness in her voice could not be masked—"of my disguise."

The Gypsy picked up Kalial's limp hand and led her inside the wagon where a soft pile of furs made a bed on one side. "You wish you were male in truth then?" the Gypsy queried. With a sigh, Kalial sank down on the fur pile for she was unaccountably weary.

" 'Twould be so much easier. I fear he would not accept me if I were to show myself to him. These men, they cannot accept strength of spirit and body in women. They wish to have a female to coddle and cosset instead."

The Gypsy softly brushed Kalial's sun-streaked hair while she considered her answer. "Yes, the men, they do seek to care for a woman. You will not yet be able to be a woman fully, golden girl. You cannot let this man have power over you because you do not yet understand that once he has power over you, you have power over him. Once you do, however . . . ah, such will be the backbone of all your strength and it is infinitely more powerful than solitary force. Now you think you have only you, but soon you will see what it means to trust another, to love another. And you seem very possessive of this McTaver . . ."

"He is mine," answered Kalial firmly, with an edge to her voice. "Through him I will rebuild my home. Your other talk is rubbish. I am the princess as I was born to be and I have the power of my duty and magic. That is all there is, that is all I have ever needed. Yet, I'll not relinquish Ronin until I am ready to do so, for my own reasons." She looked behind her and golden eyes clashed with black ones.

"My dear," laughed the Gypsy, "he is not a pet like your jaguar! You cannot control him! You must give him the freedom to choose, and this night he chooses to spend his time with a woman, not a scrawny boy-child like you! 'Tis not possible to have both. You will be his friend as his squire or his lover as his woman. Not both, for that is not the way between males and females."

"It is the way of the jaguar and the wolf. They act as teammates and life mate together," Kalial answered. "You seek to give me a lesson yet it seems I must teach you. Humans are abysmal at achieving true bonding. Look to the animals to comprehend how interdependent two creatures can be. Both may be strong—indeed must be—and both may love." Her head dropped and her eyes lowered.

"Bah. I am not to be compared to the beasts of the forest, and you have no right to speak on a subject with which you have no experience. Me, I choose to be a lover because I am a Gypsy and I can act on my desire. You, you choose to be a friend and companion to Ronin, so accept that and leave the rest to me, eh?" Kalial remained silent. The weariness of her body spread to her mind and she slumped forward helplessly. Before she slipped into sleep, she cast her mind out and located the black cat, asking for her comforting presence.

The wagon rocked slightly as dhu Cait leapt in on silent pads. The Gypsy woman started, then backed away as the great cat slunk closer. The cat lifted her upper lip and showed her teeth with a small hiss.

"Remember," the Gypsy whispered, "my role is clear. Your warrior has lusty needs tonight, as do I. Sleep the dreams of the innocent while I entertain your master." Kalial sank down and curled up into a ball, breathing deeply. The last thing she remembered before she fell into a deep slumber was the wagon flap closing behind the woman and the comforting heat of dhu Cait's body cuddled beside her.

CHAPTER 6

Kalial slept until the sun was high in the sky. The exhaustion of the past several days made her sleep complete and seamless. She awoke to the sounds of music and laughter. Stretching languidly, she felt the furs against her bare skin. She yawned widely and opened her eyes. Romeo sat next to her, stirring a small bowl of something black. Kalial grabbed at a fur to cover herself.

"Oh, sweetheart, please do not hide your beautiful body from my eyes. You give me life just by letting me gaze upon you in repose." He smiled warmly and reached out to touch her hair. Kalial jerked back and frowned at him. "Do you hear the festival? Our families have reunited at this lovely place and will dance and play for days. Your fearsome cat stalked off when the sun rose. I trust she will keep to the trees until the noise dies down?

"I fear I am always asking you if you need refreshment. Here is a plate of berries and bread. The only thing to drink is our specially blended wine." He handed her a cup, which she did not immediately take. "It would be insulting if you drank anything else while we celebrated," he said reproachfully. "You had some in your tea last night." Kalial still did not move to take it. She pulled the furs more tightly around her and sat up. She had no idea how incredibly appealing she was with her tousled golden hair and her sleepy yellow eyes. Romeo set the cup down and contemplated her.

Kalial finally asked, "Where is McTaver?"

"He is in Mariella's wagon."

"Mariella?" Kalial questioned, although the black-eyed Gypsy woman came to mind.

"The king's daughter in the second wagon. McTaver passed the night there. He is embracing the celebration. If you listen carefully you will hear his laughter next door." Kalial narrowed her eyes and strained to hear. When a sudden trill of feminine giggles was followed by the low sound of Ronin's voice, she glowered. Recalling her embarrassed dunk last night she silently renewed her pledge to pay him in kind for his mockery. She frowned at Romeo, reached for the wine, and tossed it back in one gulp. The corners of Romeo's mouth turned up as he refilled her cup.

"What are your plans today, sweetheart?" he asked.

"Revenge," she replied instantly. "He angered me last eve and humiliated me fully. I do not accept such actions!"

"Of course not. Such unprovoked punishments are despicable . . . yet you did end up with the choicest bath of the evening." His voice trailed off and he grinned to soften his teasing. "How do you intend to draw him away from Mariella and complete your revenge dressed as his squire?"

Kalial drew her brows together. "I will just tell Mariella to go away."

Romeo laughed. "And you think that will be successful?" he queried.

"Why not? She is nothing but a Gypsy girl while I am his squire. He has a duty to me."

Romeo shook his head at her naiveté. "How much experience do you have with men, sweetheart?"

"What do you mean? I work alongside men at all

times. They are my comrades." The fur slipped slightly down her shoulders as she reached for more wine, revealing the fleshy curves of her ripe breasts. The crescent of her pale pink nipple was visible.

"I believe," Romeo said gently, "that as a squire you would find yourself trussed up and dumped in the ocean the next time you displease him by interfering in his business. As a woman, however . . ." He let his voice trail off so that Kalial would listen carefully. She stared at him uncomprehendingly. He sighed in exasperation. "As a woman you could easily entice him away from Mariella. No man with a sane mind would refuse your invitation."

"Explain," Kalial commanded. She shook the hair out of her eyes. The arrogant tilt of her chin was proud and masculine, as was her strong voice, yet the golden eyes fringed by dusky lashes were purely feminine.

"You should join the festival," he began huskily. "Dance and enjoy yourself. Ronin will notice you; everyone will notice you. As long as you look like a Gypsy, he will be fascinated—intrigued—drawn to you—and will abandon Mariella's side to seek yours." Kalial looked skeptical. "Trust me, he will," he ended.

"I know not how to dance, I look not like a Gypsy and I know not how to entice him or any male," Kalial complained. She could hear Ronin laughing on the other side of the wagon flap as he and Mariella walked by. Romeo grimaced and leaned over to Kalial to speak softly while reaching over and pulling her fur up so as not to let the view distract him.

"You will be able to dance when the wine takes effect and you let your natural sensuality flow. Your heart beats like a man, full of daring, pride and strength, yet your soul whispers a feminine song. Do you not long for the stroke of a hand upon your thigh? I cannot be near you without feeling your heat, yet toward me you show no interest. If you cast your attention upon McTaver, your supple body, your sexual eyes, your sweet breath will entice him."

"I cannot. I am his squire. He sees me as his boy. I need his instruction and can not jeopardize my dependence upon him and his faith in me." Her hand went to her throat to stroke absently. A sigh hung in the air and Romeo smiled.

"I can make you look like a Gypsy." Romeo leaned back and watched her absorb his statement. She stared back. An image of silk covering her body as it did Mariella's made her squirm slightly, guiltily. Her hand dipped lower, deliberately brushing down her flesh, testing, teasing. She reached up and pulled on her telltale flaxen strands. She ran a hand through them, then paused and looked at the pot of black material Romeo was stirring. Comprehension filled her eyes.

"How would that exact revenge on him?" she began, and Romeo heard the hesitant capitulation in her voice. His lips spread widely in a grin.

"You tease him, mock him by making him want you as a woman when he knows naught that you are his boy squire. Such will be your secret knowledge that he may be clever in many matters, but around you he is a dolt." Then he added with a shrug, "Of course, once your blood is hot, you come to me." Kalial looked at him dubiously until he remarked, "Well then, do not seek me out, but still, reject Ronin at his most vulnerable moment. Make him squirm to know you more, make him ache in unfulfillment. It does not matter as long as you leave him wanting something he can not have."

Recalling the image of Mariella's hand placed possessively upon Ronin's arm a moment ago, Kalial made her decision.

"Let us do it, then. Just as I vowed, I will fight him with his own weapons, just not the ones he is expecting. I will be in control and will tease him as he has taunted me. I will get him away from that girl, and dance with him. Perhaps I will even let him kiss me. But then I will spurn him to make him feel as humiliated as I did last night when he dumped me in that water in front of her. Yes, this could be fun."

She grinned up at Romeo and took another deep swallow of the wine. The ruby color stained her lips, inviting Romeo's caressing fingertip to slide over the rich, red color. She caught and sucked his finger mischievously and then stood up, dragging the coverslip with her. Romeo felt the wet tug and silky suck of her tongue on his fingers and was instantly aroused. He looked up at her tall figure draped in furs standing in his wagon and felt powerful regret. How he wished this lovely and spirited girl were meant for him. Alas, her fate was already set, and he was but a helper in her path.

"I am afraid that your golden hair will be entirely too recognizable. This mixture will stain it dark brown but will wash out the next time you get wet." Then, lighthearted he added, "Limit your antics as to not upset him such that he tosses you into a water bath again." Romeo grinned and Kalial laughed at his joke. "You could stain your skin as well if you wish, but I would not recommend it for purely selfish reasons." Kalial looked at him questioningly. "I adore your white skin. Do you know that it glows in the moonlight?" Kalial looked away from the warmth in his eyes.

"I will leave my skin as it is. It will be covered by clothing anyway," she said. Romeo's eyes twinkled but he did not refute her.

"Come here, then. Put this robe on and lean your head over while I paint the dye on." For the second time in two days, Kalial felt strong fingers massaging her scalp. When all of the strands were covered, Romeo wrapped a towel over her shoulders. She sat upright and he carefully brushed her hair out to dry. "I adore the curl in your hair, my wild one. It hangs thick and full until I touch it. Then it springs around my brush like a marvelous caterpillar clinging to a twig."

"You speak like a silly flatlander, Gypsy," she answered. Her heart was accelerating as she anticipated the eve.

"I speak like a Gypsy man in love," Romeo said, but Kalial shook her head at him in disbelief. "You wound me with your giggles, wild child. How am I to prepare you for love when you do not even respect my declaration?"

She attempted to rearrange her features so as to appear sober, but the wine had loosened her lips and they broke into an impish smile. Romeo's belly flipped at the way her countenance glowed. He imagined a Gypsy garb appropriate for her strong, exquisite beauty. Kalial ate her meal in the dim light of the wagon while Romeo rummaged around, producing a cornucopia of silken scarves, satin clothes and ornamented jewelry. He removed Kalial's fur draping with only token resistance from her, and stared at her naked form assessingly. Kalial lowered her eyes in shyness, but allowed his perusal. He lifted his hands as if to stroke her, but his finger simply swept the air in front of her while he rocked back on his heels, tilting his head this way and that.

He finally selected a white satin blouse and placed it over her head. It was gathered at the low neckline in a wide curve, exposing the swell of her breasts and the shadowed cleavage between them. The sleeves were made of loose lace that trailed down to her wrists. He tied the shirt edges together just beneath her breasts so that a wide expanse of Kalial's alluring belly was revealed. He then placed a golden chain about her waist. When he clasped it around her, many links trailed down from her navel to hang between her legs. The cold metal startled her and her thighs quivered.

She swayed slightly from the effects of the wine and the rocking of the wagon caused by Romeo's movements. She lifted a languid hand to brace herself against a wooden strut and dropped her eyes to the kneeling Gypsy.

He next hung fifty golden clasps to the chain, evenly spaced. Each clasp was unique. A master craftsman had lovingly created and carved each one. Some bore the head of an animal—of the wolf, the cat, the horse or the falcon. Others were simple stones in delicate settings. Still others held carved rune symbols, rubbed with black. Each was worth a small fortune.

From each of the clasps he hung scarves. Although he held up a multitude of colors, he eventually settled on mere white. A few of the scarves had finely worked golden embroidery along the edges in a lacy, intricate design. These he placed as a front panel, along each hip and draped in a sweeping curve over her derrière. The other scarves were either a crystal clear white, a filmy pale chiffon or a shimmery golden satin. Fifty in all hung from her waist as a skirt and blew around the tops of her ankles. When Kalial spun around, they flared out and allowed erotic glimpses of her creamy legs.

Finally, Romeo pulled out golden jewelry. Kalial gasped at the beauty of the pile Romeo so carelessly placed in front of her. When she seemed dumfounded, he took over again and placed many golden bands around each wrist so that they jingled when she moved. He placed a filigree anklet covered in tiny bells around one ankle. She picked up her foot and shook it experimentally, marveling at the jingling sound. By this time her hair was dry, so Romeo pushed her head down such that the locks hung to the floor and he brushed the underside thoroughly. When she sat up, tossing her hair back, it was fluffy and full, a rich sable brown that gleamed almost black in the darkness, and contrasted sharply with her ivory skin and pink cheeks.

Romeo continued to ply her with the special wine. She felt peaceful and loose. She forgot her reason for dressing this way and instead reveled in the sensations. Never had she allowed herself such indulgences; never had she appreciated her sexual nature. The delight was all-consuming and she touched herself with tiny movements just to feel the silk and satin of her new clothes. A bit later, Romeo led her out of his wagon and into the late-afternoon sun.

She blinked several times until her pupils constricted and the light no longer blinded her. Without the black pupils dominating her face, her eyes became even more golden and exotic. Romeo breathed out. He held her hand and drew her over to a group of Gypsies throwing daggers into a target. They parted and let the twosome enter into their midst.

"Romeo! My brother! What foreign, fascinating creature have you discovered?" A man looked over Kalial with glittering hazel eyes. He was all Gypsy, from his swarthy skin to the red silk scarf around his neck. He bowed extravagantly to her, then spun and tossed a dagger into the center of the target. He grinned while his friends hooted and cheered. He picked up a large wineskin lying at their feet and took a deep draught. With the rim still wet, he handed it to Kalial. She pulled her hand from Romeo's and placed both hands around the skin. Tipping her head back, she exposed her long and slender throat. She took deep, slow swallows, one after another, until the men around her started to whistle and clap. Romeo bent his head and placed his lips against her exposed neck. Tremaine, the hazel-eyed man, did the same to her other side. While they nibbled, Kalial downed the last of the wine with a flourish. Another Gypsy behind her picked her up and swung her around. He buried his face between her breasts where the white satin lay and breathed in her scent, mixed deliciously with bath oil.

"Mmmm, jasmine and honeysuckle." He returned her to her feet and she laughed out loud. The musical tones cascaded over the surrounding men and they responded with smiles all around. "I dub thee, 'Jazy'," he said with embellishment.

"Jazy?" cried the men in unison.

"Of course, Jas for jasmine and ey for honey. Jazy," he repeated triumphantly, not unaffected by the wine himself.

Kalial pretended to concentrate. "Jazy," she said with a contemplative air. Then, more firmly, "Since I have no name today, Jazy it is." Tremaine grasped her by her warm waist and tossed her to Romeo. He laughed and caught her, catching a lock of her sable hair in his teeth. He looked into her happy eyes and threw her to the next man. That man lifted her to ride on his shoulders and wrapped her long, slender legs around his neck. The others made to run at him and he took off at a gallop with her still riding high. She threw her head back and laughed while the two of them dashed through the camp with a herd of complaining men chasing behind them.

When he dashed under a tree, Kalial reached up and grasped a low branch. She swung up and looked down at the men below. They teased the man who had lost his prize, cuffing him on the shoulder.

Kalial looked over at Romeo. His eyes were warm and pleased and tinged with the light of desire. She giggled and tossed her hair back and forth over her back and swung her legs to make the bells on her ankle tinkle. Tremaine began to scramble up the tree. When he was about to reach her, she stood up and leapt lightly to the ground. Her wine stained lips spread wide in a grin at the dismayed expression on Tremaine's face.

"I thought you were having a knife-throwing contest, not a tossing contest!" she trilled. The men nodded and laughed. With masculine bravado, they made their way back to the target area with Kalial, scooping up new wineskins along the way.

"Romeo, you must go next," said Tremaine, "but let me move the target back a bit to make this more interesting." He looked at Kalial. "No one has ever beaten me," he bragged. Kalial lifted a delicately arched brow.

"Women are not always impressed by your bragging, my brother," cautioned Romeo.

"But most are! Watch this!" He flung a knife sideways and it landed dead center. Romeo shook his head and took careful aim. His knife landed heavily only a half-inch from Tremaine's. Other men tossed their daggers. Those that hit the center cheered and clapped each other on the back. The daggers that went astray were collected with laughs and friendly gibes. The target was moved back again and the process repeated. Suddenly Tremaine shouted, "The winner gets a kiss from Jazy!" The nearby men thundered their approval while Kalial shook her head adamantly.

"Come, sweetheart," said Romeo, "give me a reason to beat this bear of a brother I have. Grant a poor, starving soul a tiny kiss."

"Kiss, kiss! Kiss, kiss!" chanted the men. Kalial threw up her hands in surrender. Heavy feet stomping signaled their approval. The dust rose and Kalial waved her hands in front of her face.

"Let Jazy move the target!" shouted Tremaine. The men roared. Kalial skipped up to it and looked around. Seeing a tree five yards to the right, she pointed to a vee in the trunk, partially obscured by leaves. Several men groaned.

"Take pity, mistress."

"Just a wee bit easier, fair lass."

"Ah . . . sweetheart." The men grumbled good-naturedly. Two men who were already disqualified struggled to fit the target into position. Even Tremaine scratched his head and peered dubiously at it. When it was in position, the men stepped back and started shouting encouragement to the first contestant. The first three men missed the target completely. The fourth hit it on the very rim. The man reached for Kalial and made to kiss her. She ducked with a laugh. The other men, Romeo and Tremaine, scolded him.

"You cannot claim the prize yet! 'Tis unfair, we have yet to try!"

"I am confident not even you can hit the sawdust beast, Tremaine," Romeo shouted while puffing up his chest. "I might as well begin now!" He grabbed for her again, but Kalial good-naturedly kept her distance and motioned for the next contestant.

She felt unlike her normally reserved self. The tightness that she maintained as a forest protector slipped away and along with it the mannerisms of a male. Her body began to sway as she walked and she felt a slow sensuality infiltrate her spirit. Even her firm lips melted into swollen softness as she brushed them against the back of her hand to wipe a drop of wine away.

Romeo took his position next. He stood solemnly and tested the wind, then took careful aim. With a soft glance at Kalial, he tossed his dagger. It sang through the air and landed five inches from the center. Everyone shouted at once. Kalial sauntered over to him and smiled up into his black eyes.

Tremaine stalked up to the mark and both Romeo and Kalial turned to face the target. Tremaine blew Kalial a kiss and spun around on the balls of his feet in a full pirouette. Once facing the target, he let his knife fly through the air. It landed on the other edge of the target, five inches from the center.

"Ho-Ho-HO!" shouted the assembly. "Rematch," they cried.

"No, it is my turn," said Kalial sweetly. The men grinned, glancing among themselves at the odd but exciting thought of the golden-eyed woman being skillful with knives. They stepped far away from the target.

"What do you get if you win, sweetheart?" asked Romeo.

"I get to chose on whom I bestow a kiss," she answered with a purr. The men started a rhythmic clapping as Kalial took her dirk from between her breasts. It was warm and fit comfortably in her hand. She closed her eyes for a moment and let her senses guide her. She smelled the salty air and felt its sweet caress against her bare midriff. She shook the lace away from her wrist. Opening her eyes, she threw the dirk.

It sailed through the air with hardly a sound, flashing quicksilver before landing directly in the center of the target. The clapping around her exploded into applause. The men surged around her, clamoring to be her choice. Almost instantly, Kalial felt a cold breeze sing by her ear, as a new dagger whizzed past her head and landed almost on top of hers. The clapping suddenly died. From five yards farther back, Ronin stood with another dagger in his hand.

The Gypsies parted, leaving Kalial standing between Ronin and the target. He flung the next dagger in front of her as she started to move out of his way, causing her to freeze as it whistled past her and landed just beneath her dirk on the target. Another and another he threw, skimming close to her body as she remained motionless, and each knife landed with equal precision to form a four-sided cage around Kalial's slender dirk.

Then Ronin pulled out a short sword. It was one and a half feet long, double-sided and rapier sharp. Ronin lifted it a few times and balanced it in his hand. He stared at Kalial, who stood transfixed. His brilliant blue eyes flicked toward the target as he shifted the sword into a throwing position. With minimal movement and catlike grace, he cast it through the air. It hummed, turning end over end, tumbling past her head. At the last moment, it flipped point first into the target with such force that Kalial's little dirk was flung aside. The small sword vibrated in the center of the target where the dirk had been, surrounded on four sides by his matching daggers.

The men were silent. Ronin lifted his hand and crooked a finger at Kalial. She drifted forward without thinking. Ronin reached an arm around her waist and pulled her body flush with his. The heat between them caused the men nearby to step back. He used his other hand to lift her chin. Golden eyes met aquamarine as Ronin's brightened with passion. He brushed his lips over her eyes, then down her cheek to her parted lips. He felt them quiver underneath his and it caused his hips to twitch forward.

He leaned over her and slipped his free hand into her thick hair. Gripping it at the base, he tugged so that she was arched backwards over his supporting arm. He deepened the kiss by sliding his lips over hers to feel their soft fullness. He felt her breath coming in small gasps and he drank in the intoxicating fragrance. He licked at the corner of her mouth and felt her weight sag as her knees buckled. His hand tightened in her hair and he pulled her fully against his body so that she could feel his manhood straining to reach her.

His tongue slipped between her lips to skim along her teeth. Kalial reacted by pushing his tongue away with her own. Ronin caught the offending tongue and sucked on it with a gentle pull. He then stroked it with his own. Each slippery movement explored more of her mouth until she gave in and allowed him full access. He took immediate advantage and deepened the kiss further still. Kalial's eyes fluttered shut and her hands came up to grasp his silken shirt. She gripped the lapels tightly and pulled herself closer to him. Ronin's mouth slid off hers to make a wet trail down her throat where he nipped her. He then stood back while steadying her on her feet. Kalial opened her eyes in confusion. Their golden depths were flecked with lighter highlights. Ronin ran a finger over her golden arched eyebrow. A thick tendril of sable brown hair flew across her brow. Ronin frowned slightly.

Suddenly, he was grabbed from behind as the men flung him on their shoulders. A thunderous cheer went up. In the ensuing crowd, Ronin lost sight of Kalial as he was carried over to the beach where a bonfire was just being lit. The Gypsy men laughed at his desire to go back to her, but teasingly forced him to lose her to the crowd. With grace, Ronin gave up and joined in the merrymaking.

Kalial wavered on her feet. Romeo came over to her and put an arm around her waist for support. She leaned against him and lifted her desire-glazed eyes to his. With a groan, Romeo leaned down and took advantage of her unsatisfied passion. His lips came down on hers forcefully, as if he could wrest an equal response from her, but her mouth was dull and unresponsive. He quickly pulled away and smiled wryly at her. "It is time for eating and dancing. We could go to my wagon if you would prefer? . . ." he asked with a hopeful voice.

Kalial looked over to where the camp was congregating and absently shook her head. "No, I think I would like to dance." She looked up at Romeo and smiled softly. He nodded, then retrieved her dirk from the ground. The sword remained in the target, an arrogant declaration of Ronin's possession.

CHAPTER 7

Kalial stood alone in the shadows, watching the Gypsy girls dance to the fiddles. When one found a man that she wanted, she pulled a scarf from around her waist and wrapped it around him. She would then drag him away from the light while the man pretended to protest. Occasionally two women would pursue the same man. Furious dancing would ensue until the man would grab at one girl's scarves and she would leave with him triumphantly.

Ronin was away from the site of the dancing. She could see him leaning against a tree with several other men, talking and laughing. A few of the older women offered the men food and drink. Ronin allowed them to place the meat in his mouth and tip the wineskin to his lips. The night sky darkened to black. The moon still lingered low on the horizon, barely casting its glow upon the Gypsy festival. Pinpoint specks of silver stars dotted the sky. The reflection of the bonfire shimmered off the ocean where gentle waves broke in a timeless rhythm. The fire shone on Ronin and caused his midnight hair to gleam with blue-black highlights. His eyes scanned the gathering casually.

Ronin felt tense. His body ached with unfulfilled longing. He adopted a relaxed pose and conversed with the other men, but he watched for the white skirt of silken scarves that belonged to the beautiful woman he had kissed earlier. He still wondered why he had taken the challenge to claim her kiss. If the Gypsies had been in a less congenial mood, he might have ended up in a bloodthirsty fight for daring to show up a Gypsy man and for kissing an unwilling maid. Still, he did not regret his actions for he could still taste her on his lips and feel her body pressed against his. Where had she gone? Was she already paired off with someone? He had not missed the innocence in her kiss and his body thrilled at it. Even though he told himself that no Gypsy girl could remain untouched at her age, he could not tamp down his desire to be the one to caress her breasts and touch her womanhood.

Awareness caused the hair on his arms to lift. He turned toward the fire and saw her slowly walking into the light. Her eyes were half closed. Someone dumped a bundle of herbs onto the fire next to her and they started to spark. Flaming embers cascaded around her without touching her. Then a pungent smoke rose from the fire and surrounded her in its haze. It was a heavy smoke, so it soon settled around her feet and lower calves. When she moved, swirling eddies spun up and around her, then shifted and clung. A rich scent of jasmine mixed with other, unknown, herbs wafted over to him. He saw her draw a deep breath and turn a slow, full circle with her hands outstretched. He could not move. He was spellbound.

Underneath the rapid tempo of the fiddles, a lone violin picked up an undulating melody. Ronin noticed it immediately for its cadence matched her swaying body. He saw her belly ripple as she moved with the violin's rhythm. Her navel was a vertical slit that winked at him as she began rolling her hips. Her arms swayed in the air. The golden bracelets adorning them clinked and sparkled. The cascade of white lace produced delicate patterns against her creamy skin. She bent over once, to gather up an armful of smoke and toss it in the air. Her gathered neckline gaped open for an instant, revealing the fullness of her breasts and the puckered tips of her nipples.

Ronin's mouth went dry. She spun around as the smoke fell down her body, slipping over her skin like a lover. The scarves at her waist flared out. He saw her long legs and imagined them opening for his invasion. She started to dance with more purpose, concentrating on the music. She ran her hands over her throat and the tops of her breasts. She then picked up a golden-embroidered white scarf from her bellychain. Disentangling it, she began to wave it in the air. Her movements were hesitant, shy, but incredibly erotic. She did not swing around with the practice of the other girls. Her movements were slower, less emphatic. She was like a new fawn taking its first steps on a crisp, dew-covered morning. A swirl of other girls surrounded her and momentarily blocked her from his sight. He leaned forward but when her form was visible again, the man Tremaine stood in front of her.

Ronin reached for his sword before remembering where he was. He felt a wave jealousy hit him and forced himself to turn his back on them. They were Gypsies. He had no real place here and certainly no claim to one of their women. He made himself walk around and talk to other people, but the haunting melody of the violin kept insinuating itself into his consciousness. He wondered if the pair had already left together and then chastised himself for thinking about it at all.

Abruptly he found himself at the edge of the bonfire where the women danced close to the flames. She was moving naturally now, the fluidity of her movements reminding him of lovemaking. He did not notice the black-eyed Gypsy girl, Mariella, approach him. Suddenly the Gypsy Romeo strolled forward and intercepted her. Mariella gave him a slant-eyed look, cast a shrug at Ronin's unresponsive face, and started to play her scarf around Romeo.

Kalial was lost to the music. She felt freer than she had ever felt. Her bare feet moved languidly with a tinkle of tiny bells. Her unbound breasts swelled as she became aroused by a set of blazing blue eyes focused on her. The hair cascading down her back was heavy so she lifted her arms to sift through it while her body dipped and swayed to the music. The tendrils dripped off her fingers to swing behind her in a curtain of rich sable. Of their own volition, her steps brought her infinitesimally nearer to Ronin, as if the pull of his gaze could physically move her.

Ronin sank to his knees when a white silk scarf brushed his cheek. Kalial's eyes opened and she gazed longingly at him while her body continued to undulate. She moved to dance directly in front of him. He could hear the tiny bells on her ankle and the jingle of her bracelets as well as the sound of her quick breaths. The oil rubbed into her skin gave off a sweet, musky scent. Her eyes were dilated, making them a thin rim of brilliant gold surrounding dark pupils. A momentary flicker of recognition wafted through his mind, and then was lost.

Kalial let the sensuality of the dance guide her movements. She twirled so close to him that the forty-nine scarves gracing her hips fluttered around him. She twisted her handheld scarf and lightly snapped it at his chest where his silk shirt was open. The scarf left a small red mark but Ronin did not flinch. Kalial reached up to her shoulder and pulled the gathered neckline down so that her shoulder was bare. Her ivory skin glowed. Ronin's eyes deepened to the aqua color she had seen earlier. She turned her back to him and looked over her shoulder. She ran her hands down her hips, slipping inside the curtain of scarves to slide provocatively over her heated skin.

Ronin's eyes followed her hand movements yet he remained still. The rule of this dance was clear. He could not choose her, she must choose him. Although his every muscle ached with the effort to keep from taking her, he disciplined his body to obey. He could not risk the chance of scaring off this exquisite creature, no matter how much she provoked him.

He finally felt the soft wisp of her embroidered scarf twirling around him. His face was level with the juncture of her thighs and he could smell her arousal. She swayed closer so that his nose was touching silk. Unbidden, his tongue snaked out and licked at a glimpse of bare skin below her pelvic bone. She tipped away from him and he feared for a moment that she would leave. He looked up at her face with passion-filled eyes and waited for her next move. Her dance slowed and Ronin held his breath. She wound the scarf around her hand, then used it to stroke his cheek. She carefully wound it around his shoulders so that he was snared within its boundaries.

With the symbolic gesture completed, Ronin lunged to his feet and grabbed her hard up against him. He ground his hips into her so forcefully that she stumbled back several steps. He stalked her, the hunter instead of the prey. Kalial's eyes widened and her arms came up to ward him off. Ignoring her feeble protests, he scooped her up and headed for the darkened beachfront. Behind them the lone violin swung up from its sultry rhythm to a vivid staccato beat that matched the pounding of Kalial's heart.

Ronin found a small grassy knoll nestled between the dunes. The heat of the bonfire still reached them, along with the mounting frenzy of the music, but they were hidden in semiseclusion. Kalial's eyes were faintly glassy from the wine and smoke. She gazed up at him, drunk on passion as well as spirits. He stood for a moment, just looking at her. Some memory threatened to break through the erotic fog in his brain and he looked at her face intently. Kalial saw him staring at her and did the only thing she knew that would distract him entirely. Knowing that she didn't want him to stop, not yet, she reached her hands up, cupped his head, and pulled it down to her lips. *One kiss*, she thought, *I deserve one kiss before I walk away*. She closed her eyes and sank into his embrace.

The second he felt the moist warmth of her mouth, he was in heaven. His hands burrowed into her hair and he lifted her slightly to better fit against his frame. Kalial slid her arms down his shoulders to his biceps. Her fingers could not span half the distance around. She kneaded them and Ronin felt her nails dig into the muscles. He groaned his need for her. She replied with a soft whimper from deep within her throat.

Ronin pushed Kalial down on her knees while holding onto the back of her hair so that her eyes could still meet his. Her body resisted slightly but her eyes told of her mounting desire. It only excited him further.

"You can say 'no' and I will stop. But if you do not say it now, I will do whatever I please with you until the dawn."

"The tide will come in before the dawn," Kalial whispered.

"Then I will touch you when you are wet, from within as well as from without." Ronin's voice was husky. "You have only this moment to answer." His eyes bored into hers. Kalial pulled against his restraining hand and stared up at him, but did not say a word. She debated within herself, her mind trying furiously to stop her body, reminding herself that this was only meant to be a tease. But her delicate senses yearned for his touch. The wildness in her soul, the womanly core, ached to be possessed by this powerful man. A one time chance, a one time event, her traitorous thoughts whispered to her. She licked her lips as she looked up at his tall, muscular frame. Her eyes flickered a challenge into his. Ronin grinned wickedly. He was more than ready to respond. "Undo my breeches," he commanded.

Kalial was not certain why she did not stop him. She had only meant to taunt him, perhaps kiss him once or twice. Maybe because he asked. Maybe because she was flirting with freedom and swimming in sexual suggestion. Maybe because she did not want to stop. Maybe because, for the life of her, she could not.

She felt Ronin loosen his tight hold on her hair. She tilted her head down to stare at the bulge in front of her. She could see it jump and swell beneath her gaze. She leaned forward and grasped the ties of his breeches with her teeth. She tugged. Ronin felt the heat of her breath through the cloth. He swayed closer to her mouth. Kalial kept her arms dangling by her side but clenched her fists tightly. She continued to bite at the strings until she felt them loosen suddenly. Ronin's cock sprang out and hit her lips. She froze. She stared at the huge member thrusting in front of her. She felt incredibly excited but also terribly frightened. What was she to do?

Her small, shallow breaths blew hot air over his manhood. Ronin looked down. He could see and feel himself resting on her moist mouth. The delicate face of this Gypsy was hidden underneath a fall of sable hair. He reached down and gently pushed it behind her ears. He could then view her brow, her pert nose and her panting mouth. He slid a thumb over her lips. He could feel them tremble. They were red and swollen from his kisses. He liked that. He insinuated his thumb into the corner of her mouth and carefully pried it open. She trembled and looked up at him in fear. Ronin pulled his hips away from her and looked down at her upturned face. Her gorgeous eyes held a mixture of heady intensity and sweet innocence.

He let go of her and stepped back, reveling in the picture of her kneeling in the plush oasis, highlit by the risen moon, which now caressed the ocean behind her in a series of rippling reflections. He pulled his silken shirt over his head, feeling its texture as too rough compared to the luxury of her skin. The blaze of desire in his blood roared higher as he saw her eyes widen with unveiled appreciation.

She could hardly breathe! He was more than handsome. He was tough, scarred, hard and honed. He was powerful, potent and intoxicating. To have such a man . . . she hesitated no longer. She devoured him with her eyes, her mouth open as she panted in short, soft, sweet gasps. Immersed in the new experience, she felt no surprise when he sank down beside her and shoved her onto her back.

She toppled over and fell in rhythm with a large crash of the waves. A fine mist of sea spray settled over her body, molding the fine silk to her curves. Ronin ripped his breeches all the way off. He looked down at Kalial sprawled beneath him and was arrested. Her thick hair lay like a dark cloud around her face. Her skin shimmered and he thought for a moment how unusually light her skin was for a Gypsy. He reached down with both of his hands and grasped the collar of her blouse. With one rip, he tore it from her body.

Kalial's breasts heaved. His motions were more than simply violent, they were the actions of a man who knows his woman needs his power, needs to feel his domination so she can float free in safety. Her full, rounded breasts looked innocent and untouched in their unblemished whiteness. They were tipped by a round rim of apricot that tapered to a bright pink, hard nipple. Her waist was decorated by the gold chain and ornamented clasps which held the multitude of white scarves in place. One leg was bent slightly and angled out, giving promise of open thighs waiting for his hardness.

Another crash of an incoming wave sprayed her,

wetting the scarves. As they dampened, they became translucent. Ronin watched as each wave successively exposed more of her slender legs. They dipped enticingly into a deep valley, drawing his gaze. He straddled her legs and began to carefully brush aside each scarf. He felt as if he was unwinding layers from a precious gift. Each time a bit of bare skin was revealed, he bent and licked and kissed it.

Kalial arched off the ground. Her breasts were lifted and her belly button stretched. She squirmed because her legs were trapped by Ronin's weight. She wanted him more than she had wanted anything, yet she was beyond thinking, beyond knowing how to achieve her desires. Instead, she let him take her body. She willingly relinquished her control to him and let his fingers guide her movements. Ronin was distantly aware of her lack of skill, yet he was so lost in her web of sensuality, he could not slow his assault.

Finally the skirt of scarves was fully pushed aside and Ronin could see the center of her womanhood. His looming shadow cloaked her in semidarkness, so he used his fingers to discover her folds and valleys. He stroked her, feeling her tight curls wrap around his fingers. Kalial moaned. Ronin marveled at the soft texture of her hair and he brushed his cheek against it as all thoughts were swept away, leaving only sensations. The rich aroma of her arousal stimulated him. He sat back up and picked up the dangling end of the waist chain. Running his fingers along its length he pressed it against her wet entrance.

The shock of the cool metal mixed with the electric heat of his hand made Kalial lose the last of her control. Her head rocked back and forth and her hands reached up and gripped his shoulders. Ronin began to rub her with his fingers in different ways, watching her face. When her eyes suddenly flickered and she caught her tongue between her teeth and her body convulsed, Ronin repeated his motions. Kalial let out a whimper that soon escalated into a purely feminine scream. Ronin lightened his touch. He laughed throatily at her punishing grip on his shoulders and angry expression. His hands slipped up her belly and he leaned down to lap at the small pool of salt water gathering there. Her skin was so wet, he trembled from the eroticism of the moment.

He turned his attention to her succulent breasts. He blew on them and watched a fine pebbling of goose bumps ripple across her flesh before her own heat warmed them away. He tilted his head sideways and dipped his tongue into the hidden undercurve of her breast. She tasted like honeysuckle and he nipped her for daring to be so perfect.

He could not wait any longer. He sat back and pulled her out from under him to straddle his hips. The jingling of her bracelets and anklet mingled with their heavy breaths. He wrapped her legs around him so that her dripping center was widely exposed. He slipped a supporting arm around her waist. Her eyes opened and she stared at him shyly. His erect penis leapt and found her opening, yet the petals surrounding the entrance bared his penetration. His shaft pushed at her, determined to sink into her body. A splash of an incoming wave broke over their interlocked hips and provided the key to unlocking her virgin passage.

He slid into her naturally sex-slick channel. He groaned while she moaned. The tightness surrounding him squeezed and pulsed. He could feel the folds caressing him. Heat gushed around his cock and he barely refrained from losing control before even completing the act.

Kalial felt the forceful probing of his thickness along with the salty waves washing over them. The sudden stretching of her vulva caused her to perversely clench down, wrapping tight and hard around him. She was held spellbound by his dark blue eyes. The aqua color of his desire was so deep that she could hardly make it out in the night sky. Another wave splashed over her legs and swirled between them. Its force against Ronin's back pushed him farther inside her. She let out another small scream and dropped her head back, pressing her breasts and hips forward while closing her eyes.

Ronin felt the barrier of her maidenhead and shouted with surprise. His supporting arm pulled her up closer and he claimed her lips with his own in a possessive kiss. His tongue plunged deep into her mouth and he lightly bit her lips, then kissed her harder and sucked at the tender fullness. He shook her so that her eyes opened and she stared at him. He wanted her to see who claimed her. He wanted to see her eyes as she was possessed fully for the first time.

When he had her attention, he thrust into her. The barrier held and Kalial gasped in pain. She began to struggle. A flicker of sympathy crossed his eyes, but was immediately replaced by manly desire as Kalial's inner muscles twitched and quivered at the unknown sensations. He pushed at her again, in rhythm with the waves that now crested over his back. He held her roughly as she arched and twisted.

"Hold on, my sweet, just a moment more and you will find the ecstasy I have promised you," he murmured, his voice harsh and throaty. Pushing once again, he slid his cock roughly past it, and plunged deep within her, up to its considerable hilt.

"Stop, let me go," she cried out softly, a thread of uncertainty already entering her voice. Ronin held her without moving. He could feel her muscles trying to eject him from his rightful home. However, along with the conscious expulsive spasms, a subtle, undulating ripple of her flesh gripped him and sought to milk out his precious seed. He shifted out a few inches, and then sank powerfully back in. Kalial's cries changed in tempo. She gasped with shocked pleasure when he thrust, and trembled when he pulled out. Her eyes rolled up and Ronin let her arch her back down to the ground.

Keeping her legs well spread, he moved on top of her. Using his mighty strength, he ground her pelvis into the beach with his thrusts. Waves rolled over them, not quite reaching her shoulders but drenching her legs. The pain was gone and incredible bliss swept over her. She cried in passion again and again while Ronin exalted in her sounds. His own groans mounted and he pushed at her faster and faster. Kalial felt her toes go numb, then tingle madly. Her thighs were clenched so tightly around him, they hurt. Her nails scoured his back, leaving reddened trails. He loved the feeling. It was incredible, so completely fulfilling.

Kalial could not understand what was happening to her body. She ached and tingled and burned. She felt a heaviness settle in her stomach and she rocked with the desire to ease it. Her rhythm matched his and she felt the pace rise to a frantic level. A starburst began to spark from her wet depths and her muscles started to convulse. A flood of warm fluid came from deep within her and drenched her passage from the heated friction of his cock's movements. The sparks shot out faster and closer together. A blinding white light suffused her brain. When she heard a shout of triumph above her, the light and sparks exploded into a cataclysmic climax.

Ronin felt her swollen vagina spasm and gush out a creamy, feminine ambrosia. He sank into her again and felt himself contract. He felt as if he held the world in his arms and she existed for him alone. He felt that he owned her body and possessed her spirit. With a shout, he poured into her just as she reached orgasm. His seed continued on and on while the waves crashed over his head and the woman beneath him cried out in ecstasy.

He collapsed against her as the wave sank back. He gasped as did she. He bit her stomach, then licked it in apology. He wanted nothing better than to lie buried within her, but the encroaching waves made that impossible. He regretfully slipped out of her and rolled onto his back. A splash covering his sweat-drenched body made him laugh and close his eyes for a moment. He slowly rose before turning to help the sable-haired Gypsy woman he had claimed for his own. His mouth dropped open in shock when he saw that she had scrambled away, and was gone.

CHAPTER 8

Kalial stumbled over the dunes, through the milling people and to Romeo's wagon. She ducked inside and then stilled her breathing to listen for pursuit. When she heard nothing, she collapsed on the fur-covered bed and sobbed. Her bones still felt weak, her heart still shuddered and tiny aftershocks still convulsed the center of her womanhood. She yearned to go back to him, to feel his strong arms hold and protect her. More than anything this strange and overwhelming feeling was why she had run away from him.

She had meant only to tease him, to fight him with a newly discovered weapon, but she had seriously miscalculated. She had never felt anything so uplifting, nor anything remotely resembling the searing joy she had discovered in his arms. Yet a sense of guilt made her flee from his handsome face to the relative safety of this wagon. She was born to be a ruler, she chided herself, not a woman who lay in the sand with a strange warrior! It was only once, she answered herself, not much to ask for a lifetime of loneliness. She rapidly blinked as the tears in her eyes mingled with the seawater dripping from her hair.

A drop of brown colored water trickled from her temple to her chin. She swiped at it angrily, then plunged her entire head into a bucket of water and swished it back and forth to remove the last traces of the dye that was already patchy from the splattering of the ocean waves. She swung her head up, sending a splash of water against the wagon canvas. Spotting her washed and dried tunic, breast strap and leggings, she yanked them on after dropping the belly chain and scarves to the ground and kicking them into a corner. She bound her chest tighter than usual. Either that or her breasts were still swollen from loving and ached at the confinement. A slim pair of leather boots was pulled on next. She roughly swept her wet hair into a low ponytail with a length of tan rawhide.

As she dropped her hand, the wagon flap was flung aside. Ronin stalked in, a thunderous expression on his face. He had pulled on his breeches but laced them only partway. He carried his shirt, boots and belt under his arm. Kalial shrank back against the canvas. Ronin's eyes stung her as they swept her attire.

"Well, at least I still recognize you," he barked. Kalial stared at him, trapped. "Although I will never understand why you prefer those rags to nice clothing." He ran a hand through his mussed hair. The smell of salt and sex still emanated from him. "We need to go, but first you must help me look for someone." When Kalial said nothing, he slipped his shirt on and thrust his feet into his boots. "We are looking for a girl in white. She has brown hair and a voluptuous body." His voice softened as he described her. Then it rose again in anger. "We must find her."

"What? Why?" Kalial asked in a small voice. She stepped forward. A small sparkle of light lit her eyes.

"Because she is mine. I intend to keep her."

"Keep her?"

"Yes. I will set her up at my cousin's castle until I return for her. She is an exquisite creature and I want to be the man to develop her sensual talents. I intend to be her first and sole benefactor." Confused, Kalial stood still and stared at him. The tremors in her body made her bite her lip to keep from crying out to him. Her golden eyes flickered with vulnerability. Ronin looked over at her with a touch of curiosity. "What is wrong with you?" he asked impatiently.

"Wr . . . wrong?" she stuttered, still dumfounded that he could not feel her presence after such incredible closeness.

"You look like you just came in from a fight or something. What is that on your neck?" he queried and moved over to her, rocking the wagon. Kalial almost leapt to the other side in her haste to keep him from touching her. She mumbled under her breath and clambered to the door flap. Ronin turned around, his dark eyes suspicious.

"Where are you going? What are you up to?" he accused her, stalking forward. Kalial practically fell out of the wagon in her haste and tumbled into Romeo who was walking up. She gasped and froze. Ronin descended after her. "Kal!" he demanded.

Romeo grasped Kalial and pushed her behind him and turned to face the distrustful expression on Ronin's face. "Ah, my friend, my guest. I have been looking for you for an hour past," he remarked pleasantly, but Ronin was not deceived by his mellow voice. Immediately forgetting Kal's odd behavior, he focused on Romeo.

He bowed slightly and replied, "I am at your disposal, mine host."

"There is a certain lass I have been waiting for, and it has come to my attention that you may have spent some time with her," Romeo said. He smiled, but a glint of warning flashed in his eyes.

Ronin became wary. Knowing the Gypsy jealousy, he said nothing.

"The moon has risen," Romeo continued mildly. "It is a good night for traveling."

Ronin nodded and looked around. Several other men lounged with seeming nonchalance around the wagon. His eyes skimmed over Kal and he again appreciated the boy's nervousness. He beckoned to him. Kal hesitated.

Romeo smiled. "I would consider it fair, and we are always fair in our dealings are we not, *guest*, if you would leave us this fine lad. He fits in so much better with us and is more than welcome."

The flare of anger in Ronin's eyes was intense. His eyes narrowed to slits and he snarled. Several of the men, including Tremaine, stepped forward.

"We are particular about who sleeps with our women, McTaver. You know the rules. If you take something of value of ours without our consent, then we can demand payment in return. The girl was not yours to take, so we will take your squire in exchange."

Kalial looked back and forth between the men, unsure of their intentions. A flicker of irritation coursed through her and she drew her brows together.

Ronin reached behind him and drew his sword. His voice responded softly, but with menace. "The girl came with me willingly, and was treated with courtesy. Do you not allow your women their freedom to choose?"

"Aye, we do. But seduction of the innocent is the man's treachery," said Tremaine with a hiss of anger.

Finally, irritated at being discussed, even if all the participants did not know she was their subject, Kalial broke in. "The Gypsy girl did what she wanted to do at the time, and, even if she regrets it now, McTaver cannot be held responsible." Ronin stared at her in surprise, as did Romeo and Tremaine. "If it is payment you seek, then take my dirk and be done." She glared at Romeo, the gold in her eyes snapping in the moonlight.

Romeo hung his head. "My apologies. I was not considerate of your . . . of her wayward desires. It is me who needs to offer reparations for placing you in this uncomfortable position. Take a token from the golden belt that the Gypsy girl wore this night, the night that she became a woman. You may have it, but guard it well for it is costly."

"I have no need of it," Kalial grumbled, but Ronin, stunned at the sudden twist in circumstance, nodded once again. Escaping the men, Kalial ran into the nearby trees until she was out of sight. She stood silently for a moment but her body and mind were numb. She walked over to the glen where the warhorse was hobbled, picked up some dry grass and rubbed him with it while mentally reaching for and feeling dhu Cait's presence in the tree above, then listening for the night sounds of the owlet.

With a deep breath, she stretched her hand up and scooped the baby bird out of the branches where she had placed him earlier and then settled him on her shoulder. The tiny talons pricked her. Instead of shifting the bird, she welcomed the slight pain, hoping it would distract her from her situation. Kalial then sank down on the saddle blanket that rested on the grass and leaned back against the saddle. She closed her eyes and prayed for the healing tincture of sleep.

Moments later, Kalial was roused by the owlet's peep of warning. She knew the approaching person was Ronin by the sound of his stride. She stood up and waited.

Ronin was angry. Angry and frustrated. Despite the near fight, he had asked about the girl, hoping to find her and discover why she had run away. He was concerned, yet other than the few men of the contest, no one had heard of Jazy. They all claimed that they did not know where she had come from or to whom she belonged. No one knew where she was. It was impossible to disappear in the middle of a deserted stretch of beach, but he could find no trace of her.

Romeo had located the golden chain that the Gypsy had been wearing and had given him two pieces from it, a jeweled cat and a burnished wolf. Their soft jingle was muted within the velvet bag strung at his waist. Romeo's cryptic words—"You are more likely to discover her than I am to ever see her again, so keep this as a memento and let it help you see the truth"— still echoed annoyingly in his mind. Ronin was irritated by Romeo's interference but kept the clasps nonetheless. They were worth a king's ransom and he could sell them if necessary.

His eyes were bloodshot when he broke into the clearing where Kalial waited. He had his belt in place and his sword slapped against his leg. The silk of his shirt rippled as he strode forward. Kalial blinked at the remembrance of another moment when she had watched him just like now. It seemed eons ago. She deliberately deepened her voice and spoke to him, pushing the words past the lump in her throat. "Did you find her?" she asked.

"No," he said shortly. "The sun is breaking. It is time to move on. Forget the girl. My first duty is to my family and to you. We should not have dallied here. We must make all haste to Rath-thuaidhe, whether the Serpent army is still there or not." He looked at the owl on Kalial's shoulder and with a smile, reached out a finger to him. His large eyes blinked and his head swiveled. Ronin turned his hand up and revealed a pile of fresh, thinly sliced meat. The owlet hopped over and rapidly downed the food, then settled on Ronin's massive shoulder. His claws snagged the silk until Ronin gently moved him to his bare forearm.

Ronin's eyes lifted and he looked warmly at Kalial. "He is perfect, Squire Kal. Thank you for the gift of him, and thank you for waiting for me. I apologize for my unkind words. You are a good soul and deserve my respect, not my mockery. We have a difficult road ahead of us and I would like to know that we have no secrets or resentments between us. If we are to trust our lives to each other, then we must have complete faith in each other. Do you agree?" He looked deeply into Kalial's eyes and waited for her response.

She began to choke. As she sputtered and coughed, Ronin clapped her on the back with words of concern. Finally Kalial managed to croak out, "There are no secrets in trust, McTaver, just as there is no faltering in loyalty." Ronin ceased his motions and eyed Kalial carefully for a moment, unsure if she was agreeing with him or not. With a shrug, he swiftly blanketed and saddled the horse.

"All right then. We will ride together until the outskirts of town." He swung up and reached down for Kalial. She took a steadying breath and placed her hand in his. He swept her up behind him and set the horse in a steady trot along the costal road. Dhu Cait bounded after them, as silent and watchful as ever.

Kalial could feel the tension in Ronin. His shoulders were tight and his hands were fisted over the reins although he often fingered the velvet pouch hanging from his belt. Despite his cavalier words, he was clearly upset about the loss of his Gypsy. A small part of Kalial's heart relented. She bit her lip and debated his talk of honesty. Should she reveal herself to him?

Finally, Ronin broke the silence. "Rath-thuaidhe is about a day and a half's ride away. As I told you earlier, once there we will sail to Tregaron. My ship is scheduled to be seaworthy within the fortnight. Mayhap it is already. She is having her hull scraped and sealed. Tregaron is down the coast, past a large, craggy mountain range that is difficult to travel through by foot, although it can be traversed. Sailing is by far the easier and quicker route for smaller parties. Once I convince my cousin to send men with me, we may have to return by way of the mountains unless he grants us use of another ship. I suspect that he will resist committing that favor as he depends hugely on sea trade." Ronin smiled faintly. "I will have to be rather persuasive." He then asked as an afterthought, "Have you ever sailed?"

"No."

"Of course not, my apologies. I often forget that you never set foot outside of the forest until a few days ago."

They were silent for several miles. The sun climbed up the horizon and spread faint rays across their shoulders. The owlet fluttered, beginning to exercise his wings. Pinfeathers peaked out of the down undercoat, giving him a scraggly appearance. Finally Kalial asked a question that had been troubling her.

"Ronin? Tell me about this treasure the Serpent desires. What is it?"

Ronin cast a quick look over his shoulder at Kal, dragging his thoughts from last eve to the present. "It is an old story about a treasure called the Scottish Gold." When Ronin fell silent again, Kalial glared at his back. Not noticing the expression, Ronin continued. "It is something he wants that is a part of my family history." He frowned mightily. "I can not speak of it."

"Did you not moments ago speak to me about revealing all secrets?" Kalial held her breath, waiting for his answer, ready to tell her hidden truth should he be open with her.

Despite wanting to confide in his comrade, Ronin was bound by a lifetime of familial duty and loyalty; therefore his tone was harsher than he intended. "You know nothing of what binds my tongue. I can not divulge hundreds of years of fiercely held information to a person I barely know. You may have no understanding of what it is to hold back your thoughts, but I must, so do not ask it again."

Kalial jerked away from him as if hit. The warhorse snorted at the abrupt movement and sidled quickly to keep her mounted. "I have no understanding of secrets!?'' Kalial shouted, angrier than before. "I am perfectly able to keep secrets from a lout such as you!"

"Come now, Kal, I do not intend for us to argue again. I have had a long night. I keep nothing but this one fact from you, and I am bound by duty to keep silent on the subject. Surely you can appreciate that I must not betray my family as their bodies lay rotting in open graves? I have nothing, no home, no mother, no father, no siblings . . . nothing but this stray secret that I must hold from the man who took everything else from me. If I tell you, and you are caught and tortured, I will have lost the secret as well as lost you, my only friend."

Kalial's anger faded and she dropped her eyes to the road beneath them. She, too, held secrets, secrets he did not even know she held. Not only was she the Gypsy woman he sought, but she also held the secret of Loch Nidean. Bound by the same duty, the same loyalty as he, she could not reveal its nature to him, just as he would not open up to her. She did understand; it was simply that she was used to being the only one with a secret to protect, and it was odd to be confronted with a man whose sense of duty was equal to her own. Despite the distance that silence created between them, she felt a bond develop, strengthen, deepen as she privately acknowledged what they shared.

When she did not answer, Ronin turned his thoughts to war strategy, never suspecting that her silence indicated that she understood his dilemma all too well.

Kalial let her mind wander, searching for her jaguar's comfort. Her own sense of loss was triggered by Ronin's words, and she sought the companionship of her McCat to soothe her heart, yet the animal's presence only partially calmed her. Unconsciously, Kalial snuggled close against Ronin's back. Feeling the strong chest breath in and out, Kalial relaxed peacefully. But Ronin felt her warmth, and became subtly uncomfortable with the softness of her resting weight.

A scent of jasmine and honeysuckle surrounded him and he shook his head roughly to clear the smell, thinking that his remembrances were becoming too real. A stab of longing went through him, and he closed his eyes and relived the moments of heaven he had just left behind.

With a sigh, he opened his eyes and sat up, shifting Kal. "Let us not travel in silence. You are from a strange land and"—he gestured to the owlet and the black cat—"you have unusual companions. Would you tell me about your life? Your family?"

Kalial sat up and looked at the back of Ronin's thick black hair. She fought an impulse to touch it. Instead she crossed her arms and began to speak quietly. "I have lived by legends all my life. We tell and retell the stories daily in every aspect of our lives. When a new pot is made, the clay is chosen to remind us of a particular season, and the engraving tells a tale. When we prepare food, we chant a story of a time when the fates say we will have none. When we rise in the morning and see the sun, we sing the legend of when the trees were grown to shield us from its glare."

Her strange accent curled around the words, making them seem exotic. With the owlet perched on his forearm, and the ebony cat that was as large as a small pony pacing alongside, Ronin suspended his disbelief and listened.

"I was taught the legends and I know them all. My mother taught me some, the elders taught me others, but most I learned from village life. The legends tell of events that occurred before I was born and of what will happen after I am gone. One tale is told in the autumn, when the leaves are gold and red and the santeen moss begins to burn from within."

Ronin recalled his experience with the sparking moss and snorted through his nose. Kal's voice got softer as he continued his tale. "One legend involves a stranger, like you. Hundreds of years ago, a woman from our lands was stolen by a man dressed as a wolf. He had stalked her for months, trying different costumes. When he was a rabbit, she tried to shoot him with an arrow for dinner. When he posed as a great cat, she fled from him in terror. When he slithered in the form of a snake, she did not see him hidden in the grass. But one day, he took on the skin of a wolf and pounced upon her as she gathered berries. The man-wolf gripped her hair and pulled her into his lair where he mated with her. She, thinking that she had lain with a wolf, wept, because she had fallen in love with her beast.

"For many years she lived with him in their den, loving him yet feeling that she had betrayed her family. Then one day a real wolf came out of the forest, attacked and killed the wolf-man. The woman found him and held him, seeing her love as a man for the first time, but too late. She was now a prisoner of the real wolf and her heart lay buried in the grave of her lover.

"In despair, she escaped the evil beast and returned to her forest. But the wolf chased her, his horrible fangs glistening. She ran past the berry patch where she had been seduced, she ran through the trees that had been her home, and finally she ran into the waters of Loch Nidean from whence she never returned. Now her lonely soul is buried under the nebulous waters of Loch Nidean."

Ronin halted the horse and turned to look behind him. "I have never heard such a tale. My people speak of Loch Nidean forest much differently." He looked carefully at Kal, considering the tale he had told. The boy's golden eyes were soft and misty and Ronin felt a flicker deep in his soul. He sensed something . . .

Shaking his head, he blinked and urged his horse forward.

"The legend is one of the oldest." She looked at his back with a sidelong glance. She saw the midnight black hair and recalled for a second how it had felt between her fingers. "I am not certain of its true meaning, but I avoid the lake," she murmured.

Ronin laughed, then exclaimed, "You live within the forest named by the tale you speak! Surely you visit its shores?"

"No. I do not travel to that section," she answered with a tilt of her chin.

A sharp whinny from over the next dune drew him abruptly from his retort. Ronin could hear the jangle of many bridles and the hoofbeats of many horses. "Bloody hell," he grumbled. A sickening feeling swelled up his gut. There was no place to hide, no where to run. He smelled the wind and his eyes turned hard as he recognized the scent of many unwashed bodies mingled with the tang of steel. The smell, so much more evocative than the visual memory, dragged thoughts of blood and carnage through his mind. A shudder swept through him, formed from fear and rage. The muscles of his body instinctively flexed and his warrior reactions surged to the fore.

Kalial felt his body clench, and hers reacted similarly. When he dropped his hand to his sword, she gripped Ronin's waist as an anchor.

Ronin whipped around at Kalial's grip and nearly drew his blade across her throat before he acknowledged her frightened face. He froze, staring into the golden fringed eyes and felt a sudden whisper of emotion flicker through his soul like a recognition that his mind could not place. He dropped his eyes to where Kalial's delicate fingers wrapped only partially around his hips. Involuntarily he twitched and heard Kalial gasp in response.

A raging heat pulsed from his skin as the sounds of

the approaching men became louder. He looked up once again and saw the smooth, unblemished skin and the trembling lips that seemed to beckon. Not knowing if he reacted to the memory of his family or because of his vow to protect his charge, he cruelly shoved Kalial to the ground.

"Slip into the water," he growled, ignoring her hurt whimper as he flung her away from him. "Stay there, no matter what happens. Promise me this. If I do not survive, you will continue to Tregaron as planned and tell my cousin all that has happened. Enlist his help. Demand it in the name of the Laird of Roseneath." He shook the owlet off his arm. It spread its newly feathered wings and tried to flap yet only hung for a moment in the air before spiraling down to crash into Kalial's lap. A squawk of protest signaled its safe landing. The great cat grasped the back of Kalial's tunic and began to drag her to the shore despite her struggles to free herself.

"No! I will stand with you. Let me go, dhu Cait— Ronin! You can not fight them all, let me help," she pleaded. "Two are twice as powerful as one!"

"Two are not enough. I need you to do as I bid. Get yourself to Tregaron. Here." He swung off his charger and quickly unsaddled him. He ripped the leather ties that held the saddlebag in place and flung most of the supplies out onto the sand. Then he rolled the dirty saddle blanket up tightly and stuffed it and the velvet pouch in the bag and tossed them at Kal.

"Use the clasps as needed for bribes and coin. Lie low until you see a ship that sports the plaid of the McTaver. She will be called the *Bonny Evelyn*. You must be careful around the sailors. They can be an unruly lot but they should grant you respect if they know you stand in my favor. Ask for the first mate, Dugan Trask. Now, get going before the army crests the hill!"

"Please do not send me away. I must tell you something!" Kal's voice rose as Ronin placed the saddle upon the bare back of his steed.

"Go! The only thing that is important now is to get my message to Tregaron." Ronin stared hard at Kal as he swung atop the warhorse. "That is important to you, is it not? The return of your forest and the resurrection of your way of life? You will have a family and home again."

Kal fell silent. Long seconds filled the air between them. The boy's hair had broken free of its ponytail and floated about his shoulders. He had a streak of dust on his nose and along his cheek and his glittering golden eyes were filled with indecision.

Ronin felt his heart give. "Go on, sweet Kal. You are too young and full of life to die today. Fulfill your duty to your lands and help me do the same." The hard warrior-face melted slightly as he looked at Kal with fondness. "I ask you as a new-found friend, please. Go to the ocean, forget your fears and run along the coast. Do not look back. Find my ship and give them my instructions. Keep my saddlebag safe, for it is very important to me. There is something I must do, and confronting Lothian may be the best way to do it."

With a soft cry, Kalial ran forward and briefly touched his leg, then she turned and fled down the beach, her strong and slender legs carrying her into the waves just as the tops of the Serpent banner could be seen broaching the dune.

Ronin watched the boy's retreating form for a moment longer and then searched vainly for the black hide of dhu Cait blending into the shadows of the beach grass. His mahogany horse stood battle ready. His neck was arched; his tail was held high. The flaxen hair rippled in the slight breeze. He chomped at his bit and a bit of foam could be seen in the corner of his mouth. His ears were rigidly forward and he stood

with his haunches slightly camped under, ready to
spring at the slightest touch of his master's heels.

Ronin felt the breeze slide over his skin, slipping
inside the vee of his shirt. The caress reminded him
of the Gypsy woman. He sat relaxed in the saddle,
content to confront his fate. He deliberately recalled
her form, and he branded it to his eyelids so that her
sweetness would be with him. His own black hair ruffled and his blazingly blue eyes were rich, strong and
intelligent as he watched the army approach.

"That be he! That be the one I did see earlier, yes!
I told ye that he could nay be far." The ugly man who
had dragged Quinn to his death spoke rapidly. His
filthy beard shook in his agitation and he spurred his
mount forward to charge Ronin, his stupidity and embarrassment making him reckless. As his horse galloped abreast of him, Ronin swung his sword up and
under the man's helmet, neatly severing his neck and
partially decapitating him. The man collapsed to the
ground, gurgling in his own blood. His horse cantered
for a bit, slowed, and then lowered its weary head to
the grass.

Ronin did not move other than to bring his sword
arm back to a position of deceptive stillness. His pristine white silk shirt was marred by splotches of red.
His gaze fused with that of the army captain who
raised his hand to halt the two hundred men marching
behind him. The first row of mounted riders split and
the one-eyed, white-haired leader of the Serpents rode
forward. His pale eye glowed with satisfaction.

"You are very clever, *Laird* McTaver." His voice
dripped with sarcasm. "Heading into Loch Nidean to
escape my men . . . very clever indeed. Of course, I
will not be gainsaid by mere trees or pathetic forest
people, as you no doubt discovered. I am so pleased
that you made it out alive. I feared for a while that I
had lost you, but no, here you stand, ready to fight

my entire army." He chuckled evilly. The sound ended in a harsh cough and his wandering eye turned up into his skull before dropping down again. "What? Just you? I thought you would be better prepared than this. I am looking forward to renewing our discussion." He dropped his sarcastic tone and leaned forward in his saddle.

"You sacrificed your family, your lovely little sister, to save the Secret, but now it is mine!" He sat up and motioned his riders forward. Ronin watched them dispassionately until his mahogany stallion reared in an unusual show of disobedience. Ronin crooned to the horse, asking its forgiveness for riding it to this bloodbath. When the horse's feet touched the ground, Ronin released his hold on the reins and they shot forward. He raised his sword and swung mightily at the closest man.

The mercenaries shrank back, out of his range, and Ronin pulled up in surprise. He narrowed his eyes and leaned forward to engage another soldier but that one sidestepped away with a glance at the Serpent. Ronin watched in fury as the men slid their swords into scabbards and instead pulled out clubs and cudgels and began swinging them at their sides. Ronin eyed the sheathed, deadly swords and had a moment of sick understanding. This was to be no clean kill, but a long, drawn-out beating—a punishment for escaping. He looked up at the Serpent in hatred.

"You will not grant me the warrior's right to die in battle?" Ronin shouted. "If that is your wish, then come forward and meet me, man to man!"

"We will have our time, Lord McTaver," he hissed. He nodded to the men, and they closed in on Ronin.

Kalial watched in horror as the men thrashed Ronin, dragging him from his horse and beating him endlessly with their clubs while kicking him with their armored boots. The scene continued incessantly until she was certain that the limp, reddened thing on the ground could no longer be living. Tears streamed down her face, merging with the salty ocean. She jammed her fist into her mouth to keep from screaming. With Ronin's parting plea to her echoing in her mind, she yanked her eyes away from his body and dove under water, swimming underneath the waves until her lungs felt as if they would burst. She broke the surface to gasp in more air, and dove under again. As she swam, she brushed through a mass of stinging jellyfish, but could not feel the physical pain for the wrenching that tore at her soul.

PART II

Castle Basingstoke

CHAPTER 9

Kalial kept to the shadows of the town of Rath-thuaidhe. She had debated about bringing dhu Cait into town with her, but had wisely decided that the cat would garner more curiosity than she needed here. Thus it was that two nights after separating from Ronin, Kalial was slinking along the streets, alone.

As dusk descended, a new crowd of people began to emerge. The daytime bustle of ladies and house servants, vendors and artisans gave way to a colorful array of prostitutes, soldiers, beggars and, of course, sailors. A young woman traveled the road ahead of her with hurried steps. A small reticule dangled from her wrist and she carried a package in her arms. She looked around frequently and almost tripped in her haste.

Three men lounging against a street post also saw the woman. With several pokes and laughs among them, they began to trail her. Suddenly a small boy dashed up to the woman, pushed her down and pulled on her package. She struggled only for a second, then let go of her burden with a soft cry. The three men approached the woman just as she struggled to her feet. One reached out and smoothly slid the purse from her wrist while kissing her hand. She yanked away from him so quickly, she stumbled back into another man, who caught her around the waist and leaned down to whisper in her ear. The woman's terrified pleas were barely audible.

Kalial pulled out her dirk and began to run toward the woman. Meanwhile, the woman broke free of the man's hold and leapt into the back of a passing wagon. When the man attempted to follow, the driver good-naturedly snapped him with his driving whip.

"Now there, Charley, she be with me now. Get thee gone, boys!" The wagon lurched onward, carrying the frightened woman out of immediate danger. Kalial slowed, then stepped back into the shadows as the men turned in her direction. Grumbling and angry conversation followed among the men as they strolled down the street toward a nearby tavern.

Kalial took several deep breaths. She pulled her wide hat down even lower and checked to make sure all of her hair was safely concealed. She affected a swagger like that of the sailors and tried to stroll nonchalantly behind the men. One glanced back, cast a quick eye over her form, and then turned away to resume his conversation. Kalial felt her teeth begin to chatter and she bit her tongue in an effort to still them.

Everything about this town sickened her. She detested the smells, the noise, the sheer number of people. She hated the rotten tasting food she had been able to scavenge. Sleeping in town was unthinkable, so she rested instead in a grove of trees beyond the walls. She thought longingly of her forest and the sweet, clean freshness of her lands. A splash of refuse falling from above broke her reverie and she wrinkled her nose in disgust as she continued following the sailors.

One of the men turned again and glanced at Kalial with more interest. "What you doing, boy? No pick pocketing here, understand?"

Taking a fortifying breath, Kalial tilted her head up

and stared at the men levelly. "I have no intention of
robbing you. I am looking for men from the *Bonny
Evelyn*."

"They willna hire a novice like you. That ship is
captained by McTaver, and he only runs with experienced crew. You'd have better luck with the Turks!"
The men guffawed, amused by the picture of the
pretty lad beset upon by the sodomizing foreigners.

"I want to speak to someone from the *Bonny Evelyn*. Do you know any of them or not?"

With narrowed eyes one of the men nodded and
jerked his head toward the open tavern door. "Dugan
Trask be drinking inside."

Kalial nodded and walked by the suspicious men,
thankful to get clear of their mistrustful glances.

The doors to the tavern were swung wide and
propped open by two anvils. She eyed the massive
doors warily and was pleased that she was not required to push them open. She slipped inside and
quickly shuffled to the far side of the room where the •
light was dimmest. Raucous shouts and laughter filled
the tavern, making listening to one's own thoughts
near impossible. Many tables were littered with half-
full tankards, but everywhere else women in skimpy
clothing gyrated for coins. Their harsh voices often
rose above the din to call for coins and to suggest
lewd positions. Kalial stared in utter amazement.

In due time a harried barmaid stood in front of her.
She took one look at Kalial's shocked face and said,
"New in town, honey? What you want, whiskey or
ale?" At Kalial's stupefied look she leaned down and
whispered, "If'n you look like that, honey, you be
robbed before ye blink. Better'n you keep your head
down and look mean and don' invite no stranger's
talk." She stood up and cocked her head. "Whiskey
then?" she said loudly, "and I don' take the stairs for
no un, no time, so don' be askin' agin." She winked
broadly, then turned toward the next table.

Kalial closed her mouth and lowered her head. She drew her brows together and focused on acting generally unpleasant and unsociable. Two fingers of watered whiskey found their way to her table and Kalial tossed them back with a cough. She felt the warmth spread down her arms and legs. Her resolve strengthened, she listened to the ebb and flow of conversation around her.

The barmaid came over again and plunked another drink in front of Kalial, then sat down with a tired sigh. "What ya doing here, lad?" she asked softly. "You don't look like our sort. You a cabin boy? A page? A messenger?"

"Here," Kalial said while pressing one of the jeweled clasps into the barmaid's hand. The maid gasped and quickly covered it by closing her fist. "Blimey! What is this for?"

"I need to find Dugan Trask of the *Bonny Evelyn*. Do you know who he is?"

"Of course, luv. I know them all! Let me introduce you. Come on. And, sweetie, me name is Florie."

Kalial found her arm pulled as Florie dragged her across the tavern. "My name is Kal," she gasped as Florie presented her in front of a large, dour man.

He looked up, his irritation obvious. "I'm not hiring. Get him gone, Florie."

"He's not lookin' to be hired, are ye hun?" Florie replied.

"No," Kal responded, finally catching her breath. "Are you Dugan Trask of the *Bonny Evelyn*?"

Dugan glared at Kal. "Get lost, boy! I have other things on me mind."

"I come from Ronin McTaver with a message," Kalial retaliated with heat, annoyed with his grumpiness.

"Doubt that!" Dugan replied, equally angry.

Infuriated, Kal leaned down and faced Dugan nose to nose. "I have information about your clan leader, and I have instructions that you are to follow. Now, if it were up to me, I would leave this sorry town and go my own way, but I made a promise and I will not let your stubbornness make me break it."

Dugan slowly rose, his tall form towering over Kalial. "You had best watch your tongue, young boy," he thundered until Florie slipped between the two antagonists, facing Dugan.

"Just listen to the lad, Dugan. What harm will it cause? Mayhap he tells the truth."

Dugan glared over Florie's head into Kalial's snapping golden eyes. With considerable ill grace, he resumed his seat and nodded.

Gritting her teeth, Kalial sat down as well. "Ronin McTaver bade me tell you to go to Tregaron to see his cousin."

"For what purpose? He arrives shortly to inspect the ship for a run to the Orient."

Kalial took a deep breath and told what she knew of Ronin's family's misfortune. "The Serpent massacred his family, and only Ronin escaped. He now seeks to gain an army of men from his cousin and return to reclaim his lands."

Half rising again, Dugan's voice rang with accusation. "Where is he now? Why is he not here himself?"

Florie shushed him and motioned toward several soldiers in the tavern. "Keep your voices low, me lads. The Serpent's men are growing strong and have begun to rule over the port."

"Where is he?" Dugan repeated, softer but with intensity. Kalial simply shook her head, her eyes sorrowful. Dugan rose fully, his body trembling. "We will find him," he said quietly. "Come, Florie, bring the lad and we will talk on the ship."

Florie smiled at Kalial's dubious expression. "Do not mind his bad manners. I will join you after I finish my shift."

*   *   *

It was black. Very black. At least he was spared having to watch the rats chew on the dead body in the corner, though he could still hear them and that was bothersome. Ronin curled his spine so that he faced the wall. A shaft of pain lanced through his ribcage. Or maybe it was his head. Oddly, in the dark it was sometimes difficult to determine what was hurting. The pain swelled and he decided that perhaps both his ribs and his head were the cause of his discomfort. He heard a shuffle behind him, a few grunts, and then gagged as an overpowering stench of human offal permeated the cell. Several inmates protested halfheartedly, but most just accepted it. Ronin wrinkled his nostrils before recalling the tenderness of his broken nose. A small groan escaped his lips before he clamped his jaw shut. Blackness. Just stare into the blackness, he told himself.

A shaft of light penetrated his dark blanket and Ronin winced.

"Get up, you lazy bastard!" The guard kicked Ronin in the back. He glared at the guard, his blue eyes spitting cold fire. A swift punch in the jaw rewarded his insolence. Ronin rubbed his jaw briefly, then stood up painfully, towering over the guard. His expression flashed contempt for the little bully.

The guard raised his fist again, then thought better of it. Instead, he poked Ronin with an iron in his hand. "Get movin'. You're to be questioned again. Hope you enjoy it." The guard cackled at his humor while pushing Ronin down the corridor with hard jabs from the spiked iron pole. Ronin saw a chamber loom up ahead and his face paled beneath his tan.

"Ah, my favorite warrior," hissed a voice from the shadows. Ronin kept his eyes trained on the far wall, the thin line of sweat that broke out along his brow the only indication that he was far from calm. He squared his shoulders and walked steadily into the chamber. "Are you ready to talk to me, McTaver? I slept poorly last night after our last meeting. I could not finish my roast duck because I was so distressed that you and I had not come to an understanding." Lothian stepped forward into Ronin's line of sight. *"Tell me!"* he whispered while his sightless eye shivered in its socket and the flesh hanging from his throat shook in his agitation. "I seek the Second Hunt, the second clue to the Scottish Gold, and I know that you have hidden it. Every day you will be tortured and maimed until you have told me where it is. Only by telling me your secret will I grant you absolution."

He paused and stared into Ronin's blank eyes. "Do you deny that you stole it from me? I deserved it as the spoils of your castle rightfully taken. The law is on my side, you fool. I can do things to you that have never been done before in this chamber of hell." His tone became wheedling. "Come now, McTaver, what is the point of living anymore? Your family is dead, you have nothing, no one. Just tell me and you can rest."

The whisper of the truth made Ronin's insides tremble. The lack of food, the beatings, the dark, the rats, the memories all swam in his mind like a mass of slithering serpents. He felt his mind weaken at the evil words.

Then out of the darkness memories of his friend, Kal, came to him, fortified him. Ronin took a deep breath and recalled his many conversations with the boy. He remembered the trials they had both already overcome, and the bond they had forged. They had vowed to help each other, and Ronin would not succumb to torture for he was certain that Kal would never have yielded. Emboldened, he turned to the Serpent with an arrogant look. "I do not have the tapestry, nor do I know where it is."

"You *do* know where the Scottish Gold is!" shouted the white-haired man as he stomped around the chamber.

"You killed my father for nothing," responded Ronin. "The tapestry is only a piece of cloth that is part of an old legend. Its meaning was lost long ago. There is no treasure to be found."

"Bah! I am tired of this game. I have the first tapestry and have determined that the Scottish Gold consists of emeralds, rubies and sapphires. I have seen the weave that depicts the pile of riches you hide. Your piece will tell me where it is hidden!"

Ronin shook his head. "The Scottish Gold is a fable. Leave it, Lothian. There is no pile of wealth."

"I will torture you!" the Serpent shrieked. He glared and cursed, but finally left the room. He returned moments later with a carefully preserved tapestry. With rising curiosity, Ronin watched Lothian unwrap the piece.

"See? Can you now doubt that the Scottish Gold should be mine? Your father, Robert McTaver, held the second tapestry unfairly. It should belong to my family!"

Ronin stared at the brilliant tapestry in shock. Woven amid gilded jewels and sparkling gems was an unmistakable castle tower. The tower held no resemblance to Roseneath. Instead, it evoked the image of Lothian's stronghold.

Kalial sat in her usual spot in the tavern. The barmaid, Florie, sidled up and dropped her weary body into a chair next to her. She heaved a sigh. Kalial looked at her in mild surprise. "Is not Sullivan going to be angry if you rest?" Kalial had formed a small friendship with the barmaid over the last several days and she knew that the heavy hand of the tavern's owner would find the maid's backside if he was displeased.

"Well, he don' have ta know that now does he?" Florie replied. Kalial shook her head. Some soldiers came in and Kalial watched them carefully. They swung off their capes, revealing the black and red design of the serpent.

Kalial's face froze. At last! she thought. After days of waiting, someone who might know the fate of McTaver! She leaned forward slightly, her body tense. The soldiers moved easily through the crowd, people shifting out of their way with nervous nods, and ascended the back stairs.

"Has Dugan had any word of McTaver?" Florie asked as she fanned herself.

"Where are those soldiers going?" interrupted Kalial urgently.

"Upstairs to the table room, I bet. They talk about all kinds of things up there."

"I need to listen in."

"What?" exclaimed Florie. "You canna just barge up there and make a fool o' yourself. Only Serpent men go up there. Them an' no others, you hear me? Jus' the filthy, slimy Serpents. You should continue searching the beach for McTaver's washed-up body, I'm thinking."

"The table girls," said Kalial quietly. "They go upstairs with customers all the time."

"Well, yes, but it'd look mighty strange, you jus' walking right up all alone."

"Then come with me." Kalial stood. Florie gaped at her.

"I canna do that! I be just a barmaid."

Kalial looked down at her in moderate confusion. "Are you not allowed to entertain the customers?"

"Entertain . . . well, I never! No one'd pick big Florie with the likes o' the pretty girls around." Florie waved her hand toward a table dancer.

"Let's go upstairs now and listen from the next room." Kalial's voice was hard and commanding. She strode over to the stairs without looking to see if Florie followed her. After a second's incredulous pause, Florie scrambled after her.

"You know, for a wee thing that didna know much about town a week ago, you seem to have gotten pretty haughty! Never mind," Florie grumbled at Kalial's hurt expression, "I'll go up with you. It willna do us any good though."

At the top of the stairs, Florie led Kalial to a small room off to the left, where a man and woman were just getting dressed. "Hurry up now!" said Florie, "I've got a randy one here and it don' do to make him wait." The girl looked at Florie quizzically but slipped her shoes on and left the room. The man was a bit slower but he, too, soon quit the room. Florie swung the door shut behind him and dropped the bar. Kalial was already pressing her ear to the wall.

She heard a low murmur of voices interspersed with a few feminine giggles. Kalial looked over at Florie in surprise.

"What?" Florie asked.

"It sounds like there are women in there."

"Well, of course.'Tis a tavern. What did ye expect?"

"I thought you said that only Serpent men went into the conference room."

"Women don' count, laddie. Everyone knows that pretty ladies go places that normal folk don'. Coursn' they figure that girls canna understand what they be talkin' 'bout."

"Can you get in?" asked Kalial hopefully. Florie guffawed.

"I said pretty girls." She shrugged and wiggled her big behind, then patted it with a slight grimace. "The likes o' me don' pass. What do you need? Maybe I could get a friend to help us or mayhap I have heard them talkin' 'bout what goes on in there." Florie smiled openly. Kalial turned her back to the wall and slid down so that she was sitting on her rump with her knees pulled up.

"Perhaps they know what happened to him." Kalial's voice sounded lost even to her ears. "I should not have left him . . ." Her eyes filled with tears. "I went back after the Serpents left but I did not find his body so I do not know what has happened to him."

"I know, dearie, you told us all that on the ship."

"Trask and his men think I did wrong by leaving him. I could see it in their eyes."

"Trask is a fool. You did what the laird commanded. You came here, told Dugan to go to Tregaron and protected his belongings. I'm thinking it's time for Dugan to do what ye bid him do and set sail."

"McTaver told me to continue on our journey, but I . . . we can not go without him if there's any chance he's still alive." Kalial blinked rapidly to clear the tears and she risked a quick glance up at Florie. The barmaid's friendly eyes were full of concern.

"Now, you know that no 'un survives a confrontation with those beasts. Your man is no doubt lying against some dune out there feeding the vultures. It does no good to be hopin' for the impossible, laddie."

Kalial listened with a heavy heart, sighed and then said resolutely, "I know I must complete his orders and reach Castle Basingstoke in Tregaron, but I must know his fate for certain before I leave. I . . . owe it to him."

Florie rubbed her chin and scratched at her ear. "You seem awfully loyal for a paid man," Florie remarked. Her sharp eyes looked over Kal and she noted the sculpted cheeks and aristocratic nose shaded beneath the wide hat. She waited while Kal stared at her unblinkingly. When the boy said nothing, Florie tisked.

Florie looked at Kal askance. "You stay here awhile and mayhap I'll ask one o' the girls for some help."

"Do not let the men know I am here," Kal cautioned. "Make sure the girl you talk to does not sell word of my existence to them." The boy jerked his head toward the wall. Florie drew herself up, affronted.

"O' course not! We stick together we do, so don'

fear. I be askin' Elsie. She is a soft-lookin' thing that the gents think is dumb as a turnip but she was a schoolmaster's daughter before she hit a bit o' hard times. Believe me, she'd no sooner rat on ye than fall in love with a snake." Florie propped her hand on her hip and nodded her head for emphasis, then lifted the door latch and slipped her bulk out the door. Kalial rose, relatched the door and returned to her vigil against the wall.

An hour later, Florie knocked at the door. Kalial admitted her and a winsome young girl in heavy face paint.

"This be Elsie. Tell what you heard, girl." The girl flopped down on the bed and closed her eyes. "Come, come, time for sleeping later. Tell yur news!"

Elsie opened her eyes with a moan. "Oh, let me rest a bit, Florie, I be fair tired." She looked over at Kalial's tense face and relented. "Oh, all right then, I'll tell ye." She sat up and rolled her neck, rubbing at it with both hands. "Och, them men toss me around frightful." She dropped her hands. "I heard tell of a black-haired man they keep in the prison for questioning. Only thing is, they been torturing him pretty bad." Her voice had dropped to a loud whisper.

"He is alive then?" Kalial asked frantically. "He has survived?"

"Aye, survived all right. The rumors are that he is now a temporary guest of the Serpent, but as soon as he tells the Serpent what he wants, he will be hung in the yard."

"Have they set a time?" asked Kalial.

"Yae," Florie answered, "tomorrow. That nasty man has no patience, and he figures that if he does na get the information he seeks, it must mean the McTaver don' have it no more."

"I must go and tell the ship's crew. We must prepare to rescue him!" Kalial's eyes glittered and she smiled widely. "My thanks to you both. I will never forget your help."

"You'll nae be forgetting anything, for I'm coming wit ye," replied Florie with a large grin.

CHAPTER 10

Kalial and Florie raced to the dock and hailed the *Bonny Evelyn*. She was sleek and narrow, with an upswept prow and two masts that held broad, square sails when in the open sea. She had two rows of oarlocks along her hull and a dinghy lashed to her deck. After several minutes, the small rowboat was lowered and then brought to shore. Soon it bumped along the piers and Dugan glared out at the pair.

"Should not you be at the tavern, Florie? And you, sleeping in that grove with your odd animals? I am too busy to tend to women and boys right now."

"Too busy to hear our news then?" snapped Florie while Kalial's eyes narrowed to slits. When Dugan said nothing, Florie grinned excitedly. "Kal was ever so clever and found a way to gather information. We know where McTaver is!"

Dugan swung his gaze to Kalial incredulously. "What have you heard, boy? What have you heard?"

Kalial did not waste time. "He is in the prison, and though he lives now, he will not by sundown tomorrow. We need rescue him from the prison before they execute him."

"So he lives?" Dugan asked, still stupefied.

Kalial stomped her foot in frustration. "Not much longer if we dally here," she replied.

"I will get the crew and we will storm the prison!" Dugan cried and shoved the boat away from the dock.

"Do not be a fool, Dugan Trask," Florie admonished. "You'll never get him out alive with that strategy. You needs think with more cunning."

"The Serpent men allowed a woman into their conference room, which is how we discovered McTaver's whereabouts," Kalial explained. "I'm thinking that a woman might be able to get into the prison easier than a man."

"What good would that do?" Dugan responded in disgust. "We need force to get him free."

"Not necessarily," Florie interjected. "The prison whores get inside every night at midnight. No one suspects them."

"I could not disguise myself as a whore!" Dugan responded angrily.

"I could," Kalial whispered. "I am small enough."

"And what would you do once you were inside, Kal? Leave him to die once again?"

The dock echoed with silence. Kalial's face was frozen and Florie was stunned into silence. Even Dugan had the grace to look ashamed for his remark.

Finally Kalial licked her lips and took a deep breath. "I will not leave him again," she said. The set of her jaw dared him to contradict her, and Dugan did not. "I will get the guard to open McTaver's cell. Then you and your men can come in and help him escape. The less commotion we cause, the more likely we will succeed without loss of life."

Dugan frowned but nodded nonetheless. "Perhaps you should hire a real prostitute," he remarked. "The best distraction for any man is a woman. No man—guard, sailor or captain—can see straight when his dick is hard." Dugan laughed loudly at Kalial's affronted look, then slapped her on the back in a small token of friendship. "You should bring your beasts to the ship now so everything is in readiness for immediate sail in case the rescue does not go as smoothly as you hope."

The threesome spent several more minutes confirming their plan, then split up to make preparations. Just before Florie and Kalial parted, Florie pulled Kalial aside and spoke quietly to her.

"I think you should be the one to act the part of the prostitute, for Ronin trusts you."

"But I don't know how," Kalial replied, doubts overtaking her.

"Come now, I know your secret. Perhaps men are oblivious to your feminine attributes, but as another woman I can see them clearly."

Kalial stared at her, frightened. "You won't tell . . ."

"Don't worry, love, I won't tell anyone. In fact, I will assist you. I'm thinking you will need a lot of help in the days to come if you succeed in rescuing this man of yours!"

A milling group of whores pushed and shoved at the prison gates. These were the women that could no longer make money on the streets due to age, lack of looks or overt disease. Every night at midnight they poured past the prison gates to service those inmates who had items to trade. The women stank, their teeth were yellowed and they cared only for themselves. The arrival of several newcomers hardly caused comment, especially since they kept to the back of the crowd.

Kalial crouched down and tried not to gag on the rank odor billowing out of the prison yard. She pulled her leg behind her and slowly shuffled in through the gates and across the yard, walking with a feigned limp. She shuffled unsteadily, unaccustomed to the skirts that flowed around her ankles.

Transactions flourished among the prostitutes, prisoners and guards. Payments included coins, food or trinkets. Through the bars, the prisoners offered bits

of their clothing or even their threadbare blankets in
exchange for touches between the metal barriers. The
women bit the coins, tugged on seams and told, in
explicit terms, what each prize was worth.

Kalial scurried along, sidestepping the hands reaching through the bars. Her heart ached at the desperate
expressions on the prisoners' faces. So many called
out the names of their mothers, seeking a moment of
solace from her arms. Guards who were not yet occupied waved coins in her face. She ducked, pulling a
shawl tighter over her head, and hurried along. She
thought rapidly, trying to remember the list of directions from Florie's contact in prison. *Through the
courtyard, down the first set of steps, then turn right
and find a second set of dark stairs. Pick up a torch
and head down, then follow that corridor around . . .*

Kalial paused to get her bearings, trying to still the
trembling in her hands. She crept down the first flight
of stairs and located the second. Then she lifted a
burning torch from the wall, and carefully descended
the stairs, one step at a time.

The sound of footsteps along the corridor woke
Ronin. He carefully opened his eyes, his body weak
and debilitated from the constant torture. The Serpent
was tired of questioning him and was going to hang
him tomorrow. Ronin twitched, fear vying with anger
at his fate.

"Whot's going on? Who ye be?" gruffly questioned
the guard positioned just out of Ronin's vision.

"I be sent here to see to the man afore he gets
hung. The Serpent sent me." A woman's form was
silhouetted against the wall and Ronin looked up to
see her limp over to the hunched and deformed body
of the guard. "I have been paid and want to get it
o'er and done with."

"I heard naught about this, whore," the guard
grumbled.

"Well then, tell the Serpent yurself that ya sent me away. I don' care, I get paid no matter."

She turned to shuffle away when the guard called her back. "Yur going to have to do it in the hallway then."

The woman shrugged. Ronin stood up and took a step back, not wanting to bed a filthy whore in his last moments on this earth. "Go away, woman," he called out. "I do not want you."

"Hah!" cackled the guard. "You will do the whore or I'll cut off your cock and you can die without it. The Serpent says fuck and I says fuck, so fuck the whore you will."

"Come now, great warrior, do not disappoint me," the woman wheedled. "We just go a few feet down the passage, yes?" Ronin could not see the woman's face, but her accent arrested him. Without further protest, he let the guard lead the woman around the corner and into the dim cell.

Kalial trembled at the sight of Ronin's battered face. She peered up at him, her golden eyes sorrowful. "I am . . . I am so sorry, Ronin," she whispered.

Ronin stared down at her in shock, not sure what he was seeing. The arched brows, the topaz eyes, the strong bones . . . they were of Kal, his male friend and companion, yet the soft swell of breasts that filled the dress so naturally and seductively were purely feminine. He shrank back against the wall, certain that his mind was finally slipping.

"Who are you?" he cried out angrily.

"Please," Kalial whispered again, "now is not the time to be angry. I am to pretend to give you release on your final night. While we distract your guards, your sailors will infiltrate the courtyard to aid in your escape."

Ronin stared down at the blond beauty uncomprehendingly. "Who are you?" he stammered again.

"Enough talk!" yelled the guard. "Get on wi' it. We don' have all night."

Ronin leaned down and brushed his lips across the fair maid in front of him, suddenly certain that he did not care what visions his mind conjured up as long as the images continued to be so sweet and lovely. The taste of her surprised lips made his head spin. He smelled her hair, then pushed it aside and kissed her neck.

"Hurry up, I don' hear any grunting! If'n you don't put it to her quick, I'll come do the job myself," the guard taunted.

Kalial turned, trying to avoid Ronin's touch, but he captured her shoulders and held her with surprising strength. "Do not leave now, miss. If I am to have my illusions, I insist that you stay to share them with me."

Kalial pushed and Ronin stumbled back, weakened from his ordeal. "Oh!" Kalial gasped as she gripped his arm to hold him steady.

Ronin braced himself and shook his head, trying to clear the foggy tendrils that slowed his brain. He stared at the woman, sensing that he was not understanding something, but too debilitated to unravel his confusion. Then her scent encircled him and he became suddenly, blazingly aroused.

With a smothered oath, Ronin shoved her against the shadowed wall. He lifted her hips and spread her legs around his waist. "I have dreamed about you," he murmured. "I need you now, quickly."

Kalial was so startled she did not struggle. She lifted her arms to hold his neck and gasped at the abrupt press of his shaft against her thighs. The heat of his passion sparked her own and she melted into his arms.

"Take me then, Ronin, take me fast and hard," she answered huskily while clenching his hips with her knees. "We do not have much time." She moved her hands to his shoulders and kneaded them like a cat making her bed. Her dirty skirt rode high on her hips and she wore no underclothing to bar his entrance. Ronin growled and groaned, his staff already hard and pulsing. He smoothed his hands down her body, reveling in the luscious curves, and she arched in response.

The flicker of torchlight made their shadows stand out upon the passageway wall where it curved away. Ronin glanced at it and at his treasure, unsure of what was more erotic, watching her undulate against the orange wall, or watching her black shadow ripple.

The guard licked his lips as he listened to the harsh breathing coming from down the hall and a bit of saliva dripped from one corner of his mouth. His bloodshot eyes strained in the dark, trying to see around the curve. He heard the woman's voice plead, and he imagined her begging him. The guard started to hop from one foot to the other in excitement, ignoring the prison entrance entirely.

Ronin's senses overwhelmed him and he bared her nipples with his teeth and licked them. Kalial surrendered, admitting silently that this was exactly what she wanted, what she had been longing for. She pressed her back against the cold wall and gasped. Lifting his head momentarily, he fixated on the shadow of Kalial's breasts swelling out of her blouse and the reflection of his head bent to devour them. He saw her breasts heave in agitation as the coolness of the prison air blew across her skin and caused her nipples to pucker.

He found the shadow of her incredibly exotic. It was like making love to a wraith in his dreams, yet she was hot and soft in his arms. He shifted her slightly, watching her reflection. Her shadow blurred until suddenly he saw the perfect outline of breasts, bared, with nipples so hard he could even see them as black buttons against the orange torchlight.

He pushed her against the wall with his hips, holding her there with his powerful thrust while his hands reached up and swept over her skin. When Kalial opened her eyes, she, too, saw the shadow dance and was captivated by it. Ronin stroked her neck and collarbone, then brushed lightly down her breasts. He flicked his thumb over her nipples, then reached under her skirt to grasp her buttocks.

Kalial moaned and began to rock, her body remembering the motions while her mind slipped away. She did not feel the rough wall scratch her back, nor the cold air rush down the passageway as the outer door opened. She only knew that she wanted him inside her once again, and she would scream if he didn't satisfy her immediately.

Kalial reached down and slid her skirt higher over her hips, baring her body completely. Ronin reached his fingers inside of her, feeling the drenched readiness. His heart sped faster and he fumbled with his breeches while holding her against the wall. Forgotten were the shadows and the foreplay. Now he wanted to plunge inside her.

A sudden noise coming from around the corridor made Ronin growl. "Not yet," he muttered, his cock springing loose of its confines and bursting with passion. Frustrated, he reached down and yanked her thighs apart, pinching their inner surface in his haste. Kalial cried out but let him separate her legs with only minimal resistance. She arched off the wall in an unconscious protest. The cry struck him. His gut clenched and he thrust forward, plunging into her heated core.

Kalial bit her lip as she desperately tried to quiet her passion-filled cries. She was still tight, and the immense size of him hurt her even while it pleasured her. She squirmed against him, oblivious to the sound of many feet pounding down the hall toward them. Ronin buried his face in her neck, bucking against her powerfully, rapidly, desperate to bring them both to heaven before they were torn from each other's arms. He drove hard and heavy, grasping her waist so forcefully it left bruises. Just as many men rounded the curve, Ronin felt her insides grab hold of him, gripping, releasing, pulsing, and he held her as she twisted wildly in climax. Ignoring the men for a few more seconds, he pushed into her and released his own desire in a rushing explosion deep within her glorious body.

The sailors stopped, stunned at the shadow tableau of their captain interlocked with a woman against the prison wall. They shuffled anxiously, glancing behind them, then back at Ronin and the woman, exhausted and unmoving. "Captain?" one whispered uncertainly. "Captain, we must go. The whore was only meant to be a distraction. You need not have bedded her. No telling the diseases she carries."

Ronin jerked his head up at the familiar voice of one of his crew members. "Please," the woman whimpered. "The ruse has worked. Go now and escape with your men."

"Come with me," he urged, his body still throbbing within hers.

She wriggled, trying to get loose. Her actions caused him to harden again and she abruptly stilled her motions. "Go!" she said again, more urgently.

"Come with me," he repeated, angry now. He slid an inch out of her and then back in, punctuating his demand.

"Stop," she hissed. "You will ruin everything."

"Who are you?" he asked once again, trying to see her face in the semidarkness.

She shuddered and turned away, hiding her face underneath her hair. "For now you must leave with your men or you will be hanged and your Castle Roseneath will be in the Serpent's hands forever."

Ronin jerked at the reminder of his home and duty. With a shake of his head, he pulled out of her and pulled his breeches up. Kalial pulled her blouse back in place and shook out her skirts. Her legs were wobbly and she leaned back against the wall while motioning Ronin away.

"Go!" Her pleas were supplemented by the sailors' as they hustled Ronin down the corridor, up the stairs and into the prison courtyard. Kalial resumed her limping gait and moved down the passageway well behind them.

As they reached the square, an alarm sounded and pandemonium broke out. From every corner, men jumped out and attacked the guards. Prostitutes shrieked and ran toward the gate. Ronin's first mate grabbed his arm and yanked him forward. "What ye be doing? Come on, Captain, we only have seconds!"

"The girl," began Ronin.

"The girl was hired by your lad. She is nothing but a whore. We must escape."

"She risked herself for me. I must help her," responded Ronin and he turned to head back into the riot.

"Captain McTaver, she is only one girl among a hundred. The guards know nothing of her. She will be fine! What good will you be dead?"

With a last look, Ronin finally relented. The sailors pulled him along, supporting his weakened body as they shielded him from stones and clubs. Once they broke free of the prison gates, Dugan pushed Ronin into a wagon. When he protested yet again, Dugan reached out and punched Ronin in the temple. He slumped forward in a daze.

Back in the corridor, the guard grabbed Kalial and flung her on the ground, using his bulk to hold her helpless. She could not breathe. The weight of the man was suffocating and his stench overpowering. Suddenly she could not bear it and she shoved with all her strength. The man slid away from her and cursed. He towered above her prostrate form as she crawled crablike on her hands and feet. Kalial cringed but raised her leg to kick him.

The guard breathed deeply in satisfaction. "Ah knew you were a purty thing by the way ya smelled running by me. Now stop fightin' and ah will make it worth yur while." He flopped down on top of her again with a dumb expression of contentment.

"Let me go, you beast, I am not for sale!" Kalial cried, but the man ignored her pleas. In mounting rage, she kicked with all her strength and contacted him in his most vulnerable spot. With a yelp of surprise and pain, the man rolled off of her and curled into a ball. Kalial leapt up and kicked him once again in rage. Then she spit on the man and ran up the steps and into the courtyard.

As she exited the corridor, she slammed into another person. Cursing her luck, she balled her fist to fight off yet another man when she saw a strut of iron descending through the air. She leapt out of the iron's path just as it clanged onto the flagstones. She spun, expecting another attack, and was stunned to see Florie's surprised face.

"Oh, miss! I am sorry, I am! Did I hurt ye?" Kalial grinned and shook her head. With a sigh of relief, Florie grasped her hand and pulled her toward the gates. "Good, then let's get a move on. The ship is already making sail and we need to both get on afore we lose her."

Kalial stopped, jerking Florie to a halt. "What do you mean?"

Florie turned to her, hands on hips. "Don't think you pulled the wool over my eyes. I told you, I knew who you were by the second day and I want to be gone from this place so I'm helping you and you are going to take me with you on that there ship."

Kalial smiled brilliantly and hugged the amused Florie. "Well, I could never ask for a better partner, Florie. But our lives are complicated and I do not want you to become mixed up in something that may bring you harm."

"Don't you worry about me. I'll nay say anything to anyone. I'll just be everlasting thankful to leave this dirty town."

"All right then, we'd best get moving," Kalial responded, excited to have a friend.

Florie and Kalial reached the dock just as the great ship was pulling anchor. The clanging of the anchor chain echoed down the deserted streets, rousing a few souls from their beds. A grumpy man with red-rimmed eyes flung an empty flask at them from his second-story room and shouted at them to be quiet.

Kalial ducked under an awning. She yanked her skirts off and quickly dressed in the familiar tunic and breeches after binding her breast yet again. When Florie looked at her quizzically, Kalial shrugged. "I am not sure how Ronin will react to me in a dress. I feel safer in my usual garb. Will you keep my disguise secret from the sailors?"

Florie put her hands on her hips. "Have I not already?"

Kalial smiled and nodded. "Look, the ship is sending a boat out for us." The two women waited on the dock as the small rowboat bumped against the piers. They climbed in and the sailor immediately set off for the ship.

In the distance they heard the thunder of approaching men on horseback. Florie looked anxiously back at the shore. "They're coming!"

"Pick up that set of oars and put your back into it, boy!" grumbled the sailor.

Kalial nodded and lifted the heavy oars. After a few fumbling attempts, she was able to drag them through the water without banging into the sailor's set. Just as the soldiers approached the dock, the threesome reached the ship and clambered aboard. With all the lanterns shuttered and the sails fluttering in the dark night wind, the *Bonny Evelyn* slid silently out of the harbor as the Serpent's mercenaries swarmed the shore, searching for their escaped prisoner.

CHAPTER 11

Ronin woke to the creak of timbers and the rock of the ship on the waves. He looked around. His chamber was spacious, although the large bed, a table and two chairs along with a pair of trunks occupied most of the space. Three portholes graced the curving hull. He sat up and waited until the dizziness passed, then rose and walked unsteadily to a window. Faintly visible was the line of the craggy mountain range south of Rath-thuaidhe.

After sponging off from a basin of water left for that purpose, Ronin donned a clean, white shirt, although he left it unbuttoned. He dragged on a pair of clean breeches and dunked his head in the soapy water before rinsing his hair briefly and running his fingers through it. Although his ministrations greatly improved his humor, his muscles still trembled with weakness.

He paused and braced his hands against his desk while tightly closing his eyes. Kal . . . he was certain he had seen Kal in the darkness of his prison cell, yet his body remembered other sensations. He could still feel the woman's wet cocoon wrapped around him, her tight thighs encasing him. His confusion and disbelief warred with his anger. Self-doubt rippled through him. He opened his eyes and stared at the curved wall as he came to a wrenching conclusion.

His eyes hardened into blue-tinged steel and he slowly made his way out of the cabin and onto the deck. Though his legs rapidly became accustomed to the sea motion, he leaned against the gangway frame to steady himself. Moving slowly, he breathed in the fresh sea air and scanned the deck until his gaze came across Kal coiling a rope. Her blond hair was tied back in a ponytail but several strands fluttered about her face. Her skin was a sun-touched honey hue. She wore half breeches and a long, loose shirt with a stiff vest over it. The sleeves were rolled up to her shoulders. Her limbs were muscled and sinuous. When she tossed her head back to look at the mainsail, Ronin wanted to wrap his hands around her graceful neck.

"Captain!" Dugan Trask swung down from the captain's deck. "Are you all right? Should you not still be resting? There is no reason for you to be on deck. Everything is sailing smooth."

Kal stopped her chore and rose to her feet.

"I will resume command, Trask. What is our location?" replied Ronin. His gaze shifted from Kal to his first mate, who looked worried but immediately relinquished command.

"All hands!" he shouted, "The captain is on deck!"

The sailors saluted, pausing in whatever they were doing to acknowledge the presence of their captain. Ronin nodded back.

Answering Ronin's previous question, Dugan replied, "We are south of Rath-thuaidhe, just past the Corplan Cove."

"We have traveled overnight?" asked Ronin in surprise.

"Yes, sir. You slept hard. We had no idea you were in danger, Captain. If I had known"—he tossed an angry look at Kal as she stood facing them—"I wouda made sure they never captured you, sir."

"You could have done nothing, Trask. I was meant to die in that hole. Perhaps I should have." With that, he strode over to Kalial and glared down at her. His anger boiled as a flicker of passion surfaced, reminding him of their past encounters. His gaze swept her form, noting the soft skin, the sculpted bones. At the sight of her bound chest his anger erupted. Kal stumbled back, away from his steely gaze.

"Squire Kal," he growled sarcastically as his brows drew together.

"Yes?" she replied hesitantly, her husky voice wrapping around Ronin. The wind tossed a damp tendril of hair against her neck where it stuck wetly. He searched for the words to tell her that he had discovered her deceit, but a snort from a nearby sailor stopped him. He paused, selecting another tactic.

"You disobeyed me. I told you to set sail immediately for Tregaron. Why did you wait?"

"We had to rescue you from prison. Surely you can not be angry because we waited to rescue you?" Kal looked at him in confusion.

Ronin swore violently. His voice rose above the normal din of the sailors. "You goddamn fool! You . . . you! How dare you!" he raged while the crew looked on in disbelief. Kalial trembled in fear. She had never seen him so furious.

Ronin clenched his teeth at the sight of her frightened eyes, and reined in his temper. He looked up at the stunned sailors and located one whose name he recalled. In a voice still shaking with fury, he commanded, "Raggs, you are in charge of this poor excuse of a *lad*. Teach him what it means to be a man, for only women should look so soft and vulnerable. Work him until he drops from exhaustion and give no quarter for his apparent weakness. If he is to be my squire, he must be strong and learn complete obedience.

Never should he stray from my orders or think that he knows better than his superiors. When we disembark, I want to see those skinny arms bulging with manly vigor and a meek look in his eye." Ronin staggered slightly, then braced his legs apart.

He rounded on Kal, his eyes raking her figure with new purpose. "Speak now and I will spare you!"

She remained silent, a hand clasped over her mouth to keep from shouting back at him. She was worried for his health, for the fatigue and famine of prison showed clearly on his ravaged face. She shook her head mutely, not knowing what he wanted her to say.

Ronin spied the sweet curves of her forearm, the subtle swell underneath her shirt. He glared at her, horrified and incensed, betrayed and enraged, until she dropped her hand and braced her legs, mimicking his stance.

"Aye, Captain," said Raggs. "Ye have me word that I willna be soft on the boy. I'll be breaking that look in his eye afore the voyage is out, sir."

Ronin turned to him, instantly regretting his rash words. Looking around quickly, he saw the rough men and debated quickly. If he retracted his words, the men would see his command as weak and changeable. Then, too, if they knew Kalial was a woman. . . . Without a backwards look, he spun on his heel and disappeared down the gangway, his steps stiff from suppressed anger.

Dugan Trask and the crew looked at Kal in dismay. She valiantly raised her chin at her new taskmaster. "Well now," Raggs said with a sly grin, "first thing ye must be a doin' is movin' those water barrels ten feet yonder." He crossed his beefy arms and dared her to disobey. Trask frowned at the unnecessary work, but felt obliged not to interfere. Whatever the lad had done to warrant such fury from his usually even-tempered captain must have been substantial. He watched Kal for a moment, then turned away.

*   *   *

The days were endless for Kalial, but the nights were longer. Raggs dogged her footsteps continuously. If ever she paused, he was there, assigning her a more arduous task than the last. By the end of the day, her muscles trembled with fatigue and she found it almost impossible to lift the crust of bread to her mouth and the pint of ale to her lips. The hollowness of her cheeks brought her golden eyes into sharp relief, accentuating their glittering beauty.

Florie, on the other hand, blossomed in the clean sea air. Because Dugan made it known that she had been instrumental in saving the captain, the sailors accepted her presence despite their superstition that women on board a ship were bad luck. She and Kalial enjoyed brief moments together when they went into the hold to feed and clean the animals. While Florie could not understand Kalial's close connection with the wild beasts, she appreciated her unique talent.

"How does the cat know what you are thinking?" Florie asked one day.

"She does not hear my words," Kalial responded. "She just . . . feels what I feel."

"And you? Can you understand what she feels?"

"Yes, I can."

"What are you saying to her now?"

"I am telling her that she will not have to live behind bars much longer. I am telling her that the men above are frightened of her, and would not understand her presence walking amongst them."

"And the owl?"

"Ahhh, the owl. Him I tell that his master is a fool."

Ronin rapidly regained his strength with solid food and exercise. His pale face acquired its former swarthy color, and his weakened limbs once again bulged with power. As he recovered, McTaver remained brooding and angry at Kal. Despite her workload, he did not feel the satisfaction he sought. His anger at her deceit still ran rampant through him. The moments in the forest when he had wrestled with his guilty desires fueled his current fury. She had made a complete fool of him in front of many people. Certainly the Gypsies had known she was female, for he now knew that it had been her sweetness he had taken that night on the beach, and not some nameless Gypsy girl. Yet now, after two passionate encounters, she still dared to disguise herself as a boy!

He paced his cabin like the jaguar caged below decks. As his body healed, he dreamed of Kal's silken skin slippery with passion's sweat, of her sweet-tasting kisses. Thus he awakened daily feeling fresh fury and frustration.

One morning, as the ship rocked on white-capped waves and his dreams drove him to aroused wakefulness, he left his cabin and went on deck, searching for her. He found her still form curled up inside a coil of rope. She slept heavily for it was very early and Raggs, her taskmaster, still slept.

Her honey-hued skin glowed with a spray of seawater. Her blond hair, lighter now, shimmered with platinum highlights. Working in the sun had only increased her loveliness. He was stunned that he had not discovered her secret earlier. How could he have been so blind? How could he have not seen her for who she was?

Nudging her with his boot, her woke her with a savage expression on his face. "Get into the rigging. There is a loose rope on the topsail." Kal stifled a groan and rose to her feet. Her weary eyes looked at Ronin with a haze of matching anger. Good, thought McTaver, she needs to be as angry with me as I am with her. He saw a bruise on her jaw and a deep scrape on her arm that oozed a bit of blood. Reminded of her lost virgin blood, he stepped forward and shook her roughly. Kalial twitched out of his grasp and growled. An albatross soaring overhead squawked loudly in protest.

"Learn to follow orders, *boy*. I would only accept such sullenness from a woman, not from a scrawny, ill-formed weakling lad like you. If you are not learning well enough from Raggs, then I shall set your orders for you."

"Raggs is teaching me well, Captain. Pray do not bother yourself with giving me yet more tasks. I have had time to regret my impulsiveness in saving your hide. I should have let you die in that miserable stinkpool," she shot back at him.

"Perhaps you should have. But you did not, and here I am and here you are, in my power, aboard my ship." He leaned closer. "I detest being played for a fool."

Kalial looked at him in consternation. She considered telling him about her disguise for this was the first moment she had been alone with him since before his capture. She opened her mouth to speak, but just then a pair of sailors came stumbling around the deck. Recalling the tavern, and how sailors treated women, she fell silent.

Ronin watched the thoughts flutter over her face before making a silent decision. When she said nothing, he stood up with a feral gleam in his eye.

"Get up into the rigging. Fix the rope and wrap the sails. We are stopping for a short shore visit. Do not come down until I call for you." He shoved her toward the mast.

She scrambled backwards, getting her footing, then turned and scampered up the ropes. Everyone on board seemed to think that rigging duty was the most difficult. The heavy men feared that the ropes would snap under their weight or a sudden swell would fling them to the decks below. For Kalial, however, her time in the rigging was a blessing. She was comfortable high above the ground for she had learned to climb trees at an early age. On the mast, she felt free and unburdened from the drudgery on deck.

As she reached her goal, she looked down and watched Ronin stride angrily around the boards while she mulled over his complete change in personality. A part of her feared that the torture he'd endured in prison had robbed him of compassion. Regardless of his poor treatment of her, she did not regret giving him his freedom. She need only close her eyes to feel the whisper of his body against hers, or hear the thrill of his voice when he laughed with her, and know that she could never have left him to die. He was angry that she had delayed the ship's sailing for Tregaron, she mused. How angry would he be, she thought, if he knew of her feminine form? Or the game played on him at the Gypsy camp? Such fears kept her silent day after day as she quietly submitted to the cruelty of Raggs and the other sailors.

Although Ronin had commanded that his men break her spirit, their actions only hardened her. Never in her life had she been treated with deference due to her gender so she did not miss the tenderness usually granted a female. But she had been afforded privilege of one who is known for her powers and respected for her position, and the lack of such respect forced her to toughen yet more, causing her to hide her eyes when they started to glaze in remembered dreams and clench her jaw when her lips swelled with remembered kisses.

Kalial reached the flapping rope and tied it securely. She then wove her arms through the rigging, and relaxed. She was incredibly weary. The strain of the last several days, after a week of avoiding the raging Ronin, was wearing on her. She watched the sun rise in a sweep of colors that lasted for only moments before its heat melted away the clouds and pummeled the earth with its intensity, reflecting off the open sea as well as upon the nearby coast.

Kalial felt the heat on her skin and marveled anew. She had spent her life under cover of a thick forest canopy. The damp darkness and multihued greenery had filled her days. Now, the undulating blue of the sea washed over her and she exalted in the space and light. She found a new respect for the water and for the open spaces. The loneliness of her spirit blew away, and despite Ronin's unending anger, she felt happier than ever. She fingered her soft hair in wonder. So much of her time had been spent slathering mud over her body, trying to hide the brightness of her skin and hair. She ached to remove even her light clothes and swing free and uninhibited in the sails.

She heard Raggs bellowing at her from below. Knowing he was terrified of the heights, she ignored his call. Instead she climbed higher, busily checking the sails. The tinkle of the breakfast bell reached her faintly and she saw some of the men clamber below. Raggs tossed her a disgruntled look although Kalial could not make it out from where she sat.

The heat of the morning suddenly flared hotter and Kalial looked over to the captain's deck where McTaver stood with his legs spread wide and his arms crossed over his chest. He held a bullwhip in one hand, his sword in the other, and Kalial wondered at their purpose.

When she saw the shore boats being readied she understood. The whip was often used to scare wildlife away as its reach was longer than an arm and its noise more intimidating than a shout. She frowned down at him, wishing he would throw the blasted thing away. Every time he took it out to practice, she could not help watching his arms bulge and ripple. Annoying! She grumbled to herself as she looked down. His black hair blew in the breeze. His head was tilted back to stare at her. Without a word, he jerked his head down, indicating that she should descend. Kalial hesitated.

She looked around at the beauty of the ocean. The sense of peace she had felt for a moment slipped away. The weariness tumbled down on her again. With a great sigh, she climbed slowly down until she reached the deck. Feeling Ronin's eyes boring into her back, she dragged herself to the mess hall.

The stench of grease and unwashed bodies assaulted her. She slid over to the edge of the room and leaned against the wall. The cook passed among the first shift of men, ladling thick stew into bowls along with a hunk of stale bread. Kalial closed her eyes briefly and felt her head nod. The ship had settled to a stop as the other sailors lowered the sails, and she recognized the plop of the anchor hitting the water. Vaguely she heard the sounds of a boat being lowered and Ronin's voice issuing commands. The water casks were low as they had not been properly filled before departure. She sank lower in her corner, drifting into sleep.

A tug at her bowl made her jerk awake. A sailor, Thurston if she remembered correctly, was trying to slide the bowl out of her grasp.

"Leave be," she cried. " 'Tis my meal, not yours."

"Ye not be needing it as much as I," he answered, his eyes mocking. Many sailors turned toward her with similar expressions, although some looked on with disgust. The captain's rancor toward her had caused several members of the usually companionable crew to treat her nastily, taunting her slightness and mocking her weakness. Thurston yanked the bowl away from Kalial with enough force that most of the stew slopped onto the floor. Raggs stood up and guffawed. Kalial scooted away, bumping into the wall behind her. The two sailors closed in.

"Ye have made this voyage miserable for us by angering the captain so," Raggs declared. "We don't care what ye did, but ye are certainly going to regret it." He grabbed her by the shirt collar and lifted her off the floorboards. Thurston came up in front of her and swung a punch into her midriff. The air left her instantly, and she hung limply, gasping to draw breath.

Another sailor came forward and rudely grabbed the front of her hair. Her eyes flew open and she gulped in a breath as he sliced downwards with his dagger, neatly severing a length of her golden tresses. "These be too pretty for a lad," he slurred. "We were told to make you into a man and so we shall." Kalial scrambled for her freedom, eyes wide and fearful. The sailor held the golden lock in his fist and made to grasp more.

"This long hair bothers us sailors. It must all go." He raised his knife. Kalial twisted and slammed her elbow backwards into Raggs's chest. He grunted, loosening his hold for a second and allowing Kalial to pull herself free. She slid her dirk out of her boot and glared at the men. They stood as one, the pulse of battle beating strongly. Raggs reached for her again. Kalial swung her dirk up, slicing an open arc along his forearm. He bellowed and swung a fist against her jaw.

Kalial was slammed against the wall. She heard the crack of her teeth smash together and the world erupted into chaos. Sailors bounded over tables and chairs to pummel each other and her. She valiantly threw some punches and kicked out at her attackers. She swung out with her dirk again and felt it slide into someone's flesh. The howl of pain came right before the man twisted her arm behind her back and flung her around to press her front to the wall.

He pulled up on her arm so quickly and with such force that Kalial dropped her dirk with a cry of pain. She felt slivers bury themselves in her soft cheek. The next moment, the crew dragged her out on deck and tied her arms above her head to the main bow. Her head rang and she barely kept her feet underneath her. She felt another blow to her gut just as Thurston swung a cat-o'-nine-tails in front of her.

"Ye have caused too much trouble. If the captain won't punish you proper, we will," he threatened. With mounting horror Kalial saw him stretch his arm and shoulder while making a few practice swipes with the whip. The men stepped back and Thurston paced around behind her back. She twisted to face him when the whip came stinging down. One strap graced her neck while the others flayed the front of her shirt. She screamed.

Raggs stepped forward and spun her so that her back was facing Thurston again. "Face forward like a man, boy, or your pretty face will be sliced to ribbons instead of just your back. Cry, coward. Let's see you cry!" Kalial gulped back her scream and stared around her in terror. She heard the hiss of the whip before pain exploded along her back. Her body arched forward. She screamed again, this time in rage and pain. Her golden eyes glittered as they swept the crew contemptuously.

"You are the cowards. You are the sniveling rats that beat on those weaker than you!" she shouted. Another strike from the cat-o'-nine-tails silenced her as she felt fire race down her back and burst behind her eyes. The fabric of her vest tore, leaving only the thin cotton of her shirt to deflect the blows. Again the whip rained down on her back. She felt the thin leather straps slice her skin, bruising it in nine flaming ribbons. Her shirt hung loose around her, buttoned in front but open in back.

"What be this?" she heard Thurston shout from behind her. Her legs could no longer support her and she hung limply from her arms. The men pressed in around her and she felt the slide of cool metal slip under her chest bindings and slice them from her. Her breasts sprang free, bouncing softly as her body swung with the rock of the ship. Horrified, she felt herself slipping into a faint, although she desperately fought it.

"Cease!" Ronin sprang on deck. "What in bloody hell? Get back! Drop the whip!"

The men sank back, stupefied by their discovery. Ronin raised his bullwhip and snapped it over the men's heads, sending them scurrying out of the way. When Thurston reached out to grip Kal's breast, Ronin swung the whip into his back. Thurston jerked spasmodically, rolling on the deck while clutching his arms around himself where the bullwhip had cut his flesh.

"I left for twenty minutes and I return to find you doing this?" Ronin strode forward, his eyes blazing with fury.

"It's a woman!" cried Raggs, dumfounded, staring alternately at Ronin, Kal and Thurston.

"I am quite aware of her gender, and I expect you to respect it as well now that you are aware of it. You," he motioned to one of the sailors who had hung in the background, "untie her."

"She's fainted, Captain."

"All the better," Ronin mumbled, his ire subsiding into deep trepidation. Not waiting for the sailor, he supported her with one arm and sawed at the rope with the other, nicking her fair skin in his haste to free her. As she slumped down, he caught her in his arms. "Kal-lass, I am so sorry. I never thought this would happen. Kal-lass, Kal-lass, bonny lass, please forgive me," he pleaded. He cradled her limp form and buried his head in her golden tresses. At her faint moan he lifted his head and pinned the crew with a furious look. He took a step nearer to them when Dugan Trask stepped in front of him.

"Best get the girl below, Captain." Ronin paused, debating between his desire to kill the men responsible or to comfort Kal. He snatched Dugan's greatcoat off his shoulders and wrapped it around Kal.

"Hold her. I want her to see these men pay for their actions." Ronin carefully placed Kal in Dugan's arms, then stalked over to the crew. They pressed back, placing excessive strain on the railing. "Thurston!" he barked. Ronin grabbed him and hauled him up, trembling in his rage. He wrapped his hands around Thurston's neck and squeezed, then smashed his head against the mast that had held Kal. Thurston's cheek split open and his eyes bulged. He clawed frantically at Ronin's hands. Ronin then dragged him to the rail, lifted him high, and dropped him over the side. Thurston fell heavily, crashing into the water while gasping to draw the breath that had been denied him.

Ronin spun around, scanning for Raggs. He advanced toward him, but Raggs suddenly leapt over the railing and into the water next to the sputtering Thurston. Ronin leaned over and glared at the men, then turned once again to face the crew. His voice dropped to a menacing purr. "I do not tolerate brawling, mutiny, pillage or *rape*. My ship is my kingdom. Anyone who does not accept my law leaves now along with that scum. The coast is within swimming distance—if you can swim."

The crew milled around, looking with fear upon Captain McTaver and the black whip swinging in his left hand. A young sailor stepped forward. "We respect your woman, Captain. If we'd a' known, we would never have allowed this, sir. We just thought it was a young lad, like you told us." The faint reproach was not lost upon Ronin and he was racked with guilt.

He turned back to Kal, who was stirring to consciousness in Dugan's arms. She peered out, sensing security in the form of Ronin. She, the lonely princess, had distantly heard his pleas for forgiveness, words she had never thought he would utter. Her heart blossomed at the emotion in his face and her quaking body quieted.

Kal saw the coiled strength in Ronin's arms, tempered now as he lowered the whip. A rush of excitement raced over her body. To be protected by such a man, to watch his steely vengeance cripple men—it was thrilling, rousing. He knew her now! She did not have to hide her attraction. She could touch him, stroke him, kiss him as she wanted. She could be natural with him and let her lonely soul explore the exciting rush of freedom and sensuality he had discovered in her.

She watched the crew part before him as he came to her and her breathing quickened. He strode like a predator, stalking prey that he claimed as his own, defended as his right. He looked down at her and she could smell him—the scent of sweat and wet leather and the unmistakable aroma of arousal.

Kalial lifted gold-flecked eyes to his, and let her emotions tumble forth. Her gaze shone with approval, appreciation, yet with just a flicker of shyness. She waited for him as he stared at her, until the tempo of their breathing matched. He reached down and plucked her from Dugan, lifting her into his own arms. She wrapped her wrists around his neck and leaned over to kiss him. The kiss deepened by increments as Ronin let her set the pace until he suddenly swooped her down the gangway and into his cabin.

CHAPTER 12

Kalial gasped in pain as Ronin's hands wrapped around her back. He quickly ducked through the doorway and placed her gently on the swinging bed. He unwrapped her from the greatcoat and carefully turned her over so that he could view the whip marks on her flesh. Nine furrows marred her honey perfection, like the talon strikes of a raptor. Ronin leaned over and placed his lips on the wounds, gently, softly, reverently as he divested her of the rest of her clothing and his own. Kalial shivered. He treaded over to a wash bin and returned with it and a clean cloth. He swished the cloth in the water, then lifted it and allowed a thin stream to splash over her back. The water trickled down as it made its way over her sides and over the hill of her buttocks to dribble between her thighs.

"Kal?" he questioned softly.

"Kalial," she answered, sighing as she smiled at him encouragingly from over her shoulder. She exhaled sharply at the cool sensation of Ronin's ministrations.

"Kalial . . . beautiful. The name suits you . . . strong yet fanciful." He lifted the cloth again, repeating his motions but this time starting higher on her shoulders. "I am so sorry this happened . . ." The water cascaded over her neck where another bruise marked where the whip had landed. He pressed down on her, following the water with his tongue. An insistent throbbing in his palm caused him to look at the hand that he had injured in the forest when they had first met.

He sensed the blood bond between them deepen and bloom. When he licked at her marks again, the throb in his palm burst, spreading heat throughout his body and brain. He sank lower, sliding down her body, until his questing tongue climbed the curve of her rear. Placing his hand over one mound, he felt the coolness of her skin melt from the warmth of his palm. Slick, slippery flesh, instantly misted by sweet-smelling sweat—he closed his eyes, reveling in the sensation of touching her.

Kalial lifted her hips, forming a curve in the small of her back, pressing her bottom up into his mouth. He nipped her, then sat back on his haunches to view her wanton movements. The fall of golden hair spread across the bedsheet, glinting almost silver. Her cheek sank into the blankets and her remarkable eyes were closed, the heavy eyelashes casting shadows on her face. Ronin ran his hands down her body, exalting in the dainty hourglass shape. Briefly he wrapped his hands around her waist. His fingertips could touch with a tiny squeeze, which he did as he lifted her body up against his.

He pulled her upright, on her knees, her back pressed against his chest. Her hair floated around her, encasing them both in a satin veil. His hands deserted her waist in favor of her belly. He stroked upwards in small circles, one on each side of her but overlapping in the center. Kalial's head sank back against his shoulder so that her quick breaths brushed air over his ear. She lifted her arms and wrapped them behind Ronin's head, rocking her pelvis forward into his seeking hands.

"You knew?" she whispered. When Ronin nodded

she added, "When? Why didn't you tell me you knew?"

Ronin continued to stroke circles upon her flesh, each brush reaching higher, broadening the area touched. He answered her huskily, "I saw it in your eyes the day you broke me out of prison, and heaven only knows why I could not see it earlier. Did you think you could keep letting me touch you and make love to you and still keep your secret?"

Kalial felt restless, aching for the sensations she knew awaited her. She felt urgent, reckless, impassioned. She felt deliciously trapped by his arms. A rising sense of rightness swept through her. She focused on the perfection of his touch, the confidence of his movements. Kalial twisted slightly and faced him. "But why did you keep silent? Why not confront me?"

Ronin looked over Kalial's shoulder and watched his hands slide over her flesh. His darkened skin contrasted with her creaminess. "Why did you not come to me? I wanted you to be the one to reveal your secrets and remove the boundaries between us. Every day that you kept silent made me angrier and I did not know what to do. I had no idea my men would harm you. Can you ever forgive me?"

Kalial arched into his hands with a sigh of acquiescence. Her breasts grew as he watched them sway, becoming engorged and heavy as she slid further into her passion. The apricot nipples blushed, sweetened, to an exquisite shade of pink-peach. The tips hardened, tightened, thrust forward as if seeking his fingers. He swept his circles larger, stroking the underside of each breast just as he brushed the first dainty hairs covering her womanhood. The thrill racing through him matched hers, and she arched more, tossing her head to and fro as his hands became rougher, circling faster. She forgot to think, forgot to question him further as her body's sensations over-whelmed her mind. In his arms, she felt so right, so perfect, she let her soul float in his palm.

He could feel tiny ridges of musculature along her middle, evidence of her hard work and athletic body. Yet the surface of her belly was softened by the silken texture of her skin. Then his hands slipped over the top of her breasts, brushing her nipples with the pads of his thumb. A shock rippled over her skin, creating goose bumps. Her nipples tightened more, and the tips darkened to red.

Ronin recognized the signs in her response as if he had always known them. He did not guess what she needed next, what she craved, what she ached for. He instinctively knew, and gave everything he could. He abandoned the large circles for tiny ones over her nipples, playing with them mercilessly. He started by tickling her, and then plucked at them as if he could take them away and devour them. A slight twist as he twirled one between his finger and thumb elicited a burst of movement from Kalial. She wriggled her body, pressing it closer to his, nestling her buttocks into his lap.

The soft caress of her ass wrapping around his cock was incendiary. Ronin gripped her and crushed her convulsively closer. Kalial felt the flames along her back spark as her bruises scraped his chest dusted with black hair. She ignored the pain, choosing instead to slide her body up and down, rubbing his cock in a most unconventional manner. Ronin left her breasts and shoved her onto all fours. Kalial kept rocking. He looked down and watched his penis slide between her cheeks until he pulled away slightly to view her glistening center, wet with liquid, spread softly, beckoning to him.

He grabbed each cheek and squeezed, much as he had with her breasts, and spread them wider. His cock stood proudly erect, swollen with need, skillful with experience. Ronin paused, debating whether to sink in slowly, inch by inch, forcing her to plead with him to take her, or to plunge in fully, making her scream with shock and desire. Suddenly Kalial tossed her head up, flinging her hair over her back. The strands were twisted and tangled from their lovemaking. The delicate weight settling on him, tickling his testicles, urged him forward.

With a roar, he gripped her waist and sank in, sliding through the tight passage, through the ripples of swollen flesh, deep into the heart of her until the tip of his cock touched her very center. The pressure, the pleasure, caused Kalial's arms to buckle and she collapsed on the bed, her ass held high in the air, impaled by his spear.

Ronin barely heard her passionate scream as he slipped out halfway, angled himself to slide against her pleasure spot hidden within her passage, and buried himself again. Once more he heard the distant scream and saw her head rolling, her hair tossing. He slipped out, then in with more force than ever, ramming his hips against hers. He heard her beg him to stop, then plea with him to never stop, and he felt her center clamp him, wrapping his pulsating penis in folds of drenched, dripping heat. When he tried to pull away, her pelvis moved with him, not relinquishing him. He withheld for a moment, feeling her internal muscles clench and grasp, trying to pull him in.

He relented because he could not help it. He thrust inside and felt himself start to pant, harsh breaths bursting out of his lungs. He felt powerful, kingly, the overlord of this glorious golden land spread before him. The feeling seared him, and he pumped faster, sliding out halfway and plunging in to the hilt. A crescendo collected in his gut, circling, sending out bursts down his legs, up his chest. His arms tightened and began to shake. He did not think to wait for her; his body knew her, they knew one another. He knew she felt as he did, that her belly tightened in anticipation of each thrust. Her thighs started to slide apart, weakening as all the blood in her body swirled around her core, heating the friction between them. She no longer moved with him, her body was too weak, too focused on reaching that pinnacle that hovered. She simply allowed him to use her, to pummel her, to love her.

He jerked and his eyes turned near black with surprise as his climax took over. His seed burst forth, sweeping down his cock, causing it to swell a tiny bit more before exploding into her. Ronin's heart thundered and fire scorched him, his testicles, his gut. He forgot to breathe while gasping for air. He exalted, he soared, he conquered. He held her so tightly because he could not let her go, yet he felt every sweep of her pleasure as if he was attuned to the strokes of a feather. He poured into her, forever, his hips locked to hers, her ass pressed powerfully tight against his body.

Kalial felt every breath, every movement, every pulse as if her entire body was one gorgeous sensation. She was not even in her body anymore—except that the sensations tumbling through her were startlingly real, dragging her back from the oblivion of euphoria. She was limp, supple, the ultimate submissive. She opened herself to his thrusts and let him control her body and her mind. Carried by his strength, she reeled, her soul clinging to his as he swept her into ecstasy. A shot of hot semen flooded her insides, drenching her. Her body clung to him, shivering as waves of emotion broke over her, sending showers of glitter over her closed eyelids. He met her at the zenith, touching her as she reached orgasm, then they both sank to the bed, exhausted.

Ronin lay atop her, heavy but welcome. She was certain that if he rose, she would float away and be lost to the wide sky above. The flush of heat that had so burned her body slipped away but he kept her warm and comforted. She felt him rub his face into her locks and sigh. With a lazy smile of utter contentment, she drifted to sleep.

He felt her body ripple occasionally with aftershocks and his cock, still nestled within her, twitched in response. He thought of rolling off of her, but she was so slight, she fit into the curve of his body where the majority of his weight did not press. He rubbed his face with her hair and breathed in her unique, honeysuckle fragrance, enhanced now that she had experienced such climax. He felt her slip into sleep. He knew her. He could feel all of her, could sense her superlative contentment, and it made him happy. He smiled softly, his blue eyes glowing in the fading light. Then he, too, drifted to sleep.

Ronin stood over Kalial, watching the even rise and fall of her chest as she slept. The bed swung gently with the rocking of the boat. A faint pitter-patter of rain danced on the deck and ocean. Cool, clean air washed through the open porthole. She was sprawled on her back, her arms flung wide and her leg bent at the knee. Her hair spread over her chest, twirling around her breasts in a decadent display.

Ronin's eyes caressed her. He saw a tiny beat in the hollow of her throat and placed his fingers lightly over it. The pulse beat in tempo with his own. He kissed his fingers and replaced them on her throat, smoothing them down and over her collarbone. He pulled a coverlet over her, and went back on deck.

The warm rain quickly soaked his head, his clothes, yet he remained standing at the bow, looking out to sea. He welcomed the shower, opening his mouth to catch a few drops. He relished the moment. Complete satisfaction, total peace. The surface of his skin was sensitized; he could almost feel her stroking him, kissing him. The wind became her breath and the rain her mouth. Even the knowledge that the sweet rain could change into a tempest at any moment reminded him of her. He spread his palms along the smooth railing, creating paths in the water. He imagined the drops finding new avenues, dripping down different spokes due to his disturbance, but ultimately finding their way back to the encompassing ocean. Their paths changing—their destination remaining.

She was his. He knew it with utter conviction. His unreasonable anger at her earlier proved that to him. The rage that had suffused him had been based on his own pride. How ignoble, how unnerving, to be fooled by a tiny woman with eyes of gold and hair like spun silver. His sable-haired Gypsy of uninhibited wantonness was his companion and squire. If she had remained in the role of a boy, she would have denied her being, her sensuality, her true heart. God, what a crime that would have been! And yes, what an incredible gift he would have lost.

He clenched his eyes shut in frustration. How thoughtless he had been, to allow her to be treated so roughly by the sailors. He had meant to teach her that she was not a man, could never be a man. Her body was completely feminine. Strong, yes, he would grant her that, but womanly. He had tried to punish her for fooling him by forcing her to be more of a lad than even she cared to be. But how that idea had backfired. He opened his eyes and gazed at the dark clouds, berating himself.

A warm glow spread along his back. He turned and saw Kalial standing a few feet from him. He braced, expecting anger or accusations. Instead her eyes were soft, misty topaz jewels that gazed at him with warmth and desire. She dropped her eyes shyly and he saw that she wore his shirt, since her own had been destroyed. The rain pelted her, turning the white cotton translucent. Drop after drop revealed her body. First her shoulders, then the tops of her arms. Next the slope of her chest transformed, molded. The peaks of her breasts were pebbled, thrusting impudently against the dampening cloth. The shirt hung down past her knees, becoming a sheer sheet of material that beckoned.

When she took a hesitant step toward him, the cloth stuck wetly to her belly and upper thighs. He could see a sinkhole where her belly button existed and a folded valley that separated her thighs. The silky hair hidden there created an intimate texture to the over-laying cotton.

Kalial hesitated, still uncomfortable with him now that her secret had been revealed. For so long she had played the boy, she did not know how to act the woman. She was unsure of how he would behave toward her, fearing that he would still be angry. *How does a woman act?* she mused to herself. *How can I be his friend and bedmate? Can I be both, or is that impossible? Will he still want me this morning?*

Ronin stood still and let her approach him. For the first time in his life he felt a touch of fear of the unknown. He held his breath, half afraid she would disappear like the fabled mermaids in the ocean. When she reached him, she pressed her body flush against his, snuggling in between his spread legs while looking up at him questioningly. He reached down then and cupped her chin in his hands to lift her face to his. He felt obscenely enormous, seeing his biceps dwarf her, thicker than her petite waist.

He ran his fingers through her hair, frowning thoughtfully at the section that had been shorn yester-day. She had bangs now. The effect was pixielike. The shortened strands in front framed her face, dancing in the meager light like a spray of diamonds. He gazed into her eyes and knew that his concerns were ground-less. She was stronger, braver and more forgiving than he had dared to hope. She was whole, untarnished, making peace with her body. She looked secure and free with him. He saw her face reflect goodness and strength. His eyes flashed with pride. Then, in an impulse of playful abandon, he swept her up and threw her overboard, diving in close behind her.

They heard a shout on deck as Dugan Trask called to drop the sails. The crew scrambled, trying to stop the forward momentum of the ship so as not to leave their captain behind. Although they worked quickly, the ship drifted around a bend in the coastline before she was stopped and the anchor could be lowered.

Kalial sputtered and gasped, treading water as she looked for Ronin to break the surface. Her hair slapped wetly against her face as she spun around, searching.

"Ronin?" she called out. Suddenly, her foot was grasped and she was dragged under the water, screeching. Flinging her arms out, she gulped in air, and found herself beneath the crystal blue ocean. Ronin yanked on her shirt, then released her. She kicked for the surface, and reached it before realizing that the water now caressed her naked skin.

When Ronin arrived next to her, she kicked, rising out of the water, and flopped on top of him, pushing him under. "Do you think to best me?" she called out, but he only responded by grinning. He slid beneath her easily, running his hands down her waist. He bit the inside of her thigh and Kalial shrieked, swimming away from him, all serious thoughts washed away with the seawater sluicing over her body. She spotted a log caught in a web of seaweed and struck out for it, Ronin close behind. She quickly turned, shoving a water cascade in his face, and laughed joyfully.

"Go on, you beast!"

"Not on your life, little miss," he called back. He tried to duck her attack, but again the water splashed his face, making him sputter. Shaking his head to clear his eyes, he sought her out again. By now she had reached her mat of seaweed and climbed half atop it. She twisted and sat down, sinking the natural net slightly. The top half of her hips, waist and upper body lay exposed to the sea air.

"This is my seaweed bed. I dare you to take it!" She smiled seductively at his amused look. The soft wind should have been chilling, but the heat inside her warmed her thoroughly. She sat still, with an alluring smile, watching as Ronin carefully swam toward her. The warm water washed around her feet, fed by a tropical current snaking up the Scottish coast. When he got too close, she kicked out, covering him in a blue-green waterfall. He backed away, grinning, and reevaluated his approach.

"You should not dare me, Kalial. 'Tis a sure way to entice me to prevail."

Kalial winked. "Then try, warrior," she challenged.

Diving under the water, he sought to dump her from her trophy by swimming beneath her, but the thick seaweed blocked him and he dared not fight the tenacious strands. Breaking to the top again, he saw that her lips were swollen from his earlier kisses. He decided that he wanted to lavage her breasts until they too showed the imprint of his passion. Swimming directly for her, he was startled by the force of her giggling counterattack. Defeated, he circled her minikingdom, debating strategy. He could not help his reaction to her seated there, pale breasts covered with water and tiny bits of seaweed. Her eyes whispered to him, their golden depths taunting, teasing.

His already hard cock began to strain and ache. He roughly ripped his own breeches and shirt off and exalted in the slide of water against the sensitive tip. One hand reached down and gave a swift stroke. Kalial's eyes widened and she bent her head, peering into the rippling water. A ray of sunlight broke through a break in the clouds, creating an unusual spray of tiny rainbows in the misty rain.

Kalial gazed hungrily at Ronin's hand and unconsciously slipped her own between her legs. Ronin stifled a cough as he saw her touch herself intimately. He stroked himself again and saw her imitate his motions on her own body. Slowly, ever so slowly, her thighs fell open as she explored this new game. Her fingers slipped over her flesh sitting partially in the water. She whimpered faintly, shocked and thrilled at the feel of touching herself while watching him touch himself. A spark of pleasure made her insides clench, heat and quiver. The tiny sounds coming from her almost broke his control. His eyes shot up to her face and he saw a rush of excitement there mingled with a brush of nervousness. She felt wanton. She wanted the touch, but part of her feared the unknown sensations.

A wave slapped against her chest, tossing her back. Taking immediate advantage, Ronin swam up to the heart of her, his head enclosed by her open legs. The sultry scent of her called to him and he buried his head in her golden hair. A sweep of slippery flesh rubbed against his lips. In surprise, he licked it. Kalial jerked, a harsh intake of breath causing her belly to sink. Ronin drew back, then licked his lips, liking the sweet taste remaining there. He tilted forward and touched his tongue to her again, brushing deeper. Her hips lifted and she groaned.

A surge of heat washed over Ronin. Reaching up with one hand he gently spread her folds open and marveled at the pink welcome. A rosebud topped the slit. It appeared soft, plush, inviting. Again his tongue took over and he spread its heat over her. The smell, the softness, the incredible intimacy transported him. He reveled in his exploration and discovery of her private body. He twirled his tongue around, drinking in her essence. Placing the nub into his mouth, he sucked gently, pulling on it, then releasing it to stroke it, play with it. He licked deeper, finding folds and crevasses he desperately needed to cover with his tongue. Kalial stared languidly up into the delicate rainbow arching over them, her mouth open. She felt each rasp of his tongue like a wand of pleasure that reached deep into her body and set every nerve tingling and shimmering. Her body rippled beneath his onslaught and her mind went numb, focused entirely upon the head buried between her golden thighs.

A splash of seawater washed into his mouth, causing him to growl at the intrusion. He roughly shoved her farther up on the net of seaweed, pulling his bulky body after her. This time he used two hands to open her. He sank the tip of his tongue deep inside her and moved it around, exploring the ripples of flesh. Although he had been inside her with his fingers and his cock, he now discovered subtle nuances of a woman's body hitherto unknown to him. He stroked and licked, slipping in and out. He swirled around her rose, wetting it with her own juices before plunging back in to drink more.

When her body started tossing too madly, he snaked an arm around her waist, holding her prisoner to his mouth. Distantly he heard her pleasure screams, the loud sounds she made as she neared climax. In his new position, the lush, slippery seaweed rubbed against him, each slick, air-filled pocket rolling along his cock, stimulating him, toying with him. He suddenly felt the thrumming in his head, the rush of blood throughout his body. His hips jerked against the seaweed, bucking into the slick fronds that folded around him. Frantically he pressed her hard against his mouth, his teeth grazing her as his tongue spun wildly. The seaweed clung to him, urging him on. A mermaid's cry of release rose above him, bursting over him as a gush of incredibly sweet, deliciously decadent fluid filled his mouth. He spasmed, thrusting his hips into the bed of seaweed and poured himself into the sea.

He felt her then, her nails gripping his shoulders, her thighs clenched around his neck. She was shaking, her body shivering in reaction to the tumult within her. He pulled her down to him, sliding her body underneath his. The rain was gently washing the tears from her eyes. She clung to him, her hair cloaking them both in a warm cape. Incredibly he felt himself rise again, and he shifted her fragile body so that he could slide into her. She faintly protested, but then relinquished control and let him enter.

Hard, but without the same urgency as before, he rocked her while holding onto the seaweed bed with one arm and holding her with the other. She sank her teeth into his neck, learning that he used his teeth often and assuming he liked the sensation himself. As his tempo increased, she sucked, first on his neck, then on the bits of chest she could reach with her mouth. She shook and convulsed, still pulsating from his earlier onslaught as he ejaculated again. This time his seed sped its way deep inside of her, seeking the core of her. He held her so tight, pushing his hips into hers so hard, she gasped. Weaving her hands into his hair, she held him for a moment, keeping him secure so that he would not sink into the ocean while he remained oblivious to the world.

Sluggishly, languidly, he raised his head and gazed into her eyes. The amber color was intensified by the sparks of their lovemaking. He searched their depths, seeking something even he could not name. She in turn watched him, enchanted by the swirling whirlpools of deep emotion caught in the blue depths of his eyes. She whispered his name with longing. He pressed his head into her hair, choking on words he dare not say aloud.

A crash of thunder surprised them both. Ronin looked up, abruptly alert. A flash of lightning to his right was followed closely by more thunder.

"We must go," he said thickly. He looked to where his ship had disappeared around the bend and saw the outline of a rowboat coming toward them. Ruefully he pulled Kalial off her seaweed island, glad that the now churning water hid some of her body from view. "Ahoy!" he called. The rower paused, looked behind him and spotted Ronin's waving hand. Altering direction, he pulled strongly and reached them just as another crack of thunder rent the sky.

"Damn foolish, Captain! We need to get the ship away from the coast or she'll be kindling soon. Florie's frantic and the damn cat is caterwauling something fierce. Should have left you here to wash up on shore," Dugan Trask finished grumpily as he yanked Kalial out of the water. Seeing her state of undress, he flushed uncomfortably, instantly shedding his coat once again to wrap around her. "You might as well keep it, lass. Apparently you need it more'n I do." Ronin climbed up behind her and Dugan glared at him. "No breeches for you either?" he questioned. "Well, ye ain't getting mine!" He swung the boat around and rowed for the ship.

The small boat was tossed in the waves. Kalial marveled that she had not noticed the change in the weather. The glimpse of sun visible earlier was now a memory as heavy, dark clouds covered the sky. As a belt of thunder rumbled around her, the rain became a heavy sheet of wetness that obscured the ship from view.

Afraid, Kalial pressed against Ronin's solid frame. He looked down at her encouragingly and reached for the second set of oars. Naked, grinning, and all-powerful, Ronin rowed, his feet braced against the gunwales. His arms and chest muscles bulged with each stroke. The little rowboat shot forward, skimming over the waves. A large swell bore down on them and Dugan and Ronin rotated the boat so that the bow dipped into the wave and rode jauntily over it. Then they turned again and pulled forward. Soon the ship rose out of the sheeting rain, massive and solid.

A shout from the deck signaled that they had been

spotted. Ropes fell down her sides. Ronin and Dugan each grasped one, wrapping them and knotting them to the rowboat. Ronin raised his arm and then dropped it swiftly. The men aboard heaved several times and lifted the boat to the level of the deck where the three of them could climb out. Then the boat was swung on deck, capsized and secured to the ship.

Ronin, still naked, began barking out orders. Florie ran forward and grabbed Kalial's arm. They raced down the gangway to Ronin's cabin, where Kalial slipped her half breeches on and wrapped another shirt over her shoulders. She tied it in front, then grabbed a pair for Ronin and dashed back on deck, leaving Florie scolding her for her precipitous frolic in the sea.

The ship rolled suddenly and Kalial stumbled. Immediately Ronin was beside her, holding her arm. He stood with his legs braced, his body moving with the ship. He pushed her back into the doorway and said something. Kalial shook her head in confusion, unable to hear him above the sounds of the storm.

"Get below!" he hollered. She shook her head and held out his clothes. With a raise of his eyebrow, he took the breeches and then pushed her away again. Turning, he missed the spark of anger in her eyes. He swiftly slipped into the breeches, leaving them untied as he jumped over to help lash a sail in place.

"To the oars! The ship is being pushed into the rocks. Every oarsman to his post! Raise the foresail to stabilize the ship or she'll keel over!" Ronin shouted above the wind, his voice powerful and commanding. The men leapt to obey him.

Kalial glared at his back, annoyed that he was sending her to the cabin after all her time on deck. The sound of a horse whinnying was rapidly followed by the wildcat's wail of pent-up fury. Pausing for a moment, Kalial closed her eyes and focused on the beast, calming it with delicate strokes of her mind.

The small sail danced in the wind until it caught a full pocket of air. Then it fairly sang with tension due to the fullness of its load, and the ship groaned. Inch by inch, it started to respond as the oarsmen pulled the *Bonny Evelyn* away from the shore.

Abruptly, the top line of the sail snapped, singing through the air until it whipped against the main mast. The ship listed, thrown sideways by the waves. She floundered. As several men ran over to right the sail, Ronin yelled for a man to climb the rigging. A sailor started to scramble up, but a gust of wind and a surge of water shook the ship and he was tossed to the deck. He slid along the wet boards to the railing, desperate to grab hold of something. Ronin jumped toward him and snagged his hand. He hauled him upright, then yelled for someone else to climb. The crew held back, looking fearfully at the swaying mast. With an oath, Ronin attempted to climb himself, but his weight was too great, and the rigging groaned. He stepped down and forcibly grabbed another sailor and slammed him into the ropes.

"Get up there and secure the sail or we will all die!" he hollered. The man quaked and tried to climb but his feet would not move. A flash of white and gold zipped by Ronin and he saw someone leap into the ropes and start climbing.

"No!" he shouted, louder than before. He lunged for Kalial, caught her, and yanked her down. "Get below! You can not be out here," he yelled at her.

She shook him off with the help of the rocking ship. "I can get up there. I can tie the sail! Let me go," she pleaded.

He shook his head and pushed the sailor back toward the rope. The ship was hit broadside by a wave and her deck was drenched. Kalial held onto the near-est solid object, as the oarsmen ducked their heads and braced their bodies. When the ship dropped into a trough, Kalial dashed up a few feet of the rigging until Ronin once again plucked her free. She shrieked in fury.

"No! You will not go up there. It is too dangerous. Get Trask," he shouted.

"There is no time, I can do it! I have been working hard on the ship for weeks. I know how. Let me go! I can help, I need to help," she cried. Ronin shook his head angrily and shoved her again. She stumbled back into the barrels. When she stayed there, eyes narrowed, Ronin turned away and ignored her. He snagged another hapless sailor and flung him at the rigging. The man started to climb, his movements painfully slow with fear.

Kalial glared furiously at Ronin. She looked above at the rigging for the mainsail. Making an abrupt decision, she jumped and grabbed the lowest rope. She hung for a second, then swung with the sway of the ship. She wrapped her legs around and lifted her body fully into the ropes. A sudden rise of the ship as it first wallowed then surged to the top of a wave caused the slowly climbing sailor to freeze, clinging tightly to the ropes. Kalial scampered up, her hands and feet sure. She rose to well above the flapping foresail, then shimmied over to the edge of the mainsail framing. A few feet below her she saw the loose rope. She eyed it with trepidation. She would have to leap through the air to reach it.

Ronin's bellow of rage distracted her and she looked down at him. His anger gave her the courage of defiance. Despite her sexual surrender she was still an able worker. She had not grown weak overnight. She did not need to be cosseted or hidden below decks while the men attempted to save the ship, especially when she knew how to climb better than anyone present.

She carefully gauged the distance and then waited for the swing of the ship to steady for a second. As it breached the top of the next wave, she sprang.

Kalial felt the ship heave just as she jumped. Knowing that she would fail to make the ropes, she relaxed her body and let the wind and rain carry her. Her hand slipped along a piece of rope but she could not hold it. She bent her knees and thrust her legs forward. Her ankle caught in the ropes, snapping her body to a stop. Swiftly she wound her other leg into the rigging, then, hanging upside down, she reached for the loose rope. She knotted it, yanking her fingers out of the way when the wind slammed her up against the sail, sending a vibration throughout the hull.

With a creak, the ship started to steady, pointing her bow into the waves. The oarsmen bent to their task with renewed strength and the ship started to pull away from the coast. A wave surged underneath the *Bonny Evelyn*, but fell harmlessly alongside of her as she began to skim over the crests. Kalial gripped the ropes and shimmied down, landing lightly on the deck.

Ronin grabbed her immediately and shook her. "Don't ever do that again!" he roared. "I'll not be having my woman act like a sailor. You are to be cared for, not to be risking your life! Never, ever do something that foolish again."

"Foolish?" she screamed back. "I saved this bloody ship. Do not tell me what I cannot do. I am not to be dictated to!"

Ronin held onto her arm, then spun her around. Flinging open a hatch on the deck that led to the hold, he pushed her in. She tumbled ten feet to the floor and looked up in time to see him slam the hatch shut and slip a bolt in place. She felt the rocking of the ship more keenly in this position and immediately felt queasy. However, she could not tell if the ship was to blame or if it was due to her anger at his betrayal.

She peered into the darkness, sensing a familiar presence. A pair of orange eyes gazed at her and she rushed over to the cage holding her jaguar. Dhu Cait was up, pacing, her head lowered and her teeth bared.

Atop her cage sat the owl, downy feathers now mixed
with rich brown and white flying quills. Kalial un-
latched the cage with a sob.

The ship crashed into a trough, flinging Kalial's
slight body against the iron bars. She cried out as a
shaft of pain spread out from her raw back. Dhu Cait
crouched next to her, pressing her warm, solid body
against Kalial's. Her nails dug into the wooden floor
and her four legs splayed for balance. Cradled in dhu
Cait's embrace, Kalial curled up and vented her anger
with harsh sobs. She felt the ship rock and sway and
heard the owl shuffle. She even faintly recognized the
sounds of horses held in stalls, whinnying in fear. But
for all that, she did not move from the comfort of her
great jaguar.

The black fur was soaked with her tears before her
cries became softer, interspersed with sniffles and hic-
cups. Dhu Cait curled her head around and rubbed
her cheek against Kalial's bent head. She purred.
When Kalial looked up, the cat gently rasped her
tongue over Kalial's face, drinking in the salty tears.
Kalial closed her eyes and let dhu Cait alternately lick
and rub her face until she felt calm enough to sit
against the bars.

The tumult of emotions raging through Kalial made
her confused, defenseless, yet dhu Cait could feel the
change in her despite her current tears. Her mistress
had changed—she had become a woman. No longer a
lonely princess who depended upon her cat for all
companionship and solace, Kalial was now full of rich,
fragrant emotions that came from freedom, excitement
and passion. She needed to learn maturity, but that
would take more time. Dhu Cait rubbed against her,
tickling her with her whiskers, acting as a friend instead of a mother. Their loyalty to each other was
untarnished, yet dhu Cait relinquished the child Kalial,
and watched as the woman took a deep breath and
calmed down.

The ship sped through the waves more smoothly now and the thunder ceased to crash. A shiver ran through Kalial and she glanced down at her wet clothes. A stray breeze snaked its way down the hatch. Instantly, her body was covered in goose pimples. She rose and stripped off her wet garments which made her feel warmer immediately, but the cool post-storm breezes continued to chill her body. Even though her mind felt just as cold, she forced herself to move over to the stalls, searching for a horse blanket. A familiar mahogany head poked over a broken beam and gave a soft whinicker of welcome.

"Are you not a lucky fellow? 'Tis special indeed that you are aboard the ship. Look at your pile of hay. Looks fair inviting. Do you mind if I join you for a bit?" Her voice was soft and crooning. The warhorse pricked his ears forward. He blew a gust of air over her face, reminding her of the first time she had met him in the forest so long ago. A ghost of a smile fluttered over her face before sadness descended again. She pulled herself up the stall door by bracing her arms and heaving her body forward. She yelped at the unexpected contact of her nipples against splintered wood and dropped back to the floor with a wry expression.

"Blast! One thing he said 'tis true—I have no idea how to be a woman in this confusing world. 'Tis so much easier to masquerade as a lad and be free. If only my soul would agree with my desires. I detest these yearnings I have to be feminine—this need I have for his touch and protection." The horse snorted in reply. "Yes, but you are a domesticated animal. You have bowed to his command by wearing a saddle and bit. You have been vanquished already!"

A flash of memory came to her then, a spray of ocean waves, a sound of thundering hooves, a powerful surge between her legs. She recalled the moment when they had galloped down the beach and knew then that the horse was not vanquished at all, but free to be strong as well as submissive to his lord. There was a tantalizing dichotomy in the horse's unquestionable superior strength combined with his willing and absolute obedience. Kalial pondered the message.

"But you forget a fatal flaw. He respects your power, he depends upon your abilities to assist him. He sees you as a partner. He can do this for an animal but not for a human. Me, he sees as either a delicate girl to touch and pamper and play with, or a lad to teach and browbeat. I want neither! I want to be me. I want him see who I am and care for me still."

The horse slipped from her mind, her thoughts too complex for him to understand. He pawed, lifting a pile of sweet straw and scattering it. She shivered and sneezed. Carefully this time, she pulled herself up the stall door, ducked under the broken beam and jumped into the stall. Spying a horse blanket draped over the partition, she pulled it down and wrapped herself up. She kicked the loose straw into a pile in one corner, taking care to avoid the mounds of manure. When she was satisfied, she sank down on the bed and pulled some straw on top of herself. Breathing deeply, she fell asleep to the rocking of the ship and the steady creaking of the oars.

CHAPTER 13

Ronin found her curled up in a heap of straw, her fine blond hair spread in a thick fan around her exquisite face. He pushed his horse away, slipping him a precious lump of sugar as a bribe. He knelt down, gazing at her. He ached to kiss the shadows on her cheeks cast by her lashes. They were darker than her hair, a rich dark blond, and so full he wondered how heavy they must be. He plucked the straw off of her, blade by blade, so as not to disturb her. Since her clothes were scattered on the floor, he expected to see golden flesh beneath the yellow straw. Instead he slowly revealed his family tapestry wrapped securely around her dainty form. He grinned at the tiny toes peeking out. They tightened and curled as the straw covering was removed. A small sigh signaled her gradual awakening but her eyes remained closed and she simply shifted position.

Ronin teased himself, trying to follow the contours of her body hidden beneath the fabric. He saw the lump that was her shoulder and traced the line that was her arm before her hand broke out and nestled under her head. He watched for the steady rise and fall of her chest, made so tempting by the rounded bulge of her breasts. The blanket dipped as it molded to her waist until it flared up again at her hips. He very softly stroked the blanket where it followed the curve of her buttocks. She shifted again, her legs parting so that the blanket pooled between them. Ronin shook his head at the golden reflection shining through separations in the fabric. Unfortunately, Kalial did not lie complacent for his investigation.

"What are you doing?" she snapped at him, her voice raw from crying. She felt rudely awoken and it did not help her disposition. "Give me that!" She yanked the tapestry away from a surprised Ronin and stood up, wrapping the cloth tightly about herself. She kept her back straight and attempted to look righteous and dignified. However, when Ronin took a step toward her, she thoughtlessly stepped back, tripped on the blanket and went sprawling at his feet.

"Kal? Are you all right?" Ronin questioned while trying to hide his amusement.

"My name is Kalial, you idiot, and no, I am not all right." Her voice was muffled under the blanket before her head broke free and she could level an angry, golden gaze on him.

"Kalial then. It suits you so much better." He smiled at her engagingly.

"I am Princess Kalial!" she replied heatedly, two red spots blooming on her cheeks.

"Princess?" Ronin narrowed his eyes. "Ah yes, I remember how the others cared for you and deferred to you. And as obstinate as you are . . ." A guilty flush rushed up her neck to her hairline before fading with a rosy residue. "Damn," he murmured, "what am I going to do with you, sweetling?"

Kalial bounded to her feet again, oblivious to her disarray. "That is just it! You do not have to do anything *with* me. I have taken care of myself for many years and I certainly do not need your interference now."

"Many years?" he scoffed. "What? Six and ten, seven and ten?"

"And you?" she retorted, stung by his tone. "You must be well nigh over four score to be so wise!"

He laughed, his head tilting back in his mirth. "If I was four score, my heart would have stopped during our little games of yestereve."

Kalial gasped, then spun around and dove into the straw again. Her yellow eyes snapped with fury. Ronin reached out and snagged the tapestry from her, pulling it roughly and leaving her naked. She gaped and sputtered, but instead of handing the blanket back to her, he swung himself over the stall door and carried it to the ladder. Leaning down, he scooped up her damp, discarded clothes, flipped them over his shoulder, and climbed up onto the deck. He heard Kalial's shriek of anger behind him. As a precaution, he pulled the ladder up after him and looked down the hatch. Dhu Cait watched him with a mysterious grin.

"Although I would love to wrap you in expensive clothes, this blanket is far too valuable to be rolled in the stables," he called down to her.

" 'Tis your horse blanket, you fool!" she cried as she ducked behind the stall door.

Ronin held the blanket up to catch the light. Streaks of gold glittered. He stroked the cloth and marveled at its fine quality. He recalled Quinn, the weaver from Kalial's village, and how he had wanted to lay his head upon the blanket. Trust a weaver to recognize true workmanship, thought Ronin, even when it was covered with horsehair.

"Ach, lass, it means a bit more than that." He grinned down at Kalial. "It is part of my family heritage!"

He stepped back from the hatch and thus missed the sudden intensity of Kalial's expression. Ronin's tapestry in the bright sunlight instantly roused her interest, for the workmanship was familiar to her. Quinn . . . or one of Quinn's ancestors must have woven it! The placement of the threads, the arrangement of the figures . . . she recognized the family artistry that Quinn's grandmother had passed to her eldest daughter, who in turn had passed it on to her eldest son, Quinn.

She gasped, her mouth open. Now that the tapestry was clean, she recognized the place and the meaning depicted in the weave. This was the blanket Ronin had bade her watch carefully and keep safe. This was the blanket Quinn had tried to show her as he lay dying. Her mind raced as she desperately tried to determine how Ronin's family had acquired a piece woven by a forest follower. She reached out, wanting to catch Ronin, but his shadow was already gone. She closed her mouth with a snap. After his cruel treatment, she had no intention of revealing her new knowledge of his precious tapestry. Sheer obstinacy stilled her tongue.

Above deck, Ronin flicked the cloth out on the deck and looked at the figures woven into the fine fabric. He saw a man and a woman riding animals through a dense forest. The shapes of the animals were indistinct but if one looked carefully, there appeared to be hundreds spread throughout the tapestry, skillfully woven into every section. He guessed that there was a giant lizard, a wolf, a horse, a ginger McCat. He saw birds, dragonflies, rabbits, foxes. The list was endless. They were all running to and fro and the people were leaning forward as if they, too, were running. The woman carried a pail and a knife. The man was reaching into the heavens with one hand, grasping a shaft of lightning, while the other held a strung crossbow. Along the top were various trees swept with wind. A granite boulder dominated the upper right-hand corner. Golden threads were woven throughout the tapestry but appeared to converge at the base of the rock. When sunlight hit the threads, they sparkled with the sun's reflection, creating cords of streaming gold.

Ronin stared at the figures with a puzzled frown.

He picked up an edge and carefully scrutinized the craftsmanship. One hand's breadth was made of hundreds of individual threads and each color was vibrant and rich. The magnificence could not be overstated. He stared at the piece again, this time looking for tiny details that might indicate the maker, the guild or year from whence this blanket had been created. In dull brown, noticeable only because it stood out against the beauty of the other colors, was a set of symbols gathered at two opposing corners. The Roman numerals "II of III" stood at the center of the markings.

Ronin ran his fingers through his hair. The black strands slipped and curled around his fingers then lay in a tousled mess against his forehead. Although he had known of the tapestry's existence since his father had revealed it, he had never taken the time to scrutinize it. If the Serpent had not come for it, it probably would have remained buried in the church until he bequeathed it to his own son, years from now.

He looked out across the ocean. He thought back, recalling the pattern on the Serpent's piece that he had seen while in prison. That tapestry had been labeled with the Roman numerals "I of III," and had depicted a glorious riot of colors, symbolizing exotic emeralds, sapphires, rubies and amethysts. The powerful tower of Lothian's castle dominated the piece, but the sad face of a woman looking out a window created a subtle balance to an otherwise brilliant tapestry.

The woman held in her hand a tiny, golden key. A man, standing at the base of the tower, held up a lock. A lock and key. A man and woman. A treasure called the Scottish Gold. Suddenly he began to pace, his long strides carrying him quickly across the deck and back again. He returned to glare at the blanket, then strode away again. If Lothian's tapestry, the First Hunt, was describing the Scottish Gold, then the Second Hunt, his familial treasure, should tell where it was hidden. But his tapestry told of no specific location. It was simply a collection of animals rushing through a forest. And he had no idea where the Third Hunt was, nor what secrets it concealed.

He stopped in front of the hatch on one of his passes and knelt down to look into the gloom below. Side by side, gold next to black, sat Kalial and her jaguar. Sunshine amid the night. She stared up at him from her cross-legged position, her yellow eyes eerily silent and wary. Her blond hair rippled over her bare shoulders, trailed down her back and breasts and settled into a pile of silken threads in her lap. Dhu Cait lay next to her, her tail twitching faintly. She, too, looked up at him with watchful eyes.

What am I missing? he questioned the pair silently. He gazed at her, his body instantly aching for her but his mind warning him that he would not be welcomed. He remembered her kneeling in front of him on the beach, swearing to serve him. He recalled the purity of the moment, how he had felt that her oath had been a sacrament among events that swept them along. She had been clean for the first time, her golden hair shimmering in the glow of the sunrise. Her tunic, burned along the edges, had glimmered as well, announcing its quality despite its rough treatment.

Feeling guilty, he spoke in anger. "Why are you not dressed?" he suddenly snapped at her.

She responded with a delicately arched eyebrow. "Do you think that I would sit here as a naked maid if I could get to my garments?" She lifted her shoulders in a tiny shrug and turned her palms up with a flick of her wrist. "Do tell when you see fit to return them to me and I would be pleased to put them on again."

Ronin grew preoccupied with the apricot nipples peeking through her hair. "You should be wearing dresses, not britches," he said.

Kalial's eyes grew hard and her voice became scornful. "Since I have neither, it is a moot point." She shifted, irritated by his obvious desire. "Do not be shy in your perusal, my lord. It would be a shame if anything were to distract you from your manly pursuits. Surely my simple body does not tempt you to forget your goals?" She raised her arms and shook her hair back from her face. Then she crossed her arms in front and ran her nails lightly down the opposite arm, leaving delicate pink furrows in her pale skin. Her breasts were pressed together, creating a deep and tempting cleavage. Ronin watched her sultry movements, forgetting himself in the face of such provocation. He raised his eyes to hers, expecting to see a warm glow to accompany her movements. Instead he was blasted by an icy glare, the topaz highlights piercing him with crystalline fury.

Shocked, he jerked back. When he had righted himself, Kalial was standing in her blond beauty, her hand resting on the growling head of the black cat. "Perhaps now that you are finished staring, you will see fit to return my clothes. Since you are so set on defending me, then show some of your chivalry and clothe me!"

Ronin turned and saw several members of the crew staring down the hatch, observing her with ill-disguised pleasure.

"Get back!" he barked and tossed a tarp over the iron bars of the hatchway, guarding her from view. The men quickly scurried away as Ronin stalked to the captain's deck where Dugan manned the wheel.

"Let the gal rot there for a bit longer, Captain," said Trask. "Maybe it will teach her some manners. Never should have allowed the wench on board."

"You did not know it was a wench, if you recall, Trask," Ronin reminded him.

"Humph" was his only reply.

Ronin sighed deeply. Then he swung off the deck and walked to his cabin. Opening the door, he could see the disarray left by the storm and still smell the scent of Kalial. Closing his eyes, he breathed in deeply. The sexual pull of the forest princess was irresistible. Never had Ronin felt so obsessed with a female, so that the mere scent of her could cause him to tremble. The only way to vanquish this feeling was to conquer the girl, to touch her and use her until he no longer needed her. Only then would he be free of her yellow eyes and sunlit skin.

Ronin located Kal's shapeless tunic, flung in a corner from last eve. He picked it up and returned to the deck, resolved to make amends with Kalial. He moved the tarp, dropped the ladder and stepped down into the hold to speak with her in private. Kalial stood in her natural state, her hair swinging around her torso as her body twitched with irritation. When Ronin paused, she snapped at him caustically, "May I please have my tunic to wear, Lord McTaver? I find that I am unable to feel comfortable around you thus unclothed."

Ronin smiled in a leisurely manner, then reached out to stroke one of her hard nipples. Kalial shuddered and stepped away from his hand. "My tunic, if you please," she repeated, her eyes showing a flicker of revulsion.

Ronin paused, hand outstretched. His resolution slipped as he watched the emotions run across Kalial's face. "I have seen you thus before. I have touched your sweet body and kissed your essence. There is no need to become shy now."

"Do you have no idea where I stand with you? Give me my tunic."

"Why?" he replied.

Kalial stamped her foot in vexation. The action caused her breasts to bounce becomingly. "Give it to me!" she demanded more loudly.

"No," he answered. He stepped closer to her, his muscled form towering over hers. His cobalt blue eyes bore down on her and he spoke with a deep intensity.

"You need to cease your scathing tone and speak more softly."

"I care naught for what you ask." She blinked rapidly as her golden eyes filled with shimmering wetness. "I want nothing to do with you from the moment we touch land onward. You have only done harm to me—to my body, to my soul, to my heart."

"Your heart? What do you mean, fair princess?"

"Nothing, I misspoke." She turned her head for a moment and when her eyes returned to meet his they were dry. "I want naught to do with you. I have heard tales of how you strangers treat your women and I have watched when they camped near to the forest boarders. The women would simper and cry. They were dependent upon men to find them food, protect them from wind or rain and for . . . for everything! I would never be like that. I would never be so weak and helpless."

"Our women are far from weak and helpless, Princess," Ronin responded. He spoke earnestly, looking into her eyes but keeping his hands still at his sides though he wanted to sweep her into his arms and kiss away her anger. "They are powerful in a different way. We men are the protectors, yes, as it should be. We are stronger, we are more careless with our persons and we injure less due to our thick hides. You are so lovely, so golden and precious, you cause men to bend to you by just smiling. What power is that, I tell you!"

"Yes, what power, I ask you? And what protection? I am the protector of my forest and I have no need of another to take my place. I am entrusted with the secrets of my land, not some man!" Kalial ended with a lifted head, her chin jutting forward and her swooping brows raised in question.

Ronin glared at her, all thoughts of reconciliation gone. "You know nothing of secrets," he growled. "If you think hiding your identity is protecting a secret, you have no concept of a true confidence."

"Believe me, I know more secrets that I have not revealed."

Ronin looked at her with eyebrows raised. "I am sure they mean nothing to me."

"Hah, I would not be so sure of that," she retorted but stopped abruptly as Ronin grabbed her by both arms and shook her roughly.

"Stop!" he interrupted brusquely. "A woman should not argue! This is why masculine attire is forbidden to the female race. Look what it has done to you." Kalial yanked out of his arms and snapped her mouth shut. Ronin took a threatening step forward. "Your gender should be gentle and sweet. If you have another secret that I should know, then reveal it now."

Kalial remained stubbornly silent, her eyes snapping with fury.

"This is not the time to prove your reticence, Kalial. Tell me what you think I should know."

"I shall not. My secrets are mine own and I'll not share them just because you demand it!"

Ronin spun in a circle of frustration, but when he faced her again, she still looked mutinous. Making a quick decision, he stepped forward and buried his hands in her blond hair at the back of her neck. Tilting her face upwards, he leaned down and slid his lips over her eyebrows, to the corners of her enchanting yellow eyes, along the line of her jaw and finally to her wet lips. He pressed his mouth against her softly and gathered her full underlip in his teeth. He sucked gently, then covered her mouth fully with his while sliding one arm down her back to pull her fully against him.

Kalial gave herself to the kiss, allowing her mouth to be plundered and her body to be molded, but her mind remained separate, reserved.

Ronin raised his head and smiled in victory until

Kalial spoke. "I will not tell you anything," she said softly. "Unless . . . perhaps if you ask nicely . . ."

Ronin dropped his hands in surprise, but his mind worked furiously. "I bow before no woman, Princess."

"Such is your lesson then, m'laird, for you most certainly will have to question me if you want to know." Kalial stepped forward this time, allowing her nipples to brush against the silk of Ronin's shirt. Her eyes remained light and daring and Ronin knew that she acted only to demonstrate control.

In anger he responded, "I will not do so. You must tell me if you know something important."

"Then you lose," replied Kalial. She leaned against him fully, pressing her hips into his and rotating them in a circular motion.

Ronin gasped and grabbed her naked buttocks in both hands. He lifted her and pulled her legs around his waist so that the wet core of her was spread open. He then reached down with one hand and began to unlace his breeches. Kalial laughed throatily, arching her body and letting her long hair tangle in his fumbling hands. She then looked up, her catlike eyes gleaming, as she blinked in a slow imitation of Mariella's seductive look.

She smiled in a sleepy, half-lidded way, deliberately licking her lips. She lifted her hands from his shoulder and placed them over her breasts then splayed her fingers wide so the pinkish apricot nipples peeked through.

Ronin roughly dropped her, pushing her down so that she sprawled on the ground.

"Do not play games with me!" he shouted. Even as he said the words, Ronin knew he had to retreat from the scene. Her teasing games had flustered him, and he felt his control slipping. His eyes narrowed. "If you desire games, sweet Princess, then let it be known that the field is open. I have jousted many a time and have never lost. I will make you reveal your secrets to me.

Good day, Princess." He bowed to her mockingly, then retrieved her tunic. He picked it up, patted the nose of his horse and swiftly ascended the ladder carrying it with him. A resounding clang reverberated in the hold as he dropped the hatch cage shut and locked it, leaving her naked and alone.

Ronin stomped away from the hatch, his mind swirling with half thoughts and full desires. He wanted much from Kalial. He wanted her body, her sweet kisses. He wanted her soft voice . . . he wanted her undivided trust and loyalty. She should reveal everything to him, she should trust him completely! No matter what her secrets, she should share them with him.

Ronin stood at the railing, staring across the blue ocean, watching the small ripples mar the surface as their secrets marred the bond between them. He longed to have all be as wide and pure as the sea. Instead, seaweed clogged their conversations and twisted their words into a dark abyss. Ronin's eyes darkened with pain. It was more than pride that hurt. His heart ached from her lack of openness.

Kalial glared into the gloom around her, furious that Ronin had left her so abruptly. She regretted her taunting, for the game had left her as unsatisfied as it had him. Just a few kind words . . . she wanted to hear him speak softly to her, asking for her assistance, her forgiveness. Instead he had only demanded, argued and growled. She paced angrily, repeating his harsh words in her mind, yet a tear filled her eye and her brows drew together in hurt puzzlement. She wanted something from him . . . she felt he had something more to offer buried within his warrior soul. Deep in the bowels of the ship, she acknowledged her wishes, her blossoming feelings. She regretted her quick words, and her heart ached.

CHAPTER 14

The following day, Kalial was surprised to see the ladder, then Florie, descend into the hold. She carried bread and cheese, along with a cask of water.

"Ach now, you poor thing. Here is some sustenance. The captain wishes me to tell you that should you desire to reveal all to him, he would be pleased to lend you a berth in his cabin."

"Tell him that I would rather sit here in the dark than give in to his manipulations!"

Florie shook her head, then shrugged and handed Kalial the victuals. "I figured you'd say as much. But do you mind if I stay and keep you company a bit?"

Kalial smiled sheepishly. "I would be honored. I am sorry I spoke harshly to you. The words are meant for him, not you."

"I know that, Princess. It is Princess, right? I heard McTaver talking to Trask and he said you were a princess." When Kalial nodded, Florie grinned. "I have never met a real princess afore. You are nothing like I expected."

"No, I am sure I am quite different."

"I would like to hear about your home," Florie said earnestly. "What is your life like?"

"My life is very simple, Florie. Certainly less complicated than yours. I was born a princess because my mother was one before me. I live in the forest, because that was always our home. Many, many generations ago, my ancestors followed a gifted one from the highlands in a quest to find a treasure beyond description. Once it was found, they were bound to protect it and so, for years too numerous to count, we have protected it within Loch Nidean forest."

"A lonely task, to protect riches within a forest. 'Twould seem that no treasure is worth anything unless one can share it."

Kalial looked at her new friend with surprise, then nodded slowly. "I will think on that, Florie," she said.

"Well, enough about such serious matters. I want to know what you plan to do once we reach Tregaron!"

The two women shared confidences for some time, and when Florie finally ascended the ladder, night had spread out across the horizon. She shook her head at Ronin's silent question, then left him alone on deck.

Ronin sat on the edge of the hatch, staring into the moonlight. He yearned to talk to Kal, his companion, and ached to touch Kalial, his lover. Yet, he was annoyed that she continued to hold secrets from him. How could he reveal his deepest secrets to her when she was unwilling to tell him her own? He glared down at the hatch door, unaware that she stared up, equally frustrated with him.

With a gruff sigh, Ronin left his perch that night and did not attempt to communicate with her for the rest of the journey.

A week later, Kalial heard the shout above decks announcing sight of the harbor. The scent of autumn wafted from the land, and Kalial imagined the changing leaves along the coastline as the *Bonny Evelyn* sailed into harbor. She listened to the sailors scurrying to lower the sails and man the oars to make their controlled approach to the dock.

When she heard Ronin's voice, she glared up at

the hatchway, venting a steady stream of demands, peppered with the swear words she had learned while on board. When it was clear that Ronin intended to ignore her yet again, she slumped down against one of the stall doors.

A petite pale palomino peeked its head over the stall door and nuzzled her. The fall of white mane and forelock made her look like a fairytale unicorn that had lost her horn in the lap of a maiden. She had an abundance of fine whiskers that she passed over Kalial's face, making her giggle.

Kalial settled down and munched on some bread crust and cheese Florie had lowered to her right before the harbor had been spotted. She took a few deep swallows of the clear rainwater in a wineskin that had accompanied the repast yet squirmed uncomfortably due to the grime and dust that tickled her skin. She had found another saddle blanket many days before and had initially wrapped herself in it but soon realized that there was no need. The hold was warm with the heat of the animals and the hatch was covered so no eyes could observe her.

In many ways she had felt closer to home these past days than she had since the forest fire. By the filtered light that sprinkled along the sloped floor she had explored the hold accompanied by the constant shadow of the great cat. The palomino mare remained restless with nervousness around the predator, yet her wide, intelligent eyes sought and received comfort from Kalial.

With a patience that Kalial never had for her human counterparts, she gentled the dainty steed and soothed her concerns. The owl fluttered in the relative darkness, his eyes scanning constantly for the small vermin that stowed away in the bales of hay. The pale horse readily accepted the bird's presence and was rewarded with soft touches of gratitude from Kalial's sensitive fingertips. Lounging in nothing but the drape of a warm breeze and her cloak of golden hair, Kalial began to sense the changes to her body that had crept upon her without her notice.

Tentatively, she stroked her arms, feeling the strength of muscle but also noting the softness so unlike the calloused hardness of Ronin's flesh. Crossing her arms, she swept her palms over her rounded shoulders, encircling them over and over again. Kalial located and explored a tiny mole upon her left collarbone, tracing it with inquisitive fingers. She tingled in a darkness now lit only by the glow of the animal's eyes. Night had blackened the sky and only a small lantern left on deck probed the hatch to act as her moon.

Looking up, her eyes locked into the round orbs of the owl, and a shiver of longing raced up her spine. Hesitantly, Kalial let her hands inch downwards until they slipped over her suddenly sweaty skin and brushed over her breasts. With a soft cry, she jerked her hands away from her body and squeezed her eyes closed. Whereas before she had only known one desire, one goal, that of protecting her beloved forest, now she felt many conflicting desires. She yearned to feel Ronin's hands touch her as she touched herself, yet she wanted the touch to be rougher, more abrasive and powerful.

Such thoughts angered her, confused her, and she responded by pushing them away and denying her desire. As the heat slipped away and her breathing steadied, she sought refuge in her angry thoughts and petulant demands. Consequently, she frequently leapt up, startling the horses, and shouted at Ronin, at the ship and at everyone in general. Her voice escalated and she shook her hair back and tilted her head up. Upset and at a loss as to how to handle her new emotions, she ranted intermittently, warning Ronin to come no nearer to her than the end of the ship rail and then demanding that he come down and face her directly to prove that he was no coward. Yesterday she had decided that she wanted a bath, and had spent a better part of the morning hollering for one. Of course, none had been produced. They were on a ship, for God's sake, a sailor had finally whispered down to her.

Ronin himself had let her be. She had listened to him, however, during the moments when she lay upon her straw bed. She heard his commanding voice when he issued orders and his rich tones when he discussed plans with Dugan Trask. Now with the harbor near, Kalial waited below, tearing at the crust of stale bread, and sinking her white teeth into rich, fragrant cheese while mulling over how she would discomfit Ronin once they docked.

Soon the ship bounced against the harbor and the cries of the sailors were all but deafened by the shouts from shore. Ronin stood braced on the deck, his gaze sweeping the crowd. The village was out in full force, having spotted his craft long before it had docked. This harbor was unique for its depth and accessibility, which made it a popular stopping point for all types of vessels. Therefore, the village commerce centered around the constant flux of seamen.

Merchants flashed freshly baked bread, sweet candies and sparkling trinkets. Young boys sped up and down, chasing each other and leaping over casks in a show of agility and stamina. Village lasses watched and giggled, then ignored the boys in favor of the sailors. They announced a wide array of services in voices sweet but loud. Several called to entice the men to particular taverns or saloons. Others hawked barbershops, laundry services or bathing houses. The sailors called back good-naturedly, demanding demonstrations of the welcome they would receive in the various establishments. One especially bold female flipped her skirts high, exposing a flash of red petticoats. A cheer went up from the men and the lady made a sweeping curtsy.

The sailors on deck tossed ropes to the men on shore and the ship was soon lashed to the dock. Ronin ordered the plank to be laid, selected a crew to stay aboard as guards, and walked ashore to greet the village master.

"Mr. Reed, how nice to see you again."

"The pleasure is mine, naturally, Laird McTaver. We did not receive word that you would be arriving, sir. I profusely apologize for not having time to inform Lord Basingstoke. I, of course, sent a messenger to the castle the moment your ship was sighted. He should be arriving in due time. If I could offer my services in the meanwhile?"

"I am in need of clothes for a lady," answered Ronin.

The village master started slightly, but recovered instantly. The hard glint of McTaver's eye coupled with his reputation as one of the fiercest warriors in his land caused the village master to answer quickly. "But certainly. Redhaired, brunette, blue eyes, brown? . . ."

"No, you misunderstand." Ronin grinned, although the smile did not soften the hard line of his jaw. "I need someone familiar with the trappings of a lady and capable of procuring a complete ensemble. I have a woman on board who had an unfortunate . . . accident. She is in need of clothing."

"Oh dear, is she all right? Is she a captive or a slave?" questioned the master nosily.

Despite his aversion to explaining himself, Ronin spoke briefly. "Certainly not. She is the princess of lands near to Roseneath. She . . . she is my . . . ward . . . since recent deaths on our shores have left her without family."

"My apology, Laird. I did not mean to besmirch her name. I was not aware that you had a ward, sir." The village master's prying nature was well known and Ronin took a deep breath before speaking again.

"I do. Now if you please, a casket of fresh water, a tub and the aforementioned clothes. Preferably in fine fabrics and rich colors. She is rather pale in complexion. Can you see to it?" requested Ronin as he turned away after handing the man a small pile of silver coins. The village master eagerly scooped up the money and scampered away, leaving the docks while issuing rapid orders.

Soon thereafter Kalial heard a heavy object being dragged across the deck. Curious, she drew her blanket around herself and stood beneath the hatch, staring upward in expectation. She was not disappointed. Ronin drew off the covering and looked down through the bars. He paused for a second, staring at the disheveled girl. Her instant frown brought a matching scowl from him. Gruffly, he spoke to her.

"The Lord of Tregaron, my cousin Percy Basingstoke, will be here within the hour. I will tell him you are under my protection as my ward. You will have to pretend to be a lady, but if we expect you to pull off this charade, you had best bathe and dress. It would be unseemly to appear before him thus."

Kalial's jaw dropped. She was so stunned, she could not form coherent thoughts. Her mouth worked up and down but by the time a shriek of indignation burst forth, Ronin had disappeared and Dugan had taken his place. He unlocked the hasp and drew the hatch open. The rope ladder fell down. Dugan stared at her silently from his superior height. Kalial looked around and then back up. Surely they were going to give her something to wear before she exited? How was she to climb the rope while holding onto the blanket?

She tried to ascend a few rungs with only one hand, but the ladder began to spin from her unbalanced weight. She twisted and swiftly switched hands, but the blanket slipped down her shoulders. She shrugged and wiggled, trying to raise the covering. Glancing up, she saw that Dugan observed her dispassionately, making no move to assist her. Kalial stepped up another rung and snagged an edge of the blanket with her foot. The blanket was wrenched from her struggling hands another several inches. Trying to lift her other foot, she found that she had effectively snared it in the cloth. Thoroughly disgusted, Kalial swore and dropped to the ground with a thud.

Suddenly Ronin's face reappeared beside Dugan's and he said mockingly, "Lord Basingstoke is arriving sooner than expected as he was already in town. If you find you cannot get up the ladder to bathe, I will toss the hot water down on you through the hatch. I'll not have my new ward presented as if she had slept in the stable for the past several weeks."

"How dare you! You are the one who locked me in this hold. I am—"

"Can we cease the conversation? He will be boarding the ship at any moment. It really is time for you to stop playing games and get into my cabin where your bath awaits. I did hear you demand one earlier, did I not?" Ronin's voice was short and clipped. Kalial was amazed at his impertinence.

"Fine," she said in dangerous tones. "You want to make an impression on your cousin, the great Lord of Tregaron? So be it." She calmly dropped the blanket, tossed her hair over her shoulders and climbed the ladder. Before everyone's startled gaze, she emerged from the hold, a blond, shimmering, naked nymph rising from the depths. Kalial stood poised for a moment, looking down her nose at a furious Ronin, feeling the cool sea breeze on her flesh. She then strode quietly to the gangway and down to the captain's cabin where she softly closed the door behind her.

"That bitch!" Ronin ranted as Dugan leapt to grip his shoulder. "Why does she do things to anger me so? What fool struts around a sailing vessel bare assed? Tell me! What idiot! Does she have no concept of right and wrong?" Ronin shoved Trask's restraining arm aside. He glared at his first mate but did not reprimand him for had Dugan not stopped him, he was certain he would have throttled her.

Just then, Ronin saw that his cousin had boarded the ship. Percy Basingstoke tore his gaze from the doorway and collecting himself rapidly, he walked over with a warm greeting.

"Cousin Ronin. What a surprise. What brings you to my trading port? Have you brought your lovely mother, Evelyn, or any of your sisters with you?" He glanced back at the place where Kalial had disappeared and lifted his brows.

"You can not possibly think that *she* is a sister of mine," Ronin replied to the unasked question.

"Ah, I thought not. Then who is she? Do not tell me you have taken a bride without telling me?"

"No! I am calling her my ward, taken under my protection after her clan was destroyed. She is . . . undisciplined. Since I hear you have recently married, I hope that your wife will be able to teach her some manners."

"But of course. We are at your disposal. And the McTaver! Is your father with you?" Percy's voice lifted in a question.

"Deceased, my cousin. As are my sisters. I have much to tell you and here is not the place. But I have need of your hospitality this winter. Can you grant it?"

"Of course. As I said, I am happy to welcome you and your lively ward. Shall we unload your livestock and supplies while the fair maiden prepares to travel to the castle?"

Kalial pressed her back against the closed door and finally took a breath. She started trembling and abruptly sat down on the floor. Burying her face in her hands, she could not decide whether to laugh at the commotion she had caused or to cry in embarrassment. She ended by doing a little of both before looking up at the sound of a small cough coming from the other side of the room.

Kalial lifted her head and sprang instantly to her feet.

"Well, that was a way to make an impression," Florie remarked.

"Oh, Florie, I am so glad to see you! I am nervous. Are you sure you can help me?" questioned Kalial. She spread her arms wide and looked down at her naked form.

"No fear, I know what I am about. I told you before, I used to be a personal servant to a lady afore she married and left me behind. I'll help ye for sure. I'll do me best to make you look like a lady, but it will be your job to act like one. But first things first, lass. Plunk yourself in this here tub and clean that horsy smell off o' ye."

Kalial took Florie in a great hug. She smiled and laughed. "At the very least it should be an adventure!"

Florie shook her head in despair. "Come on while the water is hot. Get your bare buns in and I'll be pouring the scented oils in the tub. Pick a fragrance you like, *m'lady Princess*." Florie picked up a tray and presented it to Kalial. At her look of confusion, Florie sighed and selected a light, springtime scent. "All ladies have a special perfume, one that announces them before they enter a room, and clings to the clothes of the man she presses against. 'Tis a way of primitive marking where the female stakes her claim. You must decide what you like."

"How do I know what I like?" Kalial asked as she sank into the deep, steaming water and closed her eyes in contentment.

"Well, I suppose you determine what you want to be represented as, or what flower you like the most, or even what sweet food you crave above all others."

"Honey," Kalial said with a sigh.

"Honey?"

"Yes, I crave wild honey, harvested in the spring while the bees are spinning around my head." Kalial dipped below the water to drench her hair.

Florie smirked. "Of course, Princess Kalial. Honey it will be, just because it is hard to find. Perhaps you will make a fine lady after all." She ambled over to the door and called out to the cabin boy. She gave him a silver coin and instructions to find a pot of fragrant honey. The boy scrambled out and leapt on the dock. His search was rapid and fruitful. Within ten minutes he returned.

Florie scooped a small handful of honey into a pail of steaming water. It thinned and liquefied, forming a sweet, diluted scent. Next, Florie allowed four drops of the spring oil mixture to fall into the water. She took a deep sniff, paused, shook her head and glanced back at her tray. She returned for a moment, shifting the vials and clinking the glass in her effort to find the perfect scent. Finally Kalial looked over at her.

"Is this really necessary? It seems odd to wash and then cover one's self immediately with oil and honey."

"Do you want to be a lady?" answered Florie as she picked out two vials and brought them over to Kalial. "Here, smell these and choose one."

Kalial sniffed and smiled. "They are both lovely," she said. Florie frowned.

"You need something special, not plain lovely. Something that makes you feel as if you are floating, that you are beautiful, that you are a princess. You must feel as if the scent reflects your inner self. Now here, choose one." She held the entire tray out. Kalial shrugged and sat up in her bath. Water sluiced off her shoulders as she carefully picked up the first bottle. She uncapped the vial and smelled. With a grimace, she set it down, looking at Florie in disgust.

"This could become tedious. How many times will I have to do this?"

"Only once if you get through with it. Now come

on, keep looking. The water is cooling." Florie pushed the tray at Kalial yet again.

Suddenly, they heard a pounding at the door and Ronin's angry voice. "Hurry up and get out here, Kalial. Your cat is disrupting the dockside!" Kalial looked up in annoyance until she heard the faint but unmistakable sounds of feminine shrieks and masculine shouts overriding the roar of a displeased jaguar. Kalial gasped and made to rise until Florie pushed her firmly back into the water.

"Not until you are done. You certainly can not go out there as bare as you came in! They will have to manage," said Florie with emphasis.

"Oh, for heaven's sake, I have no idea what oil to use. Let's get this done with and get me dressed," cried Kalial. She grabbed one at random and shoved it at Florie. Florie looked at the choice and frowned harder.

"You shall not wear rose," she announced. " 'Tis far too common. If you will not choose, I will ask Laird McTaver." With that she marched over to the door, opened it a crack and pushed her nose into Ronin's face. "She will not be coming out until she is dressed, unless you want to cause more of a commotion than there already is." She paused as Ronin shook his head. "And," she continued, "she can not get dressed until you tell me what flower she reminds you of."

Ronin was nonplussed. The image of her tearing out of the room without the benefit of concealing clothing still left him shaking his head, but Florie's question distracted him. Unbidden, the exotic scent of jasmine wafted though his mind and he said it aloud without thinking. The door was slammed in his face before he could recollect his thoughts. He had picked up his hand to bang on the door again when he heard Percy's voice in the hallway behind him.

"I trust your ward is faring well? You left us standing on the dock to deal with that angry Scottish McCat. Can I assume it belongs to her?" he asked.

"Yes," replied Ronin as he turned away from the door, "she alone can control the beast. Where is it now?"

"Ah, an exotic beast for a wild woman. How appropriate. Here is the package you requested from the village master. 'Tis your luck that a trunk of women's clothing had just arrived in port. 'Twas a dowry trunk, but the lass is already heavy with child and will not need the clothes." As Ronin retrieved the package and knocked once again to deliver it to Florie, Percy continued. "And to remind you, your ward's jaguar is pacing along the dock, that owl upon its back. The villagers are panicking. I am a bit afraid one will try to kill it."

Ronin grunted and went on deck after a final glower at the cabin door. He saw dhu Cait striding slowly down the pier, scattering people before her. Her mouth was ajar so that her teeth sparked in the sunlight. The hair along her back was raised, causing her to look almost twice her normal size. She swung her head at the sound of Ronin's voice and glared at him, then spun around and set off at a lope, straight into the center of town.

Ronin cursed as he ran down the plank after her. A fishing net caught his eye and he picked it up without breaking stride and flung it over his shoulder. He watched in shock as ripples of villagers spotted her sleek form and instantly went crazy, dashing every which way while screaming at the top of their lungs. Some attempted to climb night posts while others curled up in balls in the gutter. A baker flung his basket to the ground, turned and ran into a wall whereupon he bashed his head and dropped to the ground, unconscious.

The owl flapped his wings and lifted off dhu Cait's back. He swooped over the fallen bread and grasped a loaf. The baker's wife shot out of the bakery, fists raised threateningly until a hiss from the jaguar sent her scurrying back inside. Meanwhile, Ronin followed behind at a run, the net bouncing on his back. Abruptly, dhu Cait turned right, then right again so that she was headed back toward the sea. The owl tilted his wings so that he, too, turned. Sweating with the effort, Ronin chased the pair until they reached the dock. The chaos erupted yet again as the people spotted the return of the cat into their midst.

Dhu Cait sprang up on top of a fallen vendor's booth. She looked around and let out a terrifying yowl, midway between a roar and a child's scream. Ronin came to within a few feet of her and halted. He swung the net off his shoulders and swiftly untangled it. The cat sat back and flattened her ears. Her tail swished angrily. She hissed as she swatted the air in front of her with a black paw, deadly claws extended. She crouched down, orange eyes narrowed, muscles shivering as she eyed his careful approach. Both front paws repeatedly lifted off the ground with tiny jerks as she drew her haunches deep underneath her body.

Ronin steadied his breathing and focused on the jaguar. Her black hide shown in the sun with stripes of deeper black. Ronin blocked out the sounds of the people around him and channeled all his actions. He took one step closer and slowly lifted the net. Dhu Cait yowled again, her lips drawn back, her long canines gleaming. Ronin took careful aim and waited for a split second. In that moment, dhu Cait leapt right at him.

Her powerful muscles sprang her high above Ronin, higher even than the net he flung. She bounded well above his head, landing with a thud several feet behind him. Ronin spun, expecting attack. Instead he saw her walk forward disdainfully, her coat smooth, her tail hung low and her nose inching upwards. Ronin lifted his gaze and saw Kalial standing on the plank of his ship, her golden hair shimmering in the light and her body encased in a sweeping dress of white and copper.

CHAPTER 15

Ronin froze. His heart stopped, then thudded heavily. She stepped forward. A copper circlet graced her hair. A matching hand-pounded girdle lay around her hips, emphasizing the narrow shape. Narrow sleeves caressed her shoulders before falling in a full bell down past her waist. The cloth gleamed richly and was dotted with tiny crystal beads hidden in the copper embroidery. She bent over and her hair slipped over her shoulders to swing freely. She reached a hand down with a graceful movement and lay it delicately upon the jaguar's head. Leaning forward, she placed a petite kiss on dhu Cait, then stood and gazed at Ronin.

A deafening silence fell as the crowd grew suddenly still. Ronin stared at Kalial, his eyes riveted by her beauty. A slight breeze ruffled her hair which, he now saw, was still damp, although a few dry tendrils fluttered about her face. With the breeze came the scent of honeysuckle mixed with a subtle bouquet of jasmine. His nostrils flared and an ache started in the pit of his stomach. He stepped toward her.

"I see you have tamed the beast," Lord Basingstoke said to Kalial, lounging a few feet from her. "I am Percy Basingstoke, your humble servant. And you must be my cousin's lovely ward."

Ronin jerked his eyes from Kalial and turned them

on Percy. He felt a stirring of jealousy at the look of lust and admiration on Basingstoke's face. "Cousin," he mumbled, "please meet the Princess Kalial. Kal, this is Lord Basingstoke."

"That is quite the pet, m'lady. Wherever did you get such an animal?" Percy questioned with a charming smile.

Kalial dragged her gaze away from Ronin's intense stare, her hand still resting on dhu Cait's head, and faced the new stranger. A stray ocean breeze fluttered her hair. She stood still, her chest lifting slightly with each breath. The great wildcat stood proudly beside her, her jet black color a startling contrast to Kalial's lightness. The circling owl swooped down and perched on her shoulder.

Percy Basingstoke's reddish blond hair shone in the sunshine. His hazel eyes sparkled with invitation. He was clearly a seasoned fighter with a strong, muscular build and a powerful sword at his waist. He was richly attired in embroidered clothes that allowed free movement and amply displayed his form. He winked at her and then laughed at her startled expression.

Ronin McTaver stood slightly behind and to the right of Percy, Basingstoke's opposite in appearance. His expression was stormy. The blue of his eyes resembled the color of a tumbling sea. Two thin lines of sweat trickled down his face and over his neck. His midnight black hair drank the sunlight, absorbing it completely. With an angry motion, he thrust his hand into his hair, tossing it out of his eyes. His dirty white shirt clung to his chest. Kalial dropped her eyes, seeing the tight breeches encasing his thighs and his calves and observing the worn boots that covered his feet. A single small dagger was strapped to his boot.

Ronin watched Kalial assess and compare the two men. Suspecting that he fell short in her eyes compared to his cousin, he became unaccountably angry. Percy was handsome and knew how to sweet-talk the women around him until they fell willingly into his bed. His good looks, his rich lands and his irrefutable charm were an irresistible combination to females. In fact, his recent marriage had surprised everyone, for Percy had been fond of his liberty. Ronin usually found his cousin's ability to lure women amusing. Today he did not.

He stepped forward and Kalial's gaze snapped back to his. His expression made her fall back slightly and become tangled in her skirts. As she tripped, Percy leapt forward to catch her. A loud and threatening growl from the jaguar stopped him in his tracks just as Ronin reached out and roughly grabbed her arm and hauled her upright.

"If you cannot keep your beast contained, I'll have it walled up in a cave where it belongs," he said. "I'll not be racing around trying to catch it anymore. You should have been taking care of it, not preparing yourself as if for an audience with the king himself. What were you thinking, to allow a wild animal to terrorize a village of good citizens? And for what, to get dressed up in clothes that you cannot even properly walk in?" Ronin glared down at her, his pupils wide and his nostrils flaring.

Kalial's eyes instantly filled. Great pools of tears threatened to spill over onto her cheeks. Her pink lips parted in a quick gasp before her teeth bit harshly on her lower lip. Ronin felt her slender form shiver and shrink in his rough hands, causing a painful wrench to his gut and making his heart stop beating for a long second. He softened his hold and rubbed his thumb over her arm to still the spread of goose bumps. He started to pull her closer while frantically searching for words to ease the hurt he had unthinkingly inflicted.

As his mouth opened, he heard Percy's voice directly behind him. "You poor child, to have to deal with such an uncouth guardian. Anyone would quail under his baleful glare. Come here, *chéri*. Would you not like some solid land under your feet? I swear I, too, will fall over if I must endure the rocking of this vessel for a moment more." His soft eyes were kind and Kalial gazed at him in gratitude. She blinked rapidly to clear her eyes.

She pulled away from Ronin's hand with a jerk that shook the owl. He clamped his talons down to keep from falling, causing Kalial to wince. Ronin instantly lifted the animal from her shoulder and placed it on his own; however, before he could check to see if the sharp talons had caused damage, Percy motioned to the plank and Kalial carefully lifted her skirts to precede him to the dock. Ronin watched them move away, the ache in his heart unfamiliar and unwelcome. He turned abruptly and harshly ordered his supplies to be loaded onto a wagon, where Florie and a few others were waiting. He himself lashed his familial tapestry to the saddle of his warhorse.

"Your horse is right here, m'lady." Percy motioned to a narrow, winding road leading away from town. "My castle is not far. May I help you mount?" He glanced at the cat and back to Kalial with a grin. "Perhaps you might ask your pet to stand back?" he suggested with a light tone.

The sight of the barren road ahead sent a ripple of unease up Kalial's spine. Nevertheless, she motioned at dhu Cait to step back while she reluctantly allowed Percy to assist her in mounting the palomino mare.

Lord Basingstoke stepped forward and grasped her hand. With one eye on the wildcat and one on her, he kissed her hand, then mounted his own steed. Before she could adjust her skirts, Ronin stepped up and slid her knee into the correct position. His gaze was shuttered.

"You have not used a saddle before," he murmured. "Try not to let it show. Ride behind Percy. I will follow." When Kalial said nothing, he mounted his mahogany warhorse without another word.

Percy turned to Kalial. "How is it that such an exquisite lady like you should be placed in the protection of my cousin? Certainly you have family, or perhaps a betrothed?"

Kalial looked to Ronin for assistance, but he turned his head away and gazed out over the hills. A rising sense of unease clogged her throat and she struggled to speak. "How far must we travel?" she asked, ignoring Percy's questions. The thin note of fear in her voice brought Ronin's sharp regard.

"Why, only half an hour, maybe less, m'lady. My lands are vast but the castle sits close to the ocean so that it is well situated for commerce and defense. The road is even and smooth. Do not fret, m'lady." Lord Basingstoke reached toward her and softly touched her cheek. Ronin clenched his teeth in anger, even as a sense of concern for the fear in Kalial's eyes aroused his protectiveness.

As they exited the village and rounded a curve, Percy increased the pace. Kalial rapidly became comfortable, and they cantered up the hillside, leaving the wagon behind. The horses stretched out as the road steepened. The clatter of their hooves reverberated in Kalial's ears. She bent her head and tried to calm her fears, uneasy with Lord Basingstoke's stares, Ronin's palpable anger and the unfamiliar surroundings.

Ronin slowed his horse with a disgusted grunt and looked to the sky. Overhead he saw the owl twist and turn in the wind. Watching him, Ronin became aware of the high cliff to their right. The wall was dry and crumbly and tiny bits tumbled down as they passed.

Kalial looked back uneasily, and Ronin wondered at her uncharacteristic nervousness. His nudged his horse closer just as Percy slowed to cross a bridge.

" 'Tis best if we go one at a time," Percy said. "The princess should follow directly behind me, with you a bit farther back."

Ronin's eyebrows rose, but he pulled his steed to a halt and let Lord Basingstoke direct the crossing. Kalial shifted, her lashes fluttering. The owl cried as it circled the overhanging cliff and Kalial gasped in fear. She looked back at Ronin, but his closed face prevented her from speaking.

Lord Basingstoke crossed the bridge and then motioned to Kalial. She looked behind her at the black cat and swift communication raced between them. The cat hissed and lifted her lip but sat down on her haunches. Kalial set her dainty mare in motion, and they gingerly clattered over the bridge.

Ronin held his breath, disturbed by her odd behavior. When the cat refused to cross, he squeezed his horse's flanks and started over. Another cry from the owl above startled him and he paused partway. A small rock tumbled down the cliff, bounced on the bridge and then fell into the canyon below. Ronin watched its haphazard descent as it crashed against the canyon walls and finally came to rest upon one of the many ledges that jutted from the slope.

Suddenly, a large crack resounded throughout the canyon, and the bridge supports sagged. Ronin's horse whinnied sharply as it scrambled to keep its footing.

"No!" screamed Kalial. She kicked her mare furiously, and they both surged onto the disintegrating bridge.

"Get back!" Ronin cried. "For God's sake, get back!" He jumped off the stallion and gripped a beam for support as the horse fell to its knees. The bridge shuddered again, and wood started to cascade down.

"Princess!" shouted Lord Basingstoke. "Don't be a fool! Get off the bridge. It is collapsing!"

Kalial ignored them both, sending her mare galloping across the structure. Another huge crack resounded and a cascade of dirt and pebbles began raining down on them from the cliff above. Kalial reached Ronin and leapt from her mare. Her eyes were wide with fright as she grasped frantically for Ronin.

Together they catapulted from the bridge. Ronin grasped her around the waist while twisting in midair. They hung suspended for a moment as they fell. A large ledge broke their descent, and Ronin landed heavily on his back with Kalial slamming into him on top. A high-pitched whinny sounded above him as both horses thrashed amongst the falling debris, then followed their downward path.

Ronin bent around Kalial, rolling from underneath the horses's flailing hooves. The great warhorse leapt with his hind legs to avoid crushing Ronin and Kalial. His massive body bumped the small palomino mare and she stumbled upon landing. Scrambling, she flung out her fore hooves to heave herself up and struck Ronin in the process. She lunged forward, kicking Ronin repeatedly as her long legs remained tangled in her efforts to right herself on the shaking ground.

Ronin protected Kalial, taking the multiple blows, feeling the crack of his ribs under the mare's weight. Kalial's body lay limp in his arms, unconscious from a blow to the head from one of the falling beams. The horse finally freed herself and stood a few steps away, sides heaving and her head hung low. A final cascade of falling rock, wood and debris tumbled down, then the dust hung in the air in a thick, rolling cloud.

Ronin slowly lifted himself off Kalial and groaned. He felt a piercing pain in his chest and a deep ache in his abdomen. Levering himself up, he heard the crunch of broken bones in his arm. Ignoring his injuries for the time being, he reached his other arm forward toward Kalial and put a finger to her throat to check her pulse. The strong and steady beat greatly relieved him. He looked her over but found only a rising lump on her forehead. Her beautiful dress was dusty but not torn, whereas he was covered with

scratches and bruises and his shirt was all but
shredded.

Rising painfully to his feet, Ronin stared up at the
destroyed bridge. High above him he located his
cousin, who was struggling to maintain control of his
panicking horse.

"Ronin! Princess!" Lord Basingstoke called out.

When Ronin tried to answer, he found he could not
gather the breath to shout back. He lifted one arm
and tried to signal.

"Is the princess hurt?" Percy yelled. When he heard
no response he continued. "Try to get down to the
stream bed, then travel upstream until you locate a
goat herder's path. I will go for help. Do you
understand?"

Ronin nodded halfheartedly, the pain of his injuries
making him light-headed. He motioned to his horse.
When the palomino came too, he glared at it and tried
to push it away. The mare nickered and nudged Kalial
gently with her nose.

"Go on, horse. At least let me get to her," Ronin
said, shoving at her ineffectively. The horse moved
over, stepping delicately and prettily over Kalial's out-
flung arm. Ronin grimaced. "Fine, fall on top of me
but do not so much as brush against her. Agh . . ."
he groaned as he tried to lift Kalial's limp form. A
deep rumbling in the earth beneath him gave him
added incentive and he finally lifted her. With a painful heave, he tossed her over the back of his mahogany
horse and then leaned against the animal as coughing
racked him. Ronin wrapped his arms around his rib
cage until the pain subsided. A bitter, metallic taste
in his mouth made him spit out blood. He wiped his
mouth with the back of his hand.

A soft growl of pain came from his right and Ronin
glanced at the limping cat walking toward him. She
shook herself and set a dust cloud in the air. Above,
Ronin saw the owl circling. For a split second he felt

an odd shifting in his vision, a lengthening and sharpening that was completely foreign. Then his vision cleared and he saw the owl swoop down, wings back and talons outstretched as it landed with a powerful grip upon a twisted piece of dead wood.

Drawing shallow breaths, Ronin stared at the owl, uncertain what he had seen. The crumbling of the bridge . . . as seen from above? Ronin's head throbbed and he blinked slowly. No visions, he told himself. No sights from the owl's eyes were possible for a warrior.

With waning strength, Ronin grasped some mane and clambered aboard his horse behind Kalial. Gently he drew her upright against his body. He placed one arm tightly around her and put his hand over her left breast where he could feel the steady beat of her heart. When his head began to sag against her neck, the sweet freshness of her skin acted as an elixir and he jerked awake again. A nervous whinny from behind caused him to glance around. The pale mare was prancing, the white tufts at her fetlocks dancing. Ronin's vision began to blur. The ground beneath them shifted. With a slight squeeze, he urged his warhorse down the sloping canyon to the stream bed far below.

Darkness had began to fall when they finally reached the splashing river, and Ronin sighed in relief. Struggling to remain conscious, he turned them upstream and searched for the small paths that zigzagged up the canyon walls. Dhu Cait followed, her sharp senses attuned to the surroundings, while the owl took long, slow strokes with his wings, gliding along while watching for danger with his sharp eyes.

Finally, Ronin located a clear path, and they slowly climbed up the far side. As they drew up above the rubble and headed farther inland, the Castle Basingstoke could be seen in the distance. Ronin wrapped his hand in the horse's mane, gripped Kalial tightly, and sagged forward over her body.

*   *   *

Kalial awoke to the sounds of a busy courtyard and the lights of a score of torches blazing. An oppressive heaviness weighed her down and she pushed upward. Her action caused the unconscious Ronin to slump, falling heavily from their horse and onto the courtyard stones. She gasped. Ronin was covered in blood and his arm lay at an awkward angle.

A finely dressed woman rushed forward, flanked by a pair of hearty male servants.

"Oh my!" she cried, "Oh my goodness! Oh dear . . ." She trailed off, wringing her hands in distress and regarding Kalial helplessly. "I have not a clue what to do. Percy left an hour ago to search for you two. I am Lady Basingstoke, Percy's wife. Come in, come in!" She fluttered her hands, waving at the castle doors.

Kalial regarded her in amazement. Lady Basingstoke had glossy black hair and doelike brown eyes that looked helpless and vulnerable. The tiny woman was everything Kalial was not and Kalial was momentarily stupefied.

She slid down from the horse and held her head for a moment to still its spinning. She glanced up at Lady Basingstoke. "My name is Princess Kalial. And this is Ronin McTaver, your husband's cousin." She knelt next to Ronin, certain that if she did not help him, this woman would not.

"Oh yes, I know who you are. We were warned that you might come, and we are prepared for you." Her lips curved into a smile that did not reach her eyes. "Is he dead?" she asked.

Kalial glared at the woman. "No, but he will certainly perish if we do not assist him." She turned to one of the men standing nearby. "Can you carry him to a bed?" she asked. At his nod she looked at the woman. "Can you also find a healer?"

The woman looked faintly uncomfortable, but then smiled tremulously. "You may bring him to the green room. It overlooks the valley and has a darling little solar for you to sew in. I will send up some tea and refreshments. Will that be satisfactory?"

Kalial frowned at her in annoyance, then, abashed, replied, "Yes, thank you for everything. Hot water and clean clothes would be best. I fear his arm is broken and needs to be set . . . I do not know how he managed to get us here . . ." Kalial's voice faded as she followed the servant into the castle.

They entered through a large archway. Kalial barely had time to notice the multiple armaments that graced the niches and walls. She hustled after the servants carrying Ronin as they swiftly ascended the stone staircase. It branched into a Y at the first floor. They took the right branch to the eastern section of the second floor. The left side curved to the west.

Multiple windows covered with thin animal skins pierced the walls, allowing a soft light to brighten the hall. The servants entered through the third and final door. They carried Ronin to the large bed, then stepped back and one asked, "Pardon me, m'lady, but me mother be from McInnish land, nearby to the McTaver lands. I am Ian McInnish. Our family thinks highly of the Laird McTaver, and I'm a thinking that you may want to take care of him yourself for a bit until the surgeon sobers up." He looked down at the floor, waiting for her reaction to his bold words.

Kalial looked first at him, then at Ronin. A lump filled her throat and she struggled with her thoughts, assailed by conflicting feelings. She was angry with Ronin for boxing her in the hold, frustrated that he would not bend his pride and ask for her help. She also felt other things that she couldn't name or describe. Clearly he had saved her life again, and for this she was grateful. But it wasn't gratitude that made her shudder at the thought of an incompetent doctor handling him. She resolved immediately to tend him herself, for she had often cared for the injured in Loch Nidean forest.

Just then a young maid came to the door with a pot of steaming water and strips of linen over her arm. Behind her Kalial could hear a man singing in a slurred voice. The doctor followed the maid in, finishing his song in a loud, off-key crescendo.

"Well, I am here to see to the boy. Where is the lad?" he asked, peering around the room. When he spied Ronin on the bed he frowned. "Now that man had best go somewhere else so I can use the bed for the bleeding." He turned around abruptly and looked down the hall. "Come here, you slow fool. I need that bucket of leeches for the lad! Hop to now!" He turned back to the room and twisted his lips in what appeared to be a smile.

Kalial felt the color leave her face. She quickly turned to the servant that had spoken earlier and whispered, "Please get him to leave, then procure a splint of some sort, a rope, some wet mud and then come back to help me." She hurried over to the bed and smoothed a lock of hair from Ronin's face.

Behind her she heard the servant say, "The lad be in the west wing, sir. You took a wrong turn at the stairs. This is the lady's room and you are distressing her with talk of leeches."

The quack changed his expression to one of apology and started toward Kalial. At her look of alarm, the servant stepped in front of him and motioned to the door. "I think it be quite urgent, Doctor. The mistress bade me to ask you to hurry." The doctor's face got ruddy at the mention of the mistress and he weaved his way out of the room. Kalial looked at the servant with gratitude.

"I will return in one moment, m'lady," he said to Kalial and quickly left.

Meanwhile, Kalial beckoned the maid over and together they pulled the ragged shirt from Ronin's body. With infinite care, Kalial washed him, cleansing the dirt from his many abrasions while the maid rinsed each cloth after it became soiled. While cleaning his chest, Kalial discovered the two broken ribs. She washed his upper abdomen where the imprint of a horse's hoof discolored the skin. She then wiped his face, gently moving over the scratches that ruined the perfection of his features. She leaned over and placed a chaste kiss upon his cheek, her eyes closed.

Ronin slowly roused to consciousness. He felt a soft caress against his skin and a cool touch upon his face. A delicious scent of summer flowers and honeysuckle made him take a deep breath.

Instantly, he felt a sharp pain in his chest and began to cough. Instinctively he forced himself to lighten his breathing and smother his cough but the spreading pain snaked down his shoulder to his broken arm. He opened his eyes and tried to sit up. A fresh surge of bloody froth filled his mouth and he was forced to spit it out over the side of the bed. His gaze met Kalial's frightened eyes.

He stared at her, trying to soothe her with his silence. He breathed lightly and ignored his painful arm. He pretended he did not feel his bruised and battered body. Finally he spoke to her.

"You saved me yet again, Princess."

Kalial wrinkled her brow in distress. "Not I! You are the injured one. I have not a scratch. You saved me."

"But had you not raced to my rescue, I might be dead. Please," he paused for a breath, "please accept my thanks."

Kalial laid her head against his chest and listened. She heard harsh sounds on one side, but none on the other. The lack of breath sounds terrified her. She knew that a broken rib could lacerate a lung and cause it to collapse. If the condition worsened, he could die from suffocation.

"We must bind your ribs so they do not cause more damage," she said He tried not to move as Kalial placed a tight bandage around his chest to keep the ribs stable. He felt another urge to cough, but firmly suppressed it.

Instead he concentrated on his arm. He felt it gingerly with his other hand and winced at the sensation of bones scraping against each other. His muscles were in a tight spasm around the break, making it difficult to reset the bones. Gamely, Kalial grasped his wrist and placed traction on the arm. Ronin gritted his teeth and bored his eyes into Kalial's golden depths. He relaxed his mind, letting it drift over his memories of Kalial and drawing solace from her presence. Peripherally he became aware of another person in the room. At the edge of his vision he saw a servant come forward and place a rope around his wrist with Kalial's help.

Together, Kalial and McInnish passed the rope up and over the bed canopy and slowly placed tension on the broken section of Ronin's arm. Ronin felt lightheaded with pain. His muscles strained against their efforts so he consciously relaxed them, bit by bit. As they pulled, he felt his body begin to be lifted from the bed. He sank down, assisting them by using his weight and the pull of gravity to separate the overlapping bones. Ever so slowly he felt the muscles relax their disfiguring hold and allow the reduction of the fracture. Finally, the bone ends slid past each other and then snapped end to end in clean alignment.

Immediately, Kalial placed a pair of splints on his arm and began wrapping padding around it. Roll upon roll of padding secured the splints and cushioned the break. Next Kalial applied wet mud in a thick layer around the padding, smoothing it gently as it dried to a solid firmness. At last, she lowered the arm so Ronin could lean back on the pillows. He did so with a shallow sigh of relief.

Florie appeared at the door bearing a tray of fruits and nuts.

"Florie!" Kalial cried. "How grateful I am to see you!"

"And I you, Princess. I heard what happened. The castle folk say that bridge should never have fallen. It was solidly built."

"Obviously, they were wrong. How did you make it here?"

"The wagon went another way, over a longer but safer route. But enough. How fares the McTaver?" Florie discreetly withdrew a flask of strong spirits hidden underneath a napkin. With a smile, Kalial brought it over to Ronin, who drank deeply from it. He kept his eyes on Kalial and even grinned when she eyed the fruits longingly.

"Go ahead. Eat something. Percy's kitchen is unsurpassed," he told her.

Kalial smiled hesitantly, then picked up the tray and placed it and herself on the bed next to Ronin. She stayed beside him, munching on delicious food, while he drifted off to sleep and she, Florie and Ian conversed.

"How came you to be in this household so far from home?" Kalial asked Ian as she leaned over and checked the cast. It had hardened well and she was confident that the arm would heal correctly. Listening to Ronin breathe with difficulty, however, filled her with great concern.

"I was traded, m'lady. In a card game with Lord Basingstoke. He saw me fight in the lists and decided to barter for me."

"How horrible!" Florie exclaimed. "But why are you now in the house? You should be out training."

"This house has its own rules and I do not try to

change them. For now, I am to serve the lady of the household."

"Serve the lady? What does that mean? Is that the norm?" Kalial asked. Ian only grimaced and motioned the women out of the room so as not to disturb the sleeping Ronin. He closed the door behind them.

" 'Tis my duty, m'lady, for now. However, I promise I will stay with you and guard you until Laird McTaver is better."

Just then Kalial heard several pairs of footsteps approaching. She looked up into the concerned faces of Lord and Lady Basingstoke.

"Princess! I feared greatly for you. One can not imagine my relief when the signal fires drew me home to find you safe," Lord Basingstoke exclaimed. "Why ever did you leap from the safety of solid ground and on to the bridge?"

Kalial felt her customary reluctance to speak to strangers surface with powerful awareness. She reached down for dhu Cait's reassurance until she recalled that the cat had not followed her into the castle hall. The fear she felt on the bridge threatened her again and her eyes shifted to the side, looking for an escape.

Percy watched her hesitancy and wisely backed away a few steps while opening his empty hands to wave toward the closed door. "Laird McTaver is well?" he asked while watching the wariness in Kalial's eyes turn abruptly to concern.

"No, indeed he is not. I am terribly worried about him. I seek only to verify the comfort of my beasts and then I shall return to care for him." She took a stride toward the stairs, but her feet became tangled in her cumbersome skirts and to her dismay she felt herself falling. Briefly, she saw the displeased look on Lady Basingstoke's face before she was enveloped in the arms of Lord Basingstoke.

Percy grasped Kalial's tumbling form, pulling it close to his body so he could feel the contours of her form against his. A stab of desire ripped through him as he purposely placed a hand on her backside and gripped her buttocks. Kalial struggled against him. Still off balance herself, the action only served to arch her lower body closer to his, where she had no doubt of her effect on him. A shrill laugh next to the struggling pair caused them both to freeze. Kalial suddenly found herself freed and supported only by the strong arm of Ian McInnish. In confusion, she looked around and saw Lady Basingstoke staring at her with fascination.

"My goodness," she said, "I daresay you almost flopped upon the floor!" Kalial flushed deeply, her shame at her lace of grace complete. "Wherever did you learn your deportment?" continued the lady as Kalial lifted her skirts and stumbled past the pair and down the steps. Percy watched her flight, his soft eyes now glowing with unguarded hunger. "The poor child, I shall have to teach her how to behave as it is clear she has need of feminine guidance," remarked Lady Basingstoke.

Kalial hurried from the hall and paused in the moonlit courtyard. Hearing a step behind her, she whipped around, crouching in defense. A man's form materialized from the shadows, revealing the welcome visage of Ian McInnish. Kalial sighed in relief.

"Princess?" he asked.

Kalial stood slowly upright and grimaced. "I fear I am acting like a nervous old woman," she answered the unspoken question. "I simply am not used to these grand surroundings."

"Perhaps you would feel more comfortable seeking your wild companions in the stable," he suggested. Kalial flashed a genuine smile of thanks. Ian grinned back and then led her to a side door of the nearby stables. A whicker from the pretty palomino mare was followed by a rumbling purr from the wildcat lounging on the straw. A silent exchange between Kalial to dhu

Cait revealed that the owl was out hunting. Ian watched while Kalial's delicate form, swathed in copper and white, curled into a ball next to the menacing black beast. Her tired mind slipped immediately into sleep while Ian crouched down in the doorway to keep watch.

CHAPTER 16

When rays of sunlight peeked into the stable, Kalial
sleepily rose. Sweeping up the corner of her dress, she
looped it in the copper girdle at her waist while she
swiftly cared for her animals. Then bidding dhu Cait
to wait for her, she struck out for the castle, intent on
going directly for Ronin's room.

A shocked gasp halted her midcourtyard. A maid
carrying two buckets stared at her exposed legs. Kalial
quickly pulled the skirt down and glared at the maid.
In a huff, the maid continued along her way.

Kalial tried to slow her pace as she carefully negoti-
ated the hall steps in her long skirts. From above,
Lord Basingstoke watched the tableau. He stroked
himself as he watched her golden legs slide like satin
against each other before Kalial hid them from view.
Her slow, unhurried pace caused her hips to sway enticingly and the flecks of straw in her golden hair
glinted. The heat building inside him made him turn
gruffly toward the other man in the chamber.

" 'Tis more complicated now," he said.

"Nothing is complicated. You have a duty to per-
form, or have you forgotten your debts so quickly?"
the man replied.

"The princess adds more danger," Basingstoke

grumbled as he returned to the window, seeking another glimpse of Kalial and disappointed when he did not find it.

"She is nothing, no one. Do with her what you want, but McTaver must die."

"She is lovely in a wild, untamed fashion," Basingstoke answered, not responding to the other threats.

"It would be easy for you to take advantage of her helplessness," the man answered. "You can consider deflowering her as a bonus."

Percy turned to look at the man, distaste upon his face. "I can not believe you have turned me into a man who would consider seducing his cousin's ward."

"Do not make yourself out to be so pure. 'Tis your own actions that have brought you to this pass. You alone made a deal with Lothian to erase your mounting debts. I myself would not have traded my freedom like you did. To marry the sister of such a man is humbling indeed. Whereas once you were a powerful lord, now you are nothing but a vassal to the Serpent. So, I am not interested in your sniveling comments. You have been given a duty, and I am here to make sure you complete it. In the meantime, if you are inclined to play with his morsel of a ward, I will not deter you."

Percy ran his fingers through his hair, then rubbed his closed eyes. "You should not have sabotaged the bridge. I could have been hurt."

"I have no instructions to kill you. Lothian will send word regarding McTaver once he hears that he survived the accident, and we must need be ready to do his bidding. Do the girl now, for later there may be no time."

Percy Basingstoke glared at the man. He stalked to the door and opened it forcefully. "You may be underestimating them," he warned. "We may not be able to manipulate them as easily as you think."

*   *   *

Ronin lay upon the bed, eyes dull with pain. When Kalial carefully tiptoed into the room, he sharpened his gaze to take in her appearance.

"Where were you last night?" he snapped. Kalial halted in surprise.

"Where was I?" she repeated in confusion.

"It is a simple question!" replied Ronin, although the nastiness of his voice was lost in the heavy coughing that followed.

Kalial raced forward, lifting her skirts, and leaned over him. He breathed deeply, filling his lungs with her healing scent. His anger subsided and he smiled at her.

"Are you all right?" she asked with grave concern. His deep blue eyes near to twinkling, he broadened his smile and, reaching with his unfettered hand, he slid his fingers underneath her golden curls, grasped her neck and pulled her down to him. He captured her mouth with his, nudging her lips open and tasting the freshness within. His grip tightened and he tilted her head back to reveal her neck. He leaned forward and devoured the flesh with sharp bites and hard sucks. A tiny peppering of red marks marred her complexion before he relinquished her.

Kalial stared at him, her expression revealing her surprise and delight. She leaned forward upon his chest to return his kisses until she felt Ronin's breath freeze and his body turn rigid with pain. Instantly she leapt away in horror.

"Get back here," Ronin growled, but Kalial backed away farther.

"I hurt you," she whispered.

Ronin dismissed her words. "I said get back over to me!" But Kalial shook her head. Ronin felt an overwhelming wave of pain and frustration yet he had no way of rising and pulling her back to his bed where he wanted her. A fit of coughing convulsed him and he felt the familiar taste of blood in his mouth. Spitting it out, he struggled to sit upright.

A knock on the door interrupted his efforts. Percy strode in without invitation, his eyes skimming the room and locating Kalial at the far end. He walked over to Ronin's bed with a friendly smile.

"Cousin! How do you fare this morn?" At Ronin's glare he continued undaunted. "You have traveled long to make it to my castle and you are now its privileged guest. Please let me know how I can serve you once you have recovered from your accident. In the meantime, please allow me to entertain your ward so she does not languish in the sickroom."

A stab of self-loathing at his own weakness rippled over Ronin at Percy's words and he glanced at his casted arm in disgust.

"By all means, entertain her." He ignored Kalial's gasp. "However, I must speak with you at once about the matter that originally drew me to your lands."

"Certainly, McTaver. Let me escort the lovely lady down to the great hall and I shall return presently."

"No," spoke Kalial, "I wish to be present for your discussions."

"Of course, my darling," replied Percy, "and you shall! For anything that is important to discuss. But for now you must realize that McTaver is dreadfully weak and does not need you here at all." As he spoke he pushed her from the room.

Kalial glanced back once at Ronin's shuttered face. A rising sense of disquiet filled her soul as the door to his room closed, but having nothing to base it upon, she meekly allowed Percy to lead her down to the hall where breakfast was being served.

Ronin's eyes focused on the closed door in frustration. The ache in his chest made each breath torture. His arm throbbed. Recalling the sweet touch of Kalial's breath across his face caused other parts to ache in unison and he growled just as the door opened again. Expecting Kalial, he tried to sit up.

"Ho there, cousin, sit easy, no need for formality," Percy said. "Your little lass is below filling her empty belly and I have come to see to your needs. Tell me what occurred. I have heard rumors but no one has traveled this far with solid information."

"The clans of McInnish, McGregor, Dougal, Evan, and McTaver were decimated by an army organized by a man they now call the Serpent, whom we both know as Lothian. He and his mercenaries would sooner slit your gut than ask your name. Under the cover of friends they swarmed our castle and killed every warrior, woman and child they could. Even our hounds felt their blades. The massacre was devastating."

"Your father, Robert?"

"He perished while giving the sign of surrender to save the rest of the family," answered Ronin. "I can not describe the viciousness of their assault." His blue eyes darkened, turning into an angry storm laden with black clouds, and although he lay supine upon the bed, his anger was such that Percy took a half step back. "To be blunt, I have need of an army to take back my lands," Ronin concluded.

Lord Basingstoke chose his words carefully. " 'Tis a lot you ask, my cousin. An army would have to travel over the mountains and around the forest of Loch Nidean. 'Twould take months."

"The forest is severely damaged. The men I spoke of burned the southern aspect to the ground. Yet now that land is open and can be traversed in half the time," answered Ronin.

Shaking his head, Percy replied, "It does not matter. Leafy trees or burned crags, the land is forbidden, and my men will not enter it. The legends are too strong, the land too fearsome for warriors to cross."

"I have the key to unlocking their fear," stated Ronin, his voice rough. "The princess is their leader."

Percy's mind raced, thinking of his brother-in-law, Lothian, and speculating about the golden woman. Finally, he asked, "What will you do with the fair princess while you wage this war?"

"She comes with me," answered Ronin emphatically, surprising himself if not Percy.

Lord Basingstoke turned away, hiding his expression as he looked out the window to the courtyard below. "Of course she would be safer far away from the conflict," he said, but the silence behind him gave him his answer. Thinking again of her silky flesh, Percy debated his options. It was a gamble . . . but there might be ways to satisfy everyone. "I must think on the matter, McTaver," he finally stated as he turned back to face his cousin.

Ronin nodded. It was only what he could expect.

Belowstairs several days later, Kalial felt the stifling attentions of Lady Basingstoke as she continued her mission to teach Kalial the ways of a lady. Florie sat nearby, offering smiles of encouragement when Kalial appeared ready to bolt back to Ronin's room, where he still lay, slipping in and out of consciousness.

"My darling, you walk far too boldly. You must slow your steps, allow the silk of your gown to sway with your dainty movements." Lady Basingstoke winced as Kalial abruptly turned toward a commotion at the door. "No, my dear, tilt your head just so if you wish to see something. By heavens, do not twist your body so forcefully!"

Percy, from the other side of the room, saw the graceful turn and felt a renewed yearning at the supple strength exhibited by her movements. Striding over to her, his rich clothes gleaming, he took her hand and turned it palm up to place a kiss upon its calloused surface. "Does something concern you?" he questioned.

She pulled her hand out of his grasp. "I wish to return to Laird McTaver, but your wife has detained

me. Please explain to her that I must tend to him."
Her voice was imperious as she sought to find the
strength to go against the rules of the castle mistress.

"Ahh, my dear Princess, perhaps my wife simply
longs for your company. You are forbidden nothing
in my castle. 'Tis just that the laird is resting and 'tis
best to leave him for a while. You do understand, do
you not? Surely the seriousness of his wounds concerns you?" He smiled as he saw the uncertainty steal
over her yellow eyes. "However, if you insist . . ." He
allowed his voice to trail off as he made to walk
toward the stairs.

"No, of course not. I was not thinking clearly. He
must rest." Kalial dropped her tired eyes while twin
spots of color dotted her cheeks before they faded to
paleness. Suddenly she looked up again, this time her
gaze strong and direct. "However, while he is indis-
posed, I must be certain that his major goal is accomplished."

Percy's eyebrows rose a fraction. "Yes?" he said
warily.

"We are here to procure an army," stated Kalial,
"and I must know what you need to get started with
the arrangements."

Lord Basingstoke's salacious grin was hidden
quickly behind a raised hand. "I am most surprised
that you are privy to these thoughts, my dear. You
need not worry about arrangements. The laird and I
will handle them."

Sensing the evasion, Kalial responded tartly, "If you
do not intend to help, then I must leave now to find
others who will." She turned and strode out the door,
swishing past the messenger who stood there, watching
her with unconcealed interest.

Percy was frozen for a moment. Then he sprang
forward, catching up to her in several strides. Reaching her in the courtyard, he grasped her hand and

swung her around to face him. With all the earnest sincerity he could manage, he drew her close to him.

"Your Highness, I apologize for insulting you. Of course my men are at your disposal. I am simply not used to talking with women about such matters. I see that I am mistaken about you. Tell me what I can do to help and I will." An odd note entered his voice, one Percy was surprised to hear. It sounded suspiciously like pleading. Clearing his throat, he finished, "I will grant the laird sixty men to train and return to me when he is done, and to you I will gift ten as a token of my desire that you remain for a time."

"I take no gifts," Kalial replied impatiently.

"Then stay ten weeks, one for each man, and grant me your companionship while the laird heals and the army trains. Is that not a fair trade?"

"And if your men do not want to leave your land?" she asked.

"Then choose the men yourself, asking if they care to follow you. However, I will seek to guide your choices as I wish to be assured of your safety when you travel across the mountains. My cousin is not always kind to ladies. The protection of your own warriors will ensure that he does not take advantage of you in the cold night."

At the mention of Ronin's name, Kalial looked up toward his window. Thinking she saw a face there, she yanked her hand away from Percy's and stepped away. Forgetting Lord Basingstoke, she turned to reenter the castle doors, but Percy caught her hand and pulled her back to him onto the castle steps.

"Do we have a deal, Your Highness?"

Kalial looked at him briefly before glancing back up at the window. "I believe Laird McTaver is awake. I will see him now," she stated and tried to pull away.

"But we must confirm our arrangement or I am not

sure I will feel so generous later. Do we have a deal?" he questioned persistently.

"Yes," she answered with an air of distraction. "Thank you. I will go tell the laird now."

"Indeed," Percy replied. "Then all deals must be sworn and sealed." He pulled her close and placed a wet kiss upon her lips. Kalial felt a ripple of revulsion. In an effort not to slam her fist into his gut, she remained still before whipping her hand out of his and heading up to Ronin's room.

Ronin saw the exchange below and doubled over coughing as his breath hissed out between his teeth. Staggering back against the wall, he clenched his middle with his free hand. Just as he was able to take a solid breath, the door to his room opened and Kalial swept in, skirts held high.

Her heart arrested at the sight of Ronin huddled against the wall, face drawn in pain. Immediately she rushed forward, amber eyes filled with tears of concern. At her look, Ronin straightened and flashed fury-filled eyes at her.

"Ronin, why are you out of bed? You should be resting and getting well."

"You expect me to sit under the bedcovers while you flounce around playing with any fool that you chance upon, is that it?" he lashed out at her, fierce anger making his eyes nearly as black as his disheveled midnight hair. His broad chest was bare and a small trail of black hair snaked underneath his breeches, making patterns over the heavily bruised and damaged skin.

Kalial quailed as he pushed himself away from the wall and advanced upon her. Reaching a chair, he braced himself against its back and glared at her. "What were you and Lord Basingstoke discussing?" he snapped.

She smiled then, glad of the news she could give him. "He has promised you sixty men and me ten."

"In exchange for what?" he demanded, his voice almost breaking into a cough before he willed it away. Kalial looked down guiltily, making Ronin snarl. He saw her blushes as a sign of her capitulation to his cousin's charm. Although he did not understand his fury, he made no attempt to confine or conceal it.

"We are to stay here for ten weeks in order to train the men," she answered, avoiding his eyes. A burst of swearing from Ronin caused her to look up in alarm. He bent over, racking his lungs, fury with her vying with his own frustration at his weakness.

"You are to stay away from Lord Basingstoke!" he commanded.

Although she always tried to avoid Percy, Kalial felt her back stiffen at the order. "I will do as I please," she answered. "I intend to train with the men. I must learn what my people will need to know to protect Loch Nidean in the future."

"Absolutely not," thundered Ronin. "You will not let his lecherous hands touch you!"

"I am not yours to command!" Kalial yelled back, her own eyes brightening with emotion. The flecks of gold in them stood out in high relief, making the orbs glitter with uncommon beauty. Distracted, Ronin watched them in fascination. When he did not reply, Kalial licked her lips nervously, drawing Ronin's eyes down to their lush pinkness.

"You will do as I say," he finally stated in a deceptively calm voice.

"No," replied Kalial, her head held high. "I can not be like that woman in the hall whose every thought is dictated by her husband. I must do as I wish. You must understand that. If you do not, you do not understand anything about me at all."

Wearily, Ronin sank into the chair he had been leaning against. "I do *not* understand you. But you will undoubtedly get in less trouble on the fighting fields than in this accursed castle. You must promise to stand clear of my cousin's attentions. Will you do that, Princess?"

Kalial's anger faded at the sight of his pale face. Anger between them did not burn so hotly anymore. It was tempered by caring. Although misunderstandings and confusions separated them physically, their emotions pulled them closer. Kalial felt warm near him . . . her heart open and soft.

Despite his grumblings and gruffness, Ronin longed for her calming presence, He did not want to argue with her anymore. He wanted to understand her, to comprehend her complexities. He wanted and needed her. He was possessive of her.

"Yes, Ronin," she said, tenderness in her heart. "I will be careful of Percy. Will you rest now?" she asked as she carefully approached to lay her hand across his brow. Feeling the sweat there, she came around him and stroked his face from behind, easing the tension in the muscles. She continued to soothe him, and Ronin let her, indulging himself in the feel of her strong hands and sensual scent. He closed his eyes and felt a peculiar feeling of trust fill his heart. Under its influence, he lay back in bed and drifted into a healing sleep.

Ronin woke the next morning feeling a minuscule lifting of the heaviness filling his chest. Experimentally he tried to draw in a deeper breath, but the effort caused his lungs to heave in protest and he doubled over in a thick, blood-tinged cough. Disgusted with his weakness, he sank back against the headboard. His mind skimmed over the past, resting briefly on the faces of his mother and father before flashing to the picture of his baby sister perishing in the climax of the siege. Wave after wave of anger pulsed through him, boiling within his heart. He recalled the verdant hills of his home and compared them to the blackened, decimated rubble of his castle as it now stood. Sickness filled his heart until naught but the determination to avenge their deaths and reclaim his land consumed him. Peripherally, he knew that he was feverish and irrational. But within his thoughts he surged on, imagining, contemplating, planning a counterattack that would annihilate the Serpent.

Above his thrashing, unconscious form stood Percy Basingstoke and the messenger of yesterday. "He will undoubtedly die. His internal injuries are too severe," said Percy.

"But you must be certain, my lord. Finish him now so I may bring word of his death to Lothian."

Ronin sat up abruptly, fixing a malevolent, glassy blue gaze at the distant wall where the man stood. He scurried back, removing himself from Ronin's feverish gaze, and giggled nervously.

"I can not simply kill him, you fool," Percy protested. "Too many people would know of my treachery. A wise commander helps the weak hurt themselves." Percy's voice dripped with sarcasm. " 'Tis a tactic your master wields well, just as he used my own weakness against me. We will let my cousin sink further into his fever and he will perish soon. You have my word." Percy spoke quietly, regret clouding his voice.

"And what of the woman with him? She tends him too carefully. She may yet save his worthless hide."

"I will keep her busy. She will not come back into this room. None save me shall tend him. I will insist 'tis his wish. Now, you must leave and send my message back to the Serpent." Percy swung around and stared at the little man with distaste. "You do remember my demands for assistance in this matter? I want my lands back in my name again and the gambling papers that he holds returned to me as well."

"Of course, my lord," the other man whined, "I am to be utterly trusted. Your words are carved into my head and will not leave my lips until I sit before my master."

"Very well," answered Percy as he quit Ronin's chamber. "Then trust in me as well." The messenger looked at him askance. Lord Basingstoke returned the little man's gaze with a superior smile, then walked leisurely down the stairs to the great hall.

As he moved into the sunlit room, he spied Kalial sitting with Lady Basingstoke. Kalial's exquisitely golden face was wrinkled in a frown of annoyance as Lady Basingstoke attempted to show her the intricacies of embroidery.

"My darling," she purred, "you must, simply must, try again. No lady can go to a husband without skills!"

Kalial sprang up in anger. "I have no need for your useless skills, nor do I have need of a useless husband who would require them of me! We are wasting time! I can not stand withering away in these dank walls one more minute." Feeling contrite at the stricken expression on the lady's face, she added, "So please excuse me, my lady." As she spun away, Lord Basingstoke stepped in front of her.

"Your Highness," he began, "pray, a moment of your time. The men you requested are available for your inspection. Do you care to see them now?" Kalial paused. She glanced up at the stairs toward Ronin's room. Seeing her glance, he added, "My cousin is sleeping now. He wishes to remain undisturbed." Kalial's brows knit together in concern, but she turned away from the stairs and strode outside in front of Percy. Her gown swirled about her ankles and a tendril of her hair escaped its braid.

"Very well," she called over her shoulder, catching his appreciative gaze before he was able to mask it. "I will see my new warriors now." Under her breath, she added, "For I have no wish to remain here for a nightfall longer than necessary."

Stepping outside, Kalial saw a crew of young men, many with cheeks as yet unshorn. Spinning back toward Lord Basingstoke, she exclaimed, "What is this? These boys are not the army that Laird McTaver seeks! They are barely as old as I. We need warriors, not children." She glared at Percy in fury. "Explain this band of boys to your cousin and see how he appreciates your generosity!"

"Your Highness, you wound me. I have given you the most promising of my newly trained young men. 'Tis true they are not seasoned warriors, but have some pity, I cannot give away all of my knights and leave my village, my lands, my wife unprotected. Surely you comprehend that. And verily, do you not have faith in your laird that he will train these young soldiers to be warriors? Methinks he would be sorely wounded to see your lack of faith in his abilities."

Kalial looked at him with confusion. 'Twas true that she knew nothing of the ways of these open-land warriors; she only knew the rules of her precious Loch Nidean. In her home, the giving of skilled trackers was valued over untried youngsters, but perhaps in this world it was not so. Perhaps Ronin would be insulted by her remarks. Feeling foolish, she shuffled her toe in the dirt.

Ian McInnish, the house servant who shadowed her movements, coughed discreetly. When Kalial looked up in question, he stepped forward and addressed Lord Basingstoke. "I would be pleased to offer my services to the princess. Perhaps she would feel more comfortable with an old, spent warrior like me guiding these youths while Laird McTaver recuperates."

Percy drew his eyebrows together and opened his mouth to reprimand the man, but Kalial's beautiful smile stayed his voice. "Yes! Please! I would feel so much more secure, my lord. I know not of these things, being not of your lands. Surely your beneficence will extend to granting McTaver a man from his own homeland?" Kalial's head tilted slightly and the soft, pleading look in her eyes melted Percy's heart. He nodded without thinking, then more firmly when

Kalial laughed with delight. "My undying gratitude, my lord."

"Then you must return to the hall, Your Highness, where we can finish our discussion. The Lady Basingstoke stated that some clothes have been sewn for your pleasure."

Kalial looked down at her white and copper dress in surprise. "Are these not appropriate?" she asked.

Percy laughed. "Ah, a lady should have many dresses. Dinner is soon. Would you like a bath?"

Kalial looked askance and shuddered when he placed a hand at her back. To her consternation, she stumbled in her long skirts when she tried to move aside, whereupon Lord Basingstoke grasped her elbow. With a slight jerk, she removed herself from his hold. Percy's eyes narrowed in annoyance, but he did not move to retake her arm.

Once in the hall, Lady Basingstoke swept forward with a nervous twitter. "My dear, my darling. Come, let us finish—"

"No," Kalial interrupted. "Ronin needs my attention. When you see Florie, could you please have her bring some broth to his room? It is all I can get him to eat, and he is weakening. I must seek some special herbs to help him."

"That is not necessary, Your Highness," Lady Basingstoke replied. "Our surgeon will give him what medicines he needs to relieve the pain. Just now he made some onion crushed in honey and ale. 'Twill certainly help."

"He needs no more of that man's cures, for they have done nothing." Kalial turned to Ian McInnish, who was almost always at her side. "Will you see to it that broth is brought? I will return by nightfall with what I can find."

"Aye," Ian replied and nodded as Kalial left the castle.

She strode quickly to the stable and located dhu

Cait lounging in the rafters. "Come, my friend, we must search the countryside. You will be pleased to get out of these tight confines, will you not?" The cat yawned and leapt down, then rubbed her whiskered cheek against Kalial's leg. "I thought so," Kalial replied.

Soon, they had left the courtyard and climbed the nearby hills. Kalial walked slowly, examining the ground for plants she recognized. Many were unfamiliar to her, but as the landscape became more wooded, she started noticing familiar flora. Small plants with white flowers and dark green leaves caught her attention.

"*Biadh nan coinean,* bird's foot," she murmured and dhu Cait leaned down to smell the plant. " 'Twill reduce his fever, though he will not like the taste." She continued, her eyes scanning carefully. She came across a bed of thistles, and though she marked the spot in case she had need of their properties later, she left the purple flowers for they would not ease Ronin's ailments.

She stared into the woods, looking for true maidenhair. The slender, brown stems edged with long, fan-shaped fronds grew in abundance and she collected enough to make both a tea to relieve his cough and a poultice to cleanse his wounds. She also gathered several fragrant flowers, both to sweeten the remedies and to brighten his sickroom.

Feeling much better after her sojourn, Kalial returned to the castle. Dhu Cait stopped at the edge of the courtyard and twitched her tail.

"I am certain you would prefer to stay out in the woods. Have no fear for me. I will be well." The McCat looked at her, unconvinced, but padded away, leaving Kalial alone. Kalial watched the dark beast disappear into the trees, torn between longing to join her and her concern for Ronin. "Stay near," she called out. "I may have need of you."

The cat's quiet assent reached Kalial's mind, and she sighed with relief. Turning to the castle with resolve, Kalial walked the remaining steps and entered through the massive doors.

"Princess," Percy called out. "We worried for you."

"There was no need. I went walking."

"Heaven!" cried Lady Basingstoke. "No lady should meander alone like that. You poor dear, you need to learn so much." Her voice dropped. "I heard that Laird McTaver bemoaned your lack of femininity."

Kalial bit her lip, the comment hurting her because she knew it to be true. "Ronin should accept that I am not like other women."

"Should he? Why? Should you not try to behave as you ought to instead?"

Kalial frowned, uncertain. "I am trying," she murmured. "I am wearing this . . . this dress and . . ."

"Of course you are, darling. Are those flowers for him? Really now, they are not very attractive. He would not be impressed." Lady Basingstoke smiled cruelly, pleased to see the stricken look on Kalial's face.

Florie stepped out of the kitchen in time to hear the lady's last remark. "Princess?" she asked softly. Kalial shifted her gaze, her eyes filling with tears. Florie gasped and reached out to her, but Kalial fled her comfort and raced up the stairs to Ronin's room.

She flung the door open and ran to Ronin's bedside. Sobbing, she buried her head in the linens and vented her grief. "Ronin! Ronin, I do not understand this world!" When he did not respond, she lifted her face and stared at him, noting the feverish cast to his skin and the lines of sweat dripping down his forehead. "Here I am, arguing with a silly woman while you are ill." She stood up and regarded the flowers and ferns in her hand.

A knock on the door surprised her and she stared

at the door as it opened. Florie's face peeked around the jam. "Can I come in?" she asked.

Kalial wiped her tears and nodded. "Of course. Come, bring that broth in your hand and put in near the fire. I need to prepare some medicines."

"Do not allow that lady to distress you, Your Highness. She sees nothing but what she was raised to see. You are different and that is a blessing."

"It is nothing, Florie. But I would like to prove her wrong."

"We will, we will. Let us focus on the laird now, and then we will show her how beautiful and graceful you can be!"

Kalial smiled gratefully. Then, with Florie's help, she prepared her herbal concoctions.

CHAPTER 17

The next morning Ronin woke, his mind clear. He glanced over at Kalial slumped on a chair, her usually glowing face pale with fatigue. He took a steadying breath and found that the constant tightness in his chest was less noticeable. He licked his lips, tasting a bitterness in his mouth.

"Water?" he croaked, then cleared his throat and repeated, "Water?"

Kalial's eyes sprang open and she sat up so quickly she seemed to sway. As she picked up a pitcher of water, Ronin frowned. "When did you eat last?" he asked her.

"I do not remember," she answered truthfully. "But I am pleased to see you awake. How do you feel?"

"Thirsty. And queasy," he replied.

" 'Tis probably the herbs. You should drink some broth. 'Twill settle your stomach to have some food in it to absorb the toxins. I was fearful for you."

Ronin smiled up at her, a warm glow filling him at her obvious tenderness. He slowly sat up, intending to pull her close, when Percy walked in.

Kalial brought the broth over as Percy spoke to Ronin. "I see you have managed to fight the fever, cousin. You are a strong man."

Ronin grimaced. "I feel weak as a babe."

Percy watched as Kalial spooned the broth into Ronin's mouth. Her dress conformed enticingly to her buttocks as she leaned over, and Percy licked his lips. Striving to mask his desire, he withdrew a set of knucklebones.

"Care to play, cousin?"

"I have little energy for gambling, Percy."

"Tsk, it takes nothing to play a few hands. Come, let's try."

Kalial looked up curiously. "What is that?" she asked, staring at the pig bones in Percy's hand.

"Knucklebones," he said. "Have you never played?" When Kalial shook her head, Percy drew up a chair and eagerly explained it to her. "You take the bones in the palm of your hand, flick them into the air, and then catch as many as possible with the same hand."

Kalial stood up and moved away from the men. "I will leave you to your games, for it is not something I am familiar with."

Ronin frowned at her discomfort. "Did you not play games as a child, Kalial? What a serious little girl you must have been."

She turned away with a shrug, collected her wilted herbs and exited the room, leaving the men to their gambling. Ronin remained frowning as she closed the door. "Percy," he said as his cousin threw the bones, "she is overly tired."

"Indeed," Lord Basingstoke replied absently, engrossed in the game. "She tends you at all hours. My wife says it is not good for her constitution."

"Really? Perhaps she should take a different room while I recuperate."

"She will refuse. She is an obstinate thing."

"Tell her I wish it."

Percy finally looked up, arrested. "She will be angered if you banish her from your room."

Ronin nodded slowly. "I would rather she be angry and healthy, than ill and in my company."

"I will arrange it," Percy replied. "I know of a perfect room."

That evening at dinner, Kalial rose restlessly from her untouched trencher. " 'Tis time I checked on Ronin," she said, motioning to Florie.

"Perhaps you should retire to your own room and rest," Percy answered.

"No," replied Kalial, "I have no need of a new chamber, although I thank you for your hospitality. I am needed in Ronin's room."

Percy developed a pained expression before answering her. "I have tried not to hurt your tender feelings, Your Highness, but perhaps I must be blunt. McTaver has expressly requested that you do not tend to him. He stated that your presence . . . well, he stated that it greatly displeases him and he would prefer if you were kept out of his way. He indicated that he was irritated by having to watch over you but had done so out of duty. He feels that while he is suffering pain he should not be made to suffer your person as well."

Kalial stared at Percy in shock. She started to tremble and her breath caught in her throat. Raising a hand to her cheek, she stepped backward, stumbling, until the back of her knees hit the edge of the bench. Lord Basingstoke watched with hooded eyes, taking in the pain-filled expression on her face with only a twinge of guilt.

Florie, her ample skirts swaying, rushed over to Kalial from across the room. "My goodness, what is with ye, my lass? You are white as a sheet and shaking too. What did ye just hear?" She looked at Lord Basingstoke accusingly, but he kept silent as he watched Kalial shake her head.

"Nothing, Florie. Nothing of any matter. I am . . . I am changing rooms . . . so that I may have more privacy and . . . you may sleep with me for I fear I yearn for your comfort." Kalial closed her eyes briefly, and when she opened them again, the bright amber color was dulled with pain.

Percy beckoned a servant forward and leaned down to whisper instructions to her. The maid bobbed her head and nervously moved toward the staircase, looking back to ensure that Kalial followed.

Kalial sighed when at last they entered the room reserved for them. It was located far away from the side of the castle that McTaver inhabited. The walls appeared thicker, more solid than in the other room, and a woven grass mat blanketed the floor, muffling their footsteps. Heavy tapestries graced the walls, keeping the room warm if a bit stuffy. The place where a window used to be was boarded over with a lovely flat carving of a woman in repose. When Kalial went to investigate it, she discovered that the carving was, in fact, several strips of wood hanging against each other like vertical slats. Emotionally exhausted, Kalial curled up on a sheepskin covered bench, closed her eyes, tucked her chin into her chest, and rested.

The housemaid placed an armful of wood next to the fire, then stoked it up so that it blazed. "That is quite enough, lass!" Florie exclaimed. " 'Tis warm as the midday sun in summer in here already. No need for more." She fanned herself with the back of her hand. "Leave the door open so we can get a bit of a breeze in here, if'n you don' mind."

Kalial looked up. "No," she said softly. "Please close it. I have need for solitude."

"But you don' like to be cooped up, m'lady. You like the fresh wind and the sounds of the trees. Let us ask for another room where we can see the moon and stars tonight."

Again Kalial's voice came to Florie, soft and quiet. "No," she said, "I have no desire to move again. This room will be fine. And you misread me. I have lived in dense foliage all my life. I find the warmth and closeness comforting."

The housemaid smiled in relief. "Yes, Your Highness. The master has requested a special toddy for you and I will return with it shortly?" Her voice ended in a question whereupon Kalial simply mumbled a reply. At Florie's shrug, the maid left, closing the exquisitely carved door behind her with a soft thud.

Florie shivered, despite the warmth. Opening a corner wardrobe, she discovered a wealth of satin and silk garments, delicately fashioned with bead and jewels. "M'lady, will you look at this!"

Kalial remained silent, holding her knees to her chest.

Florie frowned, then looked up when she heard a firm knock at the door. She pushed the door open with no small amount of effort. Lord Basingstoke stood on the threshold.

"Your Highness? May I come in?"

Kalial looked up finally, took a breath and stood up. Her golden hair hung with thick, heavy curls down to her waist. Percy spied the bed behind her and fought to control a wave of lust. He leaned against the door and crossed his legs. When Kalial said nothing, he jerked his head toward the wardrobe that Florie had opened.

"Please feel free to use the clothing my wife has provided for you."

" 'Tis a fortune in clothes, m'lord!" Florie cried.

Lord Basingstoke kept his gaze trained on Kalial. "I can understand your hurt feelings," he said, "and I will be sure to let Laird McTaver know that you are too beset to meet him for an after dinner repast." He smiled inwardly at the flare of anger in Kalial's eyes. "Perhaps he will take pity on you and allow you to visit," he ended.

"Absolutely not!" Kalial fairly shouted. She sprang into action, racing to the wardrobe and hastily shifting through the offerings. "I will be down shortly. You have no need to disturb the laird. I was simply pining because I was hungry. I would be ever so pleased to join you and your wife shortly."

"Wonderful," purred Percy. "I am so pleased that I misunderstood your behaviors. May I suggest the red silk gown?"

Kalial glanced over her shoulder. "I think not," she answered, missing the flare of annoyance on Percy's face. "Now please, close the door and I will see you down in the hall. And if you could, would you see about my bath? I have a need to be refreshed." She turned away, oblivious to the angry flash in his eyes before he masked it and nodded at her back in mock subservience.

"Most certainly, Your Highness. I look forward to seeing you fully." He grinned and turned away just as the maid reentered with the hot toddy. Lord Basingstoke leaned down and smelled it, a secret smile on his lips, then nodded to the maid. She placed it on a small end table, then the two of them left, pulling the massive door shut behind them.

Kalial grimaced at the closed door. "He irritates me, Florie."

"Oh yes, m'lady, I agree. Perhaps we should approach Laird McTaver—"

"No. I forbid it, Florie. You'll not speak with him about me at all, no matter what, do you understand?" Florie looked frankly disagreeable so Kalial rounded on her. "You have joined to help me. I need you to act as my assistant, teach me how to behave in this strange world. What I do not need is an interfering woman who does not know where her loyalty lies. If you do not care to remain at my side, then leave."

Florie's eyes widened, but her voice was tart when she replied, "You canna scare me with antics like that, little lass. There is no way you're gonna get these ample buns out of the door without my say-so. Now you don' wanna elicit the laird's help, so be it. But I shan't leave ya all alone in the godforsaken place. Let me help you pick out somethin' suitable to wear."

Kalial looked at Florie, then folded her in an embrace. Florie held her slight frame, feeling her shoulders shake with a mixture of tears and laughter. When Kalial pulled away, though, her eyes were dry and there was only a small, wistful smile on her face.

As they were sorting through the clothing, a tub was brought to the room and filled with steaming water. While sipping the toddy, Kalial sank into the depths. The warmth of the room and the heat of the water made her eyelids feel languid. She barely heard the knock on the door and the message that drew Florie away to the kitchens to help with last-minute preparations.

Kalial picked up her arms and watched the water skate down her fingers to the point of her elbow before running off in a stream. She breathed in deeply and smelled the honey and jasmine scent that Florie had dripped into the water before she left and smiled a rich, deeply sensual smile. She breathed again and the water encircling her breasts dropped lower so that the tips of her apricot nipples peeked out before sinking down again. Kalial looked down in curiosity. She felt oddly light-headed. A tingling was spreading through her body and her eyes were clouding over. Experimentally, she brushed a fingertip down her breast and touched her nipple. A flash of fire seared her at the intimate touch and the image of a black haired, angry man with blazing blue eyes danced before her vision. She touched herself again, imagining Ronin's hand, Ronin's touch.

Percy almost groaned aloud before he caught himself. He bit his lip while ramming his hand down his breeches. Pressing hard against the cold stone, he tried to focus on Kalial through his tiny viewing hole, but the steam from the bath clouded his vision. He watched as Kalial slowly stood, her oil-slick skin shimmering in the firelight. She stepped out of the tub with her back to him, and he saw only a glimpse of honey-colored hair between her thighs before she stood with both feet on the rushes. He saw her wiggle her toes, then bend over to feel the softness of the woven reeds.

Unable to contain his groan this time, Percy saw her bend over, her creamy golden buttocks lifted in the air. Clutching himself tighter, he imagined grabbing her from behind and plunging into her sweet tightness. A grim look tightened his face as he vowed to take her thus, right now. Slipping out of his concealed place, he stepped into the hallway and toward Kalial's door.

Kalial stood back up and walked over to the bed. Her breasts were heavy and the tingling still fluttered about her nipples. She stumbled slightly, feeling out of control of her body. Her hip knocked into the end table and the scant remains of the hot toddy splashed to the floor. Unaware, Kalial reached for the purple silk dress Florie had selected but frowned at the complex ties that crisscrossed in front and back. She sank down onto the mattress and lay her head down. Again the image of Ronin swam over her eyes and her body arched upward in unconscious response.

Her head began to toss, sending golden curls flying about her head. She opened her mouth, panting small breaths. Her lips felt dry so she licked them and then touched them with her wet fingers. An uncontrollable shivering began to swamp her body and her thighs generated so much heat that they fell open to lessen the rough contact.

A knock faintly penetrated her mind and she slowly slid her sleepy golden eyes toward the door. A husky laugh broke from her throat. With a gasp, she rolled over face down on the bed to smother the uncontrollable giggles. She heard another knock but her only response was a low groan. She gripped the satin coverlet and bunched it between her thighs, reveling in the cool slipperiness against her heated skin.

Suddenly she felt a presence beside her and she instinctively arched up toward it. She became aware of a man's harsh breathing near her, but the sound stirred her inner fantasies and she closed her eyes and smiled. A hand reached out and caressed her cheek, then slid down and ran down the side of her bouncing breast. Kalial cried out at the touch, her skin almost unbearably sensitive. She shrank away yet still arched her body closer. Lazily opening her eyes, she tried to focus on the relentlessly blue eyes of her memory. A flash of sensual pain ripped up her body and she cried out, begging for relief. The foggy shape of the man left for a moment, and she saw it pick up her toddy cup and twirl it to see how much she had partaken. In an agony of desire, she thrashed on the bed, her figure wantonly displayed and desperate for sexual appeasement.

The hazy figure returned to the bed, looking down at Kalial with a grim expression. With one arm he grasped her ankle and pulled her to the edge of the bed. Pushing her face back down so that she could not see him, he grasped her around the waist and lifted it level with his. Kalial tossed her head back, flinging her hair over her back, concealing the shadowed line between her buttocks and the glistening center below. With a growl, the man shook her, forcing the golden tendrils to slide onto either side of her waist, revealing the depths of her hidden delights. With one plunge, he sank his massive cock into her warmth, glorying in the shriek that filled the room at his abrupt entrance.

Kalial rose up on her arms, accepting, welcoming the beast who was taking her. She wriggled and arched, pulling at the bedcovers, destroying the coverlet and flinging the pillows onto the floor. The man behind her breathed slowly, trying to maintain control, never allowing her body to escape his hold. He bucked his hips, pushing in before sliding out. Kalial stilled, feeling the tingling she could not understand begin to center on the velvet caress within her. Taking advantage of the pause, the man repeated his strokes, closing his eyes at the sheer pleasure of the tight, wet passage. A low moan came from Kalial as she sank back down on the rumpled bed, her body pliant and accepting.

Overcome by urgency now, the man thrust into her harder, faster . . . watching her writhe and twist to match his rhythm. She cried out louder, moaning and panting until he felt her internal muscles begin to clench and spasm. The man's control slipped for a moment, and he leaned over her, pressing his face into the jasmine scented skin of her neck. He felt his seed rip out of his soul, drenching her insides with his essence. Kalial screamed, gripping him so tightly he could not leave even had he wanted to. She gasped and shook, her golden body suffused with a rosy glow as she shouted out Ronin's name in her ecstasy.

The man above her jerked upward at the sound. He pulled away from her abruptly, while shoving her face down into the covers. Weak and drained, Kalial lay submissively, not trying to move. The man pulled his breaches up, grabbed the rest of the toddy and dashed it into the fire, then quit the room. Struggling to breathe, he leaned against the closed door in the darkened hallway. He felt an ache, an ache that could not match the one in his arm or the one in his broken ribs. It was an ache of joy, of triumph deep in his heart, yet it was tempered by a newfound fear. With the wonderful feeling of possessing her came the awesome responsibility of caring for her. Suddenly, her safety, her desires, her needs were more important than his own. His heart was hers.

Ian McInnish joined Ronin in the darkened hallway. He regarded Ronin's sweat-drenched face with concern. "Laird?"

Ronin raised haunted eyes to Ian's. "She rests now," he answered.

Ian looked at the closed door worriedly. "I heard her scream," he stated.

"Yes, but trust me, she needed release. Her breath smelled of poppies and mullein root. I had to help her."

Ian nodded quickly. "Thank God it was you, m'laird. She is not the first female in this castle to be drawn toward ravishment with such an aphrodisiac."

Ronin's eyes slowly turned from a glowing blue to a raging, pulsing near black. "What has happened to my cousin that he sinks so low?"

"He has a sickness, a madness he cannot control. Lord Basingstoke gambles . . ."

"Yes," interrupted Ronin, "he has always gambled."

"This time he lost everything—his lands, his castle, his freedom—and now he owes all to his brother-in-law, Lothian the Serpent."

Ronin looked at him in horror. "You can not be speaking the truth."

"Aye. You fled the Serpent's arm only to race into his deadliest embrace."

"These lands are as much Percy's lifeblood as mine are to me. How could he have gambled them away?"

" 'Tis an illness he is trying to battle. He had to wed Lothian's sister in order to stay in his own home. Lord Basingstoke has given up everything, including his pride, because of his addiction to gambling."

"Has he lost his familial honor?" Ronin stared up at the ceiling for a moment. "The Percy I knew would not abandon his blood."

"He is not the same person, Laird. You must act with great caution."

"We must leave. We must leave this castle before harm befalls the princess." He took a quick breath and pounded the wall behind him. Suddenly he coughed and clutched his side where the fractured ribs dug painfully.

Ian watched the agony mixed with resolution fill McTaver's eyes as his coughing subsided. "I must get you back to your room, Laird McTaver, before Lord Basingstoke returns."

Taking an even, shallow breath Ronin answered, "I can make it back. You did right by me, my friend, to warn me of her danger. I am grateful that you have watched over her as I bid. Without you to distract Percy and warn me, it would have been him in that room instead of me." Ronin turned fierce eyes to Ian in the dark corridor. "No one touches her but me! Do not let anyone in until morning. Then we must make plans to leave shortly, as soon as I can ride without falling beneath my steed's hooves. Are you to stay in this cursed place or do you travel with me?"

"I go with you to fight for our lands." Ian's solemn face reassured Ronin who answered with a quick nod. Ian watched him go, then turned his back on the wooden door, and leaned against it. He pulled his sword halfway out of the scabbard in readiness, watching for the return of Lord Basingstoke.

Gripping his injured arm, Ronin slipped off into the darkness, toward his room on the east side of the house. As he lay down upon his bed, his body poured sweat. He trembled from his exertions, but his mind worked furiously. He glared at the darkness, cursing his broken arm, his struggling chest, the Serpent and his wide, malevolent reach. He could not trust Percy. He thought of the winter fast approaching and the mountainous trek he would be making if he had any hope of reclaiming his land. He must prepare immediately and risk the dangerous crossing. In the meantime, he would pretend to be more ill than he actually was, hiding his growing strength from any who might betray him.

Ronin stared out the open window at the gleaming moon. Kalial's loyalty was uncertain. She was unaware of the intricate politics swirling around her. She was a creation of beauty, a woman blossoming underneath a wild, new sky. He would protect her from afar and allow her to explore this world until she was as comfortable in it as she was in her own homeland. He would wait until she came to him willingly. Then, once she did, he would hold her forever.

Percy stared down at his empty cup resting upon a table with a set of black and white discs arranged haphazardly around it. He sat alone in the great hall, the firelight flickering on the stones accenting his loneliness. He thought of Kalial in her room, her drug-laced body writhing in passion, but the pull of the gaming pieces was stronger. He glared at the pieces, counting the white discs once again before swearing. He dropped his head in his hands, feeling his own fingers tremble.

"When did this obsession take control of me?" he said aloud, his voice muffled. "And why did you come to me, Ronin? What do you have that Lothian wants? Why won't you give it to him and be done with it? I do not want to be the cause of your death. I have ruined my own life." He looked up, sighing. "Perhaps 'tis best this way, my favorite cousin. You do not want to be like me, homeless within your own home, defeated yet again by the conqueror. 'Tis best you slide away peacefully, now, without more pain." Percy picked up the discs, fingering each one. He shook them in his hand, threw them on the table, and counted the white ones. Fear clouded his eyes. With an oath, he quit the room.

CHAPTER 18

When Kalial awoke the next morning, she felt tired
and listless. Remnants of a sweet dream tickled her
consciousness and she rose slowly, unsure of her memories. Soreness lingered between her thighs and her
head ached.

"Florie," she said to her companion, "I fear I slept
poorly last night. I feel ill this morning."

Florie noted the dullness of Kalial's usually sparkling golden eyes. " 'Tis time you took back some
control of your life. You have been moping around as
if you had nothing to do but wait while the men organize themselves and set things in motion."

Kalial frowned. "That is not true, Florie. I have
collected some men for Ronin's army."

"Ronin's army. Make them *your* army. Go out and
work with them, let them get to know you. You have
much to offer them in the knowledge you have. Teach
them and also learn from them."

"But I thought I should learn more of . . . of embroidery and ladylike manners."

Florie lifted a sweeping silken gown of glimmering
brown for Kalial to don. The deep color highlighted her
blond tresses and honey skin and subtly emphasized the
smudges under her eyes, giving her an ethereal look, as
if she would drift away with the dust motes.

"Learning to be a woman does not require that you lose yourself in the process," Florie admonished. "The secret to being a woman is being yourself. The man who sees you for who you are, and still loves you, will be the man you want. Come, you have been told what to do since you were born. Now is the time to make your own choices."

"Ronin made the choice to ban me from his room," Kalial replied as Florie wrapped a girdle around her hips.

"Bah, leave him to stew a bit. Show him that you can do anything you desire, be it dine wi' the lords and ladies, or romp in the woods wi' your beasts."

Feeling better, Kalial preceded Florie from the room and went down to break her fast. When she spied Ian at the lower table, she approached him.

"Ian?" she asked. "Should we meet with the men this morning?"

He nodded. "I would be pleased to gather them. We should assess their abilities and start their training immediately."

"Good. Then when you are ready, we shall meet on the high field."

"Aye. We'll be there."

Kalial smiled with satisfaction, feeling good now that she was taking action. Her gait was confident when she joined Lord and Lady Basingstoke, and she ignored the lady's gasp of affront when she stepped briskly over the bench.

"Princess!" she exclaimed. "You need to walk around the furniture, not over it!"

Kalial lifted her eyebrows and shrugged. "I am hungry, and it was the shortest way. But if my actions upset your sensibilities, I will try to be more discreet. Perhaps tonight I will act more as you want me to."

"That would be a pleasant change." Lady Basing-

stoke replied and delicately lifted her utensil and nibbled her egg-soaked toast.

Annoyed, Kalial stood up and inclined her head.
"Until then," she stated, and at a gesture toward Ian,
she left the hall.

Within the hour, they had assembled the men in the
courtyard and had instructed them to advance to the
training ground. Some of the men shuffled nervously,
unsure of themselves, whereas others looked to Kalial
eagerly. One stepped forward with her mare.

"We are honored to serve you," he said. "I know
you are concerned about our lack of experience, but
I assure you though we do not have the years, we
have the heart and all of us are ready to serve you in
any way."

Kalial smiled brilliantly, her face glowing as she accepted the horse's reins. "And I am honored to have
your loyalty so freely given. Your convictions remind
me of friends I have lost, and I understand the gift
you give by pledging to me. I, in turn, will always
stand with you. What is your name, young sir?"

"I am called Karl. This is Erik, the scout, and Jordan, the archer, my brothers." He stood back as the
other men came forward, offering their names and
individual vows. When they had all introduced themselves, Kalial looked around for Ian. Beside him stood
a man cloaked in a heavy cowl. The man stepped back
quickly at Kalial's questioning regard and Ian shook
his head in apology.

"He is a friend of mine, though he does not speak.
Will you let him train with us?"

"Of course, McInnish. If you speak for him, I will
not say nay, although he appears too old to travel
with us."

"Do not be deceived by his hunched form. What he
lacks in strength, he makes up for in wisdom and
experience."

At her smile of approval, the men walked up to the field, followed by Kalial on her palomino mare. The large McCat padded at her side, her fierce fangs adding a hint of danger to the friendly atmosphere.

Ian divided the men into three groups, and soon Kalial, Ian and the older man were demonstrating their individual skills. Kalial aimed an arrow at an archery target, and pleased the men with her proficiency. Both Ian and his friend picked up swords, and although the older man moved slowly and used his left arm, he clearly understood the rudiments of swordplay, and Kalial shortly forgot their presence. For several hours they all practiced, until the cool autumn wind swept around them, making further training difficult.

"Every day we must meet and work to improve our skills," Kalial instructed. "In my land, when we go to our homes at night, we recall what we have learned by day. We sit on the ground and close our eyes in order to picture the lessons. In this way, our minds practice while our bodies rest."

As the men nodded in understanding, Kalial remounted. She waved to Ian and pointed her mare back down the hill. Though every man watched her descent, only one man regarded her with possessive pride. That man took a slow, steady breath, feeling the ache of his weak muscles.

Several days later, Kalial walked slowly around her room under the direction of Florie. "You certainly have the grace of royalty," Florie commented.

"I hardly feel like it," Kalial responded. "I trip on my hem at least three times a day."

"But even when you trip, you do it like a princess." Florie grinned as Kalial rolled her eyes.

"Stop it, Florie, and show me once again how I am

supposed to curtsy. We are to have guests tonight and I do not want to disgrace myself."

"Bah, you could never do that. Perhaps Laird McTaver will come down and join you."

Kalial glared at her, her eyes snapping in anger. "He has not once asked for me since he sent me from his room. That man can wither in his sickbed for all I care."

"Maybe he wonders why you have not visited him."

"I have told you that I will not speak about this."

"So you have. Bend at your knees more, not your waist. And lift your skirts to the side when you sit."

"I doubt that he will come down tonight in any case. He has not descended on any other night, so why would he do so tonight?"

"I thought we were not going to speak of him," Florie responded as she picked up a brush and started brushing Kalial's hair.

"I am not. You spoke of him first."

They both fell silent, and the soft crackle of Kalial's hair was the only sound in the room.

Kalial dressed in a burgundy and gold dress that draped to the floor in ripples of expensive fabric. Her golden locks, brushed to a sparkling sheen, were pulled back underneath a gauzy veil and gleaming coronet. Her yellow eyes were bright and only a faint trembling of her lower lip betrayed her nervousness.

As she slowly descended the stairs, gripping the banister for support, the sound of many voices escalated. She entered the great room just as Percy looked up.

"Ah, Her Highness, the Princess Kalial, has finally joined us. Please, let me introduce you to my friends. Curtis Ferguson, Earl of Southshire, Mary Ferguson, Countess of Southshire, and Evan Crandel, Earl of Belington. Friends, please meet my honored guest, Princess Kalial."

Lord Crandel stepped over to her, lifting her hand

to his lips. "My pleasure. I hear that Laird McTaver has taken you under his protection."

"Indeed not," replied Kalial with a flash of irritation. "I would say that we are acquaintances of convenience only."

"Oh, how interesting," Crandel replied, looking over his shoulder.

Kalial looked up, then gasped as Ronin himself rose from a chair next to the fire. "Acquaintances of a most pleasurable convenience," he said softly, his voice like velvet.

Kalial blushed, uncertain how to respond. She looked him over, noting his cast and rough clothes. "You appear to be well," she finally said.

"Well enough," he replied with a lift of his lips. "But you would know nothing about my progress, would you, Your Highness? Other activities have taken you from my bedside lately."

Lady Southshire stepped up, rescuing Kalial. "My dear, look at you. You are exquisite. Lady Basingstoke gave me no hint of your beauty. How she teased me!"

Lady Basingstoke glowered and looked disapprovingly at Kalial's bare feet peeking from beneath her dress. "Any peasant would look acceptable clothed in a fortune's worth of silk."

Before Kalial could respond, Percy gripped her arm and steered her away. "Her Highness," he said aloud, "has a particular charm. She has a way of looking into your soul and seeing you for who you are."

"And what," interjected Ronin lazily, "does she see when she looks at you, cousin?"

Percy led Kalial to a bench softened by cushions and motioned her to sit. "I am sure she sees that I am full of admiration for her winsome ways."

"I see that you have a great love for your cousin, though I can not understand why Ronin McTaver would generate such feelings," Kalial commented.

Percy laughed shakily, his eyes darting to Ronin's. "Aye, well, he has always been my favorite cousin."

"And you mine, Percy," Ronin replied. "Blood bonds are always strongest."

"What about love?" interrupted Lady Southshire.

Ronin shrugged. "I have no personal experience of that, though my mother and father were certainly devoted to each other."

"Have you never been in love, Lord McTaver?" Lady Southshire asked.

"I do not believe so," he replied. "But what man really knows?" Kalial looked up at him, then nervously away. Ronin watched her fidget and smiled once again. "But all this talk keeps us from dining, and since I have not sat at my cousin's table in many a year, I yearn to do so now. Princess? Would you join me?"

He strode over to her, towering over her seated form. Leaning over her he added in a whisper, "Unless you do not think yourself able?"

Kalial sprang up, snagging her dress under her foot. She struggled, ripping the cloth and bumping her veil askew. Lady Basingstoke nodded triumphantly while the men looked on with amusement. Ronin frowned, displeased by the others' reactions. He held out his left arm to Kalial. "Shall we?" he asked, and led her to the table.

Kalial lifted her chin at the smirking Lady Basingstoke. "After the lady of the house," she replied sweetly.

Ronin laughed in appreciation. "You are a firebrand. Civilization has not diminished the tartness of your tongue."

Greatly encouraged by Ronin's support, Kalial swept after the Lord and Lady Basingstoke and allowed herself to be seated at the table. Although they did not speak much, Ronin and Kalial pressed close together, each acutely aware of the other's presence.

*   *   *

A week later, as frost dusted the morning grass, Percy intercepted Kalial as she left the castle to join her men on the training field. "My dear princess, you look so unsettled," he said, his head tilted to the side and his wide mouth pursed in concern. Kalial stepped back quickly, for once remembering to pull the skirts from under her feet.

"I am merely irritated with Ronin. He lies abed and will not try to recover his strength. I have not seen him since the night we dined with guests."

"His injuries are severe. That night overly taxed his strength."

"No matter, I am leaving now for the fields."

"Of course. You are to be admired for your dedication to watching their progress." His voice dropped to a whisper as she walked from the hall. "You are like no woman I have ever met, Your Highness. Your passion for your purpose is . . . exhilarating to your men, as it is to me."

" 'Tis not so with all men, I assure you, Lord Basingstoke. My manly interests are despised by others of your gender." Kalial's gaze flicked briefly at the window above their heads before returning to the stables ahead of them. Kalial stepped forward leading her palomino mare. He cupped his hands and Kalial placed her left foot in the sling he created. With a glance back at Percy, she swung up astride saddle, exposing the lower half of her calves as she did so. Percy's mouth opened and he leaned forward to place a kiss upon her bare flesh. With an oath, Kalial pulled the dagger from her waist and pressed it to his chest to stop him.

Percy froze, then looked up in stunned surprise. "I seek only to blow the dust from your slippers, m'lady." Kalial glared at him. She slowly withdrew her weapon and watched him warily.

The boy next to her, who was half Lord Basingstoke's age and a third his size, stepped in front of him. "I shall help my mistress, m'lord." Percy's face twisted angrily and he grasped the youth's shoulders and made to shove him aside. A quick movement from Kalial made him pause. She grasped the dagger and plunged in into the folds of cloth between her thighs. Both men gasped and lunged forward, startling the mare. She sidestepped quickly away from them, nearly unseating Kalial.

Holding the dagger in her fist, Kalial pulled it roughly through the fabric, tearing it from the juncture of her legs to the hem. The two sides fell gracefully on either side of the horse's pale body, concealing Kalial's legs and feet. With a triumphant toss of her head, she squeezed her legs around the girth of the horse. The mare rose up on her hind legs with a jerk. The shimmering brown dress rippled and flowed like a royal mantle. When the dainty feet of the mare struck the ground, she sprang forward in a gallop, heading for the training field on top of the hill.

Percy watched her go, his lust for her mixed with honest admiration for her courage and spirit. Watching her daily through the peephole was not enough anymore, he decided. He must stroke her body. He must waken the passion in her golden eyes. His gaze turned crafty as he sought another way to breach her room. Ian McInnish stood guard every night, to Percy's annoyance. The maid Florie slept on the pallet next to the fire. Both of the devoted servants appeared to check all of her food and drink. 'Twas difficult to think of a way to get the princess naked and willing.

Percy turned from the hillside and made his way into the hall where Lady Basingstoke scurried to meet him. "My darling!" she purred. "I simply must get your assistance on a matter of grave importance. I need you, and I am sure you would do anything for me and my brother." She smiled sweetly, although a warning flickered in her eyes.

Percy tensed. "It is my obligation to please you, wife. What do you require?"

Lady Basingstoke's face flushed and she looked at the man behind her, nodding approvingly. "You see here an apothecary. Your"—she waved her hand vaguely in the direction of McTaver's room—"your 'annoyance' is doing better despite all my efforts to hinder his progress. 'Tis time we were more *direct* in our approach. We should not want to fail when my brother arrives, now do we?"

Percy's fair eyes shone briefly with anger before he carefully concealed it. He felt his insides clench as he spotted the vial in the apothecary's hands. A memory of Ronin as his childhood companion flashed through his mind before he deliberately ignored it. He nodded coldly to the drugmaker. "Give it to me and I shall go upstairs now," he said. "But I want it to appear natural. He has many powerful friends."

"So has my brother!" snapped Lady Basingstoke with uncharacteristic tartness.

"Your brother has no friends," answered Percy, "save those he forces."

A heavy silence greeted Lord Basingstoke's words until the apothecary cleared his throat. Glancing first at the lady, he withdrew the vial of powder. "Place it in his food or drink daily for the next five days. He shall sicken and die." He looked back at Lord Basingstoke. " 'Tis not overly painful, m'lord. Simple and effective."

Percy looked down at the powder. "What is it?"

"Wolfsbane. The dried root has been ground very finely and can be easily added to his drink. His heart will become irregular and his breathing will slow. His lips and tongue may swell and he will become weak with nausea. It will seem as if the heat of his injuries has finally enveloped him."

Percy's hand shook slightly. A haunted look chased over his countenance before it was masked.

Lady Basingstoke regarde him kindly. "Think of your people, my darling. Think of the bloodshed and horror you will save them from as you avoid my brother's anger. Remember, your first responsibility is to your family lands and the people who depend upon you. If you do not do as Lothian asks, your people will pay when the Serpent descends upon them." The last sentence was said with a hardening in her voice, an iciness that Percy well remembered and understood.

"I will see to it myself," he finally stated, his voice calm and firm. "I will start it tomorrow." Then he leaned down and placed a husbandly kiss upon the lady's brow. He turned and took the vial along with a pair of dice and headed for the stairs.

Kalial thundered up the hillside to where the men trained. The motley crew of young men were clumsily practicing a series of lunges under the direction of Ian McInnish. They stood in a row arrayed in a variety of clothing, ranging from full hoods and enveloping tunics to thin leggings and vests. Kalial pulled her mare to a walk and guided her to the front of the line. Face flushed from the ride, she swept the men with a quick appraisal and smiled. A swelling of possessive pride filled her breast.

She slid off her horse and approached Ian.

"Good morning," she said. Her steady gaze did not waver. McInnish smiled in greeting. With a small nod, he pointed toward the men who were gathering together bows and arrows and propping up targets. Grinning, Kalial strode off to join them. Once everything was assembled, she watched the men fumble with the devices. Stepping up, she picked up a bow and strung the arrow. She stood beautifully tall and straight, her left shoulder pointing toward the target. Her right arm drew back even and smooth. A soft release of her fingers sent the arrow whispering through the morning air until it landed with a thud, deep into the heart of the target.

The men cheered. During the past weeks Kalial had easily earned their respect as well as their loyalty. Drawing around her, the men tried to imitate her stance and form. They accepted her quiet corrections while they trained with serious determination.

Meanwhile, the larger men, those who were more fit to wield swords, trained under McInnish. Although they practiced simple maneuvers, they were building muscles and developing balance that would be the basis for swordsmanship in the future. They too fought with intensity, occasionally hearing the princess's words of encouragement carrying over to them when she spied one particularly successful maneuver.

Only one man tightened with anger when she participated in the drills. Only one flinched internally when her voice singled him out for praise. He was the older man, his large size accentuated by his leather hood and overtunic. After weeks of practice, he moved with increasing strength now. Kalial assumed he had been a blacksmith in his previous life, for his biceps were huge. He held the sword in his left hand, practicing endlessly to improve his control. He never spoke to her, although he often spoke with Ian McInnish. He had improved quickly and was now performing more complicated drills while also assisting his comrades.

Today Kalial grew bored explaining wind speeds and trajectories. Instead, she walked over to McInnish and asked to join the swordplay. " 'Tis time I learned some skills that will benefit me in close combat," she argued when Ian refused her. "What would you have me do should I end up face to face with one of the hateful Serpent mercenaries? Think you they would step aside because I am a woman? Or be so surprised by my skill that they would give me a chance to escape?"

"Simply 'tis not what a woman should do, Your Highness. The laird would not approve."

"I care not what the laird would or would not approve!" Kalial shouted vehemently. " 'Tis partly my army we train and I am their commander." That said, she stalked over to a threesome of men holding old, rusty training swords and snatched one from a man's hands. Moving swiftly in her split skirt, Kalial lunged at another fellow, striking at him furiously. Both of them were new to the sport, and their swords clanged against each other, causing their arms to ache and their fingers to tremble. Pressing forward to prove herself, Kalial drove the man backwards until he stumbled to his knees.

Whipping around, Kalial then attacked the other man, who raised his sword at an odd angle in an attempt to defend himself. He swung wildly in return, enthusiastically engaging Kalial in the fight. A crowd of men gathered, forming a circle around the two wild combatants. Bits of rust rained down each time their swords engaged.

Suddenly Kalial pushed her opponent back and his defensive stance slipped, leaving his chest vulnerable to her blade. With a cry, Kalial held back, halting the sword from its deadly descent. As she did so, she slipped, falling to the ground. Instinctively he reached out to catch her, forgetting that his hand held his own sword.

Kalial screamed as the blade slid along her back and up her neck. The jagged cut exploded in fiery pain. Kalial fell to her hands and knees, fighting to rise, but stumbling again.

The hooded man burst through the crowd, shoving the smaller men aside like sparrows before a hawk. He roughly grabbed Kalial, who collapsed in his hold. He pushed her face down on the field and yanked her hair away from the wound. With his one good hand, he ripped open the back of her filmy dress to expose the bloody gash marring her creamy skin. With an oath, he leaned down and placed his lips over the wound and sucked, drawing blood into his mouth and then spitting it out. Repeating the act several times, he sought to draw the poison from her body before it spread. Lockjaw resulted from rust penetrating blood, and no seasoned soldier cared to witness its terrible effects.

Kalial gasped and struggled against the pain, lifting her eyes to the man who held her pinned to the ground, whose heavy hood was flung back, exposing his face. The angry blue of Ronin's eyes clashed with her surprised ones. His brows drew together fiercely as he growled at her, "Cease your wiggling. You only cause the blood to pump faster."

Surrendering to him, Kalial let her body turn pliant. She closed her eyes and breathed slowly, concentrating on the feel of his lips upon the back of her neck and the sultry tug of his suction upon her wound. She felt his mouth, the brush of his teeth against her skin, and she quivered with sudden, heated desire. She arched her back, yielding to his touch. Finally, he sat back, his own face beaded with sweat as he stared down at her bare shoulder.

"God in heaven!" he yelled. "Have you no care for your life? Must you always do what you should not? You could have been killed!"

Lunging up, he grabbed Kalial's blade and glared at the assembled men. "He who has so little control should not dare to play at swords with the princess! For your mistake, you will never wield a blade again!" He sprang at the man who had caused the accident, his face murderous. With a cry of alarm, the youth staggered backward, flinging his sword up to protect his face.

Ronin pushed him back easily, violently, using his weaker left arm as if it had always been his fighting arm of choice. The man shouted out in alarm, frantically backing up. Distantly aware of shouts around him, Ronin continued to pound at the man who had wounded Kalial, clearly intent on maiming him. With a swift blow and twist, Ronin knocked the sword from the man's hands. Violent rage building and overflowing within him, Ronin started to swing his blade at the other man's neck.

"Stop!" cried Kalial, her unique accent penetrating Ronin's fog. "Leave him be! It was only an accident and I will heal. But look, Ronin, look at the sea!" Kalial stood shakily, the torn sides of her dress hanging around her shoulders. Catching Ronin's eye, she pointed an unsteady hand toward the coast.

Ian McInnish turned to look along with Ronin and the men. An army of over a hundred men was marching along the coast road from the town toward the castle. Appearing now no larger than ants, the dust they created confirmed the rapid pace at which they moved. In the harbor, Ronin's ship was missing. Instead, four larger ships boldly waved the flag of the Serpent.

"Lothian," Ronin breathed. "We are not ready to confront him . . ."

"We must leave," Ian said, already motioning to the men. "Lord Basingstoke will be greeting his brother-in-law and then they will come for you."

"Percy is my cousin. He would not turn me over."

"Laird, he is not who you remember. We are not prepared. We must leave now."

"Winter is almost upon us. In days the snows will come. I can not risk the men crossing the mountains in winter. I will leave alone."

Kalial looked at him angrily. "Once again you do not acknowledge that others have a right to make their own choices." She turned to address the men. "You once said that you would follow me. Are you prepared to fight against the Serpent?"

The men cheered in response, their eager faces clearly demonstrating their loyalty. After a short pause, Ronin nodded, acknowledging their allegiance. He directed several men to go to the stables and procure all the horses they could, along with tack and bridles. Another group of men was sent to the weapons room to trade their practice blades for better swords. Lastly he sent men to raid the kitchens and storehouses for food and waterskins.

Kalial turned to him, a question in her eyes. "What is this about the Serpent and Percy?"

Ronin leaned close and spoke rapidly. "He was forced to wed Lothian's sister as payment for a huge gambling debt. Now Percy is under the man's power and undoubtedly has orders to kill me. I believe he hoped I would simply die from the bridge collapse, but instead I have worked hard to recover my strength without alerting anyone to my true intention. McInnish and I have been preparing for this departure, only we were hoping for one more week and a departure by ship.

"You wait here and we will all meet up again," he went on. "Because we are on the hillside, we have seen the Serpent approach earlier than the castle lookouts have. That gives us an hour's advantage over Percy. I must go and retrieve some items in my room."

"My dhu Cait! The owl!" Kalial cried, struggling to understand what was happening.

"Call to them. They will come. Do not fear." His brilliant gaze caught her frantic one. "Trust me now," he whispered.

Kalial's eyes filled with tears. "I will . . . but Ronin? Why did you hide your recovery from me?"

"That is not important now. What matters more is the Serpent. We are not ready for him here. We must leave immediately and hope that they do not catch up with us." He made as if to turn away, but Kalial clutched his arm.

"I thought you were dying. At the very least, abed.

Why did you not tell me? The Lady Basingstoke said you were sickening and not likely to improve."

"Kalial, 'tis not the time for this discussion. I have many things to do."

"But—"

"Cease!" Ronin roared. "You could not bear to enter my room these weeks past as you waited to hear word of my death. Are you disappointed that I recovered? Does it foil your plans to stay with the charming Percy?"

Kalial looked at his towering, angry form with seeping coldness followed by a rush of fiery fury. Leaning forward, the slit skirt of her gown revealing her succulent thighs and the tattered shoulders sliding to display the bold curves and valleys of her neck and breasts, she glared at him.

"I was banned from your room by your own words! You told Lord Basingstoke that I was naught but a nuisance and you wished to be rid of me."

"Nay!"

"Oh, most assuredly yes!" Kalial narrowed her amber eyes in challenge.

"I said nothing of the sort. I waited for you and you did not come!" Ronin's animosity fairly drowned Kalial, and she stood stricken with shock. As Ronin glared at her, his black hair tousled and his feet planted wide, Kalial felt her nipples harden involuntarily. She saw Ronin's eyes drop briefly, spying the puckering underneath the thin material of her gown. With a groan and growl, he spun away, grabbing the reins on the dainty pale horse and mounting her in one leap. Pounding into her as he wished to pound into the pale woman standing behind him, he raced down the hill, clenching his thighs around her waist and wrapping his hands in her flaxen mane. Kalial watched him go, her mind racing over the miscommunications that had kept them separated these past weeks.

Through a high window in Ronin's room, Percy watched events unfold. He noted the food stores slipped into saddlebags and the bedrolls lashed behind saddles. Behind him was the empty bed where pillows had been propped to simulate a sleeping form. Percy had not even checked the bed today, knowing that Ronin was not there. He knew that Ronin had ceased trusting him, and although he was worried that Lothian would punish him for failing to murder Ronin, he was secretly pleased that his cousin had recovered so fully.

Hearing the door open, he turned to see Ronin slip inside. Ronin froze at the sight of Percy standing with his back to the window, then slowly entered the room and closed the door softly. Without speaking, he walked over to the bed chest and started withdrawing his belongings.

"You are leaving now," stated Percy.

"Yes, cousin. 'Tis time." Silence filled the room again as Ronin stripped out of his rough garments that had concealed his identity and slid into his own. He struggled briefly with the right arm splint. Percy came over and assisted him.

"You have seen the Serpent land in Tregaron. You know he is coming for you."

Ronin nodded, surprised that Percy was admitting his knowledge of Lothian's plans.

"This powder is for you, Ronin McTaver. My gift to my favorite relative from my wife. It is the ground bones of a saint, and will keep you safe. Put a bit of it in your ale daily for the next five days and you will not see failure again."

Ronin glanced at the vial fleetingly. "If it is so powerful, I will give it to my ward."

Percy winced. "No. That would not be wise."

"I would not take it, Percy, nor would I give it to Kalial, for I have come to realize that you are not worthy of being called family. Your sickness has rotted your soul."

" 'Tis true we who were once the closest of cousins are now enemies. But I have no grudge against the princess. Pray do not take her on this journey. She will be safer here."

"She does not need your type of protection, Basingstoke."

"Surely 'tis better than her death. I will treat her gently, grant her wishes, and appreciate her for her true nature, whereas you two only fight against each other. You care not for who she is but for who you want her to be. Would you want her should she become like my Lady Basingstoke?"

"Kalial is nothing like your wife."

"Not even a pool of wax dripping around their feet and welding them together could make them burn with the same color flame," Percy agreed. Ronin looked up sharply as Percy continued. "I could make the child happy. I would give her horses and land and all the creatures she wanted. I would dress her in silks and ribbons."

"And if she desired leather and fur?" retorted Ronin.

"I would not deny her. Would you?" Percy answered. Ronin stared at him for a moment until he continued, "For the horses and weapons I will not follow, but leave the princess. Do not risk the mountains in winter."

Ronin felt as if a rock had hit his stomach and his jaw tightened imperceptibly. He walked to the window where Percy had been standing and looked up at the hillside where he knew Kalial waited. The image of her golden body and golden spirit filled his soul. He wrestled with the question of where she would be most safe. He could tap her on the jaw, wrap her precious body in a blanket and leave her behind. He himself could offer her no guarantee of safety. He was fleeing with seventy-one men of no experience, about to travel over treacherous mountains in winter. If the cold or advancing army did not get them, the wild animals might.

In the shimmer of the ocean, Ronin saw a reflection of the forest fire that had bound them together. In the whisper of the wind sliding between the castle outbuildings, he recalled the sound of the waves and seagulls when Kalial had knelt before him and accepted his protection in exchange for her service. A smile flickered over his face as he realized that wild animals were probably the one thing they would not have to worry about during the mountainous crossing.

Turning back to Percy, he shook his head. "She stays with me, cousin. You are right that she would be safer here than in the mountains, but I find the thought of leaving her behind unacceptable."

"Do you love her, Ronin?"

"Of course not. 'Tis just that I am accustomed to her now and she may prove useful to me."

"Good, for I would not like to see you hurt," said Percy.

"Hurt? What do you mean?" replied Ronin.

"Well, 'tis clear that she feels no love for you, for has she not avoided your room these weeks past?"

" 'Tis clear, yes." Ronin's voice was hard. "Though I am not certain if 'twas of her own accord. Even so, she rides with me." Ronin turned impenetrable eyes upon Lord Basingstoke, then picked up the folded tapestry that had been hidden underneath a mattress and tucked it under his arm.

Percy looked at the piece with one lifted eyebrow and a wry grimace. "Is that what Lothian has been searching for? You had it here all along?"

"It is only a saddle blanket," Ronin replied blandly.

"Give it to me, and I will hand it to Lothian. Then

he will not pursue you into the mountains. Come, Ronin, is it worth risking your life for whatever secrets of fortune and wealth that bit of cloth might contain?"

"Percy, you are a gambler. Can you tell me what one's pride in one's heritage is worth? I will make a bet with you. I will throw a disc into the corner. Should it come up black, we will know that you are the man I knew you to be. If it comes up white, we will know you have truly lost your soul."

"There is no gold in that bet, Ronin."

"Ah, but we are betting on something worth far more than wealth, are we not?" Ronin flicked the disc into the far corner, where it clinked against the stone wall before rattling upon the floor. With a nod of farewell, Ronin exited the room, leaving Percy to stare intently into the shadowed recess.

Ronin encountered Florie on the steps waiting for him, carrying a satchel of clothes and other items she had packed. Together they slipped down the stairs and out of the hall. Ronin set Florie on the path toward the training ground and then approached the end of the stable. Moving more quickly now, he reached a young man who held the reins of his prancing mahogany horse. Swinging up, he looked up once again at his chamber window where Percy stood looking down holding a disc in his hand. Without making any sign of acknowledgment, Ronin spun around and galloped up the hill.

The crest rapidly filled with the men. Kalial was mounted on her mare, the black McCat at her side, the owl circling. She watched Ronin approach and marveled at his powerful assumption of command.

"The Serpent army is crossing the canyon at the lower fiord," Ian told Ronin. "We have no time to lose."

"Let's ride!" Ronin shouted, and the men yelled as they dug in their heels. Ronin's battle cry echoed down the hillside and through the lower courtyard as

Kalial's small mare shot out in front. The palomino's flaxen mane and Kalial's own golden hair streamed in the wind as the entire company galloped toward the mountains.

PART III

Castle Roseneath

CHAPTER 19

When Castle Basingstoke was only a small stony prominence of the far horizon, Ronin slowed the men and motioned forward Erik, the scout.

"You take the lead," he said. "I will drop back and watch for pursuit."

"I will join Erik," Kalial interjected, ignoring Ronin's frown. She moved up alongside the scout and smiled at him pleasantly.

The young man cast a fearful glance at her jaguar. "Will the beast be safe to camp with?" he asked.

"She will not disturb you," Kalial answered. "Look, there are some bear tracks. We'd best edge to the left to avoid her feeding ground."

"Surely you are not also a scout, Your Highness?"

"I was a scout for my people in my forest of Loch Nidean."

"You are most unusual, Princess. Once again, you have skills that many a man would admire."

"Tell me that you are not like those other pompous fools who can not conceive of a woman doing useful things?" she queried. "Have I not proven my skills?"

"Your Highness, you are better with a bow and arrows than I have seen in any man, and you throw a dagger with terrifying accuracy. But scouting is dirty, strenuous work. I can not imagine you—rather, I would not *want* to imagine you doing such a job."

"Ah! But I love the earth and she loves me. I connect with her animals and often see things others miss. Why do you not give me a chance to prove myself and we shall see how well we work together?"

"As you wish, Your Highness." He pointed to a rock formation in the distance. "We are headed there, where we can slide between the rocks and onto a path that leads into the mountains. There are other routes, but this one is the best for horses ridden single file. I think it will be too narrow for the Serpent army to travel efficiently."

"Are there other paths better suited to them?"

"Oh yes, at a lower elevation. For all that, they will take longer. It is my understanding that we wish to travel fast in order to reach the other side before the winter snows set in." The young man twisted in his saddle and looked at Kalial earnestly. "We most definitely will prove your faith in us, Your Highness. To a man, we have vowed to learn faster than a fledgling fox and train harder than a rutting moose. We owe you our lives for granting us this opportunity and we will make it successful!"

Kalial smiled fondly at the man, making him blush. "I have no reservations, Erik. Now let us keep watch of where we are going."

With Kalial and Erik leading the way, the band of men traveled swiftly between the rocks and into the mountain pass before night began to fall. No sign of pursuit was evident, yet Ronin did not relax. His body was tired and his arm ached, but he walked among the men, teaching them how to make a camp that allowed for swift disassembly should the need arise. Only occasionally did he pause and flinch from the pain of his mending wounds.

Kalial changed into breeches and a tunic and pulled her hair back in a thick braid. Joining a group of men gathering wood, she cast a defiant but somewhat worried glance at Ronin. She suspected that he detested her male garb, for it reminded them both of the secret she had kept from him. She thought that he would prefer her to be graceful, beautiful and elegant, and that she was anything but that in her familiar male attire.

She felt her legs, freed from the confines of swirling skirts, take long, purposeful strides. What she did not know was that her shoulders straightened and her chin lifted as she quickly became comfortable for the first time in weeks. She could not see that natural grace flowed from her lean limbs up through her slim waist and down to her tapered fingertips as she smoothly bent to pick up pieces of wood. She was not aware of the glow of freedom kissing her cheeks, nor of the curve of her neck displayed by her restrained hair.

Ronin, however, was fully aware of her transformation and felt an unexpected thrill of pleasure as he observed her. He watched her breeches tighten over her buttocks as she bent and discovered a wistful smile lurking on his lips. Just as Kalial stepped out of his sight, he saw her look up and glare at him, her body rigid. He frowned at the interruption, wanting to continue his perusal. Kalial, seeing the look of displeasure, incorrectly assumed it was because of her attire. Her lips compressed tightly as she stalked off into the woods.

Later that evening, Ronin watched Kalial in the firelight. She stayed far away from him, sharing her laughter and happiness with the other men. He noticed she sparkled here, in the dust and dirt, as she never had in her satin and silk dresses. These men treated her with utmost respect. It appeared that they did not resent her invasion of their world, nor did they mistake her gender. Instead, they treated her as a valued comrade with skills she could share with them.

A stray thought, simple but powerful, filled his

mind. Kalial as an individual—and as a woman—was valuable, courageous. She was intelligent, skilled, respected. She was more than an equal partner to any man, and *she was his chosen partner*. A liquid melting filled his heart as he watched her and repeated the words over and over in his mind.

He could have left her behind, but he had not. Why? *Because she was his selected companion.* He wanted her near him, sharing this struggle with him. He could not imagine finding anyone else who was remotely capable of helping him, caring for him. With a secret smile, he watched her carefully, lids low so that she could not read his thoughts.

He saw her glancing at him frequently as if assessing his reaction. He could tell that his continued silence shook her composure and that she expected him to rise in anger. Her movements became more and more animated, almost forced, as if she willed him to notice her lack of femininity. Yet Ronin remained silent, electing to observe rather than interfere. Finally, Kalial rose and swaggered over to her mare and bedroll. She tossed a challenging look at Ronin which he met calmly, and then stepped into the darkness of the woods.

Ronin watched the shadows of the night shift as her jaguar slunk off her high perch and followed her mistress. Ronin saw the owl sitting upon a high branch, swiveling his head. With a flash of clarity, through the eyes of the owl, he saw Kalial lie down on her blankets in the darkness. Surprised, Ronin blinked and the image disappeared. Visions through the eyes of the owl? Again? Lost in thought, he remained by the fire until the men gradually fell asleep around him and the richness of the nighttime enfolded him.

He had laid in his sickroom for weeks while his arm mended and his lungs healed. He had concentrated primarily upon repairing his broken body. Kalial had been dressed so beautifully. But then she had ceased tending him, and he had assumed it was due to her lack of feelings. Now it was clear that Percy had tricked both of them, forcing a separation between them that had been unnecessary. First they had been held apart by her disguise, then by a misunderstanding at Castle Basingstoke. And although he was still confused by her unconventional behavior, he was not going to allow Lord Basingstoke's trickery to cause further conflicts between them. 'Twas time, he decided finally, to give her the freedom to be herself, to allow her to reveal herself to him in her own time.

He longed for her body, but he realized that he knew naught of her soul.

Rising, he too moved unerringly into the darkness, to where Kalial slept. Dhu Cait yawned at his approach, her tail flicking only slightly. Ronin placed a hand carefully upon the cat's forehead. Dhu Cait lay still and pliant to his caress. Emboldened, Ronin stroked the cat, feeling the silky softness of her midnight fur. He looked down at Kalial sleeping peacefully and silently thanked the great beast for helping him save her many months ago. He knew that his purpose in saving his lands and his castle was true, yet now he also knew that his desire to help Kalial return home was just as strong. Any land that had spawned this golden beauty of honey hair and topaz eyes . . . that land was blessed and must not be destroyed by the evil that now terrorized it.

Ronin placed his blanket next to hers and lay down upon it, his back to the earth and his eyes gazing into the stars. Kalial shifted and sighed in her sleep, and Ronin reached his left arm out to draw her near. Watched over by the vigilant beasts of the forest, Kalial and Ronin slept together, their lungs breathing at different rhythms but the pulses of their hearts beating in tandem.

Kalial woke the next morning feeling unbelievably

refreshed and enlivened. She took a deep breath of the earth and wind, and a whiff of Ronin's scent also came to her, though he had left with the dawn. She stretched, thinking that her dreams of his strong body next to hers had been soothing and more vivid because of her inner wishes. Rolling over, she looked around at the birds and spoke to them, telling them how much she had missed their presence. She caught the thoughts of a fox guarding a den nearby, and sent it reassurance that her people were not there to harm the precious family.

A cold wind whistled around the camp, swaying the upper pine boughs. Several small rodents dashed about, gathering stores in a last-minute effort to survive the coming winter. On the ground there was a thin coating of snow, which melted rapidly as the sun rose.

After tending to herself, Kalial joined the men in breaking camp. Ronin, she noticed, stayed away from her, but did not forbid her participation. Puzzled but grateful, Kalial struck out with the lead scout once again. They were headed for a large cave high up in the mountains, her companion told her.

"I have heard that it is as large as a great room in a castle and can hold upwards of one hundred men," Erik said. "They believe that the ancient people used to live there and actually housed herds within its perimeter during the winter months."

"Why do you think we are heading there and not down the mountain?" asked Kalial.

"I think we mean to stay there for the winter," he replied.

"Surely not!" cried Kalial, her peace of the morning abruptly shattered. "We must move quickly! 'Tis time I returned to my forest!" She swung her mare around and galloped back to the men a quarter of a mile behind her. She faintly heard Erik yell for her to come back, but she ignored his warning in her haste to confront Ronin.

Ronin looked up with concern when he saw Kalial's lithe frame bent over her horse, flying down the hillside toward him. He quickly scanned for dhu Cait, and when he saw her loping alongside with her tongue lolling happily, he visibly relaxed. When Kalial yanked her horse to a stop almost underneath the hooves of his warhorse, Ronin lifted an eyebrow and waited.

"Why do you not proceed with haste to Loch Nidean or Castle Roseneath?" she demanded. "Why do we waste time heading for the caves when we could easily make the other side of the mountain before the snow arrives?" Kalial stormed at him, the past anger she had bottled up flaring to life once again. "I can tell you that the snow does not come this week. You have not the knowledge of the forest that I do. The squirrels are still collecting nuts, the bears are only just beginning to settle for their seasonal rest. Let us move down the mountain now or we will in fact be trapped for the entire winter!" Her voice rose in pitch and she thumped her heels into the sides of her horse, causing the animal to spin in circles.

Ronin reached out and grasped her horse's bridle, steadying the mare. For all his newfound acceptance of Kalial, he could not tolerate her challenging his orders in front of the men. "Your Highness, I can not understand your overwrought words. Perhaps we should ride a ways together and discuss what is upsetting you?" Heavy sarcasm laced his words for he was highly irritated with her. "Perhaps it would be best to request an explanation of my strategy instead of accusing me?"

Kalial flushed with shame. Yanking the reins from Ronin, she nodded and pushed her mare into a gallop through the dense forest. Gritting his teeth at her foolishness, Ronin turned to Ian and gave him some instructions, then followed the line of broken branches that marked Kalial's trail.

He eventually came across her and her palomino in the middle of a dried wildflower meadow. He pulled his horse to a walk and looked around warily. The dried flowers were surprisingly lovely, for many retained their colors and their petals cascaded around Kalial as she stalked through them. She had dismounted and her hair had broken free. With snapping eyes she glared at him and repeated her angry accusations in an endless torrent.

Ronin pushed his massive horse up to her and towered above her slight frame. "Silence!" he thundered. Kalial fell abruptly mute, yet the glitter did not leave her yellow eyes.

"Do you think we are ready to face the Serpent's force as we are?" he questioned more gently. The sight of her petite body standing straight and unafraid beneath his horse's hooves made him swell with pride and desire. He maintained his position and looked down at her, allowing tendrils of lust to flicker in his groin.

"We will never be ready so I say we go now while we have the advantage of surprise!" answered Kalial. She stepped back slightly, and was wary when Ronin's horse followed her.

"We have no advantage now, m'lady. Do you know so much of warfare that you know something I do not? For as I see it, we are a band of young, hardly trained—"

"I have been training them," Kalial interrupted feverishly.

"As I said, hardly trained men led by a one-armed warrior and a daring but inexperienced princess. I have no wish to see us perish at this monster's hands."

"But earlier you were set to attack immediately," she answered. She stepped back again to avoid the glare of the sun in her eyes. The huge horse followed

her, shifting his body to place her in shadow. Kalial
looked at the stallion with a flicker of concern.

"Perhaps I am wiser now—about a great many
things," Ronin replied, his voice dropping huskily.

"I find it hard to believe that you would change
your mind about anything, Laird McTaver."

"I changed my mind about you."

Surprised, Kalial stepped back several more steps.
Ronin's mahogany horse leapt forward, brushing
against her and knocking her onto her back, causing
her thighs to be flung wantonly wide and her arms to
be braced behind her. She stared up at Ronin, powerful and muscled, high above her on his warhorse. His
dark hair was longer than when she had first met him
and it swirled around his forehead. His eyes glowed
with more passion than anger as he stared at her
prone figure. He leaned forward and pinned her to
the ground with his gaze, his thoughts impenetrable.
Then he sat up abruptly, and spun his horse around
on his hind legs. Without a glance behind him, Ronin
set his stallion back down the hill at an easy canter.

Watching him leave, Kalial felt a tingling in her
lower limbs where they lay spread apart. Her rapid
heart made her so light-headed, she had to consciously
slow its beat. She felt an odd satisfaction in knowing
that Ronin had found her attractive, for there had
been no mistaking his passionate expression. Grinning
slightly, she rolled over and propped her elbows on
the ground with her chin in her hands. Perhaps he was
correct, she thought. Perhaps it would be too hasty to
fly down the mountain and attack now. It might be
best to spend the winter together, training, she
thought contemplatively as she explored her feelings
for him.

She greatly admired his bravery. She understood
and shared, too, his values of familial duty and loyalty.
Despite their frequent tiffs, she had missed him sorely
during their time in the castle. Once again in the for-

est, she felt safe, and once again next to Ronin, she felt protected and secure. She smiled. To be protected was a type of freedom that she barely understood but valued nonetheless, a freedom to relax and trust another human. He was deliciously handsome, she giggled to herself, and she wanted to feel his lips again, soon. Yes, there were many reasons why they should stay in a winter cave, she decided. And during that time Ronin McTaver would be treated to the subtle but deadly onslaught of her newly discovered feminine wiles!

They reached the cave several days later through the combined efforts of Erik and Kalial, although dhu Cait actually found the entrance. The room inside was indeed overwhelmingly large, but light flickered in through a few smaller openings as well as the large opening that allowed the horses easy access. The cave was littered with bones, leaves and debris. An old firepit was discovered in a corner where a draft served as a flue. Under Ronin's direction, the cave was cleaned and stocked with wood, cut grasses were spread on the dirt floor, and food supplies were carefully stored and organized. The shelter was arranged for army living and easy defense.

Kalial led groups of men to dig roots, gather nuts and seeds, and build lookout stations high in the trees. Ronin inspected the stations and was favorably impressed with their sturdiness, weatherproofing and secrecy.

"You have an amazing knowledge of forest living, Kalial," Ronin said. "You know more about your environment than anyone I have ever known."

"And you know much about war."

Ronin looked at her askance. "It is not my wish to know so much about man's violent nature."

"I always thought that you were a warrior, interested only in defeating the enemy," Kalial responded.

"So did I. But there may be other things that are just as important."

"Like what?"

Ronin shrugged, his gaze boring into hers. "I will tell you one day. One day I will tell you why Lothian attacked and why he wrecked such devastation upon your home. Would you like to know?"

"I would be honored, Ronin." Kalial averted her eyes, suddenly shy.

"And you, will you tell me about youself someday? About your forest? About what makes it so special?"

She shifted, uncomfortable. "I am not allowed to reveal my secrets to anyone, though I would like to share them with you."

He nodded. "I have learned that not all secrets are worth protecting at any price. Think on that, and let me know when you are ready."

CHAPTER 20

Within a week, snow began to cover the forest floor and the men, horses, Florie and Kalial gathered in the cave to begin weapons training in earnest.

"Each of you must find a partner who will be your companion in battle," Ronin told them. "If you train together, you will learn each other's weaknesses and strengths and thus be able to work in tandem, fighting to win while protecting each other's lives." Ronin's voice rang out in the enclosed space. The men milled around, finding partners and smiling at each other while placing hearty slaps upon each other's backs. When Kalial moved toward Erik, Ronin stepped forward and smoothly cut off her path, grasping her firmly by the arm.

"It is best to find another whose skills complement yours, for two archers will not do well in hand-to-hand combat just as two brutes will do poorly sneaking into a fortress."

Kalial looked up at Ronin's face, which was turned away from her, and felt a flush of heat. She complied with his firm tug on her arm and moved with him around the room as he assessed pairs and rearranged partners as he felt necessary. Once Ronin turned on his heel abruptly and accidentally knocked into Kalial. He felt the roundness of her breasts against his arm and hastily dropped his hold. He looked down, expecting to see signs of anger, but instead saw her ruefully rubbing her chest and looking away from him. When he reached out to grasp her again, she stepped neatly away.

"I will not run away, Laird. You do not need to haul me about," she stated pertly. Ronin let a small smile slip free.

"Very well. I did not expect you to accept my partnership so easily."

"I am no fool, Laird McTaver. You have skills that I do not possess. And certainly, I would want to protect you at all costs with the skills I can provide."

"You seek to protect me? Could it be that you care for me, lovely Kalial?"

Kalial harrumphed, not ready to admit to him something she only faintly acknowledged to herself. " 'Tis only that you are essential to my mission, nothing more."

Ronin's eyes darkened with anger as he replied heatedly, "And I seek your presence simply because I vowed months ago that I would protect you."

"I am your duty then, m'laird?" Kalial questioned sweetly. She bent over to adjust her bootstrap and Ronin became aware of her lack of underclothes and bindings. His breath caught at the brief sight of swollen breasts before she straightened and looked questioningly at him.

Ronin momentarily forgot her question, so when he answered it was after an extended pause. "You are my duty," he finally confirmed, but the glint in Kalial's eyes made him wonder if she had been aware of his wandering thoughts.

"Then we are in agreement. We will be partners for our mutual benefit, nothing more."

Annoyed by her attitude, Ronin turned away and barked at the men. "You must sleep next to your partner, eat with him, ride with him . . . you must know his likes and dislikes, his strengths and weaknesses as much as you know your own."

"Why do we not just tie each other wrist to wrist?" muttered Kalial.

Ronin looked down at her with a superior smile. "Our princess has made a brilliant suggestion. Pray demonstrate, Your Highness."

"Do not be foolish. I was only being snide."

"Nonetheless, it is a wise tactic. How else to get to know each other than to be bound together?"

"I will not. 'Tis against my culture."

Ronin relaxed his stance, well aware of the company of men listening. "How so?" he asked softly.

" 'Tis a ceremony with us—to bind a man and a woman."

"Indeed," Ronin replied quietly, his blue eyes glowing.

"Yes, we bind man and woman for eleven days prior to their making a lifelong commitment," Kalial explained, stuttering slightly.

"Commitment? We will be committed, Kalial," he said, caressing her name. "I see no problem with that."

Kalial stomped her foot and glanced around at the men and then back into Ronin's lazy eyes. She flushed, a stab of nervousness making her weak. She knew that McTaver's pride would not allow him to give way in front of an audience, yet he obviously did not know what he was asking of her.

"Please," she whispered, "you do not understand. We have already been bound to each other for two days of the eleven. We dare not do more."

Ronin's brows drew together. "Surely you do not mean when I captured you in the forest?"

"Yes," she whispered.

"There is no possibility of that being construed as a bonding ceremony," he answered with a touch of disdain. Out of the corner of his eye he saw Florie nod her head.

"You simply do not understand me and you never will! I live by different rules! To me the silk of a spider's web is binding no matter which creature spins it. Eleven days I am allowed. Time enough to escape from one with whom I seek no bond."

"The time is cumulative then?" asked Ronin. At Kalial's brief nod, he straightened. "Then 'tis clear we can not be bound for eleven days." Kalial sighed with relief and gratefully placed her hand on Ronin's sleeve. With a soft smile, Ronin picked it up and studied the beautiful bones and silky skin of her wrist. He rubbed it with his thumb, then looked into her tawny eyes, willing her to stare back at him. Kalial felt dizzy. She lost perception of all around her except the force that was Ronin McTaver. A tiny tug on her hand pulled her a step closer. Her head felt heavy and tilted to one side. Ronin's eyes dropped to her exposed neck and his eyes darkened as he wrapped a strap softly over her wrist. His husky whisper was thunderingly loud in the silent cave. "We will only be bound for seven days."

Kalial shrieked, comprehension dawning in her eyes. "No!" She sought to pull away from him, but her wrist snapped short at the end of her tether. "No!" she moaned again, twisting her wrist this way and that, clawing at it with her other hand.

Ronin swept her up in his arms and walked out of the cave with her. Twilight cast a frosty sparkle on the trees as he carried his squirming package away from listening ears. "Do not fret, little one, 'twill not be a total of eleven days."

"Close enough! I cannot risk it. Please release me." She stilled and looked up into his face pleadingly.

"Why? Do you wait for another to tie you thus?" Ronin questioned intently.

"No—no one . . ." Her voice trailed off.

"No one? There is no man to whom you wish to be bound?" A glimmer of emotion swam in his eyes before he turned away from her and stared into the darkness.

"I am independent. I seek no one's help. I need no one." Her voice cracked at the end of the statement.

"No one even to love you?"

The silence following Ronin's question stretched out. Finally he looked down at her golden form curled in his arms. Her amber eyes were liquid pools, her gold-flecked lashes sticky with unshed tears. A firestorm of heat suddenly took them both by surprise. The warmth bounced between them and melted the nearby snow. He let her slide from his arms, forcing every inch of her to glide against him. She found her feet resting on a log, placing her head above Ronin's. He knelt, one leg along the side of her. He pressed his dark head against her breast and breathed in her scent. Kalial lifted her bound hand up to his hair and ran her fingers through it.

"Seven days—time for us to become friends." Ronin looked up. "Can you not grant me that?"

Kalial melted at his words. A wisp of snow blew around them. She nodded silently. Ronin nodded in return, words useless to them at that moment. He wrapped his good arm around her waist to help her down from her perch. He jerked his chin toward one of the lookout shelters and they both set out toward it. Kalial's strides were long and free while Ronin tempered his forceful tread so that they walked together, stride for stride. As one unit, they climbed the tree to the shelter, each assisting the other as needed. Once inside, they could see over the mountain and the valley below. They sat with him against the tree trunk and her cuddled within his thighs. Their paired wrists rested snugly in Kalial's lap. Outside, the snow fell in earnest, creating the pleasing dichotomy of winter—

freezing outside in the wind and ice, but warm and cozy inside under the blanket of snow.

They simply sat with each other, enjoying their new-found emotions. A well of trust began to spring between them, and they spent an evening of shared intimacy that was deeper than either had ever experienced before.

The next morning they awoke to the scream of a lynx. Ronin glanced down at the comfortable expression on Kalial's face and relaxed. He grinned. " 'Tis much safer living outside castle walls with you next to me," he stated playfully.

"Think you so?" Kalial looked up at him. She yawned and tried to stretch but her arm pulled at Ronin's.

"Your connection with the beasts removes much of the worry of nighttime attacks. With you as an ally, I am most heartened." His eyes were warm as he looked into hers.

"I almost think you compliment me, sir."

Ronin frowned slightly until Kalial smiled winningly. "And I am peaceful in the knowledge that you are near," she answered. The lightning flash of possession that gleamed in his eyes at her words left her breathless.

He rose abruptly and tugged for her to descend with him. Annoyed by his sudden haste, Kalial rose slowly, then rubbed her hands over her body as if to warm herself. Naturally, Ronin's hand was forced to accompany her actions. He breathed in deeply and looked away. When finally Kalial had tired of her game, Ronin reached out and rubbed the juncture of her thighs in a quick, dominating way. "If you seek to wake your flesh in the morning, 'twoud be best if every inch was burning," he answered to her gasp of feigned outrage. Then he turned and tugged on her again. This time she complied meekly.

As Ronin trudged through the deep snow, Kalial

danced along next to him, her weight barely breaking the crisp crust. He smiled at her, then without warning tossed her into a bank of freezing snow. Kalial responded by scooping up snow with her free hand and flinging it at his head. Ronin was greatly hampered by his broken arm and consequently had to use it only to shield his face from the cascading snow.

Laughing, he finally jerked her upright and pulled her into the warm cave. Inside, the men, tethered in pairs, were alternately grumpy and humorous as they worked at morning chores like three-legged calves. Florie shook her head at the lot of them, raising her eyebrows at the laird and princess covered in melting snow.

The next several days were filled with hard training. Ronin devised exercises that required precise teamwork. He taught methods of defense as well as attack that were designed to intimidate and confuse the enemy. He also set aside time for each partner to instruct the other about his or her particular skill. Thus, Ronin found himself outside, climbing trees, slowly beginning to use his injured arm and expand his tight chest. With new eyes he watched Kalial move with uncanny grace through the branches, her weight barely stirring the snow. Oddly, the more he learned to respect her strength, the more fragile and lovely she became to him.

Bound wrist to wrist, they practiced swordplay inside the cave. Ronin held a modified shield in their joined hands and a stick in his injured one. He concentrated mostly on teaching Kalial movements that accommodated her slight form and short reach. They worked intently on voice cues and sensing the other's need for support. Long after other men fell to their bedrolls, Kalial and Ronin still danced in the firelight, opposites in color and form, yet a perfectly unified team.

In the day, lookouts watched for the Serpent army,

for although they did not expect Lothian to traverse the pass with thick snow upon the ground, they remained wary nonetheless. Ronin spoke lengthily about his home, Roseneath, and the men nodded with appreciation when he advised them of where and how they would approach the castle when the time came. He also spoke of the lush fields and fat stock, promising each man his own cottage and plot should they be successful in reclaiming his land.

As the week wore on, Ronin wrapped his hard muscles around Kalial each night. She could feel the aroused length of him jutting into her buttocks, but he refrained from taking her. The power of their newfound connection was too flammable, too volatile. Each feared that to strengthen it further with intense lovemaking would push them beyond where they were emotionally ready to go.

Kalial loved the feel of him, the smell of him, the power of him. She would listen to him raptly as he instructed the others, watching the line of his jaw and the muscles in his neck ripple with his movements. As she became stronger, she also felt weaker for she knew virtually no resistance to the wave of feelings overrunning her heart.

One evening Ronin walked her over to the rolled tapestry by gently pulling on the tether. "I would like to tell you about my heritage, something I have not shared with anyone. It is time to tell you about the tapestry of the Scottish Gold. It holds a great significance to my family, yet I am only beginning to comprehend the essence of the tale. Perhaps together we can decipher it."

Kalial sighed. The seventh night had come so quickly. She had wondered when Ronin would sever the bond between them. Now, it seemed he had one more task for them to do. "Very well, let me look at it and I will try to help you. I have told you of some of the legends of my people, but they are complicated and take lifetimes to interpret. You ask for something that is simply not done."

"There must be a time for which each story serves its purpose. Why shouldn't now be the time to tell this one?" he replied.

The scope of his intelligence and intuition took Kalial by surprise. She no longer only saw an angry warrior set on a path of revenge. She saw a man of penetrating wisdom. She nodded. "You speak convincingly. Pull your blanket out and we will trace the patterns together."

Ronin withdrew the woven piece. "I have this piece, numeral two of three, but I also saw the first piece of the series when I was in the prison of Rath-thuaidhe." He smiled encouragingly. "The first piece described a great treasure composed of a multitude of gems, a treasure we call the Scottish Gold, along with a man and woman holding a lock and key. I wonder if the secret to deciphering the mystery of the Scottish Gold requires the insight of both a man and a woman."

Kalial stared, stunned, at the tapesty he unfurled.

Not realizing that her silence was due to shock, he continued. "I believe this piece shows in what general region the treasure lies. It appears to be a forest."

"The last piece, numeral three of three gives the exact landmarks," Kalial finished for him as she lifted her gaze.

Ronin nodded. "All the pieces are required to find the treasure, for the exact location does one no good if you do not know what country to look in."

"Is that all?" she asked.

"No," he replied. "Look at my tapestry. See the plethora of forest animals running throughout the weave? See the deep forest, the thick brush, the dark shadows?" He turned to her. "I believe it depicts your lands, the Loch Nidean forest."

Kalial breathed in deeply. "Why do you think this? Any forest contains animals, trees and brush."

"Ah, but none contain you, the princess of the forest beasts, the only person I have ever known of who can communicate with animals." Ronin looked deeply into her eyes. "Do you know where the Scottish Gold is buried?"

Kalial flinched at the direct question. Her gaze darted to her tunic and back before she averted her eyes.

Ronin looked at the garment questioningly, then back at her bent head. "Are you saying that you have been wearing the third piece all this time?" he asked her in disbelief.

Kalial bit her lip. "I told you on the ship that you had to ask for my help. You refused, saying you begged for no one's assistance. Now you are asking, so . . ."

Ronin hissed through his teeth, then reached over to spread the tunic out in front of them. He noticed the vee of the neck, rimmed with scalloped blue patterns. Over the right shoulder, a cascade of silver threads rippled. The arms of the overshirt were patterned after the wings of a falcon, and scattered on the left side were five stones set in an unusual pattern. The asymmetry of the tunic had always struck Ronin as odd, but he had accepted the dress as typical for her people. When he looked very closely now, he saw the roman numerals hidden in the hem, confirming that this used and damaged tunic was the final tapestry pointing to the site of the Scottish Gold deep within Loch Nidean forest. Ronin stared at the piece for a long time before turning back to her.

"I can not tell you more, Ronin, and I can not lead you to it, but I will let you explore the forest if you have the need."

"Kalial, I suspect you know much about this. Remember when I told you of the legend of my ancestors and the Scottish Gold? It was started by a woman of unusual traits, very much like you, and the first

McTaver warrior. That man was killed, leaving his brother to continue the McTaver name, and the woman was imprisoned by a feuding clan. The clan that attacked the first McTaver was the clan of the Serpent. Lothian must have discovered the first tapestry and followed it to Castle Roseneath."

Kalial trembled, her eyes pleading silently. Unsure of what she felt, Ronin continued softly. "Lothian seeks to unravel this mystery, but I do not want the treasure revealed at the expense of your forest. What I do want is to help you protect your forest from the Serpent."

Kalial nodded gratefully.

"There must be something precious there, something worth a great deal for the Serpent to want it so badly. However, if the only way to ensure that it does not fall into his hands is to take it myself, then I will. Do you understand, Kalial?"

"I am bound by the oldest legend of all, to protect what is in the forest from all outsiders. That includes you," she ended in a whisper.

Ronin froze, his heart stilling. A shadow of pain chased across his face. His instant response was to glower, to shout, to stalk away angrily and not speak to Kalial for the next week. But the tether between them prevented his escape and forced him to start breathing again, to look deep into her face and read the emotions there.

"Does it pain you to say that, little one?" he asked gently.

Kalial flung herself into his arms. "I am terribly confused, Ronin! I have lived every moment of my life chasing people like you from my forest and now you are warning me that you may be entering soon with the purpose of locating the treasure. I know not what to do." She buried her face in his broad chest and sobbed quietly.

Ronin sat still, feeling her tiny body quake within

the shelter of his arms. The miracle, he thought, was that he had stayed and listened to her. For that he had received the unbelievable gift of her love, for he knew that she must love him to consider showing him the secret of her homeland.

"We will do what is right at the right time, little princess. Do not worry. Know in your heart that I will protect you and what is important to you for all time. Should I continue to live, I shall take care of you in any way you want, either in duty or friendship. Shush. All will be well, little squire . . . *shush*." He crooned to her softly as he rocked her and her cries slowly drifted away as she slipped into sleep.

Morning brought the laughter of the men as they cut the ties that had bound them together. They joked and teased each other about their relief to be separated, but most ended up sitting next to each other again, eating as they had before and exercising as they had for the past week. Kalial, however, slipped over to Florie and clung to her like a monkey to its mother. Ronin had given her the dagger to cut the bonds without a word. The sense of confusion and desolation the independence gave her unnerved her completely. Dhu Cait had hissed at Ronin for the first time in weeks while the owl fluttered restlessly on his perch.

Florie held Kalial in sheltering arms, understanding as only a woman could what tumult those feelings could cause. She handed Kalial a large, wooden spoon and instructions to stir the stew pot, giving her a mindless task so that the fragile princess could recover in peace. After exchanging a meaningful look with Florie, Ronin departed from the cave, leaving the two women alone.

CHAPTER 21

With grim determination, Ronin intensified the training and started carrying a light sword in his right hand,
although he had yet to wield it forcefully. His lungs
felt stronger, but still he pushed himself to become
not only as powerful as before, and then even stronger.
Outside, the winter began in earnest. It was always
snowing and blowing so heavily that one could not
see. For a month they existed to eat and train. Slowly
the young men became harder and more disciplined.
Day by day they took on the look of warriors, until
Kalial felt a rush of pride when she circled among
them.

Kalial spent much of the day teaching knife throwing, for only Ronin himself could match her skill. At
other times she would join the archers. By silent
agreement, she did not attempt swordplay. Even the
light sword tired her delicate arms quickly and she
was easily outreached by even the smallest of the men.

During the day she felt Ronin's presence, was
aroused by his proximity yet constrained by her fears.
She could see the rippling power of his shoulders underneath a sheen of sweat and every day she ached
to taste his flesh again.

He, too, noticed her sensuous strength, but held
himself away from her, allowing her to dictate the

pace of their relationship. Although he desired to pull her aside and claim her body, he controlled himself and his wants. Her curves were delicious, but her heart was precious. Without a doubt he knew what part of her he wanted most, and he was willing to wait for it.

However, each evening Ronin pulled her aside for private training in hand-to-hand defense for he remembered all too well how easy it had been to subdue her the night he met her. These moments were charged with intensity for Kalial. The shared closeness of their bonding week was not easily ignored . . . Ronin knew the moment someone said something that insulted Kalial, although she did not show her hurt, and conversely, Kalial knew when Ronin's patience was about to break, although his face did not betray him. At these moments they would quietly interfere for the other, deflecting angry words or emotional disruptions with subtle grace, saving the other's face while protecting their privacy.

And although they barely spoke, every night they were drawn to each other out of mutual need. Kalial curled up in Ronin's arms, feeling safe with him at her back and her great cat lounging alongside. If they both lay awake, deep into the night, wishing for a more intimate touch, neither spoke of it.

The winter months sped by, and soon the drip of melting ice echoed in the cave. Ronin's arm was released from the confines of his cast and he welcomed the freedom it allowed him. Cabin fever began to permeate the group, and many of them sought excuses to go outside. Ian, however, found that the wet snow could not support his bulk as he accompanied Kalial on one of her daytime forays for fresh supplies.

"This bark contains a flavor of anise," remarked Kalial. "We should strip some of it for a flavored broth."

Ian grunted. His feet were cold and he wanted to return to the warmth of the cave to dry his boots. At times he sank up to his chest while Kalial still floated along the top. They broke through a line of trees into a long, smooth opening extending from the mountaintop down to the valley. Ian surmised it must be a snow-covered riverbed.

"Look! This is where some animals have foraged underneath this apple tree," Kalial exclaimed. "Surely some dried fruits remain underneath the snow where they have pawed." Kalial's happy voice made Ian smile. Surely 'twas better out here in the sunshine of Kalial's voice than in the gloom of the men practicing sweaty maneuvers. He trudged over to Kalial where snow had been tossed to and fro by the heavy hooves of elk. She handed him a branch and together they dug down to the ground where small dried, frozen lumps met with her delighted squeals.

"Keep the dung in one pouch and hand the fruit to me," she instructed. Ian looked at the lump in his hand with bemusement.

"How do I tell one from the other?" he asked.

Kalial sighed. "The dung is smooth, the apples wrinkled. Surely you are teasing."

Ian glanced down again in dismay at his particular lump. He dropped it quickly in a bag he carried and wiped his hands along his wet breeches. "Must we collect both?" he asked.

"You are acting like a youth who has never sullied his hands. We can use the dried dung for fuel."

"We have enough wood and the cave is plenty warm."

Kalial turned from her digging in exasperation. "And what will we do when we are traveling again, which surely will be soon?"

"Start fires along the way?" answered Ian.

Kalial shook her head. " 'Tis best to be prepared, Ian McInnish. Now, start gathering. Tomorrow I will take Erik with me instead of you. At least he values his lessons." With that insult delivered, Kalial briskly scooped up a pile of elk droppings and swiftly sorted them from the wrinkled apples.

After a moment she turned to see Ronin approaching. With a smile she went to him and popped a fruit into his mouth. "Now, when have you tasted such a treat before?" she asked. His grin of delight answered her and Ronin started searching for the treats with them. Finding a particularly large one, he turned to Kalial, grabbed her from behind and shoved the morsel between her lips. She giggled and chewed.

Ian leapt forward through the snowdrift, tossing some snow in their faces. "I have done the work of finding the apples. How come you both are munching on them?"

"Try one," Kalial laughingly replied, handing a piece of dung to him. When Ian bit into it with a horrible grimace, Ronin laughed heartily.

Kalial shouted and leapt onto both men, trying to knock them over. They stepped quickly backwards, leaving Kalial sinking over her head in the snow. She thrashed, trying to find the ground to push herself upwards when she felt a quivering and rumbling shake the mountain. Giggling, she lifted her head.

Ronin saw the snow dust covering her hair and leaned forward to brush it off, but the snow slid underneath his feet and he struggled to right himself. Ian, too, appeared to be losing his balance as he struck out toward Ronin.

Suddenly they heard a large crack and rumble. In horror, they looked up the mountainside and watched large pieces of snow and ice break free and start hurtling down toward them. Ronin recovered first, his cry of Kalial's name startling Ian into action. Together they sank their hands into the snow where she still floundered, struggling with iron determination to stay upright. The snapping of trees and the crashing of rocks came closer with surprising speed until Ronin looked up and shouted, "Ian! Get back!" He motioned wildly. "Get out of the path. The avalanche will take us all!"

"No, McTaver!" shouted Ian but Ronin shoved him and forced him back.

Ronin yelled back, "Go! Get help!" Then he turned and plunged back into the now swirling snow, reaching for Kalial's flailing arms.

Ian hesitated no longer. He struggled and slipped, his large weight the only ballast against the deadly current of snow that sought to throw him down and bury him. He reached the trees and turned just as the snow dumped over Ronin and buried him in a crushing tumult.

Ronin dove down, trying to avoid the crush of ice cascading around him. He curled into a ball, protecting his limbs, and let the force of nature carry him as he was certain it carried Kalial. He thought of her small body being battered by the nature she so loved, and tears filled his eyes. He prayed as he had never done before; he cast forth his inhibitions and silently screamed his love for Kalial. Blackness began to overtake him as the snow collapsed the air around him and began to suffocate him.

In the darkness a hallucination began, a dream of a great brown and snow white owl with huge eyes soaring high above, lazily flapping his wings every now and then. The owl was so large that Ronin mistook it for a beast, for flames surrounded his feathered wingtips. The black eyes reflected icy whiteness and golden sunrays in an exotic display. The flash of white and gold twisted and formed the swirling skirts of the Gypsy girl dancing in the light of the bonfire. The heat of the fire drew Ronin, and suddenly he began to struggle, searching for Kalial in the freezing torrent.

Kalial felt herself being swept under like a leaf in a waterfall. She had briefly seen Ronin and Ian reach out for her before the snow obscured her vision. Now she swam frantically, fighting the tide that sought to pull her down, to bury her in a frozen death. She cried out, feeling rather than seeing Ronin respond. She swam harder then, terrified that now he, too, would be killed. Suddenly her searching hands struck something hard, and with despair she realized that she had fought to find the air only to find herself at the very bottom. Her hands scrapped along the rocky mountain streambed. Ice shards ripped at her flesh where the frozen river weaved along its path.

Abruptly the ground fell out from beneath her and she felt herself free-falling along with the snow. Her hands reached out instinctively and again she met the ice plummeting down with her. Her clothes snagged on the frozen waterfall, catching her and slowing her decent before giving way to the avalanche.

Finally she hit the bottom of the waterfall and rolled underneath its frozen arch. Snow continued to rain down on her, but much was deflected by the ice above her. She crawled farther beneath the arch and found herself behind the waterfall itself, in a crystal and ice cave that held firm against the power of the falling snow. With a gasp, she pulled herself deeper within the fortress, then turned and watched the snow thunder down. Shuddering, shivering, she was consumed by great, whole body tremors that shook her like a rag doll. She could sense no animals near her, no living creatures at all. All she felt was a seeping cold that started from her soaking hair and traveled to her blue toes.

The heat burned Ronin. It was painful, this heat, this fire that pushed him. Fire . . . always fire . . . the forest fire, the fire of her eyes, the fire of her touch . . . the fire in his lungs . . . the fire that forced him to keep swimming, to keep struggling for he could feel her heat fading. He breached the surface once and took in great breaths of air. He glimpsed the brown and white beast hovering over him and saw it take a sharp turn to the right. Without thought, he dove after its shadow, immersing himself in the avalanche once again. Once his arm got whipped around his back and he feared it would rebreak. But it held, the strength of the bony callus stronger than that of unmarred bone. He finally reached the edge and felt himself flung free of the snow like a dragon spitting out a troublesome bee that persisted in stinging him.

Ronin grabbed ahold of a fearsomely large tree that glowered up at the avalanche, daring it to snap the huge trunk. The snow slipped around the ancient wood, forming an eddy that cradled Ronin. The tree roots dove deep into the earth, and then even deeper down a cliff forming a gnarled and treacherous ladder to the valley below. Great billows of snow crashed far below him, forming clouds of freezing mist. Sunlight glinted through the shower, forming a rainbow of yellow, orange and blue, pink and green. The colors danced in front of his eyes. Fire . . . he needed his fire . . . his fire needed him. . . . The sunshine sparkled off the back of a flying beast that dove into the rainbow, then climbed back out with powerful strokes of his great flame-touched wings.

Ronin began the dangerous descent down the slippery root system. His actions became fevered. A shivering began in his heart and the heat that urged him on faded another degree. Black, gold and white whirled in his mind as step after step he climbed down the cliff and into the boiling snow. He heard a resounding crack above him and felt the root system shake. All at once a shower of wooden shards peppered his skin and the ladder he straddled collapsed. Ronin found himself falling into a pile of rocks frozen into the base of an ice waterfall.

He shook his head and struggled to his feet, stumbling back against the hillside. The snow cascaded in front of him, forming an arch over his head. The waterfall formed an exquisite crescent with a carved-out lee behind. Ronin ducked under the overhanging icicles and entered the space.

A fission of heat reached out of the darkness and pulled him forward to where Kalial lay shivering. He knelt beside her and grasped her face in his hands. She looked up at him in the fading light and closed her eyes in relief. Outside their protected cavern of ice the avalanche slowed, having spent most of its fury. An odd light filtered through the ice wall and cast a blue tint on Kalial's skin.

Ronin stripped her of her wet clothing, then discarded his own, knowing that wet clothing was more dangerous than nakedness. He placed them as a pallet on the frozen ground and then scooped up some dried leaves and dirt wedged into crevices in the rock. A final thundering crash reverberated in their haven as the last pile of snow collapsed at the base of the waterfall, sealing the space through which Ronin had scrambled and plunging the area into pitch darkness. Ronin turned at the horrified gasp coming from Kalial. He reached out blindly for her and took a tentative step toward the sounds of her breathing.

"Hold on, little one, 'tis just dark. Reach out your hand for me . . ." Ronin stepped forward again, this time brushing Kalial's shoulder. He felt her cold skin contract at his touch. "There now, I have you." He felt for her hand and pulled her up to his makeshift pallet. There he sat down and placed her body on top of his, her legs on each side of his waist and her front pressed against his chest. Kalial gripped him fiercely, shaking uncontrollably.

"Do you think that we can have a moment together without either one of us landing in mortal danger?" he asked with a touch of irony. The blackness that surrounded them seemed to suck at them, as if it resented living beings breaking the silence. Ronin breathed deeply and turned his head into Kalial's neck. "You are safe now, my little one."

"You will become angry with me again," Kalial whispered in response.

"No, I will not."

"Yes, you always do. I am never what you want; I can never be what you ask . . . I am so frightened, Ronin." McTaver sat quietly, thinking about her words. The darkness ebbed and flowed around them and the warmth that had hurried him to this place settled around him like a blanket. He willed his heat to enter Kalial and soon felt her trembling slow. She cuddled against him, light and airy in his arms. He gripped her tighter, suddenly fearing that she would float away from him.

In the black cavern, Ronin felt freed from the roles he had been taught, felt released from his family's expectations. He carefully reviewed the image of womanhood he expected and compared it to Kalial.

"You are nothing like I expect, Kalial. You are strong, emotionally and physically. You have thoughts that are uniquely yours and you have the intelligence to pursue your ambitions. You are too beautiful for words, your passion is extraordinary. . . . My mother was sweet and loving and perfect, as were my sisters. I was raised to protect them at all costs. I was to be a warrior and a laird of the McTaver clan. You would have terrified my mother and most assuredly she would have shuddered at your clothing. But, in truth, I think she would have approved of you."

Ronin felt Kalial shift and sensed her looking up at him. He felt the brush of her honeysuckle breath through his damp chest hairs, causing his biceps to tighten reflexively.

"My mother's approval used to be very important to me. It still is, but even had she thought to turn you away from our door, I would stand up for you. You are as different from what I thought I wanted as this darkness is from your golden eyes, yet you are every-thing I now want and need. I love you. I love you for who you are—every irritating and lovable part of you."

The silence following his words was comforting, embracing. Kalial reached her hands up and slid them through his hair and Ronin leaned forward and brushed her lips with his. "I think I love you too, Ronin," she whispered tremulously in the dark.

Not seeing each other was intoxicating for it opened them to experiencing every touch, every feeling to its fullest. Kalial murmured love words and trailed her lips down his neck and along the powerful muscles of his shoulders. She licked and stroked him with her tongue. She pushed him back gently until he was braced against the frozen waterfall, then knelt over him, the slap of her damp hair exciting him.

Ronin felt the burn of the ice at his back and the scorch of Kalial's mouth at his front. She trailed down his body, exploring freely, the sexual tension of their months of repression bursting forth. She lapped at his nipples and nipped at his sides, causing him to suck his breath in appreciatively. Finally, in the darkness that absorbed every sense but touch, she knelt between his legs and took him in her mouth. Ronin jerked in surprise, ramming the tip of his manhood into the back of her throat, then growled in appreciation. His cock slipped into her mouth, resting on top of her pink tongue. She reflexively closed her mouth, encircling his member with her bruised lips.

Kalial felt a small, salty spurt spray her throat. She swallowed. She leaned back into the hand at the back of her head and looked up into the pitch blackness. Although she could not see it, Ronin had an expression of exquisite intensity on his face. His mouth opened slightly as he pushed inside her throat a tiny bit deeper, stunned that she had taken such daring initiative but overwhelmingly appreciative. She opened her mouth wider and slipped her tongue around and over in a swirling motion, exploring unknown territory with her taste buds. Ronin's eyes closed in ecstasy. He guided her into a smooth rhythm so that her mouth slipped back and forth. Kalial submitted to his teaching while adding sucking pressure each time his cock was drawn out and lapping with her tongue when it was pushed in. She lifted her hands to grip his buttocks where the muscles bulged. She ran her nails up and over them, encouraging him to plunge deeply into her wet, heated mouth.

Kalial captured him between her tongue and the roof of her mouth and drew deeply, sucking and releasing in an alternating rhythm. Ronin shifted his hands to her warm waist, and then because she was so slight, he was able to slide them over her buttocks. With a firm grip, he rocked her body onto him, moaning aloud at the sensation it created. He gripped each half of her cheeks and spread them apart, making her as vulnerable as she had ever been. Then, as the sucking became more fevered, he slid a finger into her secret place, the tight and sensitive place that had never been breached before.

Kalial stilled and tried to pull back, but Ronin forced her to continue, pressing her head back down and her ass back up. He used his finger again, and this time Kalial paused only because she had to gasp in pleasure. Ronin gripped her head with his free hand and coaxed her back into a rhythm, sliding her lips over his cock then slipping his finger inside of her. He repeated his alternating torture until they both began to sweat and pant with mutual pleasure. Suddenly Kalial felt her body clench and buck as the internal sensations flooded her, reaching her climax abruptly, powerfully. Simultaneously, Ronin arched his body off of the frozen floor and drove down her throat, lost in his own orgasm.

A flood of warmth spilled out of Kalial as she drank Ronin's true essence, gulping greedily. Her body quivered and shook with her feelings, no longer with cold.

She started to slump down, weak from reaching her pinnacle so forcefully, but Ronin caught her and pulled her across his body. There they lay, breathing deeply the scent of their love and feeling fully the depth of their commitment.

CHAPTER 22

They woke many hours later to the sound of renewed rumbling. Ronin gripped Kalial and buried her face in his chest. She struggled against him and tried to speak against the muffling of his body. Relenting, Ronin released her head but held her upper arms firmly.

"Dhu Cait!" she cried, "I feel dhu Cait! If dhu Cait has found us, perhaps she has led others to rescue us."

Ronin grinned in the darkness. "The only man brave enough to follow her would be Ian. 'Tis my wish that he survived."

Kalial jumped up in the dark and bumped her head on an overhanging icicle. "Ouch!" she yelped while Ronin laughed.

"Come, let's dress you before an unsuspecting man falls prey to your charms." A low humph was his only reply, but Kalial searched the darkness for her clothing. Their wet clothes had hardened into ice. When they beat them against the cliff, the ice broke off, creating a cold but dry garment. Another rumble vibrated to their left and Ronin and Kalial both wondered nervously if their rescue would in fact be the cause of their demise.

Kalial focused her efforts on communicating with the black wildcat. Through dhu Cait's eyes, she saw a huge mound of snow tumbled haphazardly around the base of the waterfall. The entire group of seventy men was digging with sticks and flat stones. She turned toward Ronin's breathing and told him of her vision.

"Advise them to dig up high and we will scale the back side of the waterfall. It will take them days to get through to us from the base and by then we would have no air to breathe."

Kalial looked upward in dismay. She was confident in her climbing skills on trees and ropes, but ice was quite different. She placed a hand on Ronin's back and with it, her trust.

Kalial urged dhu Cait to climb higher. The black McCat yowled in response, and the men outside became frenzied. As dhu Cait began digging with her powerful paws, Erik, Jordan and Ian scrambled up behind her and set to work while the other men set up an assembly line to clear the displaced snow.

Within the cave, Ronin turned toward Kalial. "I will have you ascend first for should you slip I can catch you but you could never hold my weight."

"Yes," she said aloud.

With a shove on her behind, Ronin lifted her up the rocky surface of the cliff. "Use the hillside as much as you can, but do not fear using the ice as well, for there will be strong hand and footholds within the folds of ice." Ronin placed one hand and foot on the dirt side and one in the ice. Straddled, he inched his way up between the surfaces, pausing for Kalial to climb ahead of him. Once, she slipped and her foot skidded on the slope until it jammed against Ronin's solid leg. With a faint cry, Kalial scrambled for a new ledge and pulled herself up. The space they were crawling in thinned as the frozen water hugged the cliff more closely. There they stopped and braced themselves, waiting for their friends. Outside, the men dug frantically. They cast nervous glances down the mountain to where a column of soldiers was slowly winding its way upward.

*   *   *

A sudden shaft of light struck Kalial, temporarily blinding her. A spray of ice and snow tumbled down atop Ronin's head as Ian broke through the ice with the tip of his sword. An unearthly roar sent shivers of delight down Kalial's arms. She responded to dhu Cait by squealing. Ronin and Kalial ducked as the men chopped away at the crystal fortress, creating a hole large enough for first Kalial then Ronin to squeeze through. As Ronin stepped out onto the snow, a shadow swept over his face and he looked up. The brown feathers of the owl flashed before him just as he landed on a nearby branch and turned large, circular eyes at the disheveled pair.

In the midst of Kalial's assurances that all was well, Ronin cast a suspicious look at Ian. "What worries you, my comrade? You should be relaxed at a job well done. Why do you still look concerned? And why is every man and horse here with none to guard the cave and supplies?"

Ian led them to a knoll where they could look down the mountain at the approaching soldiers. "They come." He pointed.

Ronin stared down at the column, his face hardening. "I had not thought they would pursue us into the mountains in the winter. Any reasonable commander would wait until the snow melted."

"Yes, any *reasonable* man would do so, m'laird," Ian replied. " 'Tis clear that Lothian is *not* reasonable."

"No," said Ronin thoughtfully, "he is blind to danger or foolishness. He only sees that he has been denied what he seeks. We will draw them down again and not give them rest. We have been relaxed and well fed and out of the blizzards whereas they must have traveled straight through. No doubt they are exhausted and hungry, wet and cold. Perhaps the avalanche will assist us after all. Make sure they see us up here, Ian McInnish."

"Sir?"

"I want a fire built so that they see us. They will have great difficulty climbing the tumbled snow, and indeed may lose some men to sinkholes. We will stay on the far side and wait until they have traveled up before we sneak down and then let them see that we have avoided them."

"A wild chase then?"

"Yes, until we find a good place to fight." He turned to Kalial. "For us, I will defeat them and give you back your sacred forest. I ask nothing else of you, little one. Loch Nidean shall be a hidden world as it has always been."

The wariness in Kalial's eyes was tempered by trust. "But 'tis first your fight, your fight for your lands of Roseneath."

Ian McInnish glanced between the two lovers, a faint smile flitting over his face. "To be sure, it makes sense to first get moving down the mountain before you argue over why you must defeat the bastard. Did we not plan on meeting Dugan down in the ports? Perhaps once we are together, then we can organize our defense."

Ronin nodded with a wry smile, then turned back to Kalial.

"I would like to ask your assistance, Princess of the Forest. Can you not see with the eyes of the owl? Feel the movements of the army with the canniness of your black beast?" Kalial tilted her head in affirmation. "Then send the winged bird high and follow their progress, leading us always one step out of their vision."

Kalial smiled radiantly. She straightened subtly and flung her shoulders back. She flicked her hair behind her and twisted it in a knot. Pulling a thong from her tunic pocket, she tied the tresses back. Occasional wisps still escaped but she was unaware of them. She closed her eyes, and the shadow of her lashes sent black spikes across her cheeks. She breathed in deeply and concentrated. After a moment, she opened her eyes and looked at Ronin.

" 'Twill be different here, for I know not all the creatures. It will be much more difficult and require much more concentration on my part. I am not certain I can do it," she finished quietly.

"You will do what you can," Ronin told her calmly. "Is it too much to ask?"

"No. I am pleased that you have requested my help. I only warn you that I will be absorbed in my task for these beasts are not familiar with people like me and are fearful when I contact them. To avoid their nervousness I must become part of them all. I must become part of the nature that exists here. I have never done so away from my forest. I am not sure I will be able to return to myself again without help. You will not leave me lost in an unfamiliar world?"

Ronin was shaking his head even before she was finished. "If it is too risky, I do not want you to do it. We will do fine without placing you in danger."

"Ronin," she said. "Ronin, I want to do this—I need to do it. I only ask if I can rely on you to bring me back."

"How will I do that?" he questioned, still unsure.

Kalial shrugged. "I know not. Just do what feels right, my love."

Ronin jerked at her words as if he had been run through with a sword, still amazed that she shared such feelings with him.

Placing her hands over her face, she breathed through her nose. The scents around her mixed and then separated. She drew her hands downwards, allowing her fingertips to glide over her closed eyelids, then down her smooth cheeks and over her full lips.

She arched her neck and let her fingers slip over the edge of her chin and over her pure throat.

As her hands passed over each feature, Ronin watched it relax. The hands then pressed against the upward swell of her breasts, then over the top of them. Ronin felt a surge of passion as he watched her delicate hands caress her own body. They swept downwards, over the peaks and down to her midsection. Then the angle of her wrists changed, twisted, and the fingers pointed down.

She continued to touch her body, instructing each section to leave the earthly world of sounds and enter the secret world of animal thoughts and senses. She pressed her hands downwards, over her slim hips and down her firm thighs. There her hands could reach no farther so they swept outwards, fingers wide, palms up. A faint fluttering of her hand drew Ronin to her and he swept her up into his arms as she became weak.

A hum began to build in the woods around them, so quiet at first that the men almost missed it. Then it grew, advancing with a regular beat, until the band of men could make out the swish of wings, the pad of feet, the clomp of hooves and the buzz of insects. Yet they could see nothing. Spinning around, they searched the trees and snow for evidence of the forest creatures but could see none. Ronin motioned for Erik to bring over the dainty palomino mare. He placed Kalial gently in the saddle and wound her hands in the mane. With a sigh, Kalial settled into her seat and then tilted her closed eyes up to the sky.

With a whoosh, the owl suddenly lifted off of his perch and swept upward. His body tilted slightly and he spread his wings wide, catching an updraft. Higher he flew, until he turned sharply and glided away, down the mountainside. With a deep hiss, dhu Cait rose from her sitting position and pinned her ears back. The men who had become accustomed to her presence

shrank back, reminded suddenly of how wild and untamed she was. Her long tail twitched angrily in the
white snow.

Kalial's horse sidled nervously, carefully balancing
her charge. Ronin motioned to the men to mount up
and he swung with ease onto the back of his warhorse.
With a final glance back at the distant army that was
trudging toward them, Ronin pressed his thighs together and followed the slinking black form of dhu
Cait that whispered through the shadows of the
woods.

Ronin felt a rush of excitement. The days of running
away would soon be over. Soon he would confront his
enemy. He began to think of strategies that would
exploit the arrogance of his nemesis while his muscles
rippled and stretched as he limbered his body.

The band moved upward at first, following the far
side of the avalanche path. They soon came to the
area where the snow had plummeted down the cliffside and Ronin looked at the height of the drop
with appreciation.

Ian said, "We came down about a mile to the left,
where a deer path had smoothed the way. It was hard
enough coming down. I do not think we can all make
it back up."

"No, it would be too trying for us all," Ronin
agreed. "Send two men to scale the mountain and
build a large, smoky fire." A small moan from Kalial
drew his attention and he saw a frown cross her face.
Remembering the fire that had destroyed her home,
he turned back to Ian. "Make sure it is well away
from brush or trees, so that sparks will fall harmlessly
on the snow." Ian nodded and swung around to instruct the men. Without further pause, Ronin looked
up into the sky to track the owl, only a black dot in
the distance. Ronin turned to Kalial. Sensing his regard, and partially immersed in her trance, she spoke
quietly in her exotic accent.

"They approach without caution. They are confident in their numbers and think that we will have been weakened by the winter conditions. Their travel is cumbersome. We should follow dhu Cait . . . she will shield us from unfriendly visions." Her voice tapered off and she nudged her horse forward. Ronin reached out and grabbed the reins to pull the mare around a sinkhole in the snow. With a rush of emotion, his eyes caressed her calm face, and he recalled the lessons he had taught her about team effort. He twisted in the saddle and spoke to the men, his voice carrying easily.

"Pair up. Find the partner that you worked with in the cave. Remember his weaknesses, strengths and capabilities. Together you are more than each individually, more than two added together. You are honor, integrity, safety and power. Draw from your reserves and understand that from here we will conquer all—not just the petty enemy without, but also the fearsome enemy within."

His eyes drifted to Kalial, sitting placidly in her golden beauty, and for once he did not see the swell of her breasts or the lure of her throat. At this moment he felt her in his heart and knew that she could look like anything, act like any manner of hoyden, and he would still have a lasting connection with her soul. The irony, he thought, was that she was not fully aware of the depth of his feelings, perhaps never would be, for he would give her back her freedom. She would disappear back into Loch Nidean forest and probably never recall him other than in a story for her children. But he did not care, for it was right to feel for her as he did, and it was right to protect her.

The menacing glare of the black cat intruded into his thoughts, but he did not shy from her. He smiled, understanding that her look was like that of her mistress. She was threatening on the surface, but docile when petted. He jerked his head toward dhu Cait and spoke to her quietly. "Move on now, and we will follow you. Lead your princess to safety and I will protect her from the rest."

Dhu Cait curled her lip, bared her teeth and hissed. When Ronin simply sat on his mount and looked at her, she growled silently and, with a leap, she set off through the woods, slinking just barely in sight of Ronin and the men. They traveled quickly and silently, the pairs of men needing no discussions between them to navigate the path. The only unpaired person was Florie, but she was pampered by many and did not feel the lack. In front walked Ronin and Kalial's mounts, one small and pretty, the other massive and strong, not unlike the people who rode them. Behind them they smelled the smoke of the fire.

In a dazed voice, Kalial related that the army had changed direction in order to approach the fire. She swayed in her saddle as she mentally pushed away a pack of hungry wolves that had started to stalk the party. An angry howl answered her plea, arguing with the unfamiliar presence in his mind. Silently, carefully, Kalial spoke to the alpha male again, requesting safe passage. A line of sweat appeared on her brow until the wolf pack gave in and turned away.

A sleeping bear rested in a den directly in their path until Kalial's soft voice urged Ronin to veer to the right, avoiding the confrontation. And when Erik suggested they cut through the meadow instead of traipsing through the woods, it wasn't until Kalial nodded that they galloped across the exposed tundra, safe in the knowledge that the army above was busily fending off the frustrated wolf pack and were not searching for a sign of their prey for the moment.

By nightfall they had descended a third of the mountain and had entered woods much less deep in snow. In contrast, the Serpent army was only midway up the mountain in pursuit of the decoy fire. They were entangled in the treacherous avalanche snow, cursing the rebel band that they pursued for their master. With dhu Cait leading Ronin's men, and the piercing eyes of the owl marking the way, they crept forward through the darkness. A rising sense of unity bound them together, especially as reports of the Serpent army's discontent was relayed to them through Kalial. As dawn approached they neared the lowlands and Ronin halted.

"If we travel through the unprotected lower fields, they will spot us easily from their vantage point just as we saw them yesterday. We have traveled well in the night for the woods are friendly to us. Thus, we will rest here 'til the darkness descends again and we can avoid discovery. Our fight will take place when we are ready and when they are dispirited from the chase."

He looked around to see if anyone had an opinion to add, but they were all nodding their agreement. With a small smile, he turned to Kalial from his superior height atop his mahogany horse. He gently untangled her hands and pulled her off her mount and into his arms. Her mare shifted away and Ronin grasped Kalial quickly to prevent her from falling. He moved his stallion away from the men, motioning for Ian to order the setting up of camp. When he was out of sight, he turned Kalial so that she sat astride, facing him.

She was still in a semitrance, her body held upright but soft and supple. Her lids remained closed and every now and then she whispered some information about their surroundings or the doings of the Serpent army. Ronin pulled her closer so that her lush breasts pressed against his chest. He then pulled her thighs farther apart so that they lay over his own. The heat from her center warmed his groin instantly.

"Kalial," he whispered. "Come back. This is exhausting you and you need to rest." Yet she was too deep in her trance to hear his voice, and she remained beyond his reach. He spoke louder and shook her slightly, but she did not—or could not—respond. Suddenly worried, he turned to search for the jaguar in the lightening dawn. The cat, nearby, was looking at her mistress with what Ronin perceived as concern.

Ronin turned back to Kalial and spoke again. "You brought us through the trickiest part of our descent. From here the lands are open and less dangerous, and soon we will enter familiar territory. Your job is done. 'Tis time to wake up."

But Kalial sat still, her topaz eyes concealed by her lashes. As she weakened, she sank backwards, leaning against Ronin's supporting arm until her head rested upon the broad crest of the warhorse. Lying thus, with her legs spread around Ronin's waist, her back arched over his arm and her breasts pushed forward, Ronin swallowed nervously. He focused on her, trying to keep sensual thoughts from his mind, studying instead the silver threaded tunic that she wore.

The vee of the neckline followed the smooth mounds of her breasts. Ronin shook his head and tried to ignore the figure in favor of the clothing that shielded it.

"You live in a world of symbolism, my Kalial, symbolism inherent in these woven threads." Ronin reached out one hand and touched the tip of her breast where the silver threads glistened. A sudden gust of snow stung his face and sprinkled over her body. The flakes melted almost instantly, forming round drops of water. The drops rippled and rolled down her chest as she breathed, forming rivulets that looked like a waterfall. Ronin raised his eyebrows at the sight.

"Ah . . . you told me once that things are never as they appear. Perhaps now I am beginning to understand you. I will wake you as my body woke you long ago. You lived in a trance of your own people's making, and I brought you to light with the thrill of ecstasy." He shifted her again, this time settling her on the warhorse's wide back that easily acted as a stable platform for her lithe body. With both hands free, he halted the horse in a small clearing where the sunrays glinted across her sprawled form. With a fingertip, he traced the shapes of the woven rocks on the side of the tunic. Underneath, he felt Kalial's heartbeat. Ronin ran his hand to the cleavage revealed there and traced the blue edging along the collar.

"Your body is like a hidden valley, its pleasures and delights secreted away from mortal men. But here," he tapped her bared collarbone and the tiny mole that graced it, and then dipped his finger inside the barrier of her clothing, "here is the path to your soul." He leaned forward and kissed the throbbing pulse in her neck, then licked between her breasts.

"This wet path is a river, my forest princess, shielded from prying eyes by your prickly defense. And I am the wolf, for the canine is the only beast that can tame the feline in you. We will defeat this serpent reptile that seeks your treasures, for he knows not what he seeks, nor where to find it. And you, for all your mysterious legends and powers, you, too, do not understand the final prize. You are too lost in your forest to understand the world."

Ronin blew on Kalial's wet skin and watched goose bumps appear on her flesh. Her eyes remained shut, her limbs limp. Ronin reached out and slowly unbuckled the belt that held her tunic in place. Placing one arm under her waist, her pulled her up while her head lolled back. Carefully holding still so that his horse would not move, he slowly drew the tunic off her body and cast it to the snowy ground. He leaned forward and knotted the belt in the flaxen mane of his horse, then brought her wrists up and strapped them above her head.

He sat back, staring in awe at the golden orange sunrise highlighting her bared breasts. Unconsciously his thighs tightened and the horse reared up, shaking his head angrily at the abrupt pressure. For an instant Kalial was above Ronin with her wrists pulling her up with the horse's head. Her body shook with the tossing, causing her breasts to shake back and forth in front of Ronin's lips. Kalial's body slid down a few inches, enough to press the juncture of her legs hard onto Ronin's groin.

He instantly hardened, engorged and painfully constrained within his breeches. As the horse settled back onto four feet, Ronin sought to hold it still. The horse complied, although it danced in place as if feeling the sudden fever that swept through his master. Kalial remained motionless, lost in her trance. With a rip, Ronin tore off the manly breeches encasing her legs and spread her thighs as wide as he could. The petals of her inner place opened to his gaze and he stared, relishing the power he had over her prone figure. Placing one hand on her middle to balance her, he dipped his other finger into the moistness calling to him. He felt brief resistance which he pushed through until he had breached her inner sanctum. Inside, the heat of her enveloped him and he felt his cock twitch in demand.

Punishing himself, he kept his clothing in place, using just his fingers to play with her unprotesting body. He stared at her, his blue eyes blazing. He shook with suppressed passion from just looking at her. His fingers spread her open, then slipped inside and out, bringing beads of moisture with them. This he spread over her nether lips, making them glisten in the newly breaking sun. He examined the rose that graced the peak of her womanhood and he touched it first one way and then another, playing with it as he had never been able to do with any other woman.

He swiftly ran his hands over every inch of her exposed flesh, even pushing his wet fingers into her mouth which remained slack and slightly parted. He leaned down then and kissed her midsection reverently, nipping the smooth surface. His tongue whispered lower, over her inner folds, swirling and touching, lapping, using soft strokes as he explored at his own pace.

"Here," he whispered, "is the secret. I have found the treasure yet to be made. Your body receives me even if your heart has not yet done so completely. I want to give you something, something warm and alive, that will always remind you of me. I want to place my seed deep within you." He sat up then, and drew the laces from the front of his breeches. His cock immediately sprang free, almost purple with passion, the veins along the shaft pulsing. Using one hand to open her wide and the other to guide him, he shoved his massive member into the delicate, pinkening center.

He gasped at the tightness, the slight raspiness of his entrance. His harsh sound and clenched thighs angered the horse and he again rose up in a tremendous rear. Kalial's unconscious body slid its weight down and over the shaft impaling her, burying its enormous dimensions to the hilt. Ronin let out a primordial cry, a Scottish shout that sent the steed crashing down to earth and springing forward in a thundering gallop. As the warhorse stretched out his neck, so was Kalial's body stretched flat, her breast jiggling with each rocking stride.

Ronin grabbed her waist and pumped into her as the horse careened down the mountain. Ronin was past conscious behavior; he did nothing to still the beast, but instead used its rhythm to slam his hips into Kalial, creating a union between them that could never be broken. Again and again he pushed his body into hers, his head flung back and the cords of his neck stark with muscular passion. His hand slid down from her waist to grip her hips, baring every part of her to his ravishment.

A flicker of tightening muscles inside her made

Ronin reach a fevered pitch, and soon his motions became uncoordinated, out of synch with his warhorse. Jerking out of control, he felt an answering warmth liquefy her inner soul, a tiny pulse of answering passion from deep inside her body. With a frenzied cry, he sank his sword into her, felt his hips twitch spasmodically, and poured his essence into her womb.

The galloping horse must have felt the sweeping energy throb through his master, felt the punishingly cruel tightening of his thighs and heard the screaming release. With a powerful bound, he leapt up a hillside, flinging Kalial yet again hard against Ronin. A second cry burst from Ronin's lips as he came again and the horse stretched and bunched, bringing its powerful body up and over a river embankment.

They crashed down, breaking through the layer of ice that formed a mirror reflection, and sent up a shower of ice shards and freezing, crystal clear water. The horse halted, tossing Ronin's body forward on top of Kalial's form. Still gripping her buttocks forcefully, and keeping his seat by the power of his legs, Ronin sank his teeth into Kalial's neck, marking her as a stallion does his mare.

He then pushed himself upright, feeling the ice sprinkle over his body, feeling it melt and begin to cool his burning skin. He looked down where his cock still throbbed with aftereffects, still buried within its home. He brought one hand up and touched the spot where they remained joined. He brushed a shaking finger around her entrance stretched wide with his shaft. He slid one finger alongside it for a moment, feeling his own cock encased in her flesh. Cascades of icy particles were caught in the blond hair that surrounded their union. He then touched her pleasure center, noticing an imperceptible tightening in response. He pulled out of her, slowly, very slowly, watching each honeyslick inch of him slide out, pulling at her netherlips until they showed the reddened rim.

When the tip of his member pulled out, he watched the darkened hole that had enslaved him close up, appearing like a swollen rose in a garden of crystal ice.

Ronin bent down again, kissing her abdomen stretched out before him. He looked up at her face, seeing the stirrings of awareness flit over her features. He lifted heavy hands and released her wrists from the belt. He then pulled his breeches up and retied them. Pulling her form upright, he placed his own shirt, musky with the scent of sex, over her shoulders. His own torso was slick with sweat. He placed her head so that it nestled in the crook of his neck, and then looked around for his bearings.

With a wry smile and a sigh of utter satisfaction, he picked up the reins of his horse and crooned his apologies for the abuse he had placed on the beast. Then together they turned around and retraced their footprints in the snow. Halfway back, they came across the wolf pack again, but this time it was Ronin who spoke to them, without words. The owl sank down from the sky and landed with an intense grip on Ronin's shoulder. And while he could not see her, Ronin knew that dhu Cait stalked the shadows in their wake.

CHAPTER 23

On the way back, Kalial woke by degrees. She began to breathe more erratically, she shifted positions to get more comfortable, and she became aware of a dull ache that was centered between her thighs. She smelled Ronin mixed with honey and jasmine and she felt contented and safe. Her eyelids sleepily rose and she gazed at Ronin's profile for a moment before speaking.

"We are yet still in the upper mountains?"

"No, we are approaching the lowlands. We traveled quickly with your help, Princess." He looked down at her and smiled. "You are a phenomenal woman, Kalial."

She looked at him in confusion and surprise, blinking rapidly. Embarrassed because she was naked, she asked, "Where are my clothes?"

Evasively, Ronin replied, "I believe they were lost during our morning ride."

"Lost? How can my clothes become lost?"

Ronin shrugged. "I am retracing our steps to find them."

Kalial looked at him in astonishment, forgetting the oddity of her tingling body at the absurd notion of having left her clothes behind. "Well then, let us locate them! I can not go back to the camp like this. I must have my tunic. And why am I unclothed as it is?"

"You told me that I was to waken you in the way I thought right. I did so. I woke you from the inside out. Are you complaining?" Ronin's voice rang with male satisfaction.

Kalial watched his face, waiting for an explanation that would give her more clues to what had happened.

Ronin looked down at her with a grin and wiggled his eyebrows. Kalial turned away with a humph. She pushed against Ronin's chest to put some distance between them, then swung one leg around so that she sat sidesaddle and not pressed front to chest with Ronin. He smiled at her efforts but did not stop her. A languid peace still flowed within him, and her mild grumpiness did not disturb him. He switched the reins to one hand and brought the other around her waist, cupping her soft belly carefully. He smirked.

Shortly they came to an area of trampled snow and Kalial spied her garment. With Ronin holding her waist, she leaned down and scooped it up, shaking it briskly to remove the powdery snow. She exchanged Ronin's borrowed shirt for it, and looked at Ronin's chest with a smile. She snuggled against him after he had replaced his clothes as well, and they moved on.

They approached the camp a bit later. The men were sleeping in makeshift hammocks in the trees, another adaptation they had learned from Kalial. The guards nodded silently to the pair as they dismounted. Kalial moved away after placing a chaste kiss on Ronin's cheek, her long legs flashing bare underneath her tunic.

"I need to sleep. Do you mind if I find Florie and share her bedroll?"

Ronin shook his head, understanding her exhaustion. Kalial found Florie, who scooted over and let Kalial slip beside her. Almost immediately, Kalial fell into a deep sleep, oblivious to Florie's snores.

Ronin watched her settle down, then took out his own blankets, including the tapestry of the Second Hunt. He wrapped himself up and drifted to sleep, secure in the knowledge that his men were well trained.

As night fell, the group of men along with the two females continued down the mountain. Kalial was alert now, communing only with the owl. The winged creature informed her that the army had finally reached the area of the campfire, discovered that it was deserted, and were now searching the woods. Another day and night passed with them still searching the upper mountains before Ronin led the band out into the meadows of the lowlands. Because the distance between the enemies was so great, Kalial called back the owl and they traveled again by day.

Within the week they reached the first coastal town of Gigean. Hardened sailors and coastal farmers populated the town, but it was smaller and more peaceful than the town of Rath-thuaidhe. They headed for the town lodgings whose doors were opened wide to them with the exchange of a gold piece that Kalial still held from the Gypsies. A group slightly over seventy strong, they overfilled the dining area and the stables as well as the neighboring tavern.

Kalial and Florie retired to a private room. A bath was ordered and soon Kalial was shoulders deep in a warm and fragrant tub. Florie leaned over her and massaged her gently.

"You have been quiet since leaving the mountains, dear," she mentioned to Kalial while her strong fingers soothed muscles tired from riding.

"I feel quiet," Kalial replied.

"You are not angry? You are usually able to be upset about something."

Kalial smiled wistfully. "No, I am not upset, I just feel content. Odd to be sure, but true nonetheless.

Something happened up there . . . something that changed me."

"Oh? You mean in the avalanche?"

"Yes, and after. I feel as if the pieces of my soul are coming together. I used to think that I had everything I needed in Loch Nidean. Now I think I need something else."

"Something or someone?" Florie questioned. When Kalial did not answer, Florie added, "You have avoided Laird McTaver for the last two days."

"I am not avoiding him, I am simply thinking and do not want his confusion near me." She turned around suddenly and looked at Florie. "Remember at the castle how you dressed me in gowns but I could hardly stand them?"

"Of course," Florie replied with raised eyebrows.

"I was not ready," finished Kalial.

"Ready?"

"I was not ready to be a lady like that," Kalial replied. "You dressed me and scented me and tried to instruct me, but I did not understand the meaning of it all." She turned back around and sighed. "I think I understand now. I think I understand what it means to want to be a woman."

Florie continued to massage her shoulders silently. She unbraided Kalial's hair and poured water over it. The harsh soap softened into a rich lather in her golden locks. As the suds were rinsed, the golden and platinum highlights sprang free, creating a subtle halo around her face. Her skin was a pale honey hue, its warmth welcoming. The amber eyes that had often sparkled in anger now glistened with maturity underneath dusky lashes.

She turned those magnificent eyes back up to Florie. "What think you that we find me a dress to wear tonight?"

Florie smiled and nodded. "Let us get you out of this tub before you prune up and I will find you something. 'Twill not be as nice as what you wore in the castle, I am afraid . . ."

"No matter. I just want to feel the sensation of skirts rubbing along my calves."

Florie drew Kalial up and wrapped her in a thread-bare towel that felt like heaven to Kalial. She then placed her in a chair facing the fire and slipped out to find some suitable clothing.

When she returned, she found Kalial standing naked in front of the fire. Kalial turned to her unselfcon-sciously. Florie pulled out a soft dress made of deli-cately flowered designs. The cloth was a very light shade of pink and the flowers were rose, white and burgundy. A tiny row of scalloped lace edged the bod-ice and the hem. At the end of the sleeves, sweet, dark pink ribbons trailed to the floor.

"I have no underclothes for you, my dear. You will have to wear your old ones until I can find some."

"I would rather wear none," Kalial replied blithely. She was unaware of the amused expression on Florie's face. In a trice, Kalial slipped on the gown. To her consternation, it bagged away from her body at the waist.

"Here now, we are not done, my pet." Florie pulled another set of long ribbons from her pocket and began threading them through loops along the side of the dress. She crisscrossed them in front and in back, forming a web encasing Kalial's slender form. At her hips, the gown fell in wide sweeps of fabric and she spun around gaily, feeling it flare out around her.

Kalial turned happy eyes toward Florie. "It is lovely," she said quietly, "and I shall enjoy wearing it tonight."

"You do that, Your Highness. You be every inch the lady you are, for it takes a very special person to be both a sturdy survivor and a soft woman."

Kalial licked her lips, then applied a bit of the scented oil Florie gave her. The oil made her lips glis-

ten in the firelight. Her cheeks were already flushed,
echoing the delicate hue of the dress. Her hair flowed
loose around her shoulders, a sparkling waterfall.
Barefoot, she skipped downstairs to the threshold of
the main dining room, then paused and walked se-
renely inside.

Ronin noticed her immediately, but he remained
still in his corner. His eyes were gentle as he looked
upon her with quiet pride. Soon the other men in the
room saw the beauty, and a rapid shuffling occurred
while they vied to provide a seat for her. She giggled
at their efforts, and gracefully took a seat in the
center.

She turned toward the men nearest her and curved
her mouth enticingly. "Perhaps one of you could find
some refreshment for a parched traveler?" Ronin
watched the ensuing scramble with amusement and he
winked at Kalial when she happened to glance his
way. The flush on her cheeks deepened and she swiftly
averted her sparkling eyes. However, she slanted another look at him and was pleased to see him watching
her still.

A strange gaiety filled her heart and she proceeded
to flirt outrageously with the sailors at her table. Her
regal bearing protected her from too much familiarity,
yet her beckoning eyes caused the men to hover
around her, waiting and hoping that they would catch
a special appreciation from her.

Ian sank into a seat next to Ronin. "Her behavior
is not upsetting you, m'laird?"

Ronin smiled and his blue eyes crinkled at the corners. "She is only experimenting as any young, beautiful lady should. She is still trying to figure out what
manner of woman she is."

"And you do not fear that she will drift away from
you? You were not so trusting with Lord Basingstoke."

Ronin turned toward Ian in surprise. "You are close

to being impertinent, McInnish. If I could not see your face I would wonder if your name was not that of my first mate's."

Ian grinned. "I mean no disrespect, sir."

"No, I am sure you do not, yet Dugan Trask would not care if he was as rude as a boar charging through a lady's parlor." Ronin watched Kalial glance up at him with a quick flash of her eyes before turning toward a swarthy fellow who was trying to gain her attention. He then answered Ian with a voice as hard as steel. "I have made her mine and no one will take her from me. Though she may not know it yet, she will always be bound to me, even should her footsteps take her far from me."

"And you," Ian replied quietly, "are you bound to her as well?"

Ronin fell silent. His eyes darkened and he glared at Kalial across the room such that she gave a start and looked at him with surprise. With an oath, Ronin suddenly stood up and strode over to her, scattering men in his path. Kalial sprang up and focused her brilliant eyes on his immense, thundering form.

"M'laird?" she questioned softly. She lifted an elegant hand to his chest and stopped his angry strides with her index finger. Ronin froze, his chest constricting at her touch.

"Come outside with me," he commanded her through clenched teeth, and then hissed out his breath in surprise when she demurely complied. He watched the lovely swish of her hips as she slowly moved toward the door. At the entrance she glanced over her shoulder. A gust of wind from the open doorway lifted the pale strands of her hair and tossed them around her face. She sent a golden, catlike look at him through the veil of her hair and Ronin abruptly strode after her.

Outside, he grasped her hand and, without a word, led her toward the docks. The feel of her tiny fingers nestled in his bearlike paw sent shivers down his spine. They walked quietly down the boards, his flare of anger gone, until they reached the end. The ocean flickered in the moonlight beneath their feet and Kalial turned toward him questioningly.

Ronin looked down at her from his height. He lifted his hands and traced her eyebrows, then cupped her cheeks. Lowering his head, he placed a gentle kiss upon her scented lips. "I . . . do not want to lose you," he whispered to her. Kalial looked at him in confusion, but Ronin only grinned lopsidedly at her implied question.

He slowly straightened and tore his gaze from her to look out over the water. "I remember the night my family was murdered . . . I can still see the blood of my father splattered against the gray stones."

"I remember the image of your dark, sweaty back moving through my forest and the sound of your horse's labored breathing the day you fled into Loch Nidean to escape Lothian's men."

Ronin nodded. "I see the agonized look on my baby sister's face as she was tied and molested. I recall the agony that sent me into your forest for I feared the legends less than I feared my failure."

Kalial's soft, exotic voice answered, "Let go of the bad thoughts, Ronin. They will swallow you. Try to think of wonderful moments, moments that changed your life for the better. Instead of thinking of the forest fire, I remember feeling your hands lifting me to safety."

With a sigh, Ronin smiled gently and replied, "Yes, that was a special moment. At that time, I wanted to protect you because I could not protect my family."

"And now?" she asked gently. "Now what do you want?"

He turned toward her. "Now I want to know why you pledged to me that day on the coast."

Kalial stared at the light skittering over the water.

"I wanted to protect you because I had failed to protect my forest family."

"Do you think that is what is between us? A common bond forged of guilt?"

"Why do you ask?" Kalial's voice was thready and uncertain.

Suddenly he turned to face her again and gripped her shoulders. "I need to know what I am to you!"

Kalial shook her head in confusion. "I don't understand what you are asking," she finally answered. She pulled away from his grip and looked out over the blue waves that mirrored his searching eyes. "This is your world. These"—she swung her hand toward the town—"these buildings, these clothes, these rules. I once felt disconnected without the closeness of my forest. I am not sure now."

Ronin took a step back. His eyes shuttered. "You want me, that I do know, and if you deny it you are denying yourself."

Kalial nodded. "Oh yes," she breathed, "I want you all the time."

They were silent, the memory of her words reverberating in their minds as they looked at each other, but the deeper questions left unanswered. Ronin finally lowered himself to the pier and pulled her delicate body into the vee made by his bent knees. Her pink dress billowed around her as she sank down. She leaned her head against his broad chest and Ronin tucked it safely beneath his chin. They sat peacefully, simply absorbing each other's presence.

Stars came out and began to twinkle in the heavens. When Ronin looked down, he saw Kalial slumbering. He picked her up in his arms, and carried her to their bed.

Kalial woke slowly to the tickle of whiskers across her face. She smiled softly and murmured an incoherent greeting to her black beast. She stretched her arms over her head and yawned. Then she rubbed her fists into her eyes and tried to open them fully. With a blink she spied the hulking form of Ronin seated at a desk across the room. He was watching her, his eyes alight with appreciation.

" 'Tis not often that a sleeping goddess awakens so sweetly that the birds are stirred." Kalial blinked again and tried to concentrate on his words. She cocked her head as she heard the twittering of songbirds outside her window. Suddenly a brilliant smile flashed across her face and she laughed aloud. Ronin grinned at her, then turned back to the maps he was studying. She arose languidly, pulled a robe around her form, and ambled over to him. The cat padded silently beside her.

"Tell me what you are planning," she said quietly.

"We will move along this pass edging the coastline until we gain Mount Sheila. This canyon is where we have skirted Loch Nidean for generations. The path is clear and easy. From there it takes five days to reach my lands if one travels along the back edge of the forest."

"It looks to be much faster if one traverses the forest."

"Assuredly," Ronin replied. "But there are demons and Druids inhabiting the infamous trees and all who have entered it have never exited." He looked at her with a raised eyebrow.

Kalial looked down at him in smug satisfaction. Her accent thicker than normal, she purred under her breath. "What good fortune then that we are in a position to have no fear."

"What good fortune indeed. With your help we will slip through the forest and gain the other side well in advance of the Serpent army. From there we will set up an ambush." Ronin's face became grim. "I shall be satisfied with nothing less than complete annihilation. The man and his mercenaries shall be devastated, vanquished such that they never dare rise up against the clans or your people again."

"But what of the tapestries? Do you need to find the Scottish Gold as well?" Kalial leaned her elbows against the table. Ronin glanced at the creamy flesh thus exposed and felt a surge of possessiveness at the telltale red mark on her neck. He reached up to stroke it but Kalial pushed his hand away. "Ronin? The tapestries?"

"They are the maps leading to riches that the Serpent covets. However, I fear that should we not destroy the man, he will not rest until he has torn your forest home apart in his quest for the treasure." Ronin looked up, his midnight blue eyes boring out under his black, tousled hair. "I will not allow that to happen, I stake my life upon it."

Kalial appeared startled, then she glowed. Reaching out to stroke his powerful arm, she watched the play of her light honey skin against his hard, dark warrior flesh as if mesmerized. She raised her eyes to his and gold met blue like the sun setting on a stormy ocean. "I trust you . . . I will show you where the treasure lies, if you need it," she murmured, so quietly that Ronin was not sure he had heard correctly.

The world seemed to stand still. He leaned forward, straining to hear her words, to see if he had interpreted her correctly, but Kalial pulled swiftly away. She gripped her robe closely about her neck and clucked to her jaguar.

Then with unconscious grace, she stepped out of her robe and reached to pick up Ronin's discarded fine lawn shirt. She leaned over and smelled it in an achingly sensual manner. Ronin's jaw dropped and he started to his feet. Unaware of his response, Kalial sighed and slid the garment over her head.

"See if you can find me today. . . ." She smiled in his direction, exited, and headed back to the room she shared with Florie.

Ronin sank back down in his seat, surprised to feel a fine sheen of sweat on his brow. He abruptly rose again and strode over to the window. The thought of her leaving him forever soon after he had accomplished his goal was terrifying. For a moment he tried to imagine keeping her . . . demanding that she stay near him . . . forcing her to remain in the open lands where he dwelled. She had adjusted well, and she appeared to enjoy the freedom she had experienced since their fateful meeting. But as swiftly as the thought came there followed the knowledge of her complete devotion to her land, her communion with her forest beasts, and he knew that he could not force her to stay with him.

He rubbed his face with his hands. The powerful breadth of his shoulders sagged. It was torture to play like this, to dally with her while every moment in her presence wound his heart tighter. He felt as if he was losing control over his emotions. His reactions to her were beyond primitive and he did not know how to handle them. A shudder went through his frame and he looked out the window into the yard below.

His band of seventy men was practicing under Ian's careful guidance. They were shaping into a fearsome fighting force, all that they had endured having melded them together. No longer mere youths struggling to wield wooden sticks, they had become men who snapped to attention and practiced their forms with powerful intensity. Along the periphery he saw several sailors and farmers watching.

Turning away, he returned to his maps and plans. He resolutely put away his thoughts of Kalial in order to fully concentrate on his strategy. It was several hours before he went downstairs to confer with Ian.

Kalial spent the day wandering the surrounding hillside with dhu Cait. She drifted softly through open meadows and felt the sun on her face. Spring was blossoming in the lowlands, and Kalial reveled in the warm air. Sitting amid a grove of bluebells, she lazily touched each flower until she found one whose color was deep enough, rich enough, to compare with Ronin's eyes. She felt oddly complete, with a sense of fullness throughout her body and soul. The time up on the mountain had given her a chance to get to know Ronin, to experience the many facets of his complex personality. He had been fierce, protective, caring. He had also been angry, demanding and unforgiving. Yet throughout it all, also unalterably loving.

She rolled over and sank her head onto dhu Cait's glossy hide. A rumbling growl vibrated from the cat's chest. Kalial pulled herself up and sat on the beast as she had when she was young. Dhu Cait glanced back over her shoulder and flicked her tail, questioning her mistress.

With silent communion, Kalial slipped off her back and they headed into the shadows of the nearby trees. A muddy creek bed circled through the glen. Kalial walked into the water, feeling the mud ooze between her toes. She sat down facing upstream. An instant arc of white water was created as the current hit her abdomen, splashed upwards and crashed into the under swell of her breasts. Tiny droplets instantly covered her hair in a fine dew. She opened her legs, parting her thighs just enough to funnel the water so that it was focused on her juncture. The water instantly gripped the thin skirt she wore. The cloth slipped up her thighs and bunched around her belly with the bulk floating downstream. A ripple of secret delight wafted through her body.

She closed her eyes, thinking of Ronin, and leaned back on her hands as her hair swirled with her skirts. Kalial closed off all her senses except those whispering, rippling in her velvet center, and concentrated on calling him to her. She breathed deeply, lifting her thinly clad breasts into the dappled light. She curled her bare toes into the mud and smiled at the wet, slick sensation. She did the same with her fingers, kneading the wet earth like a golden lion. As she stirred the mud, it swirled and eddied around her, coating her limbs with a dark paint. The ends of her blond tresses picked up the dark coloring, creating exotic streaks. The breeze that wafted through the trees was filled with a spring scent.

The current around her suddenly shuddered and built, splashing her so that water raced up and around her breasts and over her shoulders before settling back down. Yet in the aftermath of the surge, a heaviness hung near her and the musk of aroused male surrounded her. Keeping her eyes closed, she licked the water droplets that clung to her lips. A hiss of indrawn breath sounded behind her.

Kneeling at her back, Ronin took in the offering placed before him. He reached into the riverbed and sank his large hands into the muddy bed. Scooping up the wet earth, he slid his hands over her arms which braced her, covering them in a thick coat of slick dirt. The natural oils of her skin mingled with the fragrant mud and made it into a soft, slippery sheath that alternately cooled and heated. Slowly, experiencing every nuance, Ronin slid his hands over and around, exploring the taunt and supple muscles that formed her flawlessly feminine body. With another scoop, he began to coat her shoulders but deliberately avoided her breasts. He shifted and rubbed, massaging her neck and back with the slippery mud, slavering her body. Kalial kept her breathing steady, focusing on tilting her body for the flow of the water and allowing him access to all else.

Ronin progressed up her neck, then slid muddy fingers into her silver-blond hair. Kalial felt the tug upon her scalp as he spun wet loam through her hair. The weight of the mud dragged her head back farther and she felt her throat completely exposed to the man who handled her. Stroke after stroke, he coated her hair so that the blond princess was obscured and a dark, svelte nymph replaced her.

When her head was covered, he played with her hair, drew his fingers through the wet strands. Then he slid his hands over her shoulders again and Kalial felt the roughness of his callused fingers slide easily through the mud cloak. He continued down her sides and then plunged into the water between her legs.

With a sudden roughness that made her pant, he pulled her legs further apart until the water pounded not only against her nub, but also buffeted her entrance, seeking admission. With fingers clean from the creek, Ronin pushed two fingers inside her, plunging them in without asking. Kalial's heat more than welcomed him. Her insides were meltingly hot and slippery and they spasmed around his intrusion. He spread his fingers apart, opening her wide for the current. The water surged and paused, lifted and sank, plunging into her in an unending motion. Kalial gasped and her eyelids flickered.

"Keep them closed," Ronin softly commanded her, and she responded with instant obedience.

He looked down at the woman who had flirted with nature's power and was now being loved by her most precious offspring, the almighty essence of water. The pure, unbridled sexuality of her actions was so natural, just as his fighting spirit was so much a part of him. She was water, he was fire. He lived to consume yet she had the sweet power to temper his flames.

She shook and shifted between his arms, and a wave of weakness had her leaning against his chest. Every part of her was covered in mud except for her pristine wetly clothed breasts. While his one hand stayed between her legs and spread her wide for the current's lovemaking, the other grasped the edge of her bodice and yanked it down, sliding it under her breasts, pushing them up. He leaned over her and sank his teeth around her flushed nipple, causing her to yelp and squirm. Replacing his teeth with his lips and tongue, he suckled hungrily. Pulling hard with his mouth, he lifted her slightly, enough to slide his hard shaft under her body so that it nestled between the twin moons of her rear and pointed into the water that cascaded in and out of her inner sanctuary. As if scenting her in the streaming water, his member pulsed and probed and Ronin rocked his hips against her mud slick back.

Kalial felt the abrupt increase in heat and the velvet steel head rub between her cheeks and tickle the edge of her inner lips. She wriggled, trying to twist toward him, but his teeth sank into her, warning her to remain pliant to his wishes. His other hand came up and plucked at her other nipple, rubbing it and teasing it until she could not decide what would hurt more, for him to continue or for him to stop.

The water that poured inside her picked up her wet juices and washed them down, over the throbbing tip of Ronin's shaft so that they were swamped by the same current, the same sensations, the same surges of flowing water. Ronin sucked harder, then licked and laved, while he rocked harder and faster against her back, sliding his rod between her cheeks and into the throbbing water. Kalial was buffeted on both sides, in the front by the creek and from behind by his powerful strokes. Ronin's harsh breathing echoed in her ear and matching pants exploded from her own throat.

Suddenly, Ronin lifted her several inches so that instead of her hips sitting underneath the rippling water, they were held directly in the splashing stream surface. Gasping, both Kalial and Ronin felt the abrupt increase in power, the sudden fury of the water pummeling them. Ronin forgot her nipple and, closing his eyes, flung his head back along with Kalial's. He gripped her hips to force her to stay in the rapids even though her body shook and quivered very near to her release. Pushing hard against her, faster and faster, he lifted her out of the water. The sudden blast of sunshine against her shot her to the edge, yet she held back, waiting for permission to drop over the pinnacle with him.

Within seconds, or eons, she could not tell, he pulled her back down into the heavy current and allowed a fresh, full, driving surge of water to fill her inner warmth as it clasped and clung to the ridges of his shaft. With a harsh "Now!" Ronin slammed her body against his and they both exploded. Ronin's jet of release burst out and tangled with the swirling water. It was carried inside of her where her inner convulsions alternately grabbed it, then expelled it, only to thankfully receive it yet again as the water eddied and crashed. The sensations continued, on and on, as the ecstasy swept from the burst between her legs to a limpid fire all along her limbs. She felt herself floating upon his pulsing shaft that burned her buttocks, branding her.

Then, having lost all sense of time, she slowly woke, finding herself alone, spread eagled on the grassy bank with sun slanting through the leaves, the sound of the now peaceful creek bubbling nearby and dhu Cait perched on a branch watching her.

CHAPTER 24

Several days later, the company was ready to move on. Erik had seen traces of smoke in the valley below the mountain, and Ronin and Ian agreed that the army pursuing them should not be allowed time to rest and recoup from their fruitless and exhausting search on the snowy ridges. Several sailors had been sent to look out for Dugan Trask and the crew of the *Bonny Evelyn* and would meet them back at the port of Rath-thuaidhe.

Kalial and Ronin stuck close, never speaking of what they felt but constantly touching each other as if to be reassured that they were together. Ronin incorporated her entirely in his plans, something he would never have conceived of doing with a female in the past. On her part, she listened and learned from him, granting him a respect she had never before bestowed upon another.

Instead of following the well-worn but circuitous road inland, they traversed the rocky coastline, using the skills of the scout and the eyes of the owl as guides. Upon reaching the various rivers that poured into the sea, they would find a shallow area and forge across, Ronin's warhorse in the lead, followed closely by Kalial's dainty palomino mare. Ronin knew that despite her petite stature, the mare would carry her

charge safely for once again Kalial had created a sur-
passing bond with the creature. Dhu Cait was perhaps
the least amused by the river crossings, but she gamely
leapt in, swimming powerfully across only to reach the
other side with a glare and a thorough cleaning that
started at her paws and ended at the tip of her tail.
They traveled swiftly, intending to reach the port well
ahead of the Serpent army.

At night, the men practiced in deadly earnest, for
they knew that the moment was close when it would
be decided whether they died in agony or lived in
freedom. Ronin worked diligently with Kalial, teaching her self-defense and hand-to-hand sparing that
would be necessary should they be overtaken. Never,
he swore to himself, would he again allow a woman
he loved to be as helpless as his mother and sisters
had been in their time of need.

He taught Kalial how to abruptly shift the direction
of her attack and throw her foe off balance. He taught
her ways to apply pressure so that a tiny person like
her could fell a huge warrior. He also showed her how
to grasp a wrist and twist while bending it so that the
other person stumbled to his knees.

They finally reached Rath-thuaidhe about midday a
week later. Spring was in full force, and Kalial was
surprised at how different the town looked under the
cloak of leafy trees and ornamental bushes. It was
immediately clear to her that the people of Rath-
thuaidhe recognized them as a fighting force, for they
stepped out of the street and fell silent as their horses
filed past. Ronin's face was grim as he held his prancing mount in check. Memories of his incarceration in
this town weighed heavily on his mind.

Kalial, dressed in breeches, rode proudly upon her
steed. Many of the townsfolk stared at her in shock,
stunned to see a woman in men's attire. Florie knew
the town well, so it was she who led them to an area
on the outskirts of town where it was suitable to camp.

The site overlooked the ocean, the town and the road north from whence Kalial and Ronin had come many months ago. Kalial remained in camp with Ian while Ronin and four others rode back into town to pick up provisions and seek word of Dugan. Tensions remained high, with fears that the Serpent army would reach them before their preparations were complete.

Ronin glanced over at the owl sitting on a branch rigged to the back of his saddle. Pulling on a leather vest to protect himself, he whistled at the bird. It instantly took flight, a slow, lazy flap of its wings, and flew above the men and horses as they entered the township.

As he rode the streets, Ronin felt the clammy sensation of being watched, but he could not locate the culprit. Assuming it was only his instincts on heightened awareness, he tried to dismiss the tingles. The gold coins were almost gone, but there was still enough to purchase some supplies so Ronin set off for the blacksmith, the granary and the dockyards with an air of purpose. At the dock there was no sign of Dugan, but a pair of his crew quickly made themselves known.

"Captain!" one of them cried and shuffled over to Ronin in a rocking gait. " 'Tis been uncommonly long that we have bided our time on these shores awaiting word from you."

"Where is my first mate?" Ronin replied curtly.

"He's not in Rath-thuaidhe, Captain. He sailed up the coast, thinking he might have missed you. We thought you were to descend from the mountains before winter set in."

"We had to change our plans. Is all well?"

"Aye, we are ready."

"Then send a runner up and down the coast, catching every port, until one of you spots the *Bonny Evelyn.*"

"Aye, Captain."

"Tell all to meet here, quietly and quickly. The Serpent follows by only two days. When all of you have congregated, travel at the army's back. We may have need of a flank defense and a force in place to kill any Serpents who attempt to retreat." Ronin's voice dropped to a growl and his eyes narrowed. "Make it perfectly clear to all that *no one* is allowed to go free. All of them are to be slaughtered! I want the sword hand of every man that joined with the Serpent placed at my feet in the courtyard of Roseneath. Any who fail me in this goal will join the ranks of my enemies."

"Yes sir, we will pass the message along, sir. But by my marks—there will be no dissent. We will slay any straggler who thinks to escape."

"Good. We have to make some preparations, but will leave the town shortly, traveling along the pass road. That is the direction I wish for you to take as well."

A sudden clang had the men spinning toward the alley behind them. A shadow leapt from between some wooden barrels and raced down the street. With a start, other crewman chased after him. A breeze whispered past Ronin's black hair as the owl dove from his perch on a roof gable and followed the men.

His body humming with anger at this fleeing spy, Ronin turned back to the sailor. "You have your instructions. If you catch that eavesdropper, bring him to my camp. He is probably no more than a drunk, but I am not pleased that he heard our plans."

"Aye, Captain."

With a curt nod, Ronin walked away in the company of his fighters. They quickly located the blacksmith. Flashing coin, they persuaded the man and his son to pack up their traveling wagon and come out to the campsite that afternoon. Finally they approached the granary. There they did not have as much luck.

" 'Tis closed, m'laird," one man remarked needlessly.

"It should not be," Ronin answered. "Go around the back and see if you spot the proprietor." A moment later a shout signaled that he had located his quarry. Ronin strode to the back and beheld the man dangling from his shirt collar. With lifted eyebrows, Ronin indicated that he could be set back onto his feet.

"Open the store," he demanded, but the storekeeper simply shook his head and showed his yellowed teeth in a grimace. Ronin McTaver slowly advanced. "Have you reason to refuse my business, stupid man?"

"I'll no trade with ye!" he shouted and spittle shot from between his broken teeth.

"And why not, pray tell?"

"We 'ave all been warned, ya see. We no trade with the likes of ye or all our shops will be burned."

"When did you receive this warning?"

"Just a bit ago. But even w'out it, I'd no help ye for I know where the power lies and it nay be w' ye."

"You are loyal to the snake then?" Ronin asked in a deceptively mild tone.

" 'Til me dying day," the man answered with a smirk.

"So be it." Ronin inclined his head and smiled, but the humor did not reach his eyes. He turned away and paced to the back door. As he kicked it in, he heard a gurgling gasp behind him and the sounds of pummeling fists against flesh. He did not look back.

Inside the darkened storeroom, lit only by a low-burning lamp, Ronin selected sacks of grain and flour. He leisurely circled the area, finding other provisions that he felt would be helpful, among them ropes, waterskins and woven blankets.

Behind the counter, a black box caught his eye. He slowly walked around the barrier and lifted the box. He carried it to the back door where sunlight still managed to light the dim interior, and opened it. Inside nestled a necklace formed of exquisite pieces of amber interlaced with shimmering white crystals. Cushioned in the center of the necklace were two thick, golden wristbands dotted with amber and crystal and inside them a ring formed entirely of amber, displaying a crystalline diamond upon it.

Ronin lifted the ring and examined it closely. Sunlight turned the yellow stone into a glowing ring of amber fire and the white stone cleverly attached sprinkled rainbows of muted colors into the gloom. Ronin replaced it in its velvet home and picked up the bracelets. Unlike the necklace, it was made of solid material, yet wherever a stone was set, the gold had been carved out of the back so that light could filter through and cause the stones to glitter. The crystals were shaped in shards and formed into pairs of wings while the amber wove in swirls reminiscent of honeysuckle blossoms. A solder pin formed the clasp.

He stared at the jewelry, quietly contemplating the differences between Kalial's culture and his own. The ring to him symbolized marriage, commitment and ofttimes love. To her, the ring would undoubtedly mean little, yet the bracelets would mean all of that and more, based on her previous description of the elevenday bonding ceremony. He stared at the bracelets, debating.

Finally, he closed the box with a snap and walked out, carrying the box. There was a fluttering in the air and then a sharp grip as the owl landed on his leatherclad shoulders. The men with him quickly gathered up the items and left the yard.

At the edge of his vision Ronin spied a man's shadow stalking him, but he did not give chase. He simply stared hard at the shadow and lifted one brow in silent challenge. The Serpent's spies were not his main concern, for the threat of the full army loomed larger with each delay.

*   *   *

Kalial paced restlessly, feeling oddly disconnected with Ronin gone. She tried to convince herself that there was no cause for worry, but unease enveloped her, swamping her mind. Dhu Cait stalked alongside her, her supple body swerving at the ends of their self-imposed boundaries, her ears pinned to her head and her eyes glittering. The men who remained in camp avoided them entirely. In sudden frustration, Kalial stalked over to her bedroll and pulled out her tunic tapestry.

Loch Nidean and the Scottish Gold. The two legends had melded, just as she and Ronin had melded. Yet she was still bound to protect the secret of her land. But from who was she to shield it? From anyone or only from those who would abuse it? As part of Kalial's initiation as a princess, she had been rowed out to the lake where her mother had shown her the secret of Loch Nidean. It was an unimaginable treasure which she was proud to protect.

The sound of approaching hoofbeats had Kalial spinning around to locate Ronin. She saw him immediately, his massive warrior's frame atop his mahogany warhorse. A surge of emotion made her heart beat rapidly and she brought her hands up to cover her chest. Ronin did not stop until his mount was towering over her. Eyes locked together, Ronin reached down and pulled her fingers away from her body and clasped them within his. Bending farther still, he brushed his lips across her knuckles.

"I worried about you, Ronin," she whispered.

"I missed you, Kalial," he responded, his voice as soft as hers. Then he straightened and released her hand.

Moving away from her, he started directing the distribution of goods. The horses were all given a measure of grain, a treat for which they were pleased.

Several butted and tossed their heads for more, but Ronin was adamant that they not receive too much and founder prior to the coming battle.

The blacksmith wagon arrived, a bit to Ronin's surprise for he would have thought they might be warned away.

"Ho there, master blacksmith. I welcome you gladly."

"Augh, 'tis I who am pleased to leave the town and serve your needs, although I know not if I will be welcomed back into the streets after 'tis known I came out here."

"The word is that strong?" questioned Ronin.

"Aye," the blacksmith replied and a boy nodded behind him. Ronin saw a woman seated there as well. "My wife, Kathleen," the man introduced. "A good and honest woman, mother of my son, Jake. And I am Angus."

"Does she normally come on call with you, Angus?"

"Indeed no, m'laird, but I feared to leave her alone in town tonight."

"I suspect you have no intention of returning to Rath-thuaidhe, blacksmith."

The man looked down for a moment, then glanced back at Ronin with resolution. "No, m'laird, we do not."

"Have you a destination in mind?" he queried. The man shook his head. With a sigh, Ronin turned toward Kalial, who smiled at him. "We would be pleased to have your skills in our camp, master craftsman, and those of your family as well." The boy, Jake, let out a whoop of joy, then dashed to the back of the wagon to assemble the firing equipment. Florie ambled over and pulled herself up the step of the wagon until she faced the wife.

"You are a blessed addition, mistress, for I am plumb tired of doing all the cooking for these heathens!"

The woman grinned and pulled out a bag. "I brought an offering of thanks, should your laird allow us to stay."

"By heaven! Salt! The saints have brought you to us for sure! Come, I will show you where we have set up." Florie all but dragged the woman off her perch. The two older women quickly exchanged names and fell into a female prattle that was incomprehensible to the nearby fighters.

Kalial and Ronin brought out each horse and with her at its head, soothing and comforting it, the blacksmith and his son trimmed and reshod the first fifteen before darkness fell. Bone weary, the blacksmith clambered into his wagon and started examining the various weapons that needed repair. He worked until Kalial literally threatened him with her jaguar and he finally joined his family to sleep.

When she and Ronin returned to their tent, Kalial tried to talk to him about the secret of Loch Nidean. "Ronin, I have a story to tell you . . ."

Distracted and utterly exhausted, he shushed her. "Whatever you have to say can wait until morning. For now I am weary and need sleep." He dropped onto his bedroll. Biting her lip, Kalial fell silent and slipped down beside him, vowing to tell him soon.

The next day Ronin woke before Kalial. Exiting the tent, he was surprised by several other families offering their services in exchange for the prospect of a safer home away from the threat of the Serpent. All day their camp grew in size.

Kalial and Ronin worked well together, for often they would sense the other's need even before he or she realized the desire. Along with Ian and Erik and several other men, they conferred over battle strategy and organized their plan of attack. The only area in which they disagreed concerned Kalial's whereabouts during the battle. Ronin wanted her away from the fighting, for, as he said numerous times, she was better with her eyes than any other. He wanted her to use the owl to watch the battle with a bird's-eye view, giving them an exceptional advantage over Lothian. What he did not say was that he could not bear to think of her becoming injured in the fight. Nor did he tell her of his growing certainty that should she fall to the sword, he would not be able to live.

With the owl gripping Ronin's leather-clad shoulder, Kalial felt he looked quite mighty striding around the encampment. She snuck peeks at him—admiring his great breadth of shoulders, watching the way his muscles rippled from even the slightest movements, seeing his tousled hair slip over his brow. A certain bubbling played with her insides whenever she sensed him near. She even found herself smiling at unusual times and, whenever she caught his eye, he smiled back. By the end of the day, she had forgotten her intention to tell him about her forest secret, and he had forgotten that she wanted to speak to him about something.

The morning of the second day, Ronin and a set of men rode into town. Kalial watched them go with a wistful sigh, then returned to tending the foot of a bay horse that had developed an abscess. As she held the foot up and pared down to the infected tissue, the steed began to shift and twitch nervously. Kalial put the foot down briefly and placed her hands upon the trembling hide. Sensing that her manipulations were causing minimal discomfort, she bent to resume her task. Suddenly the horse snorted and jerked his foot from Kalial's tiny hands and pounded it down in agitation, directly onto her foot.

"Ouch!" Kalial yelped as she shoved his shoulder with all her weight. "Get off me, you lout!" The horse's ears flicked forward and back and his eyes rolled but instead of picking up his foot, he leaned against Kalial and placed yet more weight upon her trapped toes. "Aaugh!" Kalial grimaced, then searched quickly for the source of the animal's uncharacteristic anxiety. A black shadow flitted behind a pile of straw, causing Kalial to start with alarm. With one last nudge to the horse, Kalial freed her foot and limped around the barrier.

Dhu Cait stood on alert, her mouth open in a soundless snarl. The whiskers around her face twitched as her lip curled. Alarmed because her wildcat was so agitated, Kalial looked around nervously. She saw the warriors training, several families working at their various trades and a line of fresh wash hanging limp in the sunlight. Just as she was turning away, dhu Cait gave a deep-throated growl and glared at the end of the clothesline. Kalial spun toward the area, hopping about on one foot. A man stepped out from behind the concealment and narrowed his eyes hungrily.

"Ah, fortune finds us back together." he said, his voice low and threatening. Kalial froze, one foot in the air, and felt the blood drain from her face as she beheld the messenger she had seen skulking about Percy's castle. The man stepped closer. "I see you remember me from Castle Basingstoke. I sure do remember you. I had instructions to get Lord Basingstoke to murder Ronin, which the sniveling gambler failed to do. Lothian did not know about you. But I think you are the key to the treasure."

A question from the McCat rippled into Kalial's mind, an image of claws and teeth shredding flesh. When Kalial did not respond, dhu Cait started to slink forward. The man dropped his hands and took one step back, but his face continued to taunt Kalial. The messenger coughed once, spewing spittle onto the clean laundry.

Kalial glared at him. "You are a fool to have entered our camp. All I have to do is shout and Ronin will slaughter you where you stand."

"You don't understand. McTaver will not survive

the coming fight. You have the power to prevent his death by giving us the treasure. If you don't, McTaver will die. Is that what you want?"

The image of Ronin, dead on a battlefield, made her shake so hard her teeth started to chatter. She knelt down and clung to her beast, her stomach rolling from the sudden fear for Ronin streaming through her mind.

"He is a warrior. He will defeat you," she replied bravely.

"Are you ready to take that chance? We outnumber your force five to one. Do you think he is so invincible that no sword can draw his blood? When he falls, you will know it was your fault."

The messenger smirked, pleased that he had instilled such terror into Kalial. He tipped his cap and sauntered away. "Lothian will be here soon. You decide," he said over his shoulder.

As soon as the man left, Kalial released her cat and crumpled to the ground. "What am I to do?" she cried. "Please help me . . . what should I do?" She looked up, great tears rolling down her cheeks. "I do not want him to die. I could not bear to be the reason for his death!" Dhu Cait curled around Kalial, comforting her with her warm presence, for she had no answers to give.

Ronin returned early, feeling faintly uneasy. The sense that he was being watched had deepened and he felt an urgency to return to camp, to check on preparations and see Kalial. When he and his men trotted in, everything seemed orderly and calm and Ronin tried to shrug off his misgivings. Nerves, he thought, nerves that should not be affecting a warrior. The need to see Kalial he also attempted to ignore. A leader should not be influenced unduly by emotions, he chided himself. Kalial was strong and independent and would most likely resent his concern.

Later that evening, he finally located her as she

moved around the horses, checking them for the third time that night.

"Why do you stay so far from the fire, little one?" he questioned, his voice velvety. Kalial jumped at his approach and then turned quickly away. Abruptly concerned, Ronin reached for her and spun her around to face him. "What? What makes you so pale and nervous?"

Kalial tossed her hair over her shoulder and looked at Ronin's rich, blue eyes. She recalled the day in the meadow when she had searched for just such a color. How hard it had been! The warmth and banked fire in his gaze warmed her and she unexpectedly flung herself into his startled arms. She buried her face into his wide chest and sobbed.

Ronin held her, confused but open to her. He had intended to tell her that a scout had just arrived with news that the Serpent army had been sighted, but now he held his tongue due to her distress. He waited while she cried, then, as the tears abated, he scooped her up and walked with her to the ocean. When dhu Cait rose to follow, he commanded her to stay. Dhu Cait's growl of disagreement was met with Ronin's fierce glare until the wildcat sank back on her haunches, twitching with suppressed irritation.

Ronin carried her to the water's edge, then sat down in the sand with her curled in his lap. When Kalial did not speak, he finally broke the silence.

"Now, little one, tell me what burdens you so that you tear my heart out with your sorrow." He looked down at Kalial, but except for a brief flash upward, she would not meet his gaze.

" 'Tis nothing," she muttered, "nothing of importance."

"Nothing!" he responded incredulously. "Do not tell me such tales. What makes you cry so? I have never seen you so dispirited. Are you perhaps concerned about the fight to come?"

"I know not why I am so overwrought. Perhaps

because 'tis just what happens to women every now
and then."

Ronin chuckled and shook her slightly. "You can
not use that excuse with me, for I know your body
well. Your monthly was due a week ago and yet the
day has come and gone with no sign of bleeding."

Kalial gasped, alternately shocked and frightened.
She jumped out of Ronin's arms and turned on him,
her eyes wide and golden.

"Think you that I didn't know?" queried Ronin. "I
have felt the subtle change in your internal tempera-
ture, and the heat has burned me." He stood up to
tower over her, his voice husky. "I feel the tightening
of your breasts, I notice the sensitivity of your nipples.
I can even smell the difference in your sweat." Kalial
backed away from him as he spoke, shaking her head,
her hand fluttering to her abdomen.

"When?" she whispered.

"When?" he repeated. "When did it happen or
when did I know? Forsooth, the two are the same, for
it was when you were in a trance. Your soul was lifting
away and the only way I could bring you back was to
give you a part of myself."

"No!" Kalial cried. She stepped back farther and
Ronin frowned slightly at her reaction.

"No need to be surprised that I knew so soon. I am
sure you are worried but," Ronin reached into his
pocket and withdrew the amber ring he carried, "I
pledge to you that I will protect you and the baby for
all time." He pulled her unresisting hand forward and
slipped the ring over her finger. Suddenly, Kalial
jerked her hand back and stared at him in distress.

"No!" she shrieked. "I . . . I feel naught but shock."

"Shock," thundered Ronin. "You feel naught for
this child?!"

"No, I speak not about the child," Kalial stammered. Her voice trailed off as she looked at him
pleadingly. "Today—"

But Ronin interrupted her yet again, "You do not want the baby? Perhaps you abhor the body that made it within you? Mayhap your love was fleeting!"

"A baby?" she began again, still staggering from the unexpected news.

"Not to worry again, Princess, I shall leave you alone! I was mistaken that your tears were for maidenly joy. Now I see they are for revulsion for the state you now find yourself in because of my ardor." Kalial took a step forward, shaking her head and reaching for Ronin's arm. The wink of moonlight reflecting off the ocean flashed on the crystals in the amber ring she wore. Ronin stepped back as if slapped.

"Keep the ring, for although it means nothing to you, it symbolizes my devotion to the child, if not to the mother." He fairly spat the last word.

"Ronin, you misunderstand." She grasped him then, her fragile fingers barely reaching a quarter of the way around his bicep.

"I misunderstand nothing. I have been distracted from my duty to my family. You are not—" His voice broke for a moment, then regained its strength. "You are not mine, or part of my family. I always knew that you did not want to stay with me." He then jerked his arm out of her touch and spun away, leaving Kalial standing alone on the moonlit beach.

"Please listen to me! I am trying to tell you something," she cried after his retreating back.

"I have heard enough," he flung over his shoulder.

Kalial watched him enter camp, barking orders and causing people to leap up in surprise. Unsure how to react to his revelation, she stared after him back and slowly raised her hand to her abdomen. A baby? Despite all her teachings, she had never been taught the rudiments of human conception. She knew that others procreated from intercourse, but she had never associated the act of passion she shared with Ronin with the creation of an infant.

Filled with newfound wonder at the knowledge that she carried a baby, Kalial turned in the other direction and wandered down the beach, oblivious to her surroundings. She did not notice the lack of her feline protector, nor did she feel the sudden stillness in the animals near her that heralded the approach of another. With barely a gasp of surprise Kalial saw the form of the messenger rise up from behind a dune and punch her full force in the temple. Tiny light shards burst in her mind, then all went black.

CHAPTER 25

Ronin stalked through camp, snapping at anyone unlucky enough to cross his path. The desire to return to Kalial was powerful. He even turned and took a step back when he felt a sharp pain race through his head, but with an angry shake he turned away and headed for his tent. She would come to him if she wanted him, he growled to himself, for he would never chase her and beg her to accept him.

The night became oppressive and ominous and Ronin paced for hours, the feeling of unease thickening and strengthening. He finally left the confines of the tent and strode the perimeter of the camp, unsure why he was so restless. The horses nickered and whinnied and even his mahogany warhorse shuffled anxiously, although he discovered quickly that the palomino mare was missing. The guards remained alert, although he snapped at them anyway. The town nearby gave off the same sounds of revelry, the ocean lapped at the shore in a regular rhythm. Yet despite all signs of normalcy, Ronin could not shake off his rising sense of doom, for Kalial did not return.

By morning, the entire camp was aware that their princess was gone. Every inch and crevice was searched. Soon, Ronin sent a group into town to search the taverns and homes, but they, too, returned empty-handed. When asked what had occurred directly before her disappearance, Ronin readily admitted to their argument, guilt overwhelming him.

As people milled around, awaiting new instructions, Ronin left them and returned to the beach. Striding along, he abruptly felt a nip upon his fingers. Spinning, he drew his sword and pointed it at dhu Cait.

"Leave me be, cat of the night! I have stumbled over you all day, yea, even the night before when you should have been beside your lady. I see your accusation, but how am I to guard her when she desires me to leave?" The wildcat hissed and circled Ronin, her neck level with his waist. She rubbed against him, bumping him with a snarl just as a shark circles its victim before it strikes. In fury, Ronin kicked out, seeking to injure the beast, but dhu Cait leapt away, snapping her teeth together and twisting midair to turn on him again. Ronin lunged after her, this time with his sword, fear finding an outlet in pure violence.

Dhu Cait swiped at his arm, knocking the sword to the sand. She bunched her legs together and sprang at him while releasing a jungle scream. Her two front paws pounded his chest and he staggered under the weight. With a roar of his own, Ronin sank his teeth into her neck, leveraged his arm underneath her throat and flung her off. Dhu Cait reached up, swinging her mighty paw, nails extended, but Ronin leaned back, barely avoiding the sharp claws, and drove his knee into her exposed belly.

Dhu Cait fell back, her sides heaving, her lips curling and her fangs glistening. Ronin stepped back too, his heart racing and arms trembling. They eyed each other, then started to circle, waiting for an opening. Dhu Cait's tail flicked and sputtered, spraying sand, while Ronin crouched down, bracing himself for another attack.

A high shriek from above caused both of them to

look up just as the owl, now large and powerful, swooped down between them, circled, then landed with a painful grip upon Ronin's forearm. Ronin looked into the winged creature's eyes and felt his world tilt, shift and stretch. The flutter of feathers merged into the sway of golden hair. A shimmer of pain skirted through him. Not the anger and frustration that he now felt, but the lance of heartrending sorrow.

Ronin sucked in his breath, then forced his mind to relax. He closed his eyes and breathed in deeply, picturing her in his mind. With a shock, he saw the image of his baby sister spread on a bed with the Serpent standing nearby, his one eye rolled up showing white sclera. Ronin twitched his head, then saw that instead of his sister, Kalial lay upon the mattress, her arms spread apart and her clothes in tatters. Golden orbs seemed to reach out to him, speak to him, yet he could not understand what they said. Frustrated, Ronin opened his eyes and looked at the wildcat that now sat quiet and calm beside him. He squatted down, making his eyes level with hers.

"Help me, my friend. We both need her and blame ourselves for her loss. 'Tis time we worked together and found her." Dhu Cait looked at him with her glowing orange eyes and blinked very slowly. Ronin reached out and placed his hand upon her head, then moved closer when she remained pliant. He pressed his cheek against her neck, inhaling the animal scent that was still tinted with sweet jasmine. He felt a tremor move through the cat, then a whispering breeze as the owl took to the sky.

Row upon row of sand dunes spread out below him as he looked through the owl's wise eyes. A brief tilt, and he was heading north. Ronin fought it temporarily, urging the bird to go toward the Serpent army in the other direction, but the owl disobeyed him, bringing him closer to the Loch Nidean forest.

A small smudge of smoke twirled around his vision, but as he peered closer he saw that the fire was recently abandoned. A trail of hoofprints led away from the site and these he followed, using the wings of the owl. Within a few twists, Ronin saw many riders and tethered behind the one in front was Kalial upon her palomino mare, her clothing in rags, her hair matted and her body swaying in the saddle. Suddenly the man who held her reins turned and peered at her with his one eye. He said something, then pulled a tapestry cloth from his saddlebag and waved it in her face. When Kalial tried to turn away, he pulled a short sword from his belt and pointed it at her belly.

Ronin's eyes sprang open and he leapt up, scooping up his discarded sword and swinging it in the air. For a moment he saw the fuzzy outline of his vision, then nothing but the relentless tide creeping forward. He turned back, glaring at dhu Cait, then searching the sky for the owl.

"He has her," he whispered to the cat. "He has her and the tunic and he will force her to reveal the treasure's hiding place, or kill her trying." Ronin lowered his sword and took a deep breath. "We must find them before he reaches his goal, for should he have no more use for her he will surely run her through." Ronin looked out over the ocean and watched the gulls dip in the currents. "And she can be so stubborn . . ." With a powerful thrust he flung his sword into the sand at his feet.

"As you pledged to me on these very shores, I now pledge to you, Kalial. I am only a humble man with base emotions. I have been blessed with your company and the privilege of your closeness, the gift of your love. I ask nothing else from you, only that you grant me the power to find you, for find you I shall." Abruptly he ripped the sword from the earth. With a flash of wings, the owl settled upon his shoulder. Dhu Cait, too, rose up and stood next to him, her strength giving him added courage. As a threesome, they entered camp and Ronin swiftly organized their forces.

The army broke camp within hours. Fifty men, led by Ian McInnish, marched out to the pass road that skirted Loch Nidean forest. They traveled swiftly but not silently, for they wanted to pull the Serpent army into the lands around Roseneath. Ten men rode with the civilians, women and children. A sizable bunch, the group moved along the coast road, intending to circle the forest from the other direction, well away from the fighting. Two men remained in town, awaiting the arrival of Dugan Trask and his sailors and seeking to gather as much information about the troop's movements as they could.

The final selected men stayed with Ronin McTaver. They sped out on the fastest horses, their mounts pointed into the heart of the haunted land, an area where the fire had done little damage. The jaguar raced with the horses, her feet skimming the ground. She ran so quickly, it almost appeared that she outraced her own black shadow. Above them flew the owl, scattering swallows and songbirds as he led the way into the forest.

Night fell, and with it came a rumble of thunder as storm clouds filled the sky. A flash of lightning brightened the landscape before it was plunged into darkness yet again. With the brief illumination, Ronin saw small figures in the trees, poised to rain arrows upon their heads.

"Stop, my fellows!" he called out. "I come on behalf of the Princess Kalial. I bring with me her familiar, the black wildcat, as proof of my integrity."

A shuffling was heard in the darkness and then a small man stood in front of Ronin's warhorse. With a leap, Ronin sprang down and held out his hand. The man ignored the offer, and simply stared at Ronin, waiting for him to speak.

"I have need of your help to save her," Ronin repeated.

"It was you who took her from us," the man replied, his foreign accent making his words hard to understand.

"Yes, I did, and 'twas wrong of me. I did what I thought best at the time. Please forgive me."

"With your black hair and wild eyes you look like the wolf of legends past. Wolves mate for eternity."

"Aye, whether they live that life forever or perish early." Ronin hung his head. "My mate is not a wolf, she is a feline, a McCat of the Scottish myths with ginger hair and golden eyes. She carries the future, and I go to save not only her and our child but also this forest."

"We know where they are," a female voice said out of the darkness, "but she has bade us to stay away and we must obey her for she is our princess. She fears for our safety."

"I have no such restrictions," answered Ronin fiercely.

"Perhaps not," the first man said with a smile. "I granted you free passage once before, and I do so now again." He turned and leapt up into the branches of a massive tree. "Follow the river to its source, Loch Nidean. There you will find the valley where our princess is being held."

Ronin nodded and swung back upon his stallion. Another burst of lightning shot through the forest, followed quickly by a rumble of thunder. The sound continued long past the time when the elemental sound should have drifted away, and Ronin breathed a prayer for the armies that clashed at the edge of the woods.

The other warriors with him looked to him for guidance. Ronin stood in his stirrups, staring piercingly through the rain and trees that separated him from the rest of his men. The sound of so many horses made him feel a moment of hopelessness. Too many, he thought, too many enemies.

"You have trained them well, m'laird. Have faith."
Ronin recognized Jordan, the archer. "You have
planned well and they will execute your orders, sir.
'Tis not like the night in your castle, for the men are
prepared and ready to fight. It no matters how many,
it only matters how well, as you have told us."

"Yes, Angus, I must have faith that our men will
do their best."

The forest man looked down from the branches.
"These men that come with weapons drawn, wearing
the emblem of the snake . . . we will not let them
enter the forest."

"You are wise, my friend," Ronin replied. "They
are the people responsible for the forest fire."

The forest men looked at each other, silent communication passing among them.

Ronin nodded. Turning to his men, he motioned to
the river rippling through the trees. "Come!" With a
sharp nudge of his heels, Ronin led his band deeper
into the woods, following the elusive form of dhu Cait
as she bounded up the river and the rain poured down
in blinding sheets.

Far from the small band, Ian McInnish and the
young warriors held their positions in the pass for as
long as they were able. As row upon row of mercenaries poured down upon them, they picked off as many
as they could from their high vantage point, but soon
the enemy sped up the mountainside and they were
engaged in hand-to-hand combat. Swords swung and
blood dripped with as much force as the rain. The
Serpent army was stunned, for they had not expected
such resistance. The young warriors cut through the
army with deadly force. Back-to-back in pairs, they
defended their position with a passion that was lacking
in the advancing enemy forces.

If the numbers had been even, the battle would
have lasted less than an hour. But the numbers were

far from equal, and sheer size began to shift the battle
in favor of the Serpent. Thunder and lightning shook
the earth and rain pelted down, making the battle-
ground slick with mud. The darkness deepened and
an eerie silence in the Loch Nidean forest made the
clash of hundreds of swords even louder. The grunts
of men lunging, the screams of men falling, the harsh
breaths of men running—it all melded together beneath the pouring rain.

Ian fell, his sword arm wounded, and his young
partner leapt in front to defend him. With a roar, Ian
surged back to his feet and deflected a blow that
would have severed the boy's head. All around him,
Ian saw his warriors stumble and slide, their only advantage the night that made them equal to many a
seasoned warrior.

All at once, a flurry of arrows thudded down upon
the writhing mass, and men with the tabard of the
Serpent fell to their knees, casting haunted eyes at
the forest that had suddenly come alive. Many of the
Serpent's army spun around to retreat down the pass,
but a wall of sailors lead by Dugan Trask blocked
their path, their cutlasses and knives shining in the
wet moonlight. Caught inside the three fronts, the Serpent army went berserk, fighting with the ferocity of
cornered rats.

Again, the tide of the battle favored the writhing
snake as Ian fell once more, his leg sliced open. Gasping, he struggled to rise, but a mercenary gripped his
sword and swung it at his head. Peripherally, Ian saw
his partner step forward and engage the downward
stroke, but the power was too much and he could not
stop the contact. Ian felt his head explode and he
slumped down into the bloody mud.

The warriors fought gamely, but with Ian McInnish
incapacitated they faltered, then retreated as the mercenaries advanced.

* * *

Deep in the forest, on the southern shore of Loch Nidean, Kalial curled in her saddle, hugging the little life that beat within her womb. She did not notice that the burned and twisted stumps surrounding her had once been the trees of her beloved forest. Instead she closed her eyes, seeing the angry glare of Ronin's blue fury, and shuddered anew. A hopelessness, a despair filled her mind as she recalled the last moments with her beloved warrior. Such angry words! Such . . . such nothingness where everything should be!

Lothian held her mare's bridle, his face gleaming with fanaticism in the flashes of lightning. With him were several men, each as intent as their master on finding the treasure of the Scottish Gold. They dragged the resisting mare through the wood, slapping her haunches with their leather reins when she balked in terror.

Kalial felt strangely disembodied, her soul lost among the evil surrounding her. As distant sounds of the fighting reached her, she cried out and felt bile rise in her throat at the thought of Ronin in battle. She tried to reassure herself that his skill, his strength, his power would see him through, but her fear overshadowed reason, and tears rolled down her face. An echo from the owl filtered into her mind, but she ignored his call.

Go away! she whispered. *Go east, go west, but do not follow me!* Her words were flung wide and entered the minds of all the creatures of the forest. The rabbits froze, the fireflies sank to the ground and the forest dwellers kept their distance. *Go farther!* she commanded, as she swept the path to the river free of all creatures.

She saw orange eyes in her mind. She saw the jaguar bounding through the woods and she stabbed her with a command to stay. The big cat faltered, stumbled.

Then Kalial felt Ronin's presence and she gasped aloud, her body abruptly straightening with shock. He was near!

Without warning, Kalial was slapped across the face.

"Focus! You must be faster and make sure none are in our path or I will stick pins inside your belly and suck out your lifeblood! Hurry, I have waited too long to find this treasure, worked too hard for a measly female like you to hinder me." The Serpent raised the dripping tunic and shoved it at her face yet again. "Find this valley and I will let your man pass without loss of life."

"My child . . ." Kalial whispered.

"Shall never see the light of the sun should you fail me. Which way? The right fork or the left? Hurry."

Kalial felt the press of generations upon her shoulders. She could not betray her people, could not allow this filth to rape her forest! Then a flash of eyes, not orange as she was so accustomed to seeing, but a brilliant royal blue, burned into her mind and spread the healing power of love through her thoughts and into her limbs. Ronin! He was coming! She tried to protect him, to push him away. *Go away! I have one more secret. I love you. I can not let you be hurt. I must protect you. I want you safe so please leave!*

The cool image of his blue eyes rose up and enveloped her, cloaked her, soothed her. Kalial felt his message, *I will not leave you, I am coming for you.* Kalial mentally shoved him as she had done to her forest men, pushed him as she had done to her forest creatures, cried out against his advance. Ronin faltered, started to fade, confused by her rejection in the thoughts that swirled in his mind, and Kalial kicked harder, willing him to leave.

Ronin hesitated, stunned by Kalial's denial. The wildcat slowed to a trot, then stopped and looked back at him. The horses milled around, commanded by Kalial to go back. Dhu Cait shivered in the wet rain, helpless to ignore her mistress's decree. Ronin looked up at the angry sky and closed his eyes as the rain pelted his face. He breathed deeply and concentrated.

Whispering to dhu Cait, Ronin said, "She has such a gift of communion, but she does not understand the depth of my love for her, and knows not that these feelings are stronger." He opened his eyes and looked at the wet wildcat. "We ride," he said quietly, then spurred his horse into a gallop, swiftly diving into the rain-drenched night, instantly leaving behind his men whose horses continued to balk. Ronin ignored Kalial's mental barrier and pressed on, forcing his mount to race through the burned woods as if the tract was as tended as a manicured road. Dhu Cait sprang after him, her wild cry of joy shattering the darkness and spurring them on to an even faster pace. They reached the river and abruptly turned upstream, noting the slowly filling hoofprints that marked both riverbanks.

Kalial heard them crashing through the forest, gaining on the Serpent's men. She stared into the darkness, her fear changing to wonder. He still came for her! The legend told of a woman and her wolf who had found a love so powerful it had cast a treasure down through the centuries. Her ancestor had woven the three original tapestries as a secret map to the treasure of Loch Nidean. Together they formed the secret to riches beyond imagination. Kalial suddenly smiled in the dark rain, laughing at the idiocy of man's search for wealth when all the riches they needed were carried within their hearts.

The party reached the shore of the loch where a thundering waterfall crashed down from a sheer cliff, adding a tumult of sound to the thunder shuddering through the forest. Lothian opened his mouth, panting with excitement. "Where is it?" he screamed. "Where is it buried?"

She turned to Lothian, suddenly strong again. "It is within the loch."

"Under the water?" he asked nervously.

"Yes, underneath the black surface, resting upon the basin floor."

"Go get it!" he screamed at her, dragging her off the palomino. "Fetch it now!"

Kalial walked slowly to the edge and stared into the inky darkness. She smiled, then abruptly dove deeply, letting the current pull her, letting the water enfold her. Her hands felt along the bottom of the lake . . . mud, grass, stones . . . an oil-slick package. She gripped the wrapped bundle and shot to the surface.

"Yes! Yes!" the Serpent screamed. "Bring it here!"

Kalial slowly swam to the lake edge. With a secret smile she handed the prize to the white-haired man who snatched it and ripped the oil-soaked wrapping. In his haste, he tore his hands on the bindings until, using his dagger, he cut through the outer covering to reveal the woven message inside. He unfurled a fourth tapestry and stared blankly at the image.

Two bodies. Two bodies in an embrace. Arms, legs, flowers, sunshine . . . two lovers lost in each other, sprawled upon a wolf pelt with golden sunrays dancing upon their flesh.

"Where is the treasure?" the Serpent screamed. "This is nothing! I want the treasure! I need the Scottish Gold! Find it for me!"

"I can not find it for you, old man. This," and she swept her arm gracefully over the valley, the waterfall, the landscape. "This is all part of the treasure. The tapestries can not find the gold for you, they only point the way in an endless message to all. This emotion," Kalial stroked the faces of the lovers, "is the most valued treasure."

The Serpent abruptly grabbed Kalial, bruising her arms in his fury. "You are trying to trick me," he growled. "Mount your horse and lead me to the Scottish Gold or I will rip your man into pieces!"

Kalial jerked her arm from his hold, casting him a

disgusted glare, and mounted her palomino mare. She sat on her steed, the warmth in her heart blossoming as she felt Ronin coming closer. He burst into the clearing just as the Serpent and his men had mounted their horses. Both parties stared at each other, Ronin's men pulling to a shuddering stop at the far end of the loch.

Ronin's eyes swept the lake and goose bumps formed over his muscled arms and chest. The loch sparkled in the emerging moonlight as the water surface was pelleted by the crashing rain. More lightning lit the sky and by its brilliance, the meadow glowed. Green grass blanketed the ground, although areas contained puddles of water. The trees surrounding the glen bent and twisted in the wind, the sound of the leaves as loud as the rain itself. At the far end where Lothian, his men and Kalial stood, a huge waterfall cascaded down, its waters foaming and boiling into the lake, forming two spumes that resembled the wings of a falcon in flight. Loch Nidean. It's dark, rippling surface was menacing, forbidding. Its depths appeared endless.

Then his breath froze within his chest as he switched his gaze to Kalial. She sat up in her saddle, the small strips of white cloth remaining on her body completely transparent in the rain. Her high breasts were peaked by tight nipples, and rivulets of rainwater sped down the creamy expanse and dripped off of the hard buds. Her thighs opened around her horse's back, and Ronin could see a glimpse of golden curls pressed tightly against the slick leather. Her hair hung down her back, past her waist and onto the horse's flanks. Despite the heavy weight of water, some wet strands whipped and curled in the wind.

Kalial looked across the expanse at the warrior, her warrior. The only man who could break through her defenses, push through her forest and claim her with his eyes alone. To her he was omnipotent, with his rippling muscles and blazing eyes and strength of emotion. She saw the wild toss of his black hair, the strength of his jaw. And upon his shoulder sat the owl, the wisest, the strongest, the most feared of all the flying hunters, while beside him stood her black beast, her fur slicked tight to her skin, making her look like a gaunt night terror.

Swiftly, the frozen scene changed, and Ronin charged toward them, his sword held low but ready. The Serpent screeched and screamed at his men.

"Do not wait till he is upon us! Attack, kill him!" The Serpent's voice rose high and shrill.

The men with him leapt forward, engaging Ronin with a clash of steel on the open riverbank. Ronin barely noted their presence, so intent was he upon Kalial. With a few swings, he broke through the men and raced forward just as the Serpent raised his battle-axe to Kalial's head. She cried out, jerked away, and leaped off the mare, but the one-eyed man followed, pressing his horse against her so that she was trapped against the cliffside.

With a sudden wrench, Ronin leaned forward and grabbed Kalial's arm to haul her out of the path of a swinging axe. For an instant Ronin went faint, his face drained of color as he saw the heavy weapon sink fully into the soil where Kalial had left footprints. He shook his head to clear it, then, leaping off his horse, he lifted his broadsword to counter another attack while simultaneously shoving Kalial behind him. She stumbled back, then tripped over a long sword that lay upon the ground next to a fallen mercenary.

Lifting the blade, she darted forward and lifted her fragile steel to challenge another attacker. The mercenary glared at her, but Kalial glared back, her eyes flashing with courage. The man swung fiercely, shattered Kalial's blade. She shouted from the pain that shot up her nerveless fingers and through her shoulder, calling for Ronin's help.

With a roar, Ronin twisted, abandoning his attack upon the Serpent, and sank his sword deep into the mercenary's side, then he yanked it free and swung again at his neck. Ronin did not wait to see if his blow decapitated the man. Instead he spun to locate Kalial.

A man was grabbing her from behind, his arm crooked around her neck. She looked up, her eyes wide, and saw Ronin forced to defend himself from yet another, while his gaze bored into hers, demanding that she remember the lessons. Kalial abruptly sank all her weight down, then cupped her hands together and, using their combined force, drove her elbow into the man's groin. As he howled with pain and loosened his grasp, she spun and drove the other elbow in as well. The man stumbled back, then weakly threw a punch at her, but she sidestepped it easily. Grinning with her victory, she stepped back and bumped directly into the massive bulk of her lover.

She smiled shyly at him and nodded her head. Ronin glanced at her, his heart swelling. Suddenly, hearing a rustle behind him, Ronin turned to counter an attack. Kalial slid into the shadow made by Ronin's bulk and moved with him as they had practiced in the mountain cave. With little effort, their combined strengths of size and agility forced the attackers to retreat.

As the enemy backed away, Ronin shifted to the left, drawing Kalial with him. They stepped over a body, and Kalial reached down and picked up the long dagger that was tucked uselessly in the man's belt. She slid it into her own belt and moved with Ronin toward the remaining men. He barely glanced at her, intent upon locating the Serpent.

CHAPTER 26

Some distance away the main battle raged, swamping the young warriors despite their valiant courage. Yet miraculously they hung on, not willing to give way. Then suddenly, to their horror, another army swept down upon them from the high reaches of the mountain. The colors were all too familiar to the men, and they gasped in desperation. Basingstoke! Shouts bounded down the slopes and the Serpent army roared, certain of their victory with the addition of Basingstoke's men as their allies. The pounding hooves drowned out the thunder as the huge force plowed down the hill, trapping the young warriors between the two powerful armies.

"Basingstoke! Basingstoke!" came the cry from the descending army. The small band of warriors looked about them, seeing Ian McInnish slowly rise to his feet, one leg balancing his weight and his sword arm hanging uselessly by his side. The Serpent army sank back, laughing, allowing the fresh Basingstoke reinforcements to finish the battle. Percy Basingstoke rode at the front of his men, his hazel eyes unusually hard.

Ian shouted a hoarse command, and his men backed up, staring at the cavalry that snorted in the diminishing rain. Percy brought his steed forward and looked down at McInnish.

"Where is the girl?" he shouted. "And where is that worthless cousin of mine?"

"They are in the forest, far out of your reach, Basingstoke."

"Ah. But I am a gambling man. I may enter the forest anyway and find her."

"Yes. You have gambled many things, your goods, your property, your sense of honor," Ian challenged him.

Percy's eyes lightened imperceptibly. "Aye, all that and more have I gambled away. But that is what I am, a good-for-nothing gambler. I am everything a man should not be."

Ian looked at Lord Basingstoke warily.

"Ronin would never have gone against me, would he?" Percy asked softly.

"No," Ian replied.

"Even though he knew I turned on him," Percy continued, turning his face up into the rain.

"He knew."

"That is honor," Percy whispered in awe, looking back into Ian's face.

"Aye. He is the most honorable man I know."

"Do you think I could ever regain my sense of honor?"

Ian glanced around and saw the Serpent army regrouping. Basingstoke's men remained still, their large horses blowing in the darkness. "A man can always regain his honor, if it means enough to him."

"Ah! I am glad you said so, Ian McInnish. I think I will take one more gamble. Care to join me?" Ian frowned, watching Percy withdraw a black and white disc. "What is your color?" Percy asked.

Ian paused, unsure of the question. Finally, responding to Percy's lifted eyebrows, he answered, "White."

"Bad choice. I always lose on white." Then Percy flicked the disc high in the air, watching it turn end over end in the rain. It fell, bouncing on the ground, still turning end over end. Black, white, black, white, black . . . white. Percy looked up, grinning. "I told you I would lose." Ian stepped back, limping badly. He raised his sword, ready to defend himself, until Percy turned in his stirrups and shouted at his own men. "We are allied with the McTaver! Drive the Serpent down! Together let us rid this land of reptilians!"

The seasoned warriors from Basingstoke raised their fists along with their lord's and joined his voice. The battle cry spread into the treetops to include the forest dwellers and sped around the back where Dugan Trask and his sailors had cut off retreat. The mercenaries fell beneath the multitudes, their screams drowned as Ronin's forces shouted in victory.

As the tide of battle shifted at the edge of the woods, Kalial and Ronin continued deep within Loch Nidean, fighting back to back, searching for the next Serpent attack. Out of the brush rode Lothian, his smile gruesome in its deadliness, his white horse's hide stained with blood. His sword was slung across his back but his hands held a strung crossbow, the same one that had felled Ronin's father many months ago.

The flush of battle fury raged in Ronin's blood and his blue eyes turned blacker than his midnight hair. A ripple of muscles shimmered down his back and his arms twitched. The memory of that night coursed through his blood and vengeance was his only conscious thought. He braced himself to charge until the Serpent slowly but deliberately turned the dart of the crossbow toward the woman at his side. With sudden clarity, Ronin realized in a fraction of an instant that no matter his feud with this demon, his love for Kalial was worth more. Out of his side vision, he saw the arrow loosen, its sharp point glittering as gold as Kalial's shining eyes.

He slammed his body sideways, crashing his shoulder into her frail torso, causing her to stumble to the ground. Yet even as he felt her body give way beneath the weight of his, he knew that they moved too slowly, that the dart would penetrate Kalial's flesh. An ache rose in him, a keening horror that was vicious in its instantaneous force. In slow motion, he saw the arrow whistle through the air, its aim true. His mind reached out, trying to mentally deflect the deadly weapon when suddenly, as if in answer to his call, a swish of wings collided with the arrow. A fine cry rose at the impact, and the great eyes of the owl swiveled in mid-descent to glare at the offender. A splatter of blood sprayed the leaves and a cloud of downy feathers billowed up as the bird hit the forest floor and lay still.

The Serpent stared at the beast in shock, momentarily distracted by the motionless body that had thwarted his deadly attack. In that moment of hesitation, Ronin flung his sword with a mighty heave, directly into the chest of his nemesis. Next to him, a small dagger, deadly in its piercing sharpness, whistled through the air, sinking simultaneously into the Serpent's heart. Ronin glanced down and saw Kalial kneeling in the mud, her arm extended from just having released the deadly blade. Looking up, their eyes met, then they turned and looked to where the man slumped, sliding slowly from his horse's back, his blood drenching the Serpent tabard. The tiny dagger and the immense broadsword lay imbedded in his chest side by side, one as potent as the other.

The night was silent.

"Come," Kalial whispered. " 'Tis time to show you the treasure."

" 'Tis not necessary," he replied, his breath still heavy from the fighting. He stepped forward, pulling Kalial to him, and grasped the bridle of the white horse. He soothed it as he pulled the Serpent fully free of his stirrups. The dead man's body thumped onto the ground and lay still. Ronin yanked his sword free and turned to Kalial. "I have no need for riches. I only need you."

Kalial trembled, then shivered, her golden eyes gleaming with unshed tears. "Please come," she murmured. Ronin smiled and nodded his assent. "We must find the horses."

Taking a deep breath, Ronin moved over to the edge of the riverbed. They pushed through a wall of dense shrubs and found not only the mahogany stallion, but also the pretty palomino mare. The warhorse was sniffing the mare hungrily and she in turn was dancing in circles, her tail high and her neck arched. At his sharp command, the dark horse snorted again, but came over to Ronin obediently. Ronin swung up on his back and indicated that Kalial was to mount up as well. Again, she complied with no fire in her look but instead, a deep, immeasurable gaze that Ronin could not interpret.

"We each have our strengths." As he spoke he reached out and pulled one of her arms toward him. Using his teeth and one hand, he lashed the rope that had been around his waist in a tight band around Kalial's wrist and, leaving very little slack, tied it around his own wrist as well.

"I bind you to keep you near me, for I want you always at my side." Kalial stilled and watched him with fathomless eyes. Ronin looked at her warily, but he continued to bind her to him, for he had no intention of letting her escape him. Two days in the forest, plus seven in the caves. Nine days total. She had said that eleven days would bind them for life, and he fully intended on adding those two days to the total.

"I'll not release this tether, so do me the courtesy of not asking," he bade her roughly, expecting an argument. When she merely nodded, he clucked to the horses. Kalial wrapped her golden legs around the mare's girth, and grasped the reins in her free hand as did Ronin. Together they rode up to the river.

"Here is the valley of Loch Nidean," she motioned, "and this waterfall is the winged falcon upon my tunic. We have guarded her heart for centuries. I have no riches to give either, save that of my love," she replied softly and tenderly.

Ronin turned her face to him. "I will have you know the truth a'fore we take another step," he murmured. "I love every aspect of you, your lovely curls and your muddy cheeks, your silken skin and your rough breeches. I could never have imagined that it would be a woman's mind and the strength of her character that would seduce me, but you have, completely. I pledge myself to you, for as long as my soul lives."

Kalial's eyes sparkled as she urged Ronin forward. "There are two parts of the secret of Loch Nidean, and I know now that it is right to show them to you. This," she leaned down and scooped the fourth tapestry from the wet grass, "depicts who deserves to have the treasure."

Ronin stared at the fourth piece, shaking his head. "I thought there were only three . . ."

"There are three in the first sequence. There are many others. Come. Let me show you what inspired them. Let me show you why they were made." She led him along the path toward the waterfall. In moments they reached the edge where the thundering water crashed and splashed, drenching them with its spray. Faced with nowhere else to go, Ronin reached over and pulled Kalial into his embrace.

She nestled close to him, the water dancing around them, and looked at Ronin with great solemnity. "I, too, would have you know that I think more highly of you than I ever thought possible. I trust you. I trust you so much that I can be vulnerable with you. I accept that I can be a woman with you, yet need not fear you will devour me. I know, deep in my soul, that you will stay beside me, let me love you and cherish you as well. I speak true when I tell you that

we have the treasure that the legends speak of. The
Serpent never had a chance of gaining its worth, for
he was an insignificant lizard that knew naught that
his time was ended. It was nay gold nor jewels, it was
our love that we sought, and once we accepted each
other for who we truly were, our treasure was revealed
and made whole."

Ronin leaned back and tilted his head, causing a
damp curl to fall over his forehead. He took a deep
breath and inhaled the jasmine and honeysuckle fragrance that was uniquely Kalial. Then he moved forward and whispered huskily, "Then I am a very
wealthy man."

With a small giggle, Kalial nudged her mare forward
and beckoned to Ronin. "Still, you must come for I
want to show you . . ." As they walked their horses
forward, Kalial nudged her mare to the base of the
waterfall with Ronin following beside her.

Kalial ducked under the heavy waterfall, smiling at
Ronin's incredulous expression. Together, they bowed
their heads and closed their eyes as the shock of freezing water pounded their shoulders during the brief
instant they were underneath the fall. With one more
stride, they stepped behind the water curtain and were
enclosed in a cavern.

Ronin shook water droplets free, then opened his
eyes in wonder. A valley lay before them, bathed in
early morning light. The emerald grass sparkled with
diamonds of dew. Rubies vied with orange topaz upon
the sunrise swept cliffside. A sapphire lake shimmered, enclosed by silver boulders and bronze gravel.

Ronin gave a whoop of joy and grinned like a
schoolboy. He kicked Kalial's mare and his own stallion into a gallop down the slope. Both horses leapt
into stride, the mare flat and low but the stallion short
and controlled so that his strides did not outmatch
hers. Ronin held his reins loosely in his left hand and
gripped Kalial's wrist where the rope bound it in his

other hand. Thus linked, they let the horses gallop through the glade, one dark and menacing, the other light and airy. Ronin used his size and strength to push the branches aside, and Kalial used her sight to guide them. They came to a fallen log, and both horses gathered simultaneously and leapt over, manes and tails sailing.

Kalial tugged on Ronin gently, and he responded immediately by slowing his mount's gait to a canter. Kalial turned their course toward the lake shore. They both bent low to avoid the brush and were soon forced to slow to a trot. Their grasps on each other's wrists shifted to a linking of fingers. Although each was aware that it would be easier to travel single file, neither sought to sever the tie that bound them together. Finally they pulled in to a walk. The mare blew hot breath through her nose, eliciting an answering snort from the stallion beside her. He bunched his neck up, twisting it to nip at her shoulder. A sharp whinny from the palomino answered his action and she shot out a kick that, although landing squarely upon the dark horse's hide, hurt him not at all.

Ronin and Kalial looked over at each other, night eyes meeting daylight, and pure energy spun a web around them. A fine mist rose from the water, and a ray of sunshine peeked over the cliff wall to spread its warmth along the canyon floor. Nudging the warhorse even closer, Ronin rubbed his leg against Kalial's satin thigh and gripped her hand tighter. With a shy smile, she shifted the palomino away into the trees toward a patch of sunlight. The mare's dainty steps seemed to flutter shyly away from the stallion's overtures. Both Ronin and the warhorse responded by leaning toward their mates, seeking with hide and hand to touch the silky golden hair that glimmered in the faint light. With each step they moved into the filtered light and toward an area of brilliant, velvety grass. Both Kalial and Ronin slid off their mounts, laughing as they stripped bridles and saddles one-handed. Once the horses were freed, Ronin pulled Kalial close. From his breast pocket he pulled out the pair of gold and amber bracelets. With a soft smile, he slid the bands over her fingers and onto her wrist.

"My bond to you is for eternity. May this circlet symbolize my never-ending love."

Kalial's golden eyes gleamed underneath her fringe of tawny lashes. Her soft hair rippled down her back and around her thinly clad shoulders.

A simple noise disturbed the pair of horses at that moment, and the big mahogany warhorse pushed at the mare and bit her yet again. The mare leapt forward, free of restraints, and dashed toward the water. In dismay, Kalial reached out to grasp her, to save her noble golden horse, but she galloped away.

The stallion trumpeted, reared and struck out, nearly toppling the humans. Before they could recover, he too burst into a shuddering run. Below them, the palomino mare cavorted, then flung her head up and whinnied sharply. The warhorse shivered in response, then with a mighty heave, he bucked and thundered down the hill to catch the elusive golden horse.

She ran from him initially, then spun and fairly chased him for several strides. She arched her neck and the teeth marks of his earlier nips were visible. She spun her tail and the warhorse received a slash across his nose that caused him to stamp angrily. He stretched to his full height, easily twice that of hers, and his massive erection jutted between his legs. The mare ducked and danced away, but the stallion pursued her, using his strength to win her favor. He shoved her, nearly toppling her over, then grabbed her mane tight in his teeth to hold her still. She whinnied and shook, trying to shake him, but the scent of her arousal defied her actions. Her tail arched up and away, opening her passage, and the stallion took immediate advantage. He let go of her for a moment, then leapt up onto his hind legs and sprang the several steps to her haunches, viciously pounding her sides with his front hooves to keep her still. His enormous member sank into her, and the stallion's muscles bunched as he drove into her yet deeper.

She squealed, but braced her forelegs to help bear his weight, and her head dropped down in submission. The stallion pounded into her again and again, sweat and foam flecking his hide. He slid, losing his grip temporarily, but the swollen bulb at the end of his cock held him in place and he regained his balance and rhythm. With sudden, powerful, unsynchronized plunges, he drove into her until her golden coat became almost black with sweat. Then, with a great roar, he poured his essence into her, jerking and quivering uncontrollably.

As the heat pulsed up and away from the horses' locked bodies and rushed up the trampled grass, Ronin turned toward Kalial and gathered her in his arms.

EPILOGUE

Kalial raced up the stairs, dhu Cait close on her heels. She ran with the freedom of a reigning princess and the pride of a woman well loved.

Ronin listened to her rapid steps, pleased that she had returned from the forest early.

"Ronin! I can not find her yet again!" She paused in the doorway to the master suite and peered inside. The owl swiveled his head and looked at her just as Ronin looked up from the fire and smiled at Kalial's flushed cheeks, tousled hair and snapping yellow eyes. The owl's left wing lay useless at his side, an injury sustained many years ago deep within Loch Nidean forest when his sacrifice saved the life of the forest princess. "Why must she wander off so frequently?" Kalial sighed at her husband's amused look. " 'Tis not a game. I worry that she will come to harm some day."

Ronin rose to his feet and walked over to her. He touched her chin and tilted it upward. "Matalia will never get lost with that wolf pack that follows her around, and I would pity the soul that tried to harm her. Look out the newly finished tower, toward the ocean, and I am sure you will find her romping in the waves with her dogs."

"She is too young . . ."

"No, my princess, she is but a few years younger

than you were when I met you, and you were already leading men. Let her be. She has your wild blood."

"Bah. All the more reason to worry," Kalial grumbled as she stared out the window toward the coast.

"You have many other children to tend. I heard your forest people have called for you to attend the weaving ceremony at the full moon. The twins are causing mischief and the baby just swallowed a button. And I need your tender caresses. Leave your eldest daughter to herself today and spend your energies on me." Ronin reached forward and hooked his finger into the amber bracelet to draw her near. The heightened color in her cheeks cooled and Kalial smiled ruefully.

"M'laird, we have guests."

"No one is more important than you. Come here." Kalial giggled and tried to twist away, but Ronin pushed her into a chair in front of the fire.

"Even if that guest is your cousin, Percy? He has come to meet his new godson and view the falconry."

"All he wants to view is your backside in your famous breeches," Ronin growled in response.

"Nay—all he truly desires is a fledgling falcon trained by you. Or perhaps the owl that hovers at your shoulder?"

"Never," he said solemnly as he touched Kalial's breast, "for that beast saved my heart." Kalial looked up into his rich, blue eyes and melted.

AFTERWORD

THE SCOTTISH McCAT

The Scottish wildcats known as McCats have existed in Scotland from ancient times through the medieval era and into the early part of the last century. Also known as the Kellas cat, Wangie cat or Cait sith (fairy cat), they were fearsome battle creatures that ofttimes bonded with clans and formed formidable forces for feudal protection. Some people have speculated that Hadrian's Wall was built to keep out the fiercely territorial McCats rather than the barbarous Scots themselves.

It is said that the wail of the bagpipe strongly resembles the skirling war cries of the McCats, which struck fear into any who heard them in the thick Scottish woods. The wild McCats are said to have evolved over centuries of interbreeding between the ginger wildcats of the Viking settlers and the now extinct Woad Blue cats of the ancient tribes.

All McCats have long fur, and their faces are framed with long whiskers that resemble beards and sideburns. Although the facial hair is bright ginger in the Celtic and Viking sub-breeds, it is a distinctive black in the Gaelic varieties. The true melanistic McCat exhibits all the well-known wildcat traits, the thick, clubbed tail, wide head, large teeth and claws, and indeed, in a good light the wildcat stripes can be seen in differing shades of black in the coat. Many McCats have particularly long canines, which enable them to tackle larger prey and which, according to myth, were inherited from the ancient saber-toothed cats that once roamed the area. In recent times, a large black cat caught near the county of Morayshire, Scotland, bore a striking resemblance to the legendary Scottish McCat.

Don't miss the next book
in the
Wild Series by Sasha Lord

IN A WILD WOOD

Coming in August 2004
From Signet Books

A shaft of pain burst through Brogan O'Bannon's consciousness as he jerked his eyes open. Pandemonium
raged around him and hundreds of wolves seemed to
swarm over his outstretched legs and around his
bound body. Brogan tried to shake his head clear of
the fog, but the action made him dizzy and the wolves
around him appeared to double. Growls, snarls and
multitudes of fierce, wild sounds roared over and
around him, mixing with human screams. He ducked
to defend himself against the wild dogs, yet found that
his arms were bound behind his back around a solid
Scottish Ash tree. He yanked with his considerable
strength, but could not snap the sinew that tied him.
He was propped up in a seated position and found
that he could not rise despite his struggles. A clank
of steel against steel caused him to look up, and he
saw one of the men who had set upon him earlier
engaged in battle with a young woman.

She wore a thick skirt of blue wool that fit closely

to her body until it flared around her hips below a hammered girdle. Her hair was blacker than the darkest cave, and curled in riotous ringlets down past her waist. She leaped at the man she fought, her sword flashing. She struck him, then deliberately ran her sword through his side. As she pulled the steel free, the wolves pounced upon him and began to shred his flesh.

The man screamed, flailing against the wolves. He stumbled to his horse, and kicking out at the beasts, dragged himself across the saddle. He hauled himself upright and looked angrily at Brogan.

"You are warned, O'Bannon! Leave Scotland!" he screeched as he clutched his bleeding side. A sudden flurry of hoofbeats announced the rapid departure of the remaining attackers and the injured man swung his horse around and galloped after them.

The woman glared at their retreating backs as she waved her sword in the air. "Cowards!" she screamed after them. "Think you afore poaching on this land again!"

Brogan gasped at the gleaming turquoise of her eyes. The color was so fantastic, he could not believe it belonged to a woman of flesh and blood. A shiver of disquiet raced up his spine as he wondered if she was of the faerie people.

Matalia stared in surprise at the man trussed to the tree. She swung her sword up and placed the point at his throat, and looked fiercely into his eyes, daring him to cry for mercy. A wisp of twilight mist snaked between them, then was swept away.

Brogan felt the tip of the sword press into his neck yet he felt no fear. He noted the fine beads of perspiration that dotted her forehead and watched in swift arousal as one drop curled down her temple and into the hollow between her breasts. He felt his thudding heart send blood rushing to his loins. Instantly hardening, he lifted his eyes back to her face.

Matalia trembled slightly. Her hand on the sword wavered and nicked the man's throat, causing it to bleed. Shocked, she realized that his eyes were upon her breasts and he had ignored the cut to his skin.

"Have you no fear, trespasser? I hold a blade above your vein of life. Should I press down upon it, you will bleed to death in moments." She mocked him, her voice low and husky.

Brogan felt desire swamp him at the sound. His perusal sank lower, caressing her hips. She shifted her weight, and a fold of wool became trapped momentarily between her thighs. Brogan's eyes burned into the vee and a groan slipped past his lips.

"Ach, mi lass, untie me and I will give you liquid more precious than me blood."

Matalia stepped back as if scalded. She glared at him, her exquisite eyes snapping in fury, although Brogan detected a flicker of uncertainty in the turquoise depths.

"You are a fool to taunt me so when you are at my mercy. I will not have you speak to me so dishonorably." She raised her sword yet again and made to step forward. Brogan bore his gaze into hers so powerfully, she froze. His eyes were stone gray, lifeless and hard. Twilight mists rose again and poured through the trees, enfolding him, matching the color of his eyes. Muscles bulged in his arms and chest, visible even through the layers of clothing. With a start, Matalia realized that he was pulling at his bonds, attempting to break free. Curiously detached, she tilted her head to see if he would succeed.

As she watched him, her eyes crept slowly down his body, to the bulge between his legs that pulsed and grew as she watched it. Startled anew, she looked swiftly up into the still gray eyes.

"Come, little maiden, I'll appease your curiosity and teach you things your husband will never learn, much less share with you. Come hither, and cut my ties."

His voice was seductive and masculine. The controlled stillness of his body was like a coiled snake and Matalia felt a whisper of desire slither through her. She looked around her, at the creeping mist and darkening forest. Brogan watched her thoughts flit over her countenance and he tensed with anticipation.

Suddenly a howl burst out of the woods beside them and Brogan leaped, every muscle straining as he desperately sought to escape. "Quick!" he shouted. "Afore the wolves descend upon us again."

Another howl bounced across the clearing and three wolves stepped into the fading light. Horrorstruck, Brogan waited for them to leap upon the superb woman before him. A fierce growl came from his throat as he struggled mightily to break free. The wolves circled the woman, pulling their lips back in a hungry snarl. They snapped at her gown, grabbing it and pulling her toward the trees.

Then, as Matalia jerked her dress from their jaws, they lay in a semicircle around her, facing Brogan. Realization came to him. The hundreds of wolves he had seen earlier were actually only these three wild canines that flocked around the faerie maiden as if under her spell. He looked around quickly, remembering his own beast, and saw the wolfhound on his side, breathing deeply but still unconscious. He glanced back at the maiden and saw that she was approaching him cautiously.

"Can you not free yourself, man?" she queried softly. She leaned over slightly to look around him and Brogan saw the wool gape away from her breasts. A fine barrier of silk encased her body underneath, barring his view. He felt his head move forward as if by longing alone he could taste her flesh. She jerked back, abruptly aware of his gaze. "I asked you a question," she said sharply. "Can you not break those bonds?"

"Lass, if I could I would have done so a thousand

times over by now, and put my arms to better use than cradling this tree trunk behind my back. Take pity, love, and free me." Brogan tried to keep his voice light and unthreatening, despite the turgid pain developing in his lap. He inched his hips forward to ease the strain, but stilled as Matalia's eyes swept down to observe his movements.

With deep, unfathomable eyes, Matalia tossed her sword away and kneeled down next to him. She reached out to touch his cheek. "I find that I am interested in how you feel, trespasser. You see, I rarely meet people not of my family." She pulled back, surprised at the sudden wariness in the man's eyes. "I am interested . . ." Her voice trailed off as she touched the first button on Brogan's shirt. A mist drifted in and out of the clearing, as swift as a deer in flight.

"Release me now, faerie maiden," he whispered as she unbuttoned his shirt. "Do as I say, little lass, for I can be a tender lover or a terrible foe." His gray eyes bored into her turquoise ones and imparted his message as clearly as his words.

Matalia stopped, considering. "What mean you, lover or foe?"

Brogan smiled seductively. "Undo my bonds. I can make you feel as if the heavens have opened and the stars are colliding in the sky. But I must have my hands to slide over your precious skin, to reach inside your private heart."

She jerked back, frightened both by his words and her response to them. She felt heat warming her thighs and her eyelids blinked quickly. "You should not say those things to me . . ." she murmured.

"Why not?" he asked.

She shook her head, not sure how to answer. She slowly backed away, calling her wolves to her side. "You should not say those things," she said again with more conviction.

Brogan snarled in frustration. "Come back here!"

he commanded. "Untie me! Those men will come back and murder me. Set me free to defend myself!"

"I think not. The thieves are gone."

"They are not thieves. They are men sent by my brother to prevent my return," he said, but she was already disappearing back into the forest. He shouted at her again, infuriated that she would leave him so helpless, but she did not look back. He yanked on his bonds, then flung his head back and shouted his rage. Fifteen years of struggle! Fifteen years! And now this small, black-haired girl thwarted him with her stubbornness!